WEBB

RANDY GREEN

Dedication

To my grandson Reilly, may every day of your life you know that you are loved immeasurably and unconditionally. May you also understand that the power of that unconditional love will provide you with all the courage and strength you will ever need. I've only known you for a few days now and I already love you with a passion I could never explain.

Acknowledgements

When I started writing I wanted to write about things that I knew, things that were in my heart and in my head. I believe that if stories of your past are stuck in your head and heart, you know that they were special in one way or another. Webb Mississippi is that place for me. I loved visiting my grandmother while she lived there, I can still see and smell the house she lived in with the creaky wooden floors and the large front porch that allowed me to play for endless hours, even during the rain. That house is gone now as it burned to the ground many years ago but I can recall that my relatives were always coming and going and there was always something cooking in the kitchen. Those memories stuck with me, along with some of the adventures I encountered while I was there. Because I was relatively young when this fictional story took place, there were some grown-up details that I needed in order to complete this sequel to WEBB so I solicited the help of my cousin Peggy to describe the city of Webb in the late 60's and early 70's. I came to the opinion that Peggy should truly be a writer because she describes things from the past with such vivid and enthusiastic detail that I get lost in her words every time she sends me more details about the place she calls home. I can't thank her enough for helping to add more life and detail to the city of Webb. I would also like to thank my cousin Diane for this incredible book cover. She is a true artist and an excellent listener. I was nervous about asking her if she would design a cover for me but I am glad I overcame my nerves. She is amazing. With her artistic skill and incredible talent, she painted the images of a key moment in this book that was only available in my imagination. Thank you, Diane and Peggy, I love you both.

Chapter 1

Breakfast

HEATHER OPENED THE DOOR to Decker's room where she found him asleep with the bedside lamp still turned on. Every morning she stood at the side of his bed and watched him sleep for just a few minutes and admired the way he slept with such peace. She did find it odd that Decker slept on his back and as far as she knew, he never moved. Every morning she would find him with a book about the Civil war across his chest where he laid it. Since Jeanine started helping him with his reading, he became an avid reader. Heather was very happy to see this change in her little brother brought about by his love for a girl. With Jeannine's help, he read anything and everything he could find about the civil war and was fascinated with every aspect of it. Heather wondered if Decker would ever grow out of certain habits, like sleeping with the lamp beside his bed turned on all night. At the base of lamp would be his pocketknife he won shooting baskets at the county fair, a rabbit's foot key chain he used to keep his gym locker and house key together. She never asked him if he slept with the light on because he just fell asleep reading or did he sleep with it on because he was a little scared of the dark. She didn't care, she loved that boy more than she could ever explain.

It was well over three years now that their mother passed away. Heather for all practical purposes became Decker's mom, but she knew he hurt on the inside just like she did. Their dad became so distant and distracted that he hadn't realized that Decker was growing into a fine young man. Heather was proud of him and if she could ever get their father out of his state of depression, she knew he would be too. She didn't mind looking after Decker, she had even turned down her scholarship offer to attend Mississippi State to stay close to home and attend junior college instead. There was no way that she would ever leave Decker alone with their dad to raise him in the condition he was in. That awful week had changed her father considerably, and not for the better. His best friend Bubba was murdered, the little Buckles boy was molested and murdered, and the worst of all if there was such a thing, their mother was accidently shot after she and their dad had won third place in the dance off over in Sumner. All of that was just about more than he could take. He won his election that same month and now his four-year term was about to end. Heather was certain he would not run again, and she was certain that even if he did run, he would lose. He was so disengaged with everything that he neglected his duties as Tallahatchie County Sheriff. What was even worse to her was that he was drinking too much to care.

"Decker" she touched his shoulder and he stirred awake just as quickly as he always did. It didn't take much to wake him. He blinked his eyes and focused on his sister. He smiled like he always did. Decker Davis was a morning person all the way. "It's time to get up little brother, breakfast in 10 minutes." She smiled back at his smile and turned to leave. "Did you forget something sister?" He couldn't see her because she had already turned her back to him, so he was not able to see her smile. She spun back around but removed the smile. She placed a stern look on her face instead. "Decker Davis! You are too old to be kissed awake! You need to outgrow this soon!" She bent down and kissed him on the forehead like she did every morning. She really didn't mind since that was what their mother did for him every day of his life until she passed, she was happy to try and fill in wherever she could. She really did think he would outgrow it but every morning they played the same game. "Now get your skinny butt out of bed and come get your breakfast!" She turned again and the smile returned to her face. She was only kidding him about being skinny.

Decker was filling out quicker than anyone could ever have imagined. He was approaching fourteen now and he was already knocking on six feet. Heather had no idea how much he weighed but she knew that he could eat 6 eggs, 4 pieces of toast and 12 slices of bacon every morning. Decker had changed so much physically and mentally in the last three years, but one thing had certainly not, Jeannine Martin. She was still Decker's only friend and Heather wondered when the friendship would change from adolescent school yard stuff to full on romance. Decker was getting to that age where he would change and from the looks of Jeannine, so would she.

Jeannine was turning out to be quite the curvy girl. Heather was always struck by Jeannine's natural beauty. As far as Heather could tell, she had perfect skin, not a blemish. Decker suffered only with a few pimples so far, but not Jeannine. She was as tall as Heather already and athletic. She still outran Decker every day when the bus dropped them off. They raced like little kids and would laugh and giggle when Jeanine reached the front porch before Decker every single time. It was nearly impossible to see one without the other. She said "please" and "thank you" and "yes ma'am" and "no ma'am" just like Decker. As far as Heather knew, she was still the best student in school. Decker had become the second best, and also as far as Heather knew, Decker had not noticed that Jeannine was becoming a woman.

"Sister, can I have some more bacon?" Decker ate as quickly as he could, but he was still hungry, and the bus would be coming soon. He was always the first on the bus and he still sat in the seat right behind Mr. Johns the bus driver. "Geez Decker, we will have to kill another hog before winter if you don't slow down!" Heather was smiling when she said it and she playfully smacked him on the back of his head. When she smacked him, she drew the fingers that had just smacked his head to her nose for a quick sniff. She might have been his sister, but she had all the instincts of a mother. "Decker Davis! You have got to do a better job of getting the suds out of your hair before you get out of the shower! You still have suds in your hair!" Decker smiled as he was shoveling some of the last remaining scraps of scrambled eggs into his mouth. "I won't have to use as much soap tomorrow then." He laughed and some eggs from his mouth spewed out on to his sisters' hip. She jumped back like he had just shot at her. "Decker Davis you are acting like a Neanderthal!" She laughed and made her way back to the kitchen. She yelled from the kitchen. "You have to stop by Mac's after practice today and get a haircut!" He said something but she couldn't hear it, so she just let the subject drop.

Elmer arrived at the breakfast table just as Decker was using the last piece of toast to mop up anything that might be left on his plate. Elmer said good morning to Heather by kissing her on the top of the head. Even though Heather was pretty tall, Elmer was still tall enough to kiss her on the top of the head with no effort. He was much manlier with Decker as he sat down, he simply said: "Morning Deck," and squeezed Decker's shoulder. Heather immediately set a plate in front of her dad as it was always the same. Three eggs over easy, three slices of toast and six strips of bacon. She also sat the last jar of pepper sauce they had in front of him. Elmer loved hot food and every year he and Lois would plant an entire row of some kind of pepper plant that Decker didn't want anything to do with. The first time he tried to help pick them, he rubbed his eye and they nearly had to be taken to the doctor in Clarksdale to get his eyes washed out. He remembered his eyes burned and itched so bad that he couldn't stop rubbing them. He rubbed them so much that one of his eyes nearly swelled shut. From that day forward Decker knew he would never have anything to do with peppers. His mother would the peppers and put them in the root cellar. Decker had to admit that she canned those peppers so that his dad could have the sauce to pour over nearly everything he ate; the house smelled really good and it would make him hungry. It wasn't the same reaction for pickles though. When his mother canned pickles, he wanted to be as far away from the house as he could. It was awful! The vinegar hung so strong in the air all through the house he swore he could smell vinegar on his pillow when he laid down for the night.

"Daddy, that's the last jar of pepper sauce." Elmer reached for the jar as Decker was picking up his plate. He held it up and looked at it a long time then set it back down on the table. "You better put it back in the root cellar. We can use it on special occasions." Heather shook her head and sighed but not loud for Elmer or Decker to hear. She wished her dad would come back to her and Decker. They all missed their mother badly; but he had been in a very bad state of depression since the funeral and had never snapped out of it. "I have a better idea, why don't me you and Decker plant some in the garden this spring?" He didn't answer but shook the regular old pepper shaker over his food instead of the pepper sauce. He shook so much that you could barely see the eggs under black flakes of pepper. "Daddy, are you coming to my game tomorrow night?" Decker was returning from kitchen where he washed his plate and put it in the strainer. His sister would pinch his ear lobe if he left a mess for her to clean up. It was always playful, but he loved his sister very much and enjoyed making sure she was happy and not overworked going to junior college and taking care of two men in the house. "Son, I don't think I can, I am covering the evening shift again."

Decker never let his dad see that he was hurt when Elmer missed his games, and he was missing almost all of them now.

Decker was now the starting quarterback, punter, kicker, and middle linebacker for the junior varsity team. He was bigger than most of the kids in his grade, he wasn't bullied anymore, and he was becoming quite a star around town. You could never tell it by talking to Decker though. The junior varsity games were played on Thursday night and the varsity games were on Friday night. Thursday night was the shift that Bubba worked and since Bubba's death Elmer took that shift and never hired another deputy to replace Bubba. He told everyone that the county didn't have the budget to replace Bubba, but everyone knew it was because Elmer felt responsible for Bubba's death and simply didn't want to hire another person that he might get attached. Mac Hibdon, the barber and friend, would try to prod their dad into hiring another deputy while Elmer was in the barber chair, but Elmer never did. Folks thought that Elmer was just waiting out his four-year term because he had lost his heart for police work. "Okay Dad, maybe you can come to the game next week." Decker turned and waved at his sister then grabbed his gym bag and bolted out the door. Before the door slammed, Heather yelled, "Don't forget to get a haircut! I put two dollars in your gym bag for Mr. Hibdon!" She paused for a second then ran to the front door. "And you are going to prayer meeting with me tonight! We are welcoming the new youth minister!" She shook her head as she walked back to the kitchen. Heather stood in the doorway of the kitchen with her arms crossed staring at her father. She had tried everything to help him get out his depression. Nothing seemed to work.

Chapter 2
The Shadow Beast

SHE AWOKE IN THE DARK cold room, but it was not completely dark. It reminded her of the times she went deer hunting with her father and how he would make them wake early before the sun was up and he would say "beat the deer to the best spots." He would place her in a stand and would drive off to his stand. She would sit there in the stand, shivering, cold, and tired and would hear every wanted and unwanted noise the dark would offer. Before long, the sun would slowly begin to rise to the point where it was no longer dark, but it wasn't day either. Her dad would laugh and tell her that THAT time in between dark and light was the time she must be weary of the shadow beasts. They were the beasts that the mere scent of them in the area would cause drowsiness to set in and would later cause a deep sleep to sweep over its victims and steal their breath as they slept, and therefore the victims would miss the deer that stirred so gently in the morning sunrise. She could feel the dirt floor beneath her, and the smell of evergreen was clearly in the air. She felt dirty sitting on the floor.

She tried her best to remember how she got here, but it was unclear. Her mind was trying to get a grip on things, but her body felt sluggish. She had trouble moving without feeling like she was in thick mud. At least she was no longer bound. Her wrists still hurt from the ties that held them together. A voice came from the room. Up until this point she thought she was alone. Now she knew her dad must have been right, maybe she was in the room with a shadow beast. Maybe she wasn't supposed to be awake. Maybe she should just lie down on this dirt floor and go to sleep. She no longer cared if the deer got away.

"How old are you my child?" She tried to figure out where the voice was coming from, but she couldn't. Her head was still hurting, and she was so tired, "eleven" was all she could summon from her vocal cords. "Eleven"! My child you are not a child as I thought, you are almost of child baring age now." The voice was moving as it spoke. "Have you allowed a boy to take your gift?" She tried to think about a gift and couldn't think of any, she shook her head to try and wake herself up more, but it was so difficult. She was so tired. "I asked you a question and I demand an answer!" She felt the hand strike her face, which caused her head to smash against the side of the wall. It didn't really hurt because she was so drowsy. "Have you given your gift away?" The voice was close, and she braced for another slap that never came. It finally occurred to her what they were asking. No, I haven't been with anyone. Jimmy Anderson kissed me and touched me through my clothes, but I stopped him!" She started crying because she was embarrassed to be talking about such things with someone she couldn't see and someone that was clearly comfortable with hitting her. "The advances upon your gift will continue as you grow, they will become relentless and quite soon you will develop a fire that burns deep in you and you will willingly give your gift to some boy who will brag to his friends how he mounted and conquered you!"

The voice rose to the point where it was at scream levels and it scared her. She scooted on her butt trying not to make a sound away from the direction she thought the voice was coming from.

She stopped when her left arm brushed against what felt like a leg wearing jeans. She gasped when she felt a hand touch the top of her head and then grip her hair. "I have been sent as the hand of God to stop you from the sins of your past, present and your future!" The hand gripping her hair pulled tightly on her hair and began to drag her across the floor as her captor continued to loudly rant. "The sins of fornication have become common place in society, and I have been sent to stop it!" She cried and begged to be let go but she was sure she wasn't being heard over the screaming. "We are living in modern day Gomorrah, men taking what they want and women giving it to them so freely and eagerly!" The hand that held her hair began to lift her, it hurt as she felt her hair popping and it was clearly being pulled from her head by the roots. She screamed in pain and the hand threw her down to the floor. She was expecting to hit the hard dirt floor but instead she felt like she landed on a big pillow. "I have been sent by the hand of God to remove your gift through mortal purification and send you to meet our Father where he will warmly accept you in the kingdom of heaven!" She begged to be let go, she promised not to tell anyone what was happening, but her tears and screams did nothing to stop the pain. Just as she was about to black out, she whispered, "Are you the shadow beast?" The voice replied, "Close, I am the hand of God."

He laid there next to her for what seemed hours to her. He had his arm around her and would not release her. He spoke the entire time but he wasn't speaking to her, as far as she could tell he was speaking to no one. He rambled, he talked about God and his duties, he ran his hands all over her and she hated it. He spoke of family and a Sherriff and how he would once again rise to the top and he would no longer be treated so poorly. She cried so much that she ran out of tears and now she was trying to understand why this was happening to her.

Chapter 3
The Bus

DECKER LET THE SCREEN door slam behind him as was customary every school morning and even on the weekend when he didn't have a real place to go other than his normal chores. On school mornings he would run the entire distance from his house to the main road where the bus would pick him up and he would be the first on the bus and last one off. He liked the conversation he would have each morning with the bus driver, Mr. Johns. Mr. Johns was a small man, but he carried himself larger than he actually was. He was always neatly dressed and took his job as the bus driver very serious. He allowed no horse play and did his best to keep the bullies at bay. Decker had to admit that since Lonnie Buckles was killed the bullying on bus number nine had all but stopped. There was an occasional fight, but it was more like a scuffle. When a ruckus broke out, Mr. Johns would pull the bus over to side, turn off the engine, separate the two combatants and if he felt that seat separations was not good enough, he became the judge and jury in deciding who started it and they would be kicked off the bus. No more arguments. It may not have been the best way to handle things, but it was Mr. Johns' way. Since he had been a bus driver for nearly 20 years, no one questioned his judgement, not even the school administrators.

The double bus doors opened making a creaking sound clearing a path for Decker to go in. "Good morning Mr. Johns." Decker leaped over the first step like he always did and made the turn to get into his seat and he nearly tripped stopping himself from sitting right on top of someone that was already in his seat. He tried to say something, but he couldn't get the words to come out. This was the first time for as long as he could remember that someone else was first on the bus and worse, they had chosen inappropriately to sit in HIS seat. His mind went in a thousand directions, it was an explosion of thoughts and questions that he couldn't stop. They came one after the other: Who are you? Why are you in my seat? Where did you come from? What grade are you in? How old are you? Do you know Donnie Ray Richardson? Have you ever had that shot in your arm that leaves a mark? What did you have for breakfast? Where do you live? Can you move one stop down from my house because I like being first on the bus? Do you like football? Basketball? Track? Hurdles? Pole Vault? Of course, none of those questions came out but while he was searching for the right thing to say Mr. Johns said: "Decker this is Madelyn, Madelyn, this is Decker Davis."

Decker still didn't know what to say but manners took over instinctively. "Uh, nice to meet you Madelyn." He stuck his hand out as he was taught, and she shyly took it. He wasn't impressed with her handshake grip. It was pretty weak by his standards, but he didn't say anything. He looked around and made the decision to take the first seat on the bus across the aisle from where he normally sat. At some point he would have to talk to the new girl about the arrangements. Mr. Johns closed the bus door and released the clutch which caused the bus to lurch forward just a little which in turn tossed Decker firmly in his seat quicker than he planned. "Decker, Madelyn just moved here from Tupelo." Mr. Johns spoke over his shoulder since Decker was on the opposite side of him. Normally Mr. Johns would look in the rear-view mirror ever so often when he and Decker would talk. Mr. Johns then glanced in the mirror at Madelyn, "Decker's dad is the county Sheriff."

Luke King was next to get on the bus. He and Decker had never become friends. Luke was just someone that Decker avoided. Luke wasn't quite as mean as Lonnie Buckles, but he was a close second. Luke had a few friends, but none were as close as Lonnie. In a way, Decker felt sorry for Luke, having lost his best friend in such a terrible way. It was traumatic for Decker to understand and he hated to think how hard it would be for Luke. Up until the day Lonnie was murdered, Luke and Lonnie were two peas in a pod. On the other hand, Luke had never forgiven Decker for punching him in the nose the day they all met at Decker's fort in the woods. Decker didn't understand Luke's animosity. It wasn't Decker's fault that the boys decided to rough he and Jeannine up that day. Decker felt like he was defending his fort and his woman. At least that is what his dad told him and Luke's dad at the time. Decker put the thoughts of the new girl and Luke King aside and turned them toward Jeannine. She would be on the bus soon enough and no matter how close they got as friends, he still got nervous, his mouth went dry and his palms got sweaty. He noticed that the dry mouth didn't last as long as it used to because the minute she sat next to him on the bus, she talked nonstop. She always had so much to say. Decker liked that part of their relationship because he wasn't much of a talker, so it suited him just fine to be able to sit back, smile and nod every so often. He liked hearing her talk anyway.

He was looking out the window and could see her standing by the side of the road. There she was, he could already feel his palms getting sweaty and his mouth was going dry. "Good morning Mr. Johns." she said smiling. She held her books against her chest with her arms crossed as she made her way up the steps. Like Decker, she froze when she saw someone other than Decker in their seat. She had a slight bit of panic and it must have shown on her face. "Jeannine, this is Madelyn, Madelyn, this is Jeannine Martin." Jeannine smiled, stuck out her hand and Madelyn took it but not near as sheepishly as she had with Decker. Decker couldn't believe it when Jeannine sat down with the new girl instead of him. He didn't know what to say or do. He couldn't remember the last time Jeannine didn't sit with him on the way to school. "So, Madelyn, where are you from? What grade are you in? What brings you to Webb?" Jeannine realized that her questions were coming a little too rapidly for the new girl and she stopped. "I'm sorry, I get excited to meet new girls!" Madelyn managed a smile, but it didn't last long. "We just don't get many new girls moving to Webb." Madelyn smiled again and this time it lasted quite a bit longer. "My dad is the barber in Webb, well, he is one of the barbers in Webb. There are two barber shops in town." She paused and put her finger to her chin as if she were thinking. "Wait, let me back up. My grandfather was the barber but he got hurt and then my dad left his meat cutting job to take over my Granddad's business." The girl didn't say much but smiled every now and then. Jeannine tried as hard as she could to get her to talk but it was futile. Young Madelyn wasn't in the mood to talk.

The bus rolled in front of the school and came to a stop. Mr. Johns pulled the lever for the door to open and it did so reluctantly. The kids had already formed a line to get off even though they weren't supposed to stand until the bus came to a stop. Decker would sit in his seat until everyone filed off the bus, besides, he was not in a hurry to get to first hour class with Mrs. Milholen. She was tough and she pushed him more than any teacher he ever had. He really liked her, but he wished he had her class later in the day, his brain didn't seem to work as fast in first hour as it did in fourth hour and she demanded excellence the minute he walked in his class. Now he had to face Mrs. Milholen and he hadn't been able to spend any time with Jeannine on the bus ride. Jeannine always helped him prepare, she made him sharper.

Chapter 4
You're Fired!

DESPITE THE LACK OF LEADERSHIP from Elmer, the sheriff's office was still running smoothly, thanks to Lavera. She ran a good clean office, but she was getting tired of making excuses for Elmer. She loved him like a son, but she had her limits. Every time she would find a bottle hidden in a box or a drawer or behind a picture, she would pour it out and toss the empty in his trash can so that he could see that she had found it and that she disapproved of his behavior.

It wasn't a big office. It never really was, but the town was growing, and they were getting stretched. They were lucky that they had a deputy transfer up from Pascagoula or they would have been in terrible shape. Elmer continued to claim that there was no budget to replace Bubba and he wouldn't think of hiring another and got very irate one day and yelled at her in the office in front of the others when she broached the subject for about the fiftieth time. He actually made her cry. The Elmer she knew before his wife died would never do that nor tolerate it from anyone. She was going to tell him that day that he had a transfer request but at that moment she decided that he would never sign a transfer in from anywhere. After he was through yelling at her he went into his office and slammed the door so that everyone would know to leave him alone.

Lavera let the sting of the moment calm down, then waited a few days and took some papers in for Elmer to sign. When he asked what he was signing she told him that it was supply requests to the state for uniform replacement and a new transmission for the Scout. All of that was true so she convinced herself that she wasn't lying by blaming the error on her absent mindedness and she had simply forgotten that there was a transfer order mixed in with others. She considered the order for replacement uniforms also a requisition for an additional deputy, so it really was accurate. When Elmer saw a deputy in the office he didn't recognize, he was furious. He threw things and cussed words that Lavera had heard before but wished she hadn't. He demanded to see his transfer papers and when the new deputy produced papers that had his signature on them, he was even more furious. He actually broke the glass of one of his gun cases with his fist and got a nasty cut in the process. Lavera remembered him holding a gun cleaning cloth over his hand as he began yelling at her again. He knew she had tricked him.

"Lavera! I have had enough of your tricks and games! I said we don't have the budget for another deputy and BY GOD I meant it!" He slammed his fist down on his desk and lost the cleaning cloth that was stemming the bleeding. The cut opened again, and he started slinging blood all over the office, some of it even got on Lavera's brand new dress. She was not happy about his childish outburst although deep down she knew she had been sneaky, but she felt like she was helping the city of Webb and Tallahatchie County. Even with the new kid from Pascagoula they were still one deputy short. The request that Elmer had sent to the state for funding a new deputy had been approved. Elmer sent the request in long before Bubba was murdered. The transfer merely replaced Bubba and now they needed to hire a new one.

Elmer reached down and picked up the cleaning cloth that was soaked in blood already and placed it back over his hand. "Lavera you have gone too far! You're fired! Pack your stuff and get out!" Lavera didn't blink, she didn't move and if anyone else would have been in the office they would have seen her face change from kind and caring and perhaps a little hurt, to a face that rarely surfaced for her. A face of anger, and sheer determination. "Fine! Just fine Elmer Davis! And since I am no longer an employee of Tallahatchie County, that makes me a private citizen with unalienable rights and access to county personnel including the drunken Sheriff!" She moved from the front of his desk and shuffled around behind it so that she could be standing face to face with him. When she was standing directly in front of Elmer, she pointed a finger and poked it in his chest. "Now sit your ass down and listen to a private citizen which is a requirement of your damn job!" Elmer couldn't believe what he was hearing from her. For some reason he sat down as he was told to do. When he was in his chair she bent over and put one hand on the desk and the other hand she used to continue to poke him in the chest. "We all lost a lot that day, maybe not as much as you but pain is pain, and we are dealing with our grief the best we can." She leaned a little closer to his face. "You lost a wife and friend, and we feel for you. We lost two friends that day and the pain is still there!" It seemed impossible for her to get any closer to Elmer but somehow, she managed. "Your children lost a mother and friend, and they should not have to endure the loss of their father to a bottle!" She leaned up and took a step back. "You can fire me if you want but know this, I will love you like a son all the days of my life but I, and everyone around you have had it with your god damned pity party!" She walked back around to the other side of the desk. "If you don't want to do this job then resign but quit taking a paycheck every month for doing nothing more than keeping dust from gathering in your chair!" She started walking to the door but before she exited, she turned back around, "His name is Tom, Tom Porter and he seems like a damn good young man that deserves a hell of a lot better greeting and welcome than the one you've given him. He's been here three weeks and you are just now noticing. Shame on you Elmer Davis!" She turned and walked out the door then stopped. She wasn't finished. One more thing HIGH Sheriff of Tallahatchie County, your precious son is starting quarterback for the junior varsity squad tomorrow night, word has it that Coach Hayes is going to let him dress for Coach Bond and the varsity team Friday night against Charleston. Imagine that, an eighth grader dressing for the varsity. The last time that happened in this city it was you! Your father was there for YOU that day and by god you better be there for him!" Elmer put his head down and mumbled: "I have to work the evening shift." She smiled and gently said, "Tom is working the evening shift. I changed the schedule two weeks ago. Try and find another excuse in that bottle if you want to but stop using work as one."

She was done now and strolled out of his office. She passed though the main office where the clerical staff stood from their desks and applauded. She had said to the Sheriff what they all wanted to say. They all knew Lavera well and understood it went against everything she believed in to strike back at Elmer the way she had. They all loved her for it.

Elmer lowered his head and looked around the desk for a minute. He opened the drawer to his desk where he thought he had a bottle of Scotch, but it wasn't there. "Damn woman." He reached inside the leg of his boot and pulled his emergency flask from it and took a drink. As he was looking down, he saw the missing persons bulletins that he had neglected for several weeks. He pulled one out of the pile that gave a picture of a pretty young girl from Drew that had been missing for the last three years. He studied the bulletin then pressed the intercom button that connected his desk to Lavera's. "Lavera get me the Sheriff over in Sunflower County please." There was no reply. He tried again. "Lavera wake up and get me the Sheriff in Sunflower county." There was no reply from the intercom but there was a reply from his doorway.

"She's not here. You fired her a few minutes ago." Elmer looked up to see a nice-looking young man in a wonderfully pressed county sheriffs uniform standing in his doorway. "I did no such thing." The man in the doorway laughed, "perhaps you didn't but the man that resides in that flask of whatever you're drinking sure did." Elmer looked at the flask he was holding and put the cap back on it then shoved it back in his boot. "Sheriff Henry said you were a good man, and he was happy to see me transfer to your leadership. Apparently, he knew you before you were a . . . " He stopped short of what he wanted to say but finished differently and more respectfully, "before your troubles began." Elmer stood up from his desk and tried to gain his balance. "Who are you?" Tom walked up to Elmer and stuck his hand out, "I am Corporal Tom Porter, I've been under your command for three weeks now, transfer from Pascagoula, Jackson County. I like that you don't micro-manage."

Chapter 5

Barber Shop Gossip

MAC WAS USING THE TRIMMERS on the back of Ollie Duckworth's neck making sure to steer clear of the cyst the man had at the base of his neck. It was about as big as a fist and poor Ollie had endured rude comments all his life but now that he was well into his 70's he had mastered the art of self-deprecating humor. "Mac are you bout finished? This chair you got is pert near as old as I am. My butt hurts!" Mac stopped and flipped the clippers off so he could clearly be heard. There were three men waiting for a cut, so he had a captive audience. "Well hell fire Ollie, this damn thing on the back of your neck gets bigger every week. I ought to charge you double for having to work around that damn thing!" They all laughed including Ollie Duckworth. Nick Berry, one of the men waiting on a cut decided to chime in. "Why don't you get that thing cut off Ollie, I bet it has to cost you a fortune having a shirt made that will fit around that mountain for a mole!" The laughter was loud. Ollie fired back, "I will never listen to a man named after a razor cut!" There was more laughter, Ollie could sling it with the best of them. "Course that's probably a good name for a joint like this!" They all laughed. Mac flipped the switch on the trimmers for sound

19

effect, "Watch it bub, I will poke a hole in the thing, and we will all drown before we could get to the door!" Nick doubled over in his chair and was about to sit up when the door opened, and Donnie Buckles walked in.

The barber shop got quiet immediately as none of the men had seen Donnie since the funeral for his little brother. He was sent back to Viet Nam shortly after and was captured. He spent the last two years of his war waiting on Nixon to negotiate the release of all remaining prisoners. Some folks in town said they saw him on TV when they would show the prisoners stepping off the plane, saluting, then getting hugs from family that were elated to have them home. Mac made conversation about it one day and pointed out that after he saw Donnie come down the steps of the transport, he saw Donnie salute, turned and left the scene. Mac said that he didn't seem to have anyone there to greet him.

At first it was difficult to recognize Donnie as it was for sure that he had not seen a barber or even a razor since he stepped off the plane. Donnie's hair was well past his shoulders and his beard was at least to mid chest. Mac was the first to figure out who this man was when the man spoke, "Hey Mac, long time no see." The voice was distinct, and Mac nearly dropped his clippers. "Well, I will be damned!" He set the clippers down on the counter next to the tall glass container filled with green stuff as Decker like to call it and all the combs. "Donnie I can't believe it's you!" The other guys in the shop soon figured out who Donnie was, and they all stood up to offer a greeting. There were handshakes from everyone. Mac did the handshake and the shoulder slap at the same time, he was clearly happy to see Donnie, even if he was a hippy. "Boys this here is Donnie Buckles, and I am moving him to the head of the line!" Mac turned and looked around to see if anyone would have a disgruntled look on their face, but he knew that no one would care. Most of Mac's customers were not a on a time schedule. "Ollie you're done, get your hunch back butt out of that chair and let a Marine get a haircut!" Mac was a former Marine in World War II that always had a soft spot for veterans.

Donnie sat down in the chair that was just vacated by Ollie Duckworth. Ollie didn't leave though, he sat down in one of the waiting chairs, he wanted to hear this conversation. "Son where you been? I've prayed every day for you." All the men in the shop nodded in agreement. Mac shook out the barber apron and draped it around Donnie. He had to lift his beard to make sure the apron was neatly around his neck. "Donnie, what do you want me to do here?" Donnie was very quiet and very slow in his delivery. "Do the best you can Mac. I want to try and be normal again if there is such a thing. No flat top, I have seen enough of those in the Marines, just a simple haircut, part hippy and part nice guy I guess." Mac laughed and turned around to get the clippers. "I reckon you want me to take care of this beard? Trim it or just get rid of it?" Donnie shook his head no and his eyes got big as if he was scared of something. "Uh, no Mac, I like a nice full but shorter beard if you can." Mac laughed again, put the trimmers back down on the counter and picked up the scissors. He started cutting the back first and the hair began to pile up. Ollie piped up, "Y'all heard about that girl they found off of 82 just east of Winona?" All the men in the shop grumbled. Andy Marko, one of the guys that was waiting on a cut and shave said, "Wasn't just one girl, I heard. They found another one just north of Starkville off of 45. It's a damn shame really." Every man in shop grunted and nodded. Everyone was surprised to hear Donnie add to the conversation, "Wasn't just girls." He let that hang in the air for just a second then continued, "Found two boys, one just south of Ripley and another just east of Booneville." The barbershop got very quiet as the new information sunk into everyone. Mac shook his head, "God almighty, those poor babies, we live in a terrible time I tell you. People behave so poorly, doing God knows what to those little girls and boys then just dumping them like a piece of trash on the side of the road. Makes me sick to my stomach." Mac continued to speak as he cut. "I think you can trace the degradation of society back to that dumbass Texan we had in the White House. I swear that Johnson just screwed this whole country up." Ollie spoke up at that comment. "You don't know what the hell you are talking about Mac! It was the Irish Prince from Boston that got us into that war! Johnson just didn't know how to get out of it is all." There was chatter coming from everywhere when the door opened, and Decker stepped in. Everyone stopped and the shop got quiet except for the sound of scissors cutting Donnie's hair. Mac stopped cutting to turn and see Decker standing by the door after it closed.

Decker looked around the shop, he knew everyone there but because of the way the man currently in the chair was covered with a towel and was leaned back, Decker couldn't tell who he was. He wasn't very thrilled to be in the shop, but he was doing what his sister had asked him to do. Most of the boys in his class were wearing their hair pretty long these days but Heather was having none of it. She didn't even like any of the boys that went to junior college with her if they had long hair. Decker couldn't figure out why she was so opposed to a little more hair than normal, besides everyone was doing it. "Decker Davis! Your sister said you'd be by. Why don't you have seat, it's going to be just a bit, I have a few people ahead of you." Mac pointed at a chair and Decker shuffled over to the chair and sat down. "Thanks Mr. Mac. I am not in a hurry." Ollie decided to change the conversation now that young ears were in the shop. "Say Decker," he leaned forward in his seat, "People gossip'n all over town that you are gonna dress for the Choctaws Friday night? Any truth to that?" Decker blushed because he really didn't like people talking about him and he certainly didn't like to talk about himself. Decker nodded and slid his hands under the back of his thighs which was a habit of Decker's when he was nervous. "Yes sir, that's what coach Hayes told me, but it is up to Coach Bond." One of the guys clapped his hands together. Decker turned to look and saw that it was Andy Marko that clapped his hands. "Hot damn son that is awesome! Hadn't been an eighth grader dress for the varsity since your old man did it!" Decker nodded. Decker tried not to look nervous, but he couldn't help it. He didn't like everyone staring at him and it seemed they were all nervous by the way they were fidgeting and trying to think of something to say. Ollie Duckworth couldn't take the silence anymore, so he decided to get up and leave. "I will see you fella's in a week or so." They all waved or said something cordial, but Andy Marko decided to take one last jab at the good-hearted Ollie Duckworth: "I'll wait a few minutes after you leave and then I will say goodbye to that thing on the back of your neck." They all howled with laughter. Ollie didn't retort but he did manage a smile. Decker kind of felt sorry for Ollie. Everyone was always making fun of that big bump on the back of his neck, but Ollie didn't seem to mind.

Mac finished the hair of the man in the chair and was trimming the beard now. Decker still couldn't tell who it was, and he really wasn't looking. He found a *Boy's Life* magazine and was fumbling though it. There was a good article on the value of always carrying a scout knife which Decker made a mental note to add that to his Christmas wish list. He was always very good at dropping hints to his sister and she was always very good at remembering.

Mac finished the man in the chair and spun the chair so the man was now facing the row of chairs with waiting customers. He handed the man a mirror so he could inspect the job that was done on the back. When the man looked though the mirror and approved, he handed the mirror to Mac and that was the first time that Decker saw that it was Donnie Buckles. Decker could feel the air escape his chest and he knew that his eyes got really big. He froze and didn't know what to say. Decker had no problem with Donnie but with the trimmed beard now, Donnie looked a great deal like Brett. Decker thought that all the Buckles looked alike because they all had some kind of facial hair, except Lonnie, of course. Decker figured that if Lonnie hadn't been murdered then he probably would eventually grow a scruffy beard too.

Donnie could tell that Decker was scared and he felt bad inside, but he didn't know what to do. Donnie rubbed his beard and ran his hand though his hair, reached in his pocket for some money but Mac stopped him. "Uh, no charge Donnie. One Marine to another." Donnie smiled a little and thanked Mac then turned to Decker. "Hello Decker, it's good to see you." He paused and looked around the room knowing that everyone was looking at him. Decker was still frozen in his chair and didn't realize that he had dropped the magazine and the two dollars he had in his hand that he was going to use to pay Mac. Donnie took a step toward Decker and stuck out his hand to shake Decker's. "I am sorry about your mother." Decker saw the hand coming at him and had a flash back of when Brett was hitting he and Jeannine by the courthouse that day. Donnie started to finish what he wanted to say: "She was a . . . " Decker leaped from his chair, turned and bolted out the door. He ran as fast as he could. He knew exactly where he was going too, he was headed for library to find Jeannine. He knew she would be there, and he was not about to have anything happen to her.

The door slammed as Decker exited the barbershop. Donnie let his head drop and Mac could see that he was struggling with the moment apparently as much as Decker, but as the door was slamming, Donnie finished what he was going to say, "A good woman." Mac put his hand on Donnie's shoulder. "It's just gonna take some time. He's a good boy, I am sure he didn't mean anything by it." Donnie shook his head as if he agreed. Andy could see that Donnie's face strained as if he were gently wrestling with some demon inside him at the moment. "Yep Mac, lotta time." Donnie bent down picked up the two-dollar bills and the *Boys Life* that Decker dropped, "Mind if I take this?" Mac shook his head that he didn't mind. "Thanks for the haircut Mac. Nice work." Donnie nodded at the other fella's in the barbershop and he walked out the door. Albert stood to get in the chair as it was finally his turn. "No tellin' what terrible things they did to that boy over there."

Chapter 6
The Library

DECKER WAS RUNNING AT FULL speed and nearly ran into Mrs. Tackitt as she was coming out of Milholen's drug store. He was quick enough to avoid the collision and she yelled something at him, but he didn't hear what she said. Mrs. Tackitt lost her husband in the war or at least it was believed he was lost. After all the prisoners were released, which included Donnie Buckles, she was notified by the war department that her husband was officially listed as missing in action. She held out hope that they were wrong and maybe her husband was on the last plane to arrive home, but he was not. She was a beautiful lady, but she carried a sadness about her that made Decker sad too. He made a mental note as he was running to apologize to her the next time he saw her.

He bounded down the steps that led to the street from the sidewalk where he crossed the street without looking either way. The street was always pretty slow, so he never really bothered to look anyway but today he was determined to get to the library. He took the library steps three at a time and busted though the front door.

The library was quiet like it always was and the noise that Decker made as he rumbled through the door startled the librarian and she dropped a book she was holding which made even more noise. A huge SH-H-H-H came from where he expected it came from, right where Jeannine was sitting. He was relieved that she was there and was safe. He slowed down but not before the librarian came right up next to him and whispered, "Decker Davis! You know better than to come in here like that! Shame on you!" He turned to apologize but she was already walking away. He was breathing a little heavy because of the way he ran from the barbershop to the library. He tried to slow his breathing and he sort of tip toed to Jeannine's table. He shook his head when he saw that she was reading a quantum physics book. He loved to listen to her talk about space and space travel and how she going to get a job working for NASA and she had to read all of these kinds of books even if she wasn't required to read them in school.

He sat down at her table and he put his hand on her forearm as he always did when he sat down beside her at the library. She would pretend she didn't know he was there but, in this instance, she couldn't pretend because she had already given him a big SHUSH. She had her head down and was reading or at least Decker thought she was pretending to be reading, she loved to brush him off as much as she could. He loved to touch her arm and hold her hand if she would let him; but most times she wouldn't, but in the library, when there was no one else around, she would let him keep his hand on her hand but not actually hold her hand. His heart would beat so fast that he would be afraid to move a muscle. He wanted to have his hand on hers as long as he could. Today with his hand on her forearm he leaned over and kissed her on the cheek. This was a bold move for Decker, but he was so relieved that she was okay. "Decker Davis!" She leaned away from him, but he could see the smile on her face, and it made him smile. "What in the world has gotten into you!" He let the smile disappear from his face and whispered, "I just saw Donnie Buckles." She leaned forward very quickly and tried to whisper but it came out loud, "Where?!" Decker put his hand back on her forearm and this time she put her hand on top of his. It was the most comfortable reassuring thing that he had felt since his mother died. "In the Barbershop. I thought maybe he had come for you again. I got scared." Jeannine could see the strain on Decker's face and thought for a minute that her heart would jump out of her chest. She now understood why Decker came barreling into the library like he did. She realized he was worried about her. She could feel the tears well up in her eyes and tried to stop them, but she couldn't, one giant rolled down her cheek. All the memories of that awful day came rolling back into her mind. She saw how bad her grandad's face looked and how she thought he was going to die that day. How Mr. Davis sat with both her and Decker with his arms wrapped around them. It was the worst day of her life and she had done everything she could to put it behind her. Decker reached up and wiped the tear away from her cheek with his thumb. When the motion of his hand reached the side of her cheek, he cupped her cheek and leaned forward and kissed her on the forehead. The act made Jeannine cry and she scooted close to Decker and hugged him. He held on to her and whispered. "It's ok. I won't let anyone hurt you." She nodded her head as if she understood and said, "Let's go home". He pulled away, closed all the books on the table and got up to go put them back. Jeannine sat there and stared straight ahead. When Decker was finished putting the books away, he came back to the table, saw that her library card had fallen from the table to the floor, he bent down, picked up and put it in his front pants pocket. He would give it to her later, but he was afraid that if he gave it to her now, she would lose it again. She might have been the smartest girl in the world, but she tended to lose small things. He put his hand under her underarm to helped her up. She rose and turned and looked at him. Decker could see the tears well up in her eyes again and decided the best course of action was to hug her, so he did. When he hugged her, she immediately let out all of her tears. Decker could feel her body shake against his, but she wasn't making any noise. He knew she was crying, and he also knew that she hated to cry. She once told him that it was a sign of weakness.

Decker held the door open for her as they exited the library. He waved at the librarian as they were leaving. Once they were on the sidewalk, Decker looked both ways fully expecting to see Donnie coming after them with another baseball bat, but he didn't see anything. He still needed a haircut and knew exactly where to get one. "We have to go see your dad before we go home. I ain't going back to Mac's as long as Donnie is there, and I still have to get a haircut or Heather will have my hide when I get home." Jeannine smiled at the thought and they both started walking south towards Dub's Barbershop. They were walking side by side down the sidewalk. They walked past Milholen's drug store and Barlow's hardware when Jeannine took Decker's hand. He didn't argue one bit and as a matter of fact he found it hard to breathe for just a second. She hadn't held hands with him in public ever. As they crossed the street that led to the railroad tracks a car slowly pulled up beside them. The window to the passenger seat slowly rolled down but only about halfway. Just as Decker was about to say something, Aubrey Bigelow drove up and the car rolled up its window and slowly drove away. Aubrey pulled alongside Decker and Jeannine. He rolled down the window and Decker could clearly see him. Aubrey flipped the lights to the police car on, but he was only kidding around with Decker. "Hey kids!" He flipped off the lights and Decker turned his attention from the car that just rolled away to the police car that Aubrey was driving. "Decker are you ready for the game tomorrow? I am gonna be there! Everyone is saying that you are going to dress for the varsity on Friday! Is that true?" Decker felt his face flush a little, he hated attention like this, and he definitely hated being asked about dressing for the varsity.

He didn't see it as a big deal but apparently the town did. He was tired of answering questions about it and now wished that Coach Bond hadn't asked him to dress.

The attention he was getting was unbearable. He only wished his dad knew. Jeannine must have sensed that Decker was embarrassed, so she started talking. "I am here too Chief! You men only notice Decker these days and I think its high time you started recognizing the women of this community." She smiled when she said it and she said it in a way that was playful. Aubrey knew she was playing with him. "Now you look here young lady, this is man talk, beauty and charm doesn't cut it with me." He laughed and so did she. At least for minute the Chief had taken her mind off that day. "Listen, you kids need to watch yourself, just got a missing girl report and from what the report says, she is about your age. There are some crazy people out there and I can't have the town king and queen getting abducted!" He laughed but it was a nervous laugh. Decker could tell that he was trying to hide something, but his dad always said that Aubrey Bigelow was the worst poker player in town. "Thank you Chief, we are just going to her dad's barber shop to get a haircut." Aubrey smiled and nodded and started to drive off but stopped. "Say Decker you never answered, is it true?" Decker smiled and answered, "Yes sir it is." Aubrey pulled away but Decker and Jeannine could hear him say to himself: "I'll be darned."

Decker looked around for the car that had slowed to a stop, but he didn't see it and began walking again. This time he took Jeannine's hand in his. He had an uneasy feeling in his stomach about the car, but he wasn't for sure if the feeling was spurred on by seeing Donnie Buckles. He knew Donnie didn't have anything to do with what his brothers did, in fact, everyone in town said that if it hadn't been for Donnie, Elmer Davis would be in prison for beating Brett Buckles to death.

Jeannine never protested his holding her hand when he was brave enough to do it. Most of the time she was the one that had to instigate the affection but today, Decker was in full blown protective mode. "Decker, please don't say anything to my dad about Donnie being back in town." Decker stopped walking, turned to look at her. "You know I don't keep secrets very well; I hate them actually." She laughed and squeezed his hand. "I know you hate secrets and that is what I like most about you, but you know my dad gets really mad and he can't control his temper." Decker nodded in agreement but was still working through the potential problems of keeping this secret and really couldn't find any reason to tell her dad or anyone else for that matter. "I don't see any reason he needs to know now. I don't see that as a secret it's just information that isn't important." She smiled, stopped, and stood on her tip toes and kissed him on the cheek. Something she rarely did but he sure liked it.

Decker held the door open for Jeannine as they entered Dub's barber shop. They were both greeted by her dad who stopped cutting hair for a second and came to hug Jeannine as he always did. He rubbed Decker on the head which Decker hated but never let on like he did. Decker really thought that Bobby Martin did it on purpose because he knew that Decker didn't like it. In fact, Decker was already as tall as Bobby, so Bobby had to reach up to rub his head. Danny Reed was in the chair getting a trim and Charlie B was sitting in the second chair picking at an old Fender electric guitar. Decker loved hearing Charlie B play. He was a master at picking out any song you could think of and lots that Decker had never heard. "What are you kids doing today?" Jeannine was scared that Decker was going to explain why he was at their shop instead of Mac's, so she quickly said: "Decker heard Charlie B was in here and wanted to hear him and get a haircut at the same time!" She made sure to sound very excited about the whole thing. Charlie B smiled as he picked out what Decker thought was an old Lead Belly tune called "Midnight Special", but he couldn't be sure.

"Decker Davis, as much as you like music, I can't understand for the love of Pete why you don't pick up a guitar and go to work!"

Charlie B stopped picking his guitar long enough to make sure that Decker heard him. Decker never heard what Charlie B's last name was, he just knew that everyone called him Charlie B. Decker tried to call him Mr. B one day, but Charlie corrected him immediately and Decker never tried to call him anything but Charlie B after that. "Even if I tried, I could never play like you, sir." Everyone in the barbershop stopped for a second as Charlie B switched from Lead Belly to what sounded like "How great thou art." "Hell, I know that boy! Ain't nobody gonna ever be as good as me but it never hurts to try!" Everyone laughed at the comment, including Decker. "Decker just have a seat and I will get you next. Charlie B is just entertaining." Decker sat down and looked for a magazine, but he didn't see any he liked. Jeannine sat down beside him and took his hand. Taking his hand was something she NEVER did in front of her dad. Decker took it for a second without thinking but then he realized where they were, he let go quickly and stuck his hand in his pockets. Jeannine just smiled and rolled her eyes at him. She liked to try and embarrass Decker every chance she could. It wasn't that he didn't want to hold her hand, he loved that part, but he did not want her daddy upset with him. Everyone knew that Bobby Martin had a short fuse and Decker was not about to light it. "Decker, I hear you are dressing for the varsity Friday night, tell me that's a lie!" Jimmy, who was letting Bobby trim the back of his neck was laughing as he said it." Bobby turned the clippers off and used it to point as he spoke. "Now you look here, Decker here, is my baby's boyfriend and there ain't nobody allowed to pick at him but me." He was smiling as he said it. "Now you get up out of that chair and let me cut that boy's hair!" Bobby playfully smacked Jimmy on the back of the head with his hand and yanked the barber apron off Jimmy at the same time. "Come on Decker!" Bobby patted the chair and Decker climbed in the chair.

The tune Charlie B changed to was something that Decker had never heard, but immediately liked. It was a hard strum with some kind of upward pick, and he let his hand slide up and down the frets of the guitar so effortlessly, pressing harder on the strings when he wanted more sound and more softly when he hummed with his picking. "So, Decker, I need to tell you to forget all the talk. Play hard on Thursday and forget Friday. It's a big deal for sure but don't ever forget to play one game at a time." Decker smiled and said, "Yes sir, I don't take things too serious and I really kinda wish folks would quit talking about it. I probably won't even play Friday night." Bobby started cutting Decker's hair, but he continued to speak. "That's the right attitude young man but don't go into Friday night thinking you aren't gonna play, you need to go into it thinking you ARE going to play and prepare like the dickens so that if it happens. You will be ready." He paused for a second, looked up in the air, and then around the room, "I reckon that attitude is proper in life too. I wish someone had told me that when I was your age." Decker could see Jeannine smiling at him which made him smile.

When Bobby finished cutting Decker's hair, he threw some of that barber powder on the back of Decker's neck that he liked so much because of the way it smelled and then brushed him with that big handle soft brush that he also thoroughly enjoyed. "There you go Decker!" Bobby yanked the apron off of Decker in one swooping motion and patted Decker on the head at the same time. "That'll be two bucks, young man." Decker reached in his right pocket and didn't find the money Heather had given him. He fished in his left pocket and didn't find it there either. His hands began to dart everywhere as he tried his back pockets with no luck. Charlie B sat up in his chair with his guitar in his hand and began to pick out a song he had obviously just made up on spot. *"Man got to feel good about the way he done look"* Dun dun ah dun dun . . ."*Find him a good woman that knows how to cooks"* dun dun ah dun dun. *"go to the doctor when it hurts him to go pee!"* Dun dun ah dun dun, *"Save all his money . . .by getting' his haircut for free!"* Charlie B couldn't finish the last strum and twang before the whole barbershop burst out laughing, including Jeannine. Decker had to admit that it was pretty creative, and he was impressed with the tune, but he still couldn't figure out what happened to the money he was given for a haircut. "Decker Davis, you trying to stiff me for a haircut?" Bobby gave him a stern look but Decker sort of knew that Mr. Martin would have no problem taking payment later which is what he would have to do because Decker clearly had lost the money. "No sir, Heather gave me the money this morning and I forgot where I put it. I promise I will bring it to you." After the laughter subsided completely, Charlie B went back to pickin' a tune, Decker thought he had heard it before, but he couldn't place it. "I'm just messin' with you Decker, pay me when you find it." Bobby shook the apron out one more time, folded it and tossed it onto the bar behind him. Decker was relieved and he turned to leave, Jeannine grabbed his hand and he recoiled. He was still not comfortable holding her hand in front of her dad.

Chapter 7

Parchman

THE BUZZER SOUNDED and all the inmates emerged from
their cell. It was time for a head count and breakfast. It was Judd's
favorite time of the day. It was early and most of the inmates were
too sleepy to start trouble. He didn't feel like he had to have eyes in
the back of his head like his dad had told him when he entered. He
also liked it because he got to see Brett and his father at breakfast.
Judd was in a different cell block than Brett and his father. Judd
pleaded guilty to assault with a deadly weapon charges, but the
judge gave him less time and a lighter sentence of 4 to 10 years
because in the judges words, "Judd was a victim of simple mindedness and had been overly influenced by his big brother Brett.
Brett on the other hand was sentenced to 5 to 27 years because
again in the judge's words he was "the most spiteful, cold hearted
and downright meanest person that he had ever seen in his court-
room." The judge actually said to Brett that he wished he could
give him the death sentence, that his actions towards humanity in
general were despicable and he hoped that he could someday find
a peace that would change his black heart.

Judd took his tray and immediately found his father sitting
with Brett. There were no cordial good mornings over prison

breakfast, but Judd felt comfortable sitting with his family. "I got word last night from the guard that my ole pal is returning this afternoon and it will be time for a little payback." Donnie Buckles Sr. shoved a fork full of eggs into his mouth as he spoke. "Word has it that he tried to rob a bank over in Holly Springs and accidently shot himself in the thigh trying to put his gun back in his pants." He laughed when he said it a little bit of the eggs he was eating escaped from his mouth and landed on his chin. Judd laughed a little, not at the comment but the fact that his dad had no idea the small piece of scrambled eggs was even on his chin. Judd had no idea who his dad was talking about and really didn't care. "Yeah, he botched that deal for sure." Brett was the first to speak back to the patriarch of the family. "I was planning on taking the Sheriff's wife for my own when he was out of the way and now because those two idiots shot the wrong person, I can't even do that!" Brett had a very serious look on his face when he said it but his dad didn't take it that way. Donnie Sr. laughed out loud: "HA! That high class broad would not have anything to do with you and you are a fool if you think she would!" Brett frowned because he didn't like being put down and he was definitely being put down. "Oh, get over it, you idiot. It's a status thing. You aren't in her league and unless you strike oil in the delta you will never be in her league son." Brett still didn't like being put down like that, even if it was his dad doing it. He also knew better than to argue or back talk. His dad didn't take guff from anyone, especially his boys. "What are going to do when he gets here?" Donnie Sr. bit off a piece of bacon and then ate some bread. "It ain't what I am gonna do, it is what you and your brother are gonna do." Judd didn't like the sound of that. The last time he did what he was told was when he helped beat up that high school kid. At first, he thought he was doing what he was supposed to but when he saw Brett hitting that little girl, it bothered him. He didn't care what color she was; she was still a little girl and he just didn't think it was right to hit that girl or the

Sheriff's kid. He remembered he was about to holler for Brett to stop but that Donnie Ray kid showed up out of nowhere and started getting the best of his brother. He was always told that blood was thicker than water so he couldn't let that kid beat up his big brother so that's when he hit him with a baseball bat.

"You and Judd need to get him in the rec yard this afternoon. I have it arranged with the guards." He slid a napkin over to Brett and under it was a homemade knife. Keep this out of sight until Thursday." Donnie Sr. looked around and rubbed his forehead. "I paid that son-of-a-bitch to kill the sheriff, not his damn wife. It's been three years and he hasn't bothered to apologize or give me my damn money back!" He stopped rubbing his forehead and looked at Judd, "I get my pay back now!" Judd started to get up. "Where the hell are you going?" Donnie Sr. was always in charge and he didn't excuse anyone from the table. "I said sit down!" Judd stopped, set his plate back down on the table but stood there. "Daddy, I am up for parole in 6 months, the warden says I got a good shot at making it if I keep my nose clean." Judd looked over at Brett then back to his dad. "I can't get into this." Judd started to grab his tray from the table again, but his dad slammed his hand right down in the middle of it which made a heck of a racket. The noise around them stopped for a second but soon it became noisy again. "Let me tell you something Tinkerbelle." Donnie Sr. took his fork and pointed it at Judd, "The only reason you haven't become somebody's bitch in this hell hole is because of ME!" You will do what I tell you, you simple minded little shit. And if you do what I tell you to; your ass stays intact, if not, I will give the nod that you are fair game, and the bull queers will make you a queen for the rest of your painful time!" Judd looked at his father and he could feel his face getting red. He didn't like being threatened anymore and he sure didn't want to stay in Parchman any longer than he had to. Committing an assault in the yard would insure him at least another 4 years. He really had some thinking to do. He grabbed his tray and left the mess hall.

"You think he will help, Pops?" Donnie scratched his head as he watched Judd walk away. "First time I've seen him show some backbone. Hells bells, little Lonnie was tougher than Judd. Surprises me he did that." Brett turned to watch his brother put his tray in the slot and walk out. "I ain't gonna count on him this afternoon. I will handle it myself." Brett looked at his Daddy, "Besides, don't you think he could be handy for us in here if he were out there? Right now, we ain't got nobody bringing stuff in and your stash is gonna run out soon." Donnie Sr. stared at Brett then squinted his eyes and leaned forward, "Don't try to grow a brain on me now dipshit. I do the thinking in this family."

Judd made his way back down the hall toward his cell when he was stopped by a guard. "Hey Judd, the Warden wants to see you." Judd stopped and looked around, he knew the guard, but not well. He saw him occasionally in the yard but not often. Someone told him that he was mainly a tower guard and only rotated to the yard when someone called in sick. His badge plate said 'Murphy' but Judd really didn't care what his name was. It was going to be a long day for him. He was going to have to figure out how to avoid the deed his father wanted him to do in the yard today and how to get out of this place as soon as he could. Maybe the warden had figured out a way to help him stay on track. Murphy led him down a hallway that led to the main hallway. Judd could hear him humming as he walked in front of him. They came to an 'L' in the hallway where Judd could only turn left, so he did. When he turned left, he saw in the hallway two men mopping, he tried to avoid the wet spots, "HEY! Off my damn floor!" one of the men yelled at him and leaned on his mop handle. Judd turned to look at the guard, but the guard was gone. He knew something was wrong when he looked back at the man that was leaning on his mop handle. The man leaning on the mop was smiling. He turned quickly to run back down the hall that would lead him to the cafeteria, but his path was now blocked by two other men. He was trapped and he had no idea why. He hadn't done anything to hurt anyone. His mind raced, he hadn't taken sides, he was not with the whites or the blacks, he was very careful not to offend either. "Y'all have the wrong guy. I ain't done anything to anybody and I don't want no trouble." The man leaning on the mop just laughed. "We don't want no trouble either and I know you're a good little boy. Your Daddy is the bad boy of the family." He dropped the mop handle, and it made a loud echo when it hit the floor. "We are all gonna have a taste and send you back to your daddy all sweet and broke in." Judd didn't know what that meant but he knew it couldn't be good, so he took a swing at the first man that was blocking his path, but the man stepped free of the punch and then delivered an uppercut that sent Judd falling to the floor in a crumpled heap. He spent three weeks in the infirmary and didn't remember much about that day, but he knew what they did to him and it hurt.

Chapter 8
Prayer Meeting

DECKER WALKED INTO THE CHURCH with Jeannine. He was careful to hold the door for her. She hardly ever went to church on Wednesdays with him. She went to Sunday service several times and he reciprocated by going to her church also. They were good at switching out Sunday's and had now been doing it for so long that neither felt like a visitor in either church. "Decker, I don't want to hear about the Battle of Pea Ridge right now." Decker had just read all the facts on the Civil War battle that took place in Northwest Arkansas. He was deeply into it and loved to talk to Jeannine about it. She was so quite on the walk over from her dad's barber shop that he couldn't figure out what to say to her. He knew she was still thinking about that day and so was he, but he knew from experience that it was better to change the subject if you didn't like the subject stuck in your head. "Well, you ain't sayin' too much and I didn't know what to say. I just hated not being able to make you feel better."

Decker stuck his hands in the front pockets of his Levi's jeans that Heather had helped him buy. Heather liked to take him to look for clothes. He was growing so fast that he often outgrew his clothes before they were broke in. He hated brand new jeans too. They were too stiff and made him feel like he was walking with burlap tied around his legs. Not to mention that brand new jeans never fit right. Since Heather had taken on the duties his mother uses to have, she always bought everything too big so he could grow into it, shoes included. When he got a brand-new pair of sneakers, he would have to wear two pairs of socks for a while until his feet grew into them. That was never good either because the more socks he wore, the more his feet would sweat and then Heather would complain about his stinky feet. Jeannine smiled at him as she stepped through the door, "I don't even know where Pea Ridge, Arkansas is." He started to tell her, but she interrupted, "And I don't care where it is." He started to say something again, but she continued, "Now if you were to tell me that there was a battle of Webb, Mississippi then I would want to know all about it!" Decker laughed at the thought and started to tell her about the battle of Brice's Crossroads just north of Tupelo, but she had made it clear that she only wanted to hear about the war if there was a battle actually in Webb.

"Well hello Decker and Jeannine! It is nice to have you in prayer meeting tonight! Especially you Jeannine, we don't get to see you on Wednesday nights." Mrs. Charlene was the pastor's wife, Decker always thought that she might be the nicest person he'd ever met. She always smiled, and Decker thought she was pretty for a grown up and he liked the fact that she could sing like a songbird and play the piano all at the same time. Decker was fascinated with anyone you could play an instrument. He wasn't clumsy at all, but it seemed to him that in order to play an instrument you had to get your hands to move by themselves and get your brain to move separate from your hands. It was just too much going on. Before his mom died, she tried to get him to practice controlling his hand movements by rubbing his stomach with one hand and patting the top of his head with the other. He never could do it. Mrs. Charlene stepped forward and hugged Jeannine and then hugged Decker. That was another thing he liked about Mrs. Charlene, she always hugged him like his mother used to. She would squeeze tight and hang on for just split second longer than he did. "My goodness Decker you are taller than me now!" Decker was about to say something about his jeans being almost broke in, but Pastor Lloyd came up and announced his presence. He had a big voice and there was never any mistaking his words. He could be heard clearly when he preached his sermons. "Decker Davis, I hear you are dressing for the varsity this Friday, is that right?" He said it in question form, but it came out more as an excited statement. "I'm telling you buddy I remember when me and your daddy played on the same team but neither one of us could hold a candle to you!" He laughed and then looked at Jeannine, "Young lady I think you get prettier every time I see you and just don't see how that's possible!' Jeanine smiled and Decker could tell that she liked the attention. He liked the attention too but not about dressing for the varsity this Friday. He was getting embarrassed by all the questions about it. He honestly had no idea why he was being asked to dress because it certainly wasn't to play quarterback. The varsity had a very good quarterback already in Mike Ford and he would probably play in college next year. He wasn't as good as Donnie Ray Richardson, but then nobody was.

"Who do we have here?" A short stocky man walked up to the conversation with a smile on his face. Mrs. Charlene stepped away so that the short man could see Decker and Jeannine, "Jim this is Decker Davis and Jeannine Martin." She made a swooping motion with her arm and made a little bow as if she were introducing the queen or something but again, Decker noticed that Jeannine liked it. "Decker and Jeannine, this is Jim Johnson our new youth minister." Jim stuck out his hand for Decker to shake which Decker did easily although Decker did not like the grip this man had. It wasn't firm as a grown up should be, but he let it go. Jim then stuck his hand out for Jeannine and shook hers. Decker tried to watch and see if maybe he could tell how well the new guy was gripping Jeannine's hand when he shook it, but he couldn't tell so he just forgot about it. "It is so nice to meet you both." He stepped back a little from the conversation and looked around, "My wife is around here somewhere, and I'd like y'all to meet her." They all scanned the church as if they were expecting her to materialize soon. "Well, I don't see her, but I bet she went over to the parsonage to tidy up a little. She is nervous about meeting everyone tonight."

Mrs. Charlene looked around a little while longer then spotted her, "There she is, come on over hun!" A tall lady came over to where they were all standing. When she was next to Jim, she put her arm around him, and Decker nearly laughed out loud but he stopped himself. She was at least a foot taller than her husband. The two did not look like they belonged together at all, but Decker decided that wasn't his business at all. "Well, who do we have here?" The tall lady smiled, then it struck Decker that not only was she a foot taller than her husband, she was taller than everyone standing in the huddle. He sort of let his back heels come off the ground and stood slightly on his tip toes so he could at least be as tall as this lady. He held the position for as long as he could but then his legs started to hurt so he put himself flat footed again. "Why Janet this is Decker Davis and Jeannine Martin!" Mrs. Charlene clasped her hands together and smiled as introduced the two then said, "Decker and Jeannine are quite the couple. Kids, this is Janet Johnson."

Decker felt a hand on his back, and he turned to see his sister standing there behind him. "Well hello Heather!" Mrs. Charlene nearly knocked Decker out of the way to get to Heather where the two women hugged for a few seconds. Decker and Jeannine took the opportunity to slip away from the adult chatter although he really didn't think of his sister as an adult. He really didn't know what category she fit in now. She was a mom and a sister, and he wondered which one would show up when he told her he lost the two dollars she gave him. "Did you see how tall that woman was?" Jeannine was trying to whisper but she still wasn't very good at it. He put his finger up to his lips to help he understand she wasn't as quite as she thought she was. He whispered back, "Yes and how short her husband was." He smiled when he said it and they both giggled a little. They found a place to sit that was not on the back row, but it was pretty close. His momma wouldn't ever allow him to sit on the back row and out of respect for her he never tried, even after she was gone.

Heather came over and sat beside them putting Jeannine in the middle. Heather leaned over and whispered in Decker's ear, "I think Daddy is coming back to us. I will tell you about it tonight when we are all at home." She smiled a smile that Decker hadn't seen in a very long time and it made him feel good. He loved Heather more than he would ever be able to tell her because every time he really wanted to tell her; he got the feeling he was being just too mushy so he would stop himself.

When they all sat together this was usually the order of things, Jeannine in the middle of Decker and Heather. One other thing that Heather always did was grab Jeannine's hand and hold it during the service. Decker never asked her why she did that, but he knew that Jeannine liked it. He figured it was a girl thing. He was about to whisper something to Jeannine when he heard Mrs. Charlene begin to play the piano. That was always the signal to find your seat because service was about to begin.

Decker sat back in the pew and tried to focus on the service. He had his fingers locked together and placed in his lap when he felt a hand touch his. He looked down and saw that Jeannine was prying his fingers apart and when she was successful she locked her fingers into his, now Jeannine didn't have any more free hands to spare, the Davis kid's hands had a good grip on both of hers. He looked at her and smiled, she winked at him and they both looked towards the new youth minister.

The new youth minister stood at the pulpit where the pastor normally did his best work, but it was Wednesday and the pastor just sat back and enjoyed the sermon of a visitor, evangelist, or in this case the new youth minister. The pastor was kind enough to introduce the short youth minister and his tall wife, a fact that Decker continued to struggle with. He tried to imagine Jeannine being taller than him and he guessed it didn't bother him, so he wasn't sure why the height thing with this new preacher was stuck in his mind so much. Jeannine squeezed his hand to get his attention, she always knew when he was daydreaming too much.

"God is good, God is loving, God is truth and God is forgiving." The short pastor stuck his finger in the air as if he were pointing directly at God. He seemed to have trouble reaching the microphone with his voice and tried to adjust the stand so the microphone would lower but he couldn't do it and the microphone dropped on the wood top of pulpit and made a racket. He quickly grabbed it and flung the electrical cord around the pulpit so that he could move out from behind the pulpit. Jeannine squeezed his hand only this time it was to keep her focused. It must have just struck her how short he was, and she wanted to laugh. Squeezing Decker's hand kept her focused. He didn't mind but this squeeze was causing his knuckles to turn hard white. The short pastor stepped down from the platform the pulpit stood on and was now standing eye-to-eye with the audience and that made Decker chuckle because the audience was sitting, and he was standing!

"God has a plan for all of us, God knows what we are doing, and he is disappointed in our behavior and our children." He stopped and reached into his back pocket and took out a handkerchief and wiped his forehead. He was sweating and was clearly nervous. "I have been sent here, along with my wife, to help set the path for the youth of Webb and to help guide them back to the path of righteousness and away from the paths of sin." There were a few murmurs from the crowd, Decker thought he made out an Amen in one of the murmurs, but he wasn't sure. There weren't many head nods either. Clearly it was not starting off the way he wanted it. He walked down the middle aisle of the congregation and was starting to look and feel more at ease but as he reached about the third pew back, the cord for the microphone ran out and it yanked him back a little. The microphone hit him in the front tooth and made a high-pitched squeal. The metal smashing against his front tooth must have hurt because he bent forward and let the microphone drop to the ground. There was a big gasp from the crowd, and everything went quiet for a second. Decker could see Pastor Lloyd stand up and start to make his way towards the struggling youth minister but just as he was about to step off the podium the youth pastor grabbed the mic off the floor and stood straight up and started talking as if nothing had happened.

"Today is more important than ever that we embrace the youth of Webb and teach them that the sins of the flesh are nothing to be taken lightly and that the temptation of our youth is as great as it had ever been!" Unfortunately, he got excited that he was back on track and took a step forward which caused the microphone to hit him in the forehead this time. Even though this was comical to Decker and to Jeannine because every time the poor pastor hit himself with the mic, she would squeeze his hand harder. This time the microphone to the head took its toll and the short pastor dropped to a knee. Pastor Lloyd stepped down from the podium and made his way to the struggling pastor. The audience began to pray out loud for the health of the pastor. The prayers were meant well by the congregation, but it only made things worse. Things like: "Help that man understand his limits!" and "God help that tooth heel so fast!" and "Lord heal brother Johnson's forehead!" Decker couldn't help it and he laughed out loud. His laughter caused Heather to smack him on the back of the head which made him stop laughing quickly.

Pastor Lloyd put his hand on Jim Johnson's back as he continued to kneel. He said a prayer that wasn't loud enough for the congregation to hear in the back where Decker was sitting. He then leaned down and whispered something in the youth minister's ear. The youth minister lifted his head and looked around the congregation and slowly rose to a standing position. The congregation applauded which made Decker think of the time he saw a guy get hurt on the football field and when he finally stood up and staggered off the field with the help of coaches and teammates, the crowd cheered for him. Someone in front of Decker near the front row said, "Amen, preach it brother!" Pastor Lloyd patted Jim on the back, made a little wave at the congregation and returned to the podium and the chair where he had been sitting.

Youth Minister Jim Johnson smiled and for a second Decker thought he saw one of his eyeballs roll back in his head. It was a weird look that almost made Decker laugh again, but Decker returned his focus as he felt Jeannine's hand squeeze his very hard. The young pastor shook his head as a way clear the cobwebs out of his head. That was a term Decker's football coach would use when he would get hit hard playing football. In Decker's opinion, shaking your head never worked. Some days he would forget what happened in practice so easily that the coach would yell at him the next practice for forgetting something. "The Devil is determined tonight church!" The young pastor took a few steps back towards the podium, releasing the tension on the mic cord. He apparently had learned his lesson and understood the parameters of electronic limitations much better now. He didn't return to the pulpit though. He stayed just beneath it down by where the alters waited on folks to come pray when the mood struck them. "The devil doesn't have limitations church! The Devil doesn't have obstacles folks! The devil has victims and I refuse to be a victim of the devil tonight!" That really got the congregation going and it also breathed new life into the clumsy pastor. Decker was sort of relieved because he was certain that if he saw that pastor conk himself in the face with that microphone one more time, he would for sure laugh out loud and not be able to stop. His hand already hurt where Jeannine was squeezing it, but he didn't dare tell her. Everything seemed to go relatively smooth after that and the pastor pounded his message home to the congregation about the devil's power and how the youth are all so tempted today by television and advertising and that as grown-ups, they all had an obligation to steer the children in the right direction and ensure that they have a non-judgmental passage into heaven.

Decker stood as requested as did everyone else while Pastor Lloyd closed the prayer meeting with a nice prayer thanking God for his assistance with tonight's message. Once the prayer ended, Decker and Jeannine along with his sister stepped out into the aisle and made their way to the back of the church where the youth minister and Pastor Lloyd were waiting to greet and thank everyone for attending. When Decker got to the two men, Jeannine let go of his hand so he could shake hands with the two men but to his horror he realized that his hand was cramping now and it had taken on a closed, gnarly look to it, not to mention that it hurt. The youth minister saw the hand, "Are you alright son?" Decker tried to rub his shaking hand with his left hand to work out the cramp, but it wasn't budging. He grimaced as he spoke, "Yes sir, it's just a cramp." Pastor Lloyd laughed and patted Decker on the shoulder and was about to say something but was interrupted by the youth minister, "Might be a message from God, son."

Chapter 9
Heather

HEATHER FINISHED PUTTING AWAY the dishes. She was tired, not physically, well maybe a little but she was tired mentally. She missed her mother but more painful for her was that her mother's death had robbed her of her what she called her formative years. She felt guilty thinking this way, but she couldn't help it. She ceased to be a teenager the day her mother died. She wanted the same things that every girl her age wanted, she wanted to have fun, sneak a beer, break curfew, date a boy, make out with a boy for heaven's sake but she couldn't. Since her mother was murdered, she had been mom junior in her mind. She wasn't loose and didn't have sex like the other girls in her junior college and she wasn't sure that she even wanted to, but she at least wanted to be able to tell a boy no when he got too excited. When most boys found out that her dad was the County Sheriff, they would shy away from her. That fact alone would drive her insane because she knew that in her Dad's present state, she could get pregnant and have a baby in the middle of their living room and he wouldn't even notice.

In her mind she told herself that she did the right thing by not going away to college and staying at home and going to junior college. She hated that all her friends went off to Ole Miss or Mississippi State, she even had one girlfriend that went off to Washington State and here she was, stuck in Webb, having to try and fill the gaps she could because of her mother's death. She loved Decker and didn't mind looking after him, there was no doubt about that, but she couldn't help but want to be a kid again. She wanted her mother back and it hurt every time she thought about it, but she didn't dare show that to Decker. Decker dealt with the grief in his own way and he had Jeannine to help him. She had no one.

It hurt the most when her dad started drinking, it was a little at first but then it increasingly got worse. Neither of her parents were prudish about drinking and both enjoyed a beer or some wine every now and then, but it was always in moderation. When she caught him pouring a drink, straight shot of whiskey at 7 AM, she knew he had a problem. She tried to say something about it but she soon realized that the man she knew as her father was gone. He seemed broken and she had no idea how to fix him. He wasn't mean or violent, he simply wasn't there. She prayed every night that their family would heal from all the pain they had endured.

A year after her mother died, she took a job at Turner Brothers working around her school schedule and for the most part, Decker's schedule. She would work today but she would not work for the next few days. On Thursday she would have Decker's normal football game, but this week she asked for Friday night off. She wanted to be at Friday's game because Decker was going to dress for the varsity which was a big deal and the whole town was talking about it. There was no way she was going to miss that moment for Decker because she wasn't sure that her dad would make it to the game regardless of how big of deal it was for a freshman. She normally worked on Friday nights, but she asked off the minute that Decker told her that Coach Bond asked him to dress Friday night. She felt like she was more excited about it than Decker. He hated the attention. All those years of Decker trying not to be noticed were now gone. Even though he still tried to remain in the shadows, he was a local spotlight.

At first, she didn't like working at the store, but later it grew on her. She found she liked the interaction with customers as it took her mind off the problems she was having at home. The manager was a nice man, he was Greek, or at least she thought he was. He had huge eyebrows that took on a life of their own when he started talking. He would walk through the store and tell her everything she needed to do and was very detailed about how to do it. He would meticulously instruct her on everything from how to properly clean the bird cages in the back of the store to how to break down and clean the popcorn machine in the front of the store. He was demanding of everyone, but he was good to her and she appreciated it. He made the job interesting, but she mainly liked the fact that it took her away from her home for just a few hours.

She loved the interaction with customers so much that she wanted to be the expert reference on items. She especially loved trying to help them find things that they needed. The store was small and didn't have a lot of room for excess inventory so there was a main catalogue that they used to order things they didn't have and she would peruse it daily just so she could answer questions without having to reference it. She knew almost everyone that came into the store and was always genuinely happy to see them, except for the one customer that recently seemed to browse everything, including items specifically for ladies. At first it bothered her that he would ask questions of her about women's sizes and how they differed from men's sizes, but she figured that maybe he was buying a gift for his wife and wanted it to be a secret. It wasn't so much the questions that he asked, it was the way he seemed to look at her. She told her manager about it but not until the man had come in for a third time and was asking the same questions, he had already asked her. He bought something small every time he was there, but the questions were always the same. The Greek manager told her not to worry about it and that men always had trouble shopping for things that women would wear later. It was just human nature, and she should let it go.

Chapter 10
I'm Sorry

ELMER SAT AT HIS DESK with his head down staring at the coffee-stained desk calendar that hadn't been changed since the beginning of the year. He stared at some of the notes he had written on the January blocks and remembered all his resolutions and the notes that he made on the calendar that would help him keep those resolutions. He read the quote that he thought was from Abraham Lincoln that said, *"Whatever you are, be a good one"* that he wrote at the top of the calendar to help him stay focused, but nothing worked. Every day he wrestled with the ghost of his wife and replaying that moment where she bent over, grunted, looked up at him as she held her stomach, and collapsed outside the dance hall in Sumner. At first, he thought she had stomach cramps but then she fell forward into his arms. She didn't say anything but when their eyes met, he saw fear, and he didn't know why. His normal response was to try and stand her up, but she went limp in his arms. He felt something warm on his forearm and laid her down on the sidewalk and realized she was bleeding. He thought a car had backfired, but it hit him quickly that she had been shot. He looked around but didn't see anything. He heard people yelling and pointing at two guys that had been fighting in the parking lot. After the gun shot, both men jumped in their pickup and drove away in a hurry. Witnesses said that the two men got into a fist fight and one pulled a gun on the other. What seemed odd to Elmer at the time was why two guys that were fist fighting, fired a shot at each other then jumped in a pickup together and sped away.

The scene played over and over and over in his head. He had dreams: instead of holding the door for her and letting her walk out first that he would get shot instead of her. He dreamed about grabbing her close and kissing her a split second sooner as he was about to do because she was so excited that they had done so well in the dance contest and he was proud of her. Maybe if he had reacted on his emotions sooner, she would not have been shot. The dream where he kept her from getting shot occurred every night and he couldn't stop it.

Now he sat there at his desk dripping blood from the cut on the top of his hand, staring at a desk calendar that had become worthless, reaching for a flask in his boot and getting a lecture from a deputy he didn't even know, but had been working in his office for apparently two weeks. When the new guy told him that he had just fired Lavera and worse, he had no memory of it, he nearly broke down in tears. He would never fire Lavera. He loved Lavera like his own mother and wouldn't even consider hurting her. He didn't even remember Lavera giving him the tongue lashing of his life. It was when he had his head down and was staring at the desk calendar, he saw the missing person sheets. The little girl missing from Drew caught his eye. It was a cute picture of her with a sunflower in her hair. Without reading the details included at the bottom of the sheet he guessed she was about Decker's age, maybe slightly younger. She was a beautiful young girl, and he was certain that he had seen her. Somewhere. That's when he wanted Lavera to get him in touch with the Sheriff of Sunflower County. That's when he learned that he had just fired her in front of everyone. That's also when he decided he had had enough. It was time to start fixing things he had broken.

"Since you're familiar with my hands-off management style Tom Porter, keep your hands off my stuff, don't get dead on me and make sure the office doesn't burn down." Elmer got up, grabbed his hat and keys and out the door he went. He brushed by Tom Porter and intentionally smacked into him. There was no mistaking that Elmer was a big man and when he brushed into Tom Porter, the small but intentional collision caused Tom to fall back a few steps. Tom's expression went from smart ass to respectful and cautious. Elmer made his way out of the station and into the Scout.

He set the brake on the Scout, got out and made his way up the sidewalk to Lavera's house. The sidewalk looked like it was something out of a gardening magazine, for that matter, her entire yard looked like something out of a gardening magazine. Lavera kept the best yard in all of Webb and she was proud of it.

He dreaded this conversation, but it had to be done. Lavera's house was just a block off the square and right down the street from the church. She walked to church every Sunday because she never drove a car. She could walk to the station and she could make the quick walk downtown to Milholen's, I Peals, and Turner Brothers any time she wanted. The walk to the Sheriff's office was the longest walk she had, and it really wasn't too bad.

Elmer took the three steps up to Lavera's porch where he could see the swing. It was at the end of the porch closest to the street and the invisible wind ghost was rocking it back and forth. The screen door was closed but the main door was open. He could hear the radio playing in the house. Lavera loved to listen to her old Admiral radio. She could pick up stations all the way from St Louis on clear nights and she took great delight in her ability to stay in touch with all music. Not just the old stuff, but also the new stuff that the kids were listening to now. He thought it was that boy band from England what everyone was going crazy over. He didn't see what all the fuss was about but then he really didn't listen to music very much.

He knocked on the screen door and it kind of banged against the frame letting him know that it wasn't latched. He would get frustrated with Lavera because she never locked the house. It never even occurred to her that an intruder would consider her an easy mark. Although it was October, the weather was still very warm and Lavera loved to keep the screens open as long as she could. "It's open Elmer." His heart was beating fast and his palms were sweaty. Even though he really didn't remember the conversation he had with Lavera he knew deep down that he hurt her. It made him feel as low as he could feel. She stood by him when she didn't have to. She loved him unconditionally and he knew better than to strike out at her the way he did, and he needed to make it right. He also knew he better man up and not even think about blaming the alcohol.

He pulled the screen door open and stepped into the living room area of her Victorian style home. He loved this house from as far back as he could remember it. The floors creaked when you walked on them, it smelled a little like moth balls and fried okra or something similar. He especially loved her house when he was a boy, and it would rain. She had a porch that went all the way around the house. He could play outside and never be bothered by the rain. The house suited her well and she made it home for anyone that stepped inside it. He walked through the living room and knew that he would find her sitting at the little metal green table with the four padded chairs. She loved to sit there and read a Bible while sipping a cup of coffee. He stepped through the door frame to the kitchen and sure enough that is where he found her. "How did you know it was me?" He crossed his arms, folded them against his chest and leaned against the door frame. She never looked up from her Bible, but she did manage to sip a cup of coffee. "Your knock Elmer. You knock like a timid little girl when you are contrite, always have, always will." He smiled and looked down at the floor. "You don't miss much Lavera." She took another sip and didn't look up from her reading. Elmer really didn't think she was reading, she was toying with him now and he deserved it. "I came to say I am sorry." She set her coffee down and finally looked up. She clasped her fingers together and rested her elbows on the table. She didn't say anything but stared at Elmer. She had a stare that could melt copper and it made Elmer uncomfortable. "Aren't you gonna say anything?" Lavera never blinked but continued to look straight into Elmer's soul. "I said I was sorry; I was hoping for some forgiveness."

Lavera looked down at her Bible then back up to Elmer. "I was just reading here in Matthew in the New Testament; would you like to hear what it says?" Elmer unfolded his arms and stuck his hands in his pockets. "I think I probably should hear it regardless of whether I want to or not." Lavera took a sip from her coffee, sat the cup down and then raised the glasses she had hanging around her neck and placed them on the bridge of her nose, "says here in Matthew chapter 18 verse 21 and 22: *Then Peter came to Jesus and asked, "Lord, how many times shall I forgive my brother or sister who sins against me? Up to seven times?" Jesus answered, "I do not say to you, up to seven times, but up to seventy times seven.* Elmer took a deep breath, "so what number am I now? Have I spent up my 490?" Lavera took the glasses off her nose and let the chain catch them as they dropped to her neck again. "Not even close but you haven't apologized." Elmer took his hands out of his pockets again and pointed a finger at Lavera and as soon as he did it, he regretted it. He had a bad habit of pointing a finger at people. "I most certainly have! It was the first thing I said when I came through this door." He quickly stuck his hands in pockets again hoping that Lavera hadn't really noticed his finger pointing. "No Elmer you came in and said you were here to apologize. You haven't apologized, merely announced your intentions." She had a point and it really took whatever starch out of him that he had left. "Yes ma'am. You're right. I haven't done it proper yet." He felt a lump come up in his throat and he fought to keep it down so he paused before he started again. "I was wrong to treat you the way I did. I was wrong to fire you." He swallowed hard and no matter how hard he tried he could feel a tear roll down his face. "I'm an educated man Lavera, but I sure ain't smart enough to figure this stuff out. I am just about broke." He breathed in deep and found that he gained a little strength with the more he talked. "I love you like a mother and I need you. I need you as a friend and I definitely need you back in the office." He continued to look down until he heard her speak. "Look at me Elmer Davis." He raised his head and she stood up from the table, which in turn he also stood up. He didn't know why he stood but it was reflexive he thought. When a lady leaves the table, the man was supposed to stand. That's what he had been taught by his father and it occurred to him that he had not had any such conversation with Decker about the same outlook towards proper manners in a while. He made a mental note to correct that with his and Decker's behavior towards Heather. Lavera walked around so she could stand in front of him. She was a small framed woman but in Elmer's mind they were looking eye to eye. "Apology accepted, but you have more apologies to make." She stood on her tip toes so she could try and put her arms around him. He leaned down so it would be easier for her to embrace him and she gladly accepted the gesture. She squeezed him and his sheer power lifted her off the ground. "Don't get carried away Elmer Davis. Put me down." He chuckled a little when she said it. "Sit down. Let's talk a while." She went to the counter, grabbed the coffee pot and poured a cup Elmer.

Elmer pulled out a chair and sat down. He was relieved the hard part was over or at least the apology part was over. He wasn't very good at apologies and everyone knew it. He had a feeling that Lavera was about to perhaps go over a list of other people he would need to apologize to. "I miss Lois too; we all do for heaven's sake. But your nearly three years of sulking and mourning have got to end." She placed the cup of coffee for Elmer in front of him then moved around to the other side of the table and took her spot. "The city of Webb can survive another Sheriff since you haven't done much to get re-elected, but I can't." She closed her Bible and looked around the kitchen: "But this is not about me. This is about your family." She reached across the table and put her hand on top of his. "Your daughter is not Decker's mother, so stop putting her in that position." She paused for a second and squeezed his hand tight. "Are you coming back to the office with me now?" Lavera released his hand, leaned back in the chair and breathed in deeply, "No Elmer, I am not." Elmer leaned his head back and looked at the ceiling, "Dang it Lavera I already said I was sorry, and I was wrong. What am I missing here?" He looked directly at her. "I know and I accepted it, but I am tired Elmer. The office needs someone young and I need to rest." She took her hands off his and looked away. "Those posters and then those pictures of those girls that have been found all over the state got to me the other day. The world is a bad place and I need to get away from it." This time Elmer reached over and took her hands. His hands were huge compared to her little hands and he was careful not to squeeze too tight, but he needed her to feel what he was feeling which was nothing but love and respect for her. He also knew that he hadn't hit rock bottom yet, but he was dangerously close. He would need Lavera to help him get straightened out.

"Lavera, the flyers and the pictures of the little girls are what got my attention after I pulled that stupid stunt on you." He leaned forward more in his chair. I swear I have seen one of those girls before, but I have been in such a cloud for three years, I can't be sure." He gritted his teeth as he spoke, "If I learn that one of those girls could have been helped by ME and I didn't do it, I don't know what I will do. Whatever it is I know; I will need you to help me fix it." Lavera gasped: "Where do you think?" He leaned back in his chair and let out a deep breath, "That's just it, Lavera, I have been in a fog since that night and I just can't remember, but I know I have seen one. I think it was over in Holly Springs, Biloxi, Drew, Clarksdale but hell it could have been Tupelo. I don't remember!" Lavera got up and poured a cup of coffee and she refreshed Elmer's cup while she was up. "Well, there are several flyers on your desk, which one is it?" Elmer rubbed his forehead and leaned further back in his chair so he could reach into his back pocket. He fished a folded piece of paper out of his left back pocket and laid it on the table. He sat adjusted in his seat and sat up straight. He unfolded the paper and pressed it flat against the table. The girl was no more than 10 or 11 as best Lavera could tell. She reached for her glasses that were hanging around her neck and looked at the picture, "Jessica Lynn Muncik." Lavera straightened out the paper again and read the rest of the description. "Elmer, this says she was abducted from a playground a block from her home in Drew almost 3 years ago." Elmer shrugged his shoulders and nodded his head in agreement. "You said yourself you've been in a fog for the last three years; how could you possibly remember this little precious little angel." Lavera stared at the picture and Elmer could see a tear roll down her cheek." He reached for the paper again but Lavera stopped him. "How in the world anyone could harm such a precious little thing I will never know. It truly breaks my heart." Elmer finally got her to release the paper, refolded it and held it in his hand for a second before the slid it into his front pants pocket. "I know, but her face is burned into my head somehow. She is like a flashbulb that constantly goes off in my head and I can't get it to stop now." Lavera smiled, leaned forward, patted him on the hand and said, "It's good to have you back Sheriff." He placed a hand on top of the hand that was patting his. "Are you coming back to the office with me?" Lavera shook her head again, "No, I can't do it anymore."

Chapter 11
Welcome to Webb

TOM PORTER BOUNCED ALL OVER the state as a youngster. His dad was a bean hauler and had his own truck. He liked to pack the family up when things were lean and go work in a town that needed a handy man or carpenter. Tom's dad was a proud man that loved having his own business, but he was never too proud to do any job he could to support his family. Tom had two brothers and two sisters that he sort of kept in touch with, at least his sisters he did. The brothers were ramblers, they liked to pack up and move as often as they could. Tom always believed that it was because they had got into too much mischief and were trying to stay ahead of the town's people or the law. His brothers had a loose definition of morality. He didn't think they were bad guys but they both had no problem skipping out on debt. The last contact he had with his oldest brother Richie was two years ago when he graduated from the police academy. He was surprised to see him in Pearl that day. He didn't even realize then that Richard knew he was going to be a cop and considering that Richie was always in trouble with the law he didn't think he would approve. Nevertheless, he was happy to see him. What didn't surprise him that his other older brother James was not there.

He and James were the closest in age and had always gotten along well until they were teenagers. James became very distant, socially awkward and angry. He didn't show up for graduation day despite getting a personal invitation. Tom was the youngest of the three boys and he strongly believed that his brothers being rough and picking on him led him to be a police officer. He sometimes wished when they were beating on him, sometimes playfully and sometimes not so playfully, that someone would come along and stick up for the little guy and that's what he believed he was doing now by becoming a cop.

His two younger sisters Ruth and Rebecca came along as the product of a different mother, but he didn't care. He loved and protected them way better than his older brothers protected him. His dad married a young girl from Ruleville after their mother committed suicide with their dad's pistol. It happened when Tom was just 9 years old and he was the one who actually found her when he got home from school. He wished he hadn't raced his older brothers' home that day, but he had. Normally they would beat him, but he had discovered a short cut through the backyard of The Whitman's place. The short cut took enough time off the race that he burst in the front door and ran back to where his mother was always sewing. He wanted to tell her the good new but instead he found her slumped in her sewing chair holding a gun by her side and blood all over the sewing machine. When he tried to shake her and help her, she simply slumped further and fell out of the chair. He screamed when he saw her face, her eyes were open as if she were looking directly at him, but he knew she was dead. There was no smile that she always gave him. Since they didn't have a phone in the house, he ran out of the house as fast as he could all the way to the grain elevator where his dad was working to tell him to come home and that something terrible had happened. The manager at the grain elevator hated kids and yelled at him for being there and told him that his dad got fired the week before and to get his scrawny ass out of his elevator.

He didn't know what to do so he kept running towards town and finally made it to the post office, that was the first place he saw an adult. It was Avery Miller, the postmaster that he saw that day and luckily Avery had a phone, called the Sheriff's office and then drove Tom in one of the mail trucks back to the house where he found his older brothers both sitting on the porch crying. He felt bad that he didn't have time to warn them and they too had found their mother in the same condition. It was a memory that he wished he didn't have because there was never a night that he didn't wake up sweating with her dead face and blood matted hair staring at him.

After that, his dad took them all and moved to Ruleville which is where he first met Bobbi. Bobbi was a young girl they met when they were all chopping cotton. The work was terrible, monotonous, and hot and he hated it. His dad made them all work when there was work to be had so that they could make ends meet. Bobbi didn't look to be too much older than Richie his oldest brother, but she could chop cotton better than all of them combined. She didn't say much during the day but before the day began and they were waiting to be issued a hoe, she could talk a blue streak. She was always talking about making it in the movies and she was gonna be a big star someday. Tom didn't figure she looked like any movie star he had ever seen, and he figured she better get her a pair of shoes if she was gonna go anywhere because she never had on shoes. Even when he and his brother James ran into her at Woolworths, she didn't have shoes on.

It wasn't long before their dad brought her home one night, took her in the back bedroom and stayed in there all night. He and James knew something was up when the next morning she was in the kitchen wearing nothing but one of their daddy's shirts and cooking some breakfast. From that day on, they were instructed by their daddy to call her Mrs. Bobbi. Tom couldn't remember a day from then on until he left for college that Mrs.

Bobbi wasn't in the home. She was always nice enough to them, but she never made it to Hollywood. She ended up having Ruth a few months after she moved in with them and then about a year later, she had Rebecca.

Tom didn't finish college like he planned, he was just a few credits short of getting his criminal justice degree when the money from a couple of scholarships he received ran out. He tried to make do on his own and got a job as the night security guard at the bank which was boring as hell and most of the time he dozed off for hours at a time because nothing ever happened anyway. He just couldn't stay up all night and go to school during the day. That's when he applied to enter the police academy. The bank manager vouched for his character by writing a recommendation letter for him and it must have worked because he got in on his first try.

After his time at the academy, and since he had gone in as an independent candidate, it meant that he could be hired anywhere in any city in the great state of Mississippi. He wasn't worried he wouldn't get hired he was only worried as to where. He wanted lots of action and he didn't want to be stuck in some podunk little town helping kids in the cross walk. No sir, he wanted to solve murder cases, he wanted to get into shoot outs and put bad guys in jail but most of all, he wanted to stand up for the little guy.

He was hired by the Pascagoula police department and was surprised by the salary. It was more than he expected for sure but it would still be tough starting out. Originally, he hoped he would be in Vicksburg or Jackson, there was way more activity in those locations but being down on the coast did have its perks. He loved the area but there wasn't much going on in Pascagoula. He did routine patrols and covered shifts on a moment's notice. He worked overtime every time it was offered, and he racked up a sizeable little savings account in the process. Life was pretty good, and he was slowly learning how to be a cop during his time there, but he needed to leave. He applied over and over in the big cities, but he never got the approval. He had also applied to be detective in his own precinct and was passed over. Each time he was told he needed more experience and needed to better "control of his emotions". He didn't understand that part but got the feeling that he would never even make corporal in the Pascagoula police department. He didn't handle being passed over very well. It hurt more than anything ever had. He knew he was a good cop; he knew every rule backwards and forwards and if he didn't, he carried the small but thick police issue rule book with him everywhere he went. The police issue rule book was always in his left breast pocket and the small handbook sized bill of rights was in his right pocket. Tom was proud of being an American and he took a great deal of pride in knowing the rules of his profession and his country better than anyone.

Through his commander in Pascagoula, he found out that Jackson County had an opening for a corporal and that he met the qualifications. His commander was happy to put in a good word for him and subsequently he made the shift to the Jackson County Sheriff's Department as Corporal Tom Porter. One year later he was very happy to be standing in the doorway of Sheriff Elmer Davis's office; very happy. All he needed now was to keep a low profile for a while and hopefully something would come open in one of the bigger cities.

Chapter 12

First Kiss

AFTER THE PRAYER MEETING WAS OVER and Decker managed to work the cramp out of his hand, Jeannine talked him into walking her to her father's Barber shop where the two would grab a soda from the machine and then her dad would drive them home. She really thought that offering the soda was the only way she could convince him to walk with her, but the truth was that Decker didn't mind at all. He really liked to run home from town if he could. It was only a couple miles and he enjoyed the exercise. Decker liked the sound the soda machine at Dub's barbershop made when he put the quarter in and pulled on the bottle and he especially loved the Mt. Dew flavor. He could chug a whole bottle in just a few seconds which was never the plan. He would try and sip to make it last longer but after a few sips he would end up downing the whole bottle. The other thing he liked about visiting the barbershops was that he never had to pay for a soda at either place, although he always tried.

They walked out of the church where Decker told Heather what he was planning on doing and she hugged them both and told him to be home by 8:30 because it was a school night. Jeannine started talking about the youth minister the minute they were out of range of the church. "There is just something weird about that man, and his wife! Did you see how tall she was?" she held her hand way above her head to illustrate how tall she thought the lady was. "She was a GIANT Decker!" Decker started laughing and so did Jeannine. He tried to control himself, "I am sure they are good people, and we shouldn't have fun at their expense but dang . . . " He paused for a second and tried not to laugh but couldn't, "When he hit himself in the head with that microphone I nearly laughed out loud!" Jeannine poked him in the ribs, "What do you mean almost!" She poked and pushed him, "You DID laugh out loud! If I hadn't nearly crushed your hand you'd still be laughing at that poor man!" They walked a little while before they calmed down and squeezed the giggles out of their system.

"Decker they are a clear amalgamation of what two people can do when they love each other." Decker stopped and she took a few steps before she realized that Decker was not walking beside her anymore. She turned and looked at him and he had a confused look on his face. "What's wrong Decker?" He started walking toward her, "A-mal-guh-what?" Jeannine laughed. "We have to get you out of those civil war books and into some smarter books." She laughed as she said it, but she knew based off the look he was giving her that she would need to explain the word, or he wouldn't move much further. Decker was a sponge for information, and he hated hearing a word he didn't know. Truth be known, she had been dying to use that word in a sentence and this seemed like a good test run for her. "Decker it means a combination, a union, a mixture. It just means that the two can be totally different but as long as they love each other nothing else matters." He shook his head as if he agreed, "Why didn't you just say that? I understood that part way better." He took a breath and smiled. "And I love my civil war books." She laughed, stepped forward and hugged him very quickly. It happened so fast that Decker didn't even get the chance to hug her back. "I know and I am just glad you love to read now!" That wasn't completely true, Decker still had trouble reading he just didn't give up as quickly as he used to. Jeannine was so smart that he pushed himself to try and be as smart as her.

"I know everyone in town has asked you if it's true, but no one has asked you how you feel about it. Do you want to tell me?" Decker shook his head and looked down at the ground. "What if they play me?" Jeannine put her hand on Decker's forearm, "Then you'll play." He looked up and looked her in the eyes, "You make it sound so easy. Those guys play for real. They are big and fast, and I don't belong there." He looked down again, stuck his hands in his pockets and shuffled his feet. Jeannine grimaced because she knew that look, she knew that was the boy she met on the playground so many years ago. The scared boy that got bullied because he lacked confidence and he let them bully him. She knew that if he did get to play on Friday night and the old Decker came back, he would get hurt. He might even get killed. "Decker Davis, you listen to me, you are the best football player in the state of Mississippi, maybe in the whole United States, no wait, maybe in the whole world! You belong on that field more than anyone I know so stop with the attitude." Decker didn't look up; he kept his head down. "Decker look at me." He raised his head enough to make eye contact with her, but he didn't take his hands out of his pockets. Jeannine took a step closer to him, close enough that she stepped on his shoes but didn't remove her foot from the top of his. She stood on her tip toes, placed her hands on both sides of his face and kissed him on the lips. Decker's hands shot out of his pockets and he took a step back but since Jeannine was still standing on his feet he stumbled and fell flat on his back taking Jeannine to the ground with him. The fall was worse for Decker than Jeannine since Jeannine landed on top of him.

They both laughed at the turn of events, but it was kind of a nervous laughter. Jeannine propped her elbows up on Decker's shoulders and looked him in the eye. "I take that back, if a girl can knock you over so easy on the side of the road then you are gonna get killed on that football field!" They both laughed and this time it wasn't nervous laughter, it was real laughter. Decker sat up which caused Jeannine to roll off him. She ended up sitting right next to him. "You stepped on my foot and kissed me. I don't think any of the Clarksdale players are gonna kiss me. It just caught me off guard is all." Decker stood up quickly then held his hand out to aide Jeannine in getting to her feet. They both started walking towards Dub's barbershop, Jeannine continued to talk but Decker didn't say a word, he was still replaying the kiss right smack on the lips in his head. He was trying not to smile as they walked but he suddenly felt very light, like he wasn't even touching the ground. He couldn't explain it, but it felt awfully good.

"Say something Decker Davis." She playfully smacked him on the arm to snap him out of whatever fog he was in. She knew he was thinking about the kiss and in truth, she was too. She had no idea why she did it. They have never been intimate other than holding hands, even when he kissed her on the forehead in the library, she didn't consider that intimate. This was a kiss on the lips, and she instigated the contact! She now worried that her behavior was not ladylike and the only way she could currently get past this point was to talk and she was good at talking. Decker looked at her with his hands still in his pockets, "About what?" Jeannine rolled her eyes which she was also good at, Decker actually liked it when she rolled her eyes, "About that girl on the bus! I have been talking about her and you haven't been listening! Your mind is probably on that stupid football game Friday night, but I got news for you mister," she took a breath, "You have a game before that! You could just as easily get hurt in that game, so you better come back to earth and take it one game at a time, just like they told you at Daddy's barber shop today." He knew she was right. He was the JV game to play tomorrow and he really wasn't thinking about that and he definitely wasn't thinking about the new girl on the bus. "What about her?" Jeannine pointed at the road that led to both of their homes and said, "She lives in the old Murphy place!" Decker was trying to figure out what that had to do with anything but he couldn't so he just shrugged his shoulders. "Decker, nobody has lived in the place for years. Old Lady Murphy died 10 years ago and the place has been empty since! Its spooky is all." Decker thought about it for a second, "Well somebody was bound to move in there, just frustrates me because that makes the old Murphy place the first stop for the bus."

Jeannine, looked down the road they were walking then back to Decker, "Decker she DIED in that house and nobody knew it for days, weeks, it could have even been a month!" Decker shrugged his shoulders again; he was having trouble seeing what the big deal was. "Decker! The smell! They said she rotting away and was pretty much nothing but a skeleton when they found her!" The thought of finding a skeleton seemed kinda cool to Decker, the thought of finding a dead body didn't seem very cool to him though. He saw his mom in the casket, and he saw Bubba in the casket and he even saw Lonnie Buckles in his casket, and he didn't care much for any of it. He would be happy if he never saw another dead body again as long as he lived. He especially didn't like remembering his mother in the coffin. She just didn't look like her to Decker, she was too white, to plastic looking, she didn't seem real. He still had bad dreams about it.

When they reached the barbershop and before they went in, Jeannine stopped, turned to stand directly in front of Decker, "I'm sorry I was so forward tonight. I don't know what I was thinking. I hope you aren't mad at me." Decker was glad that it was getting dark outside or she might have seen him blush and she still may have seen him blush, he couldn't be sure, but his cheeks and forehead were currently on fire. He didn't know what to say, it seemed like a bad position for him to be in, he couldn't say he enjoyed it, that just didn't seem right but he sure did enjoy it, and he couldn't act mad because she was so forward because he had hoped and prayed many times that she would kiss him because he would never have to courage to kiss her so he thought about it and replied, "No big deal." He was trying to be nonchalant about it with his response and apparently his response was the incorrect one. "Decker Davis! You mean to tell me that ME kissing YOU right on the lips is not a big deal!" She spun around in a complete circle and as she was spinning. "I am looking for all the girls around here that you've kissed that would lead you to the deduction that MY kiss was no big deal!" Decker was completely at a loss; he knew he had said the wrong thing but he didn't know how to immediately fix it.

As she was spinning and yelling at him, she dropped her Bible which Decker saw his opportunity to get back in good graces so he bent over to pick the Bible up off the ground for her, but Jeannine decided she would pick it up also which caused their heads to slam into each other. Pain shot through the top of Decker's head and he was certain that he could see little flash bulbs going off behind his eyes and he staggered back. Jeannine had the exact same reaction and was stumbling backwards until she fell back in her backside. "Good Lord Decker! No big Deal?" She was rubbing the top of her forehead. Decker's head hurt and he could think of nothing but relieving the pain, so he was surprised to see that despite the pain Jeannine was having, she managed to hang on to the subject matter. The flash bulbs behind his eyes started to slowly go away. He could see Jeannine still sitting on the ground and he could see the Bible was still right where she dropped it, so he reached down and picked up the Bible and then bent over to help her up. She was obviously still mad, "Leave me alone Decker Davis, I can get up on my own." He had pretty much spent enough time with Jeannine to know when to be quiet and let the moment dissolve. She stood up slowly and took the Bible from his hand. She was still rubbing the top of her head and was squinting her eyes. "Come on, let's get daddy to take us home." Decker started to take a step towards the barbershop door but decided at that moment that it would be best if he just ran home. He needed the exercise, and it was only a couple miles. He figured Jeannine would help her Dad clean up the shop and if he kept a good pace, he would probably beat them home. "I think I am going to just run home." She stopped rubbing her forehead, "No big deal huh?" With that she turned and started walking toward the door. "I will see you on the bus tomorrow Decker Davis."

Chapter 13
Mythical Madelyn

"I HAVE TOLD YOU MANY TIMES over not to make friends. If your behavior doesn't change soon, we will have to go back to the old way of doing things. I seriously thought you were beyond such childish behavior by now." Madelyn stood with her face pressed against the corner of her room as she had been instructed. Usually, she would stand there until she was told she could turn around, but if she had been really bad in their words, they would whip her with whatever instrument they could find. She was not allowed to cry. If she cried, she would get whipped more and it would seemingly never stop. They were always careful not to hit her in places that might be seen in public because they didn't want any questions. There was one time back in Holly Springs that they had to practically leave in the middle of the night because someone at school reported that the little girl had a broken collar bone and needed medical care. Too many questions required too many answers that they could not give so they packed up and moved quite often. She had always been told to not make friends and if anyone tried to be her friend, she was to simply rebuff them.

She didn't know if tonight's behavior required a beating or not, but she waited patiently for the pain. The only thing she had done so far was to meet the bus driver which was required before she was even allowed on the bus and then she met the first two kids on the bus and tried her best to ignore them without drawing attention but there was no doubting that she liked them both. They made her smile because she could tell they were happy and something told her that despite their color differences, they were more than just friends. It was something about the way the boy looked at the other girl when she stepped on the bus. His expression changed completely.

She was standing in the corner with her eyes closed thinking about the encounter and trying to remember if she had slipped up, but she was certain she had not. She smiled as she remembered the girl, Jeannine was her name, and she talked a lot. She didn't have to say a word all she had to do was nod. She wanted her to go away, if SHE found out that she had a friend she would give her the whippings but if HE even thought that a boy had looked at her in a friendly way, it was much worse. He did terrible things to her and throughout it all he would constantly remind her that she was HIS. She had almost all forgotten about her childhood and all she could think about now was surviving and how not to feel so dirty every day. If she had known that she had accidently taken those two kids seats on the bus she would have sat at the back of the bus or anywhere else just to keep from getting any attention.

She continued to stand in the corner waiting on her to make up her mind if whatever she had done deserved a whipping, sometimes she would have to stand in the corner for so long that her legs would cramp up so bad, but she didn't dare adjust her stance or try to rub her legs, that action alone would be sure to make her angry and she would really get it. "Take off your clothes. I will return momentarily." Madelyn knew what that meant, and she immediately wanted to throw up. This is what made her feel dirty, no clothes meant that HE would be home, and HE would punish her. When he was finished punishing her, he would lay there with his arms wrapped around her, some-times he would sob and pray that God would forgive her for her sins and accept her into heaven. He would hold her and squeeze her until he fell asleep and then, and only then would she try and wiggle free and go wash herself. Nothing she tried, including baths and showers worked. No matter how hard she washed, where she would nearly rub her skin raw helped, but she tried. She had just about given up on God because he was not answering her prayers. All she really knew how to do now was to pray every day that God would figure a way to set her free, but he never did.

She wondered what a regular life would be like, to be like one of those kids she met on the bus and not live the way she did. She would dream, write down her dreams, and to her, that was as close as she would ever come to being normal like the other kids. Happiness eluded her but she often found she was happiest when they would bring other kids into the family. When that happened and there was someone else around, they would not pay much attention to her. It was then that she would hide in her room and write her stories. She had a vivid imagination and she put it to use writing stores about a little girl with secret powers that had been given to her accidentally when she touched an angel in her dream. She had amazing powers that could heal sickness and help people feel happy, but she had also been given powers to hurt people when the devil saw her touching an angel and decided he needed to get even. She didn't like the bad pow-ers but she knew they were there so she had to be careful not to become angry because if she did, a simple touch of the mythical girl's hand would cause the skin to burn all the way down to the bone. The pain she could cause was immense and deadly. Madelyn wished she could find a way to really use those bad powers on him and her now.

She would write until her hand hurt and then she would find creative ways to hide her stories from them because they would never approve. She would get in big trouble if they thought she was doing anything that would attract attention to herself. In all her stories, the little girl helped the children across the country to be happy, she would fix their problems and stop them from crying. She would do whatever she could to help the children in her stories stop crying. She would climb trees with them, run with them and play tag and have tea parties. If it were a boy she was trying to help, she would play football and baseball, she would even catch crawdads in the creek and dig for worms so they could go fishing together, anything to stop them from crying. She wasn't particularly fond of the boy stuff, but she did it to help dry up their tears. It was all the things she wanted to do when they would bring other kids into the house because she hated to hear them cry. They didn't stay long it seemed and for that, she was glad.

As best she knew her parents died when she was just a toddler and because she had no family that she knew of, she was placed in the custody of the state where she bounced around quite a bit. Her first memories of childhood were not pleasant and nothing much had changed. When she first came to them, she was 8 or 9, she couldn't remember exactly and at first it was a good home. The child welfare services would check on them regularly but then they stopped. About a year after the last visit, she found out that she had been adopted and she would no longer have to worry about relocating with a different foster family every three months. Now, all she had were dreams of a happy life and they were becoming fewer and fewer. She slipped up that day by telling her about the girl that sat next to her on the bus and boy that was clearly shocked to see someone sitting in his seat. She seemed in a good mood and she thought it was an innocent enough comment but apparently it wasn't. She knew the drill and today was going to be a bad day.

Chapter 14
Easy Rider

DECKER WATCHED HER GO into the barbershop, he always stood and looked at her for as long as he could. Once they were in school and in between classes he would always be late for his classes because he wanted to watch her go into the classroom. There was something about the way she always turned to look back at him, smile just a little and then shake her head and roll her eyes at him that he enjoyed more than anything he did throughout the day. At first, he would get into trouble for being tardy but soon the teacher caught on to what he was doing that caused him to be late. Everyone knew what the two had been through together and they all knew that Decker Davis was hyper protective of Jeannine and would rather be kicked out of school than miss seeing her enter the classroom.

Decker tried to be in the same classes as Jeannine, but she was into math and chemistry and all the things he hated so he stuck with his curriculum and found ways to be as close to her as possible. Decker wasn't a bad student by any stretch, in fact he was a very good student, he just hated math and Jeannine loved it. There was no way Decker could keep his GPA up the way he did if he took the same classes that Jeannine did. His objective wasn't to be 'Valid Victorian', that was a position that was surely going to Jeannine when they were seniors. His objective was to get into college with as many scholarships as he could. He didn't want to saddle his dad with the burden of paying for his school. He was pretty sure his dad wasn't going to be Sheriff for another term and after his mom died, he had really let the bait store run down. Decker was afraid they weren't going to have any money in the near future.

Once he was certain that Jeannine was safely in the barbershop, he turned towards main street and started to stretch his legs the way he did before every practice and game. Coach Hayes was adamant about working up a sweat before they every started practice, he would make them stretch and go through all the exercises until he felt like every player was limber and warm. He would yell things like, "No team of mine will ever get tired!" and "A prepared body is a successful body!" It was always a bunch of clichés with Coach Hayes, but Decker liked them. He liked hearing Coach Hayes talk because for such a muscular stocky man, his voice came out as very high pitched and almost echoed off their football helmets. Most of the other players would make fun of it when Coach was not around but Decker never did, not because he didn't think it was funny, it was, but because Decker could never make his voice sound anything like coach Hayes. When he tried it just came out like he was trying to mimic Donald Duck.

When Decker felt like he was good and limber he started out slowly running on the side of the road, he wanted to cut through main street because he liked to look at the stuff in the shop windows as he ran by. That's how he saw his Lou Brock fielder's mitt that he got for Christmas before his mother died. Back then she told him that Santa Clause brought it, but he knew better. He remembered telling her about it in the kitchen while she was making meatloaf for dinner one evening. He could hardly contain his enthusiasm and she knew it. She would laugh as she tried to make the hamburger meat turn into a loaf.

He made it to the walkway of the first store and hopped up on the sidewalk. He slowed his pace a little so that he would be sure to take in everything that was in every window. He was pretty sure he knew all the merchandise and wasn't expecting anything new and he wasn't disappointed. He started to pick up the pace because he convinced himself that none of the displays had been changed in a week for sure, maybe longer.

The streetlamps had been on for quite a while and it was quite dark; another reason Decker liked running on the sidewalk as long as he could. He would never admit that he was afraid of the dark, but he was certain that 99% of all bad things that happened to a person happened in the dark. He passed Barlow's Hardware and saw the same chainsaw in the window that had been in the window for the last three months and wondered why Mr. Barlow didn't update the display with something new more often. It seemed to Decker that most people liked seeing new things and he might sell some more stuff if he would just update his window display. As he was thinking about what he would put in the window if he owned the store, he heard his name. "Decker Davis!" He looked up and saw Jim Milholen coming out of his store with Bandit. "Hey Mr. Milholen." Decker was running at a decent pace as he passed the hardware store and slowed down to stop in front of Mr. Milholen. Mr. Milholen stuck his hand out for Decker and Decker took it like he had been taught to do.

"I see you're preparing for the big game against Charleston Friday!" Decker really didn't have that game in his head at all and again wished people would stop talking about it. He wouldn't even get to play, that much he knew for sure so he couldn't see what the big deal was. He would be standing on the sideline holding a clipboard the whole game. If it weren't for having to chart plays, he was pretty sure he could sneak off to the snack bar and get a hot dog and nobody would even notice. "Uh sort of, I actually just dropped Jeannine off at the shop and I was on my way home." Decker knelt and petted Bandit who was a

German Sheppard that belonged to Mr. C. Biggars. Mr. C was a lively old man that enjoyed the peace and quiet of his farm so much so that he hardly ever left his farm. If he had important stuff like banking to do, he might take a trip into town but most of the time he would convince the bank to come out to him. He wasn't unsociable, in fact, he was quite the opposite. He loved to have company and the joke was that he could talk the ears off an elephant. He was such a talker and a master storyteller that somewhere over time he acquired the nickname "Gabby". Decker remembered being at his farm twice, both times with his dad. His Dad would check on him almost weekly and the two men would sit under his fig tree and talk for at least an hour and if it were cold, they would talk in the tool shed where there was a pipe stove.

Decker figured that Bandit was in town to pick up cigarette's for Mr. C. Gabby taught all his dogs to go to town and pick up his choice brand of cigarettes. He would stick some money in a little holder he made specially for this task, send the dog to the Piggly Wiggly and then the Piggly Wiggly would take the money and stick the Chesterfields in the dogs' collar and send him on this way. It occurred to Decker that Milholen's didn't sell cigarettes so maybe Bandit had gotten lost. Decker was petting Bandit and obviously Bandit loved the attention because he was trying to drape his paws over Decker's shoulder and lick him on the face. Decker didn't mind, he was fascinated with Bandit and his intelligence level and even though Bandit looked ferocious with his black face and mixed black and brown coat, he was such a good, loveable dog. "What's Bandit doing with you Mr. Milholen?" Decker continued to pet Bandit. "Well Gabby has a touch of the gout and needed some medication for it. He called me right before closing and said he was sending Bandit to pick some up." Mr. Milholen turned to lock the door and then bent down and petted Bandit with Decker. "We just made the exchange and Bandit is good to go." He stood back up, "Maybe you and Bandit can run together. I don't think Bandit has ever been out this late before, the gout must be worse than what Gabby is letting on." Decker smiled at the thought. It would not be the first time that Bandit ran with Decker. It seemed like during the summer, he and Bandit found themselves on the road home almost daily. Decker had no idea what gout was, but it didn't sound too bad to him. "Sure!"

Decker knew he wouldn't be able to run Bandit all the way home because Mr. C's farm was about a mile past theirs, but he would be happy to have the company. "Say Decker, Kay Kay says that you are one fine historian." Decker was confused, he had no idea who Kay Kay was or really what a historian was. Jim could see the confusion on his face, so he continued, "She says that your knowledge of the civil war is as good as anyone's she has ever met." Decker smiled because he knew that he knew a lot about the civil war but not nearly what he wanted to. He was currently trying to find all the information he could on family's that were split up by the war more specifically, battles that may have pitted brother against brother. He was fascinated by the revolution that a brother could physically kill a brother based off a different point of view. He struggled with the concept but he decided not to tell Mr. Milholen all of that and simply said, "Thank you." Decker stood up and started to tell Bandit that he was ready to run, "Oh and Decker, Kay Kay is my wife, your Teacher . . . " He paused, "Mrs. Milholen." Decker smiled as it all made sense now. "Thanks Mr. Milholen!" Decker whistled and away they went. Bandit would run ahead to the point where Decker had trouble seeing him, especially in the dark but Bandit would always slow down and walk long enough for Decker to catch up to him.

Decker was sweating and was running at a good pace, he wasn't tired at all, in fact, he was considering picking up the pace a little to see if he could make it home faster. The road leading to his house, and technically to Jeannine's house was paved but not very well. It had potholes and cracks every step of the way, but

Decker knew them like the back of his hand. He would avoid the big ones completely or he would adjust his stride so that he would hop over them and not have to veer off course. He was thinking about the JV game coming up and keeping an eye on Bandit at the same time. Bandit knew the way back to his house which was about a mile beyond his and 2 miles beyond Jeannine's for sure, but Decker felt he needed to look out for Bandit with him being the grown up and all.

Coach Hayes put a new play in practice this week that called for Decker to break the huddle, walk to the line, and start barking out a bunch of fake play calls to throw off the defense and act like he was mad because his teammates were not adjusting to the play call well, and slowly, but not too slowly, unsnap his helmet and begin walking toward the sideline like he was going to call time out and visit with the coach. If Decker pulled the fake off correctly, he could make it to the sidelines, stop his walking, get his feet set before the play clock expired, the center would then direct snap the ball to Grant Washburn who was the fast as lightening halfback, and a very good passer, would then throw the ball to Decker who would be streaking down the sidelines unguarded. The defense would think that Decker was going to call timeout and relax just enough to catch them off guard. The Coach told Decker that the play was called "Easy Rider" based off a movie about motorcycles or something. Decker wasn't sure because he hadn't seen the movie but was also told by his sister that he could not see the movie, she said he wasn't old enough. Coach Hayes told him that the entire play depended on his ability to act and if he ever called it, Decker better get nominated for an Academy Award. As Decker was running, he was practicing unsnapping his helmet in disgust when the headlights came up behind him. He was so focused on the fake play that he hadn't noticed the car coming up behind him.

When it occurred to him that there was a car coming up behind him, he scooted over to the shoulder of the road so that they could have plenty of room to go around him. He saw the little rise in the road ahead and figured it might be dangerous for the car to swerve around him without being able to see if there was a car coming from the other direction. He always struggled with this part of the run home. It didn't seem like a steep incline when he was in the car with his dad or Heather but running up it sure was difficult. The big car cruised slowly around Decker and he waved as he did with every car he encountered. It was too dark to see if the anyone in the car waved back but he didn't care. It was habit with Decker more than courtesy. Decker continued to run as the car crested the small rise in the road and then the taillights were out of site. He was back to practicing his disgust when he heard the high-pitched squeal and he knew exactly what it was, Bandit.

Decker turned his jog into a sprint and crested the hill, he could see the taillights of the car but now they were flashing, and he could see a man bent over in the middle of the road. From the distance he could only make out a lump in the road and his stomach started to churn as he knew that Bandit had been hit. He sprinted up to where the man was bent down over a dog who was whimpering but trying to raise its head. The man had his hand on the dog and was talking to himself. To Decker's surprise it was not Bandit, but he didn't like to see any one or any animal in pain. The man had a ball cap on, and it was pulled way down over his forehead and so Decker couldn't tell who it was. He didn't recognize the car either, so he figured it was just a stranger passing through. "I didn't see it, it just darted out in front of me." His words were very soft as he spoke. Decker thought maybe the man was fighting back some tears because even though Decker didn't hit the dog, he felt bad enough. "Son, can you help him? Do you know anything about dogs?" The man didn't lift his face up he simply stared down at the dog who was whimpering. "I have a dog mister, but I don't know how to fix them when they are hurt." The man put his hand on the dog. "I am sorry little fella." He rubbed the dog for a second or two, "I think he has some broken ribs, but I can't tell." He gently rubbed some more then stopped just short of the little dog's shoulder blades, "Right here, feel right here and see if you can tell if his ribs are broken." Decker knelt to feel the dog's ribs but never quite touched the poor dog before the cloth was placed over his mouth and nose and he faintly heard: "Good boy." He knew in an instant that he was in trouble but that cloth that had just been smashed tightly in his face with what felt like another arm around his neck. He tried to yank free, but his body started to feel like lead, this arm that had him was thick as a tree trunk and his head started to spin. He knew he was in trouble, he reached in his front right pocket, dropped to one knee so he wouldn't fall over and emptied the contents of his pocket on the ground before his eyes closed and he was asleep.

Chapter 15

Dapper Donnie

DONNIE STEPPED OUT OF I PEALS clothing store feeling quite a bit different than he had felt since he returned from Viet Nam. When he finally decided to get a haircut and shave, he knew he not only needed to change his physical appearance, he needed to change the way he dressed. He couldn't remember the last time he washed the faded and worn Levi's he had been wearing and he couldn't remember if he even had another pair to put on. When he got home, he burned his marine uniform like so many other returning soldiers had done, but now, feeling different about himself, standing in front of I Peals, he wished he hadn't. He wanted badly to get back to the person he was before he saw war and the evil that men do, and this was the first step in doing so. It's the only steps he knew to take.

He looked down at the shoes he bought and worked his way up from the new jeans to the new Ely Walker shirt that Mrs. Hazel had talked him into buying. He didn't want to buy at first, but she was such a charming woman that he took her advice and more importantly took her seriously when she told him that he looked dapper in that shirt.

He felt a little stiff as he surveyed himself on the sidewalk in front of I Peals. It was late when he walked into the store, so late in

84

fact that Mrs. Hazel was about to lock the door. Mrs. Hazel was a lovely woman, well known in town and well respected. Donnie had only met her a few times because his circle of friends never connected with her circle of friends. He figured she was maybe in her 40's or 50's. It was hard for him to guess ages, but Mrs. Hazel was one of those ladies that was always so well kempt that to Donnie, she just looked young no matter what age she was. Donnie tried to back out and come back later but she was having none of it. She made a huge fuss out of seeing him and to his surprise, she hugged him like he was her long-lost son. Donnie could not remember the last time he felt the sincerity of a gentle human touch, a real sincere hug and it felt good to him. Even though he thought maybe Mrs. Hazel was spreading the happy greeting on a little thick, he enjoyed the exchange. He knew his family name wasn't quite sterling in Webb and he appreciated the way she came across as loving and sincere. Hazel outfitted him to the nine's and as he stood there with her staring at him in that full-length mirror on the back wall of the store, he hardly recognized the man that staring back at him. He was glad he worked up the courage to go into the store and begin his journey back to normalcy if there were such a thing. As he was about to turn and walk down the sidewalk towards home, he saw Decker Davis talking to Mr. Milholen and playing with a dog. He fished in his pocket and found the two dollars that Decker dropped while they were in the barbershop and took a step to cross the street so that maybe he could give the money back to Decker and hopefully he wouldn't scare him like he had earlier.

He hated the encounter at the barbershop. He loved his brothers despite their faults but he in no way condoned their behavior. The fact that Brett and Judd assaulted a couple of kids then nearly beat another kid to death with a baseball bat turned his stomach. He knew his brothers had a mean streak, especially Brett, but he had no idea they were capable of such meanness. Everyone in town knew the story of Brett lighting a cat on fire but nobody in town knew that Donnie had beat the crap out of

Brett when he found out about it. Donnie had his own reputation for being a tough guy and he knew that, but there was a big difference between being a tough guy and being a mean guy and Donnie had no tolerance for picking on someone weaker. He liked the Marines because he believed in their belief of protecting those who can't protect themselves.

Back in the day, and long before the war, Donnie enjoyed fighting. He didn't have to have much of a reason to go bare knuckles with anyone, and if he was being completely honest with himself, he often made up a reason to get into a scuffle. The fact that he was prone to fight made him well known by the local police and Sheriff's department. He badly wished he could erase those memories and somehow change the actions of his past, but he knew he couldn't. As for now he was hell bent on trying to repair whatever goodness might be left in the Buckles' name.

He stepped off the sidewalk to cross the street and take another shot at calming Decker's fears but just as he was about to the middle of the street, Decker stood up and he and the dog took off running down the sidewalk and Mr. Milholen went back in the store. He stood there in the middle of the road for a minute, looked around to see that the town was almost completely closed down now and the only car left parked at the far end of town was his flatbed truck. He hated the truck, but it was the only thing left on the Buckles' property that he could get running. Since his dad and brothers were currently spending their days enjoying taxpayer funded housing at Parchman State Penitentiary, their family farm had been severely neglected. He used most of the money that he had left over from the Marines, which was a tidy sum, considering he didn't spend a dime while he was a POW, the checks continued the entire time. He tried to try get the house back in livable shape and pay the back taxes and what was left of the mortgage. Luckily, Mr. I.D. Weathers at the bank had a soft spot for service men too and refused to foreclose on the property as long as Donnie was a POW. How Mr. I.D. Weathers found out that Donnie was a POW was a mystery to him, but Donnie was grateful, nevertheless.

He opened the passenger door of the truck and crawled over because the driver side door was stuck, and he hadn't had time to repair it yet. A driver side door that opened was a luxury he put on the back burner so that he could spend the money on the seat. The seat was really nothing but springs covered by a blanket. It hurt like hell to sit down and drive so he reupholstered the seat himself. He had never done anything like that, and he was quite proud of his work. The driver side door could wait a while. He turned the key and the engine groaned like it always did. He would turn the key, listen to it grunt and try to come to life but eventually he would have to turn the ignition off and wait a little bit. The truck was easy to flood if you weren't careful, so he took his time. This time it was taking a lot longer to start than it normally did so he got out again, popped the hood and started looking to make sure he had good battery cable connections which he did, and was about to close the hood when he heard, "Need a jump?" He turned to see a deputy he had never seen before, but he knew who he was. In a town this size, you can't have a new deputy and everyone not know him before he even goes on his first patrol.

"No, I think it is just cold and needs a little time." Donnie hadn't done anything wrong, but he felt uneasy around this guy. Maybe it was just his lifelong abrasiveness towards authority figures, but this was more. He felt like this guy was sizing him up to see if he could take him. He knew the look. It was the look a guy gave you from across the bar that is designed to intimidate you. Back in the day, that look would make Donnie smile and he would often wink at the guy trying to send the intimidating look. Nine times out of ten, the wink and smile caught the intimidator off guard and Donnie could actually see the body language change from confident aggressor to nervous participant. Donnie smiled at the thought and the deputy must have caught the smile and mistook it for something more than it was. "Something funny, boy?" Donnie reminded himself that today he had made to decision to change everything about himself and no more than 10 minutes after he had taken the first steps of that journey, his commitment to the plan was being tested. "Uh, no sir, I was just remembering a joke I heard about flatbed trucks." Deputy Tom Porter stepped off the sidewalk and entered into Donnie's personal space which Donnie took as another test of his commitment. "So, tell me the joke." Donnie closed the hood on the truck and turned to the Deputy. "I'm Donnie Buckles, I don't believe I have had the pleasure of meeting you deputy." He stuck out his hand, but the Deputy didn't take it, so he started to walk around to the passenger door, but the deputy stepped in front of him. "Ain't you gonna tell me the joke?" He said it with that smile that Donnie knew, it was the smile that was supposed to make Donnie feel uneasy. It worked because Donnie did feel uneasy, not for the reasons the deputy wanted, but because Donnie had already sized this man up and figured he could have him pummeled and bleeding on the sidewalk in less than three minutes. "I'm bad at repeating jokes deputy but it goes something like this," he paused and looked around, "Flatbed trucks are a magnet for flat chested women." The deputy laughed a little then his face went hard again. "You are the worst comedian I ever heard; you better find you a new job."

Donnie nodded and out of habit, let his face go hard. He had reached the point of no return now. This deputy was intentionally trying to push his buttons and needed to be taken down a peg. He could feel his fist clinch as the deputy got even closer to Donnie. "I know who are, Mr. Buckles. Your family name ain't worth two nickels around here. The whole bunch of you living up in Parchman and I promise you, if you try any of that cat burnin' stuff in my town, I will personally see to it that you get your own suite nest door to worthless dad and lazy brothers." The deputy obviously had his facts wrong about the family and who burned cats, but Donnie didn't care now. This deputy needed his ass kicked and it was worth it to Donnie to spend a few days in jail just to be the one to do it.

"Oh, Donnie you look so nice, young man! I just love how we got you all fixed up. I swear you look like you could be a senator from the great state of Mississippi! Mrs. Hazel nudged her way in between the two men and gave Donnie another hug. His fists immediately unclenched, and he returned the hug. "Thank you, Mrs. Hazel, I don't believe I will be running for office any time soon." She laughed but did not let him go. The hug she was giving him was clearly intended to get the deputy to step back away from the two because three was a crowd. Mrs. Hazel was a very smart woman. She saw the exchange as she was locking up the store and decided she needed to intervene. She wasn't a big woman at all, she was actually very slight and had she waited a second more, there would have been no way she could have stopped Donnie from sending this new deputy to the hospital. She had a plastic dish in her hand as she hugged Donnie. When she felt the deputy take a few steps back she released her grip and looked straight at the deputy. "You must be that new deputy from Pascagoula, Tom Porter is it?" She didn't try to shake his hand but even in the dark, Donnie could see the smile on her face as she spoke to the deputy. Right then he got the feeling that even though Mrs. Hazel had the most disarming smile and relaxing hug, you'd be ill advised to cross her in any way. "Yes mam, that's correct." She let some of the smile shrink from her face and her eyes got hard, "Deputy it is so nice to meet you and welcome to Webb." She stuck her hand out and the deputy scrambled to take it. He was very clumsy in the exchange, but he managed to get through it. "Well Deputy, I've got some business to discuss with Mr. Buckles here that's quite pressing so if you don't mind, I would like to conduct it in private before he gets away." She let the smile return to its full bloom, but Donnie could see that Mrs. Hazel was not making a statement, she was politely telling the deputy to leave. "Uh yes ma'am, y'all have a nice evening." Tom Porter turned and walked down the sidewalk towards the Sheriff's deputy car that Donnie could see was parked at the far end of town.

Donnie turned to look down at Mrs. Hazel and he shook his head. "You knew I was about ready to put him in his place, didn't you?" She stopped smiling and put her hand on his chest as if she were searching for his heartbeat. "I wasn't about to let those dapper clothes get dirty scuffling with the likes of him." She didn't remove her hand. "I wanted to tell you in the store that I know you have a good heart, and I don't know what kind of pain you are feeling on the inside and would never even try, it must be awful in there but know this," she rubbed his chest of his heart with her hand, "With a little help from God and a lot of help from friends, you can heal." Donnie felt a lump work its way up his throat and he choked it back down. He nodded in agreement and let out a deep breath. "Mrs. Hazel, I will be your friend for life but after what I saw in that godforsaken country, God is going to have to work his ass off to explain why he let that happen." She stepped forward and put her arms around him again, "He will son, give it time." Donnie squeezed her tightly then released her.

"You have some business to discuss Mrs. Hazel?" She laughed and held up the plastic bowl. "This is some homemade spaghetti that I brought to give that Heather Davis. That poor girl has been working and cooking and going to school and trying to take care of Decker and Elmer as best she could, and she is just about wore out. She is far too pretty to look as old as she has been looking lately. I forgot to give it to her when I saw her today. Would you be kind enough to drop it off for me?" He smiled, looked down at the plastic bowl, "Yes ma'am, if I can make it out to the Davis farm without eating it all myself I sure will." Mrs. Hazel playfully smacked him on the chest with the palm of her hand. "You listen here, there is a meal waiting for you at my house any time of the day or night. Don't you dare get hungry Donnie Buckles and don't you dare get those clothes dirty." Mrs. Hazel turned and made her way back up the sidewalk and with a quick spring in her step she was out of site. Donnie stood there holding the plastic bowl staring at her. He thought to himself, that's how a mother is supposed to behave, thank God for Mrs. Hazel or he would have been in jail tonight.

Chapter 16
The Replacement

ELMER PULLED OUT OF LAVERA'S DRIVEWAY careful not to roll over any of the grass on either side. He would catch hell if he accidently drove into any part of her grass. He was looking out the back window of the Scout as he backed out but hit the brakes. He turned to look back at Lavera's house in hopes that maybe she would change her mind and wave at him to stop before he left but he had no such luck. He wondered if he hadn't fired her would she have quit anyway, and he doubted it so he was racked with guilt at the moment. She was right about every-thing too, he had neglected his job, his bait store and worse his family. He missed Lois as much as a man could miss anything, but he needed to start healing and quit sulking. When Lavera reminded him that his kids lost their mother and they hurt too, it stung. He knew it but for some selfish reason he made himself believe that his pain and grief was worse than anyone else's.

He turned down main street and saw all the signs, "Elect Aubrey Bigelow as your County Sheriff. A Sheriff you can count on." He shook his head. Aubrey was a good man, but he was not a good law man. He missed too many details and he enjoyed speaking and going to parties and fund raisers more than he enjoyed solving a crime. Elmer thought it was a dangerous thing to have a man so careless in charge of all of Tallahatchie County. Aubrey started his campaign over a year ago and now that the election was just a little over a month away, he was really pulling out all the stops. "Not one damn sign." Elmer said out loud in the Scout as he drove. Lavera's words were eating at him like a fungus now. He could not believe that he had not even tried to get re-elected as the County Sheriff. It was a job that he truly loved and, in his opinion, had done a damn good job of it for almost twelve years now. He was shaking his head and at that very moment decided he needed to make Aubrey's path to the Sheriff's office a little bumpier than it had been.

As he passed Turner Brothers, he slid into the first available parking spot and set the brake on the old Scout. He took a deep breath and steadied himself. A drink would help calm his nerves for what he was about to do but he knew also that if he wanted to return to normal, that bottle of Old Harper in his boot could not go along for the ride. He reached down in his boot and pulled the pint size bottle up to his lap where he looked down at it for what seemed like an hour but it was really just a few minutes. The inside of his head was like flashbulbs going off at one of those fancy movie premiers, but each flash was a memory. A gun shot, Bubba sitting at the breakfast table, he and Lois dancing to a third place finish in Sumner, Bubba lying on that garage floor in a pool of blood, he and Decker fishing and eating bologna sandwiches, Heather graduating with honors, Dub Martin lying on the barbershop floor with his face swollen so badly you could hardly tell who he was and with each flash he could see the blows that he rained down on a naked Brett Buckles until his face was nearly unrecognizable. His breathing became hard and labored and he thought for a minute that he was going to pass out. He heard her voice in his head say, *"Your children lost a mother and they can't lose a father to a bottle."* She was painfully right.

He discreetly dropped the bottle in the trash can in front of

Turner Brothers so that no one would see him do it. He didn't even regret that the bottle was nearly full. He was done with it and he needed to make this his first stop to recovery. He still had a lot of Sherrifin' left in him and he wasn't about to give up so easily. He admitted in his head that one month of campaigning was not very much, but he still had favors out all over the county and he intended to call in as many markers as he could to change the outcome. He suddenly felt confident but even with his new-found confidence, he was going to need some help from the one person he trusted more than anyone else.

The little tinker bell on the door at Turner Brothers rang announcing his arrival and he could immediately see Heather in the back of the store cleaning a rack. The floor creaked as he walked and since there was no one else in the store it was quiet. Since Elmer was so big it was impossible for Heather not to see him enter and when their eyes met, for the first time Elmer could see the unnecessary aging that she had undergone. She looked so mature, she had bags under her eyes and her shoulders were shrugged just a little. She wasn't dressing as snappy as she used to, and he could see that she had lost the enthusiasm for curling her hair. The guilt he was feeling a few minutes ago as he sat in the Scout staring at the bottle started to overwhelm him again. His heart started racing and his mouth would have spit cotton balls if he opened it right now. She stopped what she was doing and turned to look straight at him. It was a shock to see him in the store because he never stopped by because Elmer Davis didn't shop for anything. He would get new socks only when Heather noticed his toes sticking out of them or the elastic in his underwear would fall apart when she would do the wash. She would go buy what he needed and just stick them in his drawer. He never noticed and he never thanked her.

"Daddy? What's wrong?" Because he never came in the store, Heather had a worried look on her face. Elmer could see that look and he couldn't keep it together anymore. He took the remaining few steps separating them in record time and grabbed her in a bear hug. Her feet came off the ground and Elmer didn't even notice. He stood there with his big arms wrapped around her and her with her arms wrapped around his neck. "She could feel the emotion in her father, and it made her start to cry. "What's wrong Daddy?" What is it?" He swallowed as hard as he could to choke back the quiver in his voice but there was no hiding the tears that were streaming down his face. Because he held her so tight, Heather could not see the tears, but she could feel the emotion for sure. Elmer whispered in her ear, "Nothing baby. I just needed to let you know that I love you and I need you." When she heard those words, she began to sob uncontrollably. With her feet dangling off the floor and smothered in her father's embrace she cried like she had never cried before. It was if her father had woken up and decided to squeeze all her emotions and pain right out of her on the floor of Turner Brothers. Neither could see the Greek manager standing behind the counter wiping the tears from his eyes as fast as could wipe.

When Elmer could feel that her body was no longer heaving with each sob, he slowly eased her feet back to floor and slightly released his grip on her but kept his hands on her hips because he figured if he said what he needed to say and he started blubbering again, he would just scoop her up again and hold her tight so she couldn't see him cry. "I am sorry for taking you for granted baby. You have been the rock in this family after your mother died and that was my job, not yours. I won't ever let that happen again. Not as long as I have a breath in this dumb old body of mine." He smiled and with his big hand he took his thumb and gently wiped a tear away from Heather's face. She still hadn't collected herself enough to speak, she just continued to look up at her dad with amazement. She wondered what had happened to bring him to this place. What was so urgent that he had come tell her in public. She certainly didn't mind at all but for her dad to show that style of emotion in public was way out of character for him.

"I've decided I need to keep this job I have as Sheriff; I need to get the bait store up and running again and more importantly, I need to be your dad again and I can't do any of it without you. I'd like you to come work for me, if you would." She smiled and let out a deep breath with her bottom lip closed over her top lip that caused some of her hair to fly up then slowly waft back down in her face. Elmer's eyes lit up and he laughed. That exact same motion was the same thing that Lois used to do when they were on the dance floor and the song would finish. He would joke with her that the reason she did that was that it was such a task for her to avoid getting stepped on by his feet and blowing her hair up was a sign of relief. He hadn't noticed that Heather was just as strikingly beautiful as Lois was until that very moment.

Heather looked up at her dad, "Of course I will help you Daddy. I just can't leave my job here though, they need me." Elmer looked around for the manager and didn't have to look very far, the Greek had eased up behind them so that he could better hear what they were saying. "Oh honey! You are the best worker we have ever had but it is more important that you go help your father!" He stuck his finger in the air as if he was making a brilliant point, then smile a huge grin that made his big bushy eyebrows nearly disappear into his hairline, "and besides, I do not wish to vote for the other guy!" Elmer smiled and turned his stare away from the manager and back to his daughter. "Well, honey? Will you help me?" Heather wiped another tear that was starting to well up in the corner of her eyes. "Of course, I will Daddy but what do you want me to do?" Elmer looked at the manager again, "Can she leave now?" The Greek manager nodded in approval and Elmer nodded and tipped his hat to the manager. He was on the verge of tears again and was afraid that if he actually mouthed the words THANK YOU to the manager he would start balling again. "Finish up what you are doing here baby, I will meet you out front." Heather smiled and nearly jumped into his arms again. Now she had done it. The tears he tried to choke back by not saying thank you to the manager came roaring back. Once the tears slowed down between the two of them again, Heather let go of her father's neck and slid down to put her feet on the floor. Elmer held the embrace from sort of a bent angle because he was so much taller than her and whispered in her ear because he didn't want the Greek to hear this part, "I need you to take Lavera's place." Heather's eyes got as big as silver dollars when she heard that, and she may have actually gasped. Elmer let her go and quickly turned and strolled out the door feeling lighter than he had felt in a very long time.

Chapter 17
Payback

DONNIE SR. AND BRETT STROLLED THROUGH the exercise yard with Judd following like a lost puppy. They were looking for the right moment and their intended target. They put their plan on hold after the attack on Judd. Donnie Sr and Brett would settle up with Judd's attackers in due time, but they needed to finish this business. They had paid good money for the hit on Elmer Davis and they had nothing to show for it except a dead woman. Make no mistake, they laughed at the thought of big ole Elmer squalling at the funeral of his wife and in some regard, that was kind of a payback, but it was not the original agreement. The two men they had tasked out and paid handsomely for the job were dumb enough to land back in Parchman and for sure, Donnie would not let a debt go uncollected. This time the two men would have to pay for it, and he had it all worked out.

Judd was drawn in; he hadn't said much since he was attacked. He thought everyone was looking at him now and he couldn't stand it. He hated that he couldn't get over it and move on, but he couldn't. What those men had done to him was wrong and should never have happened. He was mad at the guard for letting it happen and he was mad at himself for being tricked so easily. He knew he was just a step slower than everyone else, but he wasn't stupid. When he was in school the kids would pick on him and call him stupid and it didn't seem like things ever changed. He dropped out as soon as he was old enough to and spent most of his time with his big brother Brett. Brett could be just as mean as the other kids but at least when he was with Brett, nobody else called him names. In fact, when he was with Brett, folks seemed to be a little scared of him and he liked that. Now he was walking a few steps behind his dad and his brother, but nobody was scared of him anymore. Everyone knew what those men did to him and they laughed behind his back, some men in the yard would whistle at him like he was a girl and he hated it. "What in the hell are you doing back there Judd? Get up here and walk with us you little queer." After the attack and Judd came back from the infirmary, Brett had become as mean as he had ever been towards Judd, and his daddy let him be that way.

Judd walked a little quicker so he could catch up to his family, but he didn't want to. He was supposed to pick up the knife from a guy that worked in the metal shop, then he was supposed to slip the knife into Brett's pocket without anyone seeing, then Brett would take the knife and jam it in the target a few times while Donnie Sr. and Judd would block the view of the guard tower at the first turn. There was a proven blind spot in that location and Donnie Sr. planned to exploit it today. Originally, they were supposed to get two knives and take care of both men, but one of the men they hired to kill Elmer Davis was beaten to death down in Natchez when he made a pass at a man he thought was gay but wasn't.

"Hey queer bait, the exchange is coming up. Get ahead of us and get ready, don't drop the shiv, you idiot and make sure you get it to me." Judd could feel the hair on the back of his neck, he knew he wasn't a queer, and he hated his brother for calling him that. If it weren't for Brett he'd still be back in Webb and not in this terrible place. He wasn't cut out for prison and besides, he wasn't a criminal anyway, he only did what Donnie told him to do, none of this stuff was his idea. "Judd, Donnie said get in front, now get in front!" His dad was trying to yell but he was also trying to keep his voice down which made him spit as he talked. Judd looked down at his shoes, a habit he acquired long ago. He was not a good student because it took him longer to figure things out than most people.

Donnie Sr. slowed his walk to allow Judd to move in front of he and Brett. He wasn't convinced that Judd was ready to handle this, but he had no choice. He had unfished business and it was time that this was cleaned up. He had waited patiently for the two men that he hired to kill Elmer Davis. The day he got word they would be returning to Parchman he could hardly contain himself. He began plotting how to punish them both for not having the guts to return his money for the failed attempt. He began bribing the guards and establishing more control of the yard. He had guards all over the prison giving him information on when and where they would arrive, what block they would be housed and how best to punish them. He settled on this spot in the yard based off the information he had been given. Normally he would have had the knife ready by having Brett keep it in his bunk but when the new warden arrived two weeks ago, things changed. A shake down occurred and Brett lost the weapon he passed him in the mess hall. Now he had to depend on someone outside the family to bring them a new pig sticker.

Donnie Buckles Sr. hated Elmer Davis with every bone in his body. Elmer hounded him relentlessly when he first became Sheriff of Tallahatchie County. He thought the new young Sheriff was show-boating and trying to make a name for himself by constantly harassing him and his operation. It was a good operation too. He controlled all the gambling and most of the illegal booze while the country Sheriff at the time looked the other way. Donnie Sr. didn't know if the Sheriff was afraid to tangle with the Buckles clan or he just didn't want the headaches but either way, he rarely had any trouble with the cops. It was all a good operation, and nobody really bothered him before Elmer was elected. Everyone in the county knew that Elmer should not have been elected. If the Sheriff before Elmer hadn't had that accident while cleaning his gun, he would still be running his business and making a pile of cash. As it turned out, old Sheriff Murphy accidently shot himself while cleaning his gun one night, supposedly at the dinner table and right in front of his wife. The day after Sheriff Murphy's death, his wife packed up the kids and left town. She had the funeral in Tupelo and wouldn't even come back to a memorial the town had for her husband. She left the house, furniture and most of their clothes they had lived in for nearly 20 years and never came back to Webb.

Elmer Davis ran unopposed, everyone fawned over Elmer because of his local legendary status. Donnie Sr. hated Elmer when they were growing up together and he hated him now. He spent most of his waking hours and often his dreams watching Elmer Davis die and he intended to turn the dreams into reality. Unfortunately, because he would be locked up for life, he would never get to SEE Elmer die but he could at least revel in the act. He had a few other plans in the works that would ensure that the Sheriff of Tallahatchie County would suffer for the rest of his life. He hadn't shared a few of his plans with his sons because he could trust neither of them to keep their mouth shut. Brett was a braggadocios dummy and Judd was a simple-minded weakling. He was not about to give up simply because two nitwits failed to do the job. He was going to send the message to everyone inside and outside Parchman that he had no tolerance for failure when it came to the demise of Elmer Davis.

Donnie Sr. could see the courier of the weapon approaching and he slowed his pace, he could also see his target about twenty yards behind the courier, everything was working as planned. He took a quick glance up at the guard tower and was given the nod he was looking for. As they approached the exchange point the courier handed the knife to Judd as expected and continued walking towards them as Judd slowed his pace so that his father and brother could catch up to him and he could slide the knife in his side coat pocket where Brett would ease in behind and take the knife. Just as Brett was about to reach into his brother's pocket, he felt a sharp pain to the side of his head which caused him to stumble but not fall. The courier that had just handed Judd a knife pulled his hand from his side pocket and punched Donnie Sr. in the stomach. Donnie Sr. immediately bent over forward and then collapsed to the ground. The courier continued to walk in the opposite direction but never sped up his pace. Judd continued to walk in the direction he intended to and never saw his brother and his father on the ground behind him.

Judd was a good fifty yards away before he heard the yard sirens blare which meant that he had to get down on the ground, lay flat and wait to be cleared. He had been told when he first entered Parchman that if he moved during this time, the guards were free to shoot him. This is the first time he had actually been through this and the thought crossed his mind to move anyway. It just might be easier. He figured that his dad and brother had done what they were supposed to do and was actually relieved it was over. He hadn't done anything wrong and didn't have any weapons on him, so he had nothing to worry about so instead of moving and getting shot, he crossed his arms, placed his head in the cradle it created and waited to be cleared by the guards.

Chapter 18
Tommy Gun

TOM PORTER TURNED AND WALKED AWAY after tipping his hat to Mrs. Hazel. He was told that the Buckles clan were bad to the bone and that Donnie was the worst of them. He heard all the stories and he heard that the Sheriff, his new boss, nearly beat both younger Buckles to death with his bare hands so he already knew not to push the Sheriff too far. That would be silly to anyone, not just him. The Sheriff was a very imposing man although the experience he had with the Sheriff his first two weeks on the job only told him that the Sheriff didn't care about his job very much and he had a problem drinking but thought he was hiding it from everyone, but he didn't do as good of job as he thought he was doing.

He had intended on making a statement with his encounter with Donnie, but it hadn't turned out well and he was pissed. Mrs. Hazel interrupted his intimidation act he learned a long time ago which was to establish your territory quickly and there will be less trouble in the future. He liked trying to scare people into what he called respecting the badge. He had been told by one of the senior officers down in Pascagoula that it was important for a law man to be respected and often, that respect came with a healthy dose of fear. So, if Donnie Buckles were as bad as everyone said, he would need to establish that "respect" very quickly or in his opinion no one else in town would respect him. He would have to take up where he left off at a later time, he had night patrol.

He walked down the sidewalk passing each store. He jiggled the handle on the door at Turner Brothers and it was securely locked. He studied the window display for quite a while. There was a suit in there that he really liked. It was a soft blue seersucker that came with or without a vest. It was a little pricy for his salary and if he had to be honest, it might be made for a man a little older than him, but he knew if he had the spare cash he would go in and have the store order one in his size. He daydreamed for just a minute looking at the two mannequins in the window, the man with seersucker suit on had a nice low brimmed hat that made him think of Humphrey Bogart or Jimmy Cagney. He liked both of those guys because they were tough guys and they always got the best-looking girl, which was his plan.

The other mannequin was the woman and she had on a spaghetti strap dress that he thought was out of season and probably should have been gone a long time ago, but the mannequin still looked good. The skin tone reminded him of one Mrs. Tackitt. He hadn't been in town long, but he had already spotted her and fully intended to marry her just as soon as he could convince her. The guys in the Sheriff's office said to stay away but he knew better. They said she had married her high school sweetheart and then he went off the Viet Nam and was listed as MIA. He felt bad for the guy, but hell, most of the POW's were home now as far as he knew and there wasn't much hope of her husband making it back now. He didn't care if she was a little older than him. She was beautiful and age didn't matter.

He met her on Saturday at the weekly mercantile blowout the town always had. They would have all kinds of stuff going on to get people to come down and shop. The stores would stay open until midnight and every store would always have something on sale at a whopper price reduction. He experienced his first one last Saturday and even though he was on duty, he had a ball. They had jugglers and dunk tanks and hot dog stands but he quickly found out that his favorite stand was the snowball stand. That's where he met Mrs. Tackitt for the first time. He had just taken a big bite out of a Banana flavored snowball and it exploded then proceeded to drip all over the front of his shirt. He managed to grab a napkin from the window in the stand and get it cleaned up before it stained; but the yellow banana juice they squirted all over the ice cone to turn it yellow kind of matched his brown uniform. He wasn't too worried, and for October it was a pretty hot day so he knew it would dry fast.

Mrs. Tackitt came up to the counter right as he was wiping the drippings from his shirt. He was a little embarrassed at first, but she didn't pay any attention to him, so he introduced himself. "Hello ma'am." He reached up to tip his hat and remembered he left it in the car so he pretended to adjust his hair a little so it wouldn't look awkward, but it didn't work, he felt awkward from the get-go. She smiled and nodded then turned back to the snowball stand. "Uh, I am Tom Porter ma'am, my friends call me Tommy." She turned and smiled again then continued to order a rainbow flavored snowball which didn't seem appealing to him. He couldn't see how in the world anyone not order the banana flavor; it was simply the best. "Uh you can call me Tommy too ma'am." Mrs. Tackitt took her cone and gave the man some change and said, "Keep it." She then turned back to the deputy and said, "It's nice to meet you Deputy . . . ", she paused for a second and he could tell she was looking at his name tag on his shirt, "Porter". She then turned and walked down the middle of the street following the man on stilts until she got to Maxwell's Hardware and she went inside. Yes sir, he would marry her for sure.

He was enjoying the memory of his encounter with Mrs. Tackitt as he continued to walk down the sidewalk. He got to

Maxwell's Hardware which he was told used to be Barlow's Hardware but after that little Buckles kid was dumped behind Barlow's, old man Barlow couldn't stomach throwing the trash out anymore. He was scared to death that he was going to find another kid laying there in his sock feet with his lifeless eyes staring up at him. He had real nightmares after that, and the doctor told him he needed to get away from Webb and get somewhere where he could hopefully erase the memories of that day. He sold the store to Archie Maxwell and the last anyone heard he was living on the coast down in Alabama somewhere.

He stood looking at the window of Maxwell's and he could see the shut off dot in the middle of the TV in the display window. When he was little, he liked to turn the TV off and stare at the screen until the little dot in the middle of the screen was completely gone. He didn't know why but he was fascinated by that little dot. Then it occurred to him that the store closed well over an hour or two ago. He wasn't sure what time it was, but he was pretty sure there shouldn't be any dots left on the screen. He wondered if maybe the TV was defective and the tubes inside weren't shutting off properly. He made note of the model, it was an Admiral and decided that maybe he would steer clear of the Admiral brand if he wanted to buy a new TV someday. Well, really, it wouldn't be a new TV because he never had a TV, so he couldn't really be disposing of an old one. He was about to move on to the next store when he heard a crash inside the store. Finally, he thought, this could be a robber and he just might see some action. He unsnapped the leather strap on his holster that fit over the hammer just in case he needed to draw his gun quickly.

He tried to peer through the window, but He couldn't see anything. He cupped his hands to reduce the glare of the streetlight and placed them directly on the glass. He squinted his eyes but couldn't see anything out of the ordinary. He had already jiggled the knob on both entrance doors, and both were secure. He decided to walk around back. He took the alley closest to the store and made his way around back. He could feel his heart racing in his chest, and he tried to step as softly as he could, but his boots seemed heavy and almost pounded the asphalt leading to the back of the store.

He reached the back entrance where the deliveries were made and reached for the handle. Just as he reached for the handle, he could see that the door was slightly ajar. It was dark in the back of the store but there was no mistaking, the door was already open. He decided it was time to remove his weapon from the holster now. This was heart pounding stuff and even in his previous roles as a cop he really hadn't faced anyone in a shoot-out or even broke up a fight. He kept his back against the wall and held his pistol at his side with his right hand while slowly opening the door with his left hand. He winced as the door creaked when he pulled it open, and frustrated that it was so heavy. He had trouble pulling the door open with just one hand but managed to get it open enough for him to ease inside, remaining sideways so he wouldn't be such a big target in case he did get in a shoot-out. He stepped lightly into the store and made his way along the back wall trying to look down the rows of counters that held all the merchandise. He froze when he saw movement in the front of the store. He was certain he saw movement even if it was just for a second and he was also certain that he had been spotted because the movement he saw made it look like whoever it might be was crouching and moving quickly in front of the counters.

From his police training he knew that they were trying to flank him, so he had to be careful and not let them come up beside him. Now was the time to announce his presence and maybe by doing so he could avoid a shoot-out and any possible loss of life. He was a great shot and had scored the highest proficiency rating in Academy history so he was for certain that he could easily kill someone. "Sheriff's Office!" He screamed at the top of his lungs, "You're sealed off and there is no way out!" He took in a deep breath of air and remembered not to buy an

Admiral TV. "Don't make me shoot!" He had his gun extended out at the ready when he heard a clicking sound. That had to be a hammer cocking he thought. He was really going to get in a shoot-out, and he could see himself explaining to the TV lady over in Sumner how he dropped this bad guy with one shot and saved Maxwell's Hardware from losing any merchandise. He felt the bump against his leg and his reaction was to jump and try and turn towards the bump. When he made the awkward jump and turn, he squeezed a little too hard on the trigger and his gun discharged which immediately produced a scared yelp from the dog that was roaming free in Maxwell's hardware store.

The dog ran back towards the front of the store scared half to death at the deafening noise the gun shot made. "God dangit!" Tommy let out the breath he had been holding and put the gun back in his holster. He could see lights shining in the front window display. Apparently, the guys shooting pool at Young's heard the gunshot and ran across the street to see what happened. Three of them had flashlights and were trying to see what was going on in the store. Tommy walked to the front of the store where he saw the dog hunkered down by the register and whimpering. He decided that the best thing to do was to head off the gossip that was sure to follow and opened the front door to Maxwell's.

He stepped out on the sidewalk where he could see at least seven men all looking at him. "Go on back to your game boys, nothing to see here. Just a weapons malfunction. The men all laughed at the same time and one of them yelled, "Malfunction my ass, you was trying to kill Archie's poor little dog!" They all howled with laughter then someone yelled, "It's deputy Tommy gun!" Then came more laughter until Archie Maxwell showed up. "What's going in here?" He was fumbling with his keys then realized the front door was already open.

One of the men in the crowd pointed at the deputy with a beer in the same hand he was pointing with, "Tommy Gun here just tried to shoot a hole through poor old Jax, Archie!" They all laughed again. Archie was a calm and kind man who didn't get too excited about anything except Christmas, and all the sales he did at Christmas. He was a little frustrated with the attention his store was getting at the moment. "You fellas go on back to your pool game before the deputy here sites you for public drinking." The men in the crowd realized they had all rushed out of the pool hall to see what the shot was about and hadn't bothered to leave their beers inside. It was against the law to consume alcohol in public and they all knew it. Everyone that was holding a beer quickly moved it out of site and retreated to the pool hall.

"I'm sorry Mr. Maxwell, I heard a crash in the store and thought someone was trying to rob you." He fidgeted with this holster a little and shrugged his shoulders for a little more dramatic effect. Archie stepped by the deputy and went in the store. He flipped the light switch and the store became fully lit. "Oh Jax! The dog came up to his owner with its tail between its legs. Archie bent down and rubbed both side of the dog's face which made him unfurl his tail and begin to happily wag it. "You went and knocked over the gas cans didn't you!" Tommy looked over at the display of cans that were now scattered all over the aisle. "He's done that twice now." Archie stood up and looked at Tommy. "How did you get in here?" Tommy spun around and pointed at the back door. "The back door was open Mr. Maxwell." Archie shook his head in a frustrated way. "I really don't know what's the matter with me lately. That's the third dog gone time this year that I have plum forgot to lock the back door." He rubbed his chin then looked down at Jax. "That cat got in here again didn't he boy?" He bent down and rubbed Jax's head again, but something caught his eye in the back of the store. "You like to hunt Deputy . . . " He paused as if he was searching for a name and Tommy finished for him, "Tom Porter, sir," Archie stood up and pointed at the back of the store. Hope you like to deer hunt Deputy Tom Porter because I sure don't."

Tommy was confused and was trying to see what he was pointing at in hopes of uncovering the origin of the odd question, then he saw it. On the back wall of the store was a nicely mounted deer head that had now been shot twice, the first time was the fatal one that landed him on the back wall of the hardware store and this time was more of a humiliating shot that went through his jaw, out his eyeball and left the right antler dangling from the explosion. "You'll need to replace that for me Deputy."

Chapter 19
Honky Tonk Women

DONNIE CRAWLED IN THE TRUCK from the passenger side, slid the key into the ignition, pressed the clutch and turned the key. The engine roared to life as quickly as it ever had. He thought to himself that perhaps it may be the ugliest truck in Tallahatchie County, maybe the whole state of Mississippi, but it was the most reliable. He pushed the shifter in the floor into reverse and he eased the big flatbed out of the parking spot. He drove by the pool hall and thought about all the times he had hustled guys in that building then having to fight them when they realized he had hustled them all. He was an excellent pool player and could always pick up some money when he wanted to but at that moment, he knew he wouldn't ever hustle anyone again.

He looked over in the passenger seat at the plastic dish containing the spaghetti that Mrs. Hazel asked him to take to Heather Davis. Smelling it through the sealed container he heard his stomach rumble. He couldn't remember the last time he had eaten. He knew he had nothing at home and seriously considered eating the spaghetti, but he changed his mind. He let the heavy truck pick up some steam and shifted gears. Even though the truck didn't have a radio, it had long been yanked out and sold for some reason or another. He was sure that Brett used it for beer money, he started singing *Honky Tonk Women* by the Rolling Stones. "*I met a gin-soaked bar room queen in Memphis . . .* " He was tapping on the steering wheel to keep time with the lyrics "*She tried to take me upstairs for a ride . . .* " He paused to think about that new deputy that was trying to show his feathers. He thought about Mrs. Hazel and wished she had been his mother. Maybe if she would have been his mother, he would have turned out different, maybe he would have gone to school and made something of his life. Instead, he had a baby brother that had been molested and murdered, two other baby brothers that turned out to be bully's and were currently sitting in prison with his dad. He smiled and laughed a little when he realized there wasn't much he could do about the past and though it was silly to be daydreaming about stupid stuff, he started tapping on the steering wheel again. " *. . . she had to heave me right across her shoulder . . .* " He laughed because that image of a woman, even if the woman may have been a dude, tossing him over their shoulder and hauling up any stairs, anywhere, was simply humorous. It was the one song that he sang over and over while being held captive in Viet Nam. It got him through some really rough times. " *. . . cause I just can't drink you off my mind . . .* " He really belted that part of the verse out and laughed again. "I'd have to be doing a whole lot of drinking to get heaved over a chick's shoulder for sure, man." He started in on the chorus with gusto: "*It's a Honky tonk . . .* " He stopped singing as he crested the hill and saw a car in the middle of the road with a man closing the trunk of his white car, then scooping a little dog off the ground and seemed to be in a hurry. Normally he would just go around because this kind of stuff wasn't his business but when he decided to make a change today, he decided that everything about him had to change. He shifted down and slowed the truck to a crawl until it was directly behind the car. The man hadn't quite made it back to the driver's side when Donnie stepped out of the truck.

"Hey man, everything alright?" Donnie tried to put the guy at ease because he sure seemed nervous. "Oh yes, yes, thank you my good man." Donnie almost laughed at the guy's accent. It was funny for sure. It certainly wasn't local but something about it seemed goofy. "Do you have a flat? What's the deal man?" Donnie was trying to walk towards the man, but the man got in his car and shut the door. The window was down so the man yelled at the window, "Young Beau here just had to use the dunny. Tootle loo my good man!" Donnie was left standing in the road as the car drove off.

Well, that was just weird. That had to be a fake accent but what the hell did he need to use a fake accent with me for? I didn't even get a good look at him. He tried to make a mental note of the license plate, but the car sped away so quickly, kicking up dirt from the two passenger side tires that were resting on the dirt part of the road. All he could manage to get was HCM 4. He was kicking himself for not looking at the license plate sooner. He didn't even know why he decided to look at the license plate at all, but he did. It just seemed to Donnie that the whole encounter was just weird. He walked back to his truck and out of the corner of his eye he caught the glitter of something metallic on the ground. He stopped and bent down and picked up a rabbit's foot key chain with two keys and beside the key chain was some sort of card. It was too dark to see it clearly, so he held it front of his headlight and saw that it was a library card for Jeannine Martin. He thought about it for a little bit, the barber's daughter. He held the key chain in his left hand, and he tapped on the card with his index finger with his right hand like he was making a point in a presentation. He took the card and put it in the front pocket of brand-new Ely Walker shirt and slid the rabbit's foot key chain into his front pants pocket. As he walked back to the truck that was still running, he was thinking what kind of man says tootle loo? The string of missing girls across the state wouldn't hit him until he was later standing on the front porch of the Sheriff's house. He got back in the truck, caught a whiff of the spaghetti and wrestled with the idea of eating but quickly backed down from the idea.

He pressed the clutch and jammed it back into gear and slowly released the clutch. Even though the truck was very reliable, she had a very sensitive clutch and if you even thought about letting it out before you had the right mix of gas, she would jerk to a stop. He got the truck rolling and started his singing again. This time he picked up a little Elvis and lowered his voice to try and sound more like The King. *"Wise men say, only fools rush in . . . "* He once again laughed at himself as he tried to curl his upper lip like Elvis did. It seemed to help him sound more like Elvis, he wasn't sure, and he wasn't about to ask for opinions.

He slowed down so he could see the entrance to the Davis's drive. It was very tough to see in the dark, but he managed. He laughed again because they had been neighbors almost his entire life and yet he had never been down this road. Seeing the Sheriff was something he tried to avoid if he could and yet here, he was, driving right up to the house. After all the squabbles their families had, he started have second thoughts about this little errand he was running for Mrs. Hazel.

He eased his truck down the winding dirt road that led to the Sheriff's house. He was amazed at how far the house was back into the property. The driveway was so long that the Davis's could have given their driveway a street name. He started humming *Honky Tonk Women* but he didn't sing it. He was getting more nervous by the minute thinking about how he would make the introduction. "Hey Sheriff, good to see you when you aren't beating my brothers half to death," or Hey Sheriff, got some food for your daughter but none for you or your son." He laughed as he thought it about it. He was thinking about how to knock on the door, would he use a forceful knock or a timid one and if he were too timid, they may not even hear him and then he would just feel stupid standing on the front porch.

He slowed the truck to a stop right in front of the Davis's house. The lights were on and he could see silhouettes moving throughout the house. He killed the engine and set the parking brake. He sat there with his hands on the steering wheel tapping out the song again, but he wasn't humming or singing. He tried to exit the driver door and remembered after he jammed his shoulder against it that it didn't open. He winced a little as his shoulder and elbow protested the collision. He grabbed the plastic bowl and set it on the dash so he could scoot over and exit the passenger door. When he had his feet on the ground he reached back in and grabbed the bowl to take with him for the knock. He made his way up the steps and stood squarely in front of the door. For a second, he thought about turning around and getting back into his truck, but he was certain they had seen him or at least his head lights coming up the drive. They lived so far away from the main road; they'd have to blind not to see someone coming up their drive. He was about to knock when the door opened.

Chapter 20

Good Bye Old Harper

ELMER HELD THE DOOR TO TURNER BROTHERS open for Heather to walk out first. He turned and looked back at the Greek manager and gave him a smile which the manager returned along with a wave. The Managers eyes were still moist from witnessing the most genuine exchange of emotions between a father and daughter he had ever seen. Elmer let the door close easily as he stepped out on the sidewalk. The sun felt good, but he could feel fall in the air. He realized at that moment that he had enjoyed fall more than any season because Lois loved it so much. She would spend all day preparing to go to the football games and everything had to be just right for Decker. He loved his hot chocolate and popcorn and she loved to see the look of wonderment on his face when they would finally sit down on the bleachers. He thought she would love to watch her son play now because neither had any idea that Decker would turn out to be as good as he was at football. When that growth spurt hit him, it hit him fast and took full advantage. He also realized that he couldn't remember a single game that Decker had played since she died. He felt some shame flow over him, but he beat back by looking at his daughter who was standing on the sidewalk staring at him as he daydreamed. Her eyes were still a little puffy from the wash of tears that exploded when she finally got the bear hug from her Daddy that she missed so much.

"What are you thinking about Daddy?" He looked down at her and smiled, "More than I can share right now but I will in due time." He pointed towards the Scout and said, "I think we need to go introduce you to the office now." He held Scout door open for her to climb in and as she was getting situated, he smiled and said "Daddy, that's good to hear. I have missed that." He shut the door before she could respond. He walked around the front of Scout and noticed the Old Harper bottle he discarded in the trash and smiled. When he got in the Scout he sat still for a minute and it was very quiet in the Scout. Heather didn't say anything, she waited for her dad to speak. He depressed the clutch and turned the key to the Scout. It came to life as quickly as it ever had, and it sat running for just a second before Elmer spoke. "Today I saw a picture of a little girl that has stuck in my head." His expression changed from relief to anguish in one motion. "It is 2 or 3 years old and I feel like I have seen her. If I saw that girl long ago and could have helped her and didn't, I think I ought to be shot." Heather put her hand on the forearm that extended out from the shifter in the floor, "What girl?" He reached in his shirt pocket and pulled out the missing girl flyer that he found in his desk. He handed it to her, she unfolded it and stared at the smiling little girl from Drew, Mississippi that was just beautiful. She had a smile on her face that was hard to forget. Heather felt a rush of emotions come over her. She realized that the picture she was staring at was a young girl that had been taken from her parents. The pain they must feel, and the fear this girl must have felt, nearly caused her to cry.

"Why would you have been able to do something Pops? How would you know she was in trouble back then if you did?" He shook his head, "I don't know baby, I just know that I have seen that little girl somewhere and I won't sleep a wink until I remember where I saw her." He let out a deep breath and then looked at

Heather, "Let's go introduce you as the new office manager but we gotta go pick up Lavera so she can be there when we announce it. I got some more public apologies to make." He pulled the radio mic from the cradle, "Uh, anyone covering for Lavera? Copy?" the radio cracked and scratched a little, then a female voice came on that sounded very soft. "Hello Sheriff." He wrinkled his forehead trying to figure out who was responding. "Is that you Peggy?" It was quiet for an awkward moment before the soft voice returned, "No sir, this is Mary Alice." Elmer could never tell the two a part, not because they looked alike but because they never worked on the same day. They were two part-time workers that happened to be sisters or cousins or something, he wasn't sure. They didn't have the budget for both of them to work at the same time, so he counted on Lavera to schedule them correctly. It was another task that Lavera had done without any complaint, in fact, it was Lavera's idea to hire the two so that they could train both and would never have to worry about someone calling in sick or the office falling apart whenever Lavera took a week of vacation and went to go visit her brother in Arkansas. "Okay Mary Alice, make sure everyone assembles in the office in 30 minutes please." "Copy Sir."

The three of them walked into the office. Lavera was so excited that Elmer had shown back up at her house with Heather. She saw it as a first step on the road to recovery for Elmer and Heather. There was so much healing that needed to be done in that family and she felt like her daily prayers were being answered right before her eyes. At first, she didn't want to go back to the office with them, she would rather have just let the blow up of the day slide by and everyone would get back to normal, but after listening to Elmer and Heather explain the need to make things right before the healing could begin, she agreed. She knew they were right, but that didn't mean that she didn't still feel uncomfortable with it.

Elmer stood in the middle of the office with Lavera on one side and Heather on the other. He didn't have to announce anything, everyone had already gathered when they walked in. He looked around the room at the faces that were staring back at him. It was a moment of clarity for him. He knew each of them, Mary Alice had even called Peggy into the office because she was concerned because the Sheriff never called a meeting of all the staff. "Thank you all for tolerating me these last few years. My behavior has been less than professional and for that I truly apologize." He looked down at his feet for just a second and then looked back up and then scanned the room as if he intended to make eye contact with everyone and he did. When he finished scanning the room, he turned and looked down at Lavera and stopped. "Today I disrespected a woman that has been nothing but good and decent to all of us and I regret that very much." He turned away from Lavera and looked at the crowd. "I apologized to her at her home and begged her to come back and she unfortunately decided that now was a good time to end a very long career for the Tallahatchie County Sheriff's office." He turned back to Lavera and continued, "Fortunately for me, she forgave me and agreed to stay on long enough to help train her replacement." He turned and looked at Heather. "I know of no one more organized and tough enough to handle the job than this young lady here." He put his hand on Heather's shoulder and it hit him at that moment that she was the spitting image of her mother and he hadn't noticed until now. It was quiet for a second and Lavera quickly reassumed her role as the office manager and said, "Well don't just stand there, welcome this wonderful woman into the sheriff's office!" And with that, everyone clapped and made their way toward Lavera and Heather where they all started hugging and talking and just like that, there was life back in the Sheriff's office. Despite his size, no one noticed Elmer retreating to his office and closing the door.

He went through all the reports on missing children that were available. For the ones that he had in his Rolodex, he called each of the Sheriffs of the locations where the children went missing. Every one of them said essentially the same thing. The girls and boys were out doing normal kid things and never made it home. He collected all the information that he could from each one but the one that really stuck in his gut the most was the little girl from Drew. The Sheriff of Sunflower County, R.C. Ross was incredibly thorough and detailed on all the information that he had on her.

She was 11 years old when she went missing but she would be 14 now. Her bike and what was believed to be a hair ribbon and a bow were found on the side of the road with the kick stand engaged as if she meant to park it there. She was only a block from her house when she parked the bike. Her mother said she left that morning around 9 AM and was going to play with her cousin that lived just a street over from where they lived, and never came home. She didn't realize there was anything wrong until late in the day when she didn't return. She said she called her sister and her heart stopped when her sister told her that she never came over that day. The father was called from work where he worked in a welding shop. Sheriff Ross told Elmer that the father was destroyed by the whole thing. He spent his days looking for her; he even lost his job, but he never stopped looking for her. He managed to scrape by and make a living for he and his wife, but it wasn't long before the marriage broke up and they went their separate ways. Even though they never said it to each other, each blamed the other for the loss of their little girl and the small little fire of resentment and anger that burned inside them was too much to keep the marriage together.

By the time he was finished talking to the Sheriff of Sunflower County, Elmer had tears rolling down his cheeks. The story was awful. No family should ever have to endure so much pain. He realized that he was lucky to have two kids that loved him, and he was going to be a better dad from now on.

He thanked Sheriff Ross for all the information and promised to keep in touch because his gut told him that he knew this little girl. His intercom crackled to life as he sat there "Uh, Dad, I mean Sheriff, you have a collect call from Parchman." Heather paused for second, "Do you want to accept?" It wasn't uncommon for him to get a call from Parchman, but it was uncommon for the calls to be collect; that usually meant that it was from an inmate which again was not uncommon, however, most of the inmates that called always worked favors through the guards and didn't have to call collect. Most of the calls he received from inmates were surprisingly friendly, they would want to tell him that they had no hard feelings, and they were trying to get straight or they would ask to have the Sheriff check on a family member which he always managed to do. "Yes, go ahead and patch it through." He waited for a second and then voice came through, "Well hello Sheriff." Elmer tried to recognize the voice, but he was drawing a blank. "I'm sorry, I don't know who this is." The voice laughed, "You know us better than anyone, hells bells boy, we are your neighbors." Elmer could tell the voice was taking a drag on a cigarette as he paused, "We got payback coming your way Elmer Fudd, just thought I'd let you know." The voice laughed, "Tootle loo Sheriff." The line went dead. Elmer just shook his head and put the receiver back on the cradle. Interesting he thought.

He put the weird phone call behind him and decided it was time to meet with them. Once he straightened up his desk and threw the old calendar away, he opened a brand new one and wrote on the top of the calendar ELMER DAVIS COUNTY SHERIFF. He opened all his files and went through all the secret hiding places for his Old Harper bottles and was satisfied that he collected them all; he opened the door and asked Lavera and Heather to come into his office. Both ladies were still getting hugs from the rest of the staff while they swapped old war stories about how difficult it could be to work in the Sheriff's office, especially when the Sheriff was determined to solve a crime, he was relentless, and he tended to be quick tempered with a stinging tongue.

Lavera sat down in front of Elmer's desk and then Heather followed. Elmer held up the missing girl flyer and said "I am not going crazy, but I know I have seen this girl somewhere. I don't know if I saw her when I was over in Drew a few years ago doing something with state police but I know damn well that I have seen her." He laid the flyer down on the desk and then picked up another piece of paper that said, "Re-Elect Elmer Davis STRENGTH and INTEGRITY." He pointed at the paper and looked at Heather, "Change the STRENGTH to EXPERIENCE and I want these up all over town." He handed the paper to her and she took it. "I also want a town hall meeting scheduled for next Monday night. You can get the word out to the county through the radio station, they will give you the airtime for free and then I want time to speak at the city council meeting on Wednesday." He smiled, looked at both of them, but mostly at Lavera. "I need you to stay on as long as you can. I need Heather to be up and running just as quick as you can and oh . . . " He paused then turned back to Heather. " . . . and YOU will finish college while working for the County. Lavera will fill in for you when you have to go to class." Lavera smiled and realized she'd been snookered. She fully intended to retire and take care of her health issues, but Sheriff Elmer Davis had just given her an order and she was obliged to follow it. "Any questions ladies?" Heather smiled at her father but didn't say anything, "Heather we need to be home by six tonight so I can help you with supper. She smiled and shook her head, "Nice try Dad, but tonight is prayer meeting and we are meeting the new youth minister, you can help with supper tomorrow night though . . . " Heather paused, "or you can go to prayer meeting with us."

Elmer cleared his throat and glanced down at the trash can full of near empty bottles of Old Harper. "I'm sure I could use some praying, but I need to get my act together here first. I will just meet you and Decker at home after the prayer meeting." The two ladies got up and started to walk out but Lavera turned and said, "Don't forget the one in the hollowed-out center of the coat rack." She turned and walked out the door with Heather. Elmer was confused at first but then he stood up, went over to the corner, removed a Stetson from the top of the rack, reached down in the center and pulled out an unopened pint of Old Harper. "Damn" was all he could say.

Chapter 21
Cassidy Bayou

"PLEASE BE QUIET. PLEASE BE QUIET. Please be quiet." Decker heard the whispering in the room, but the room was very dark. His head felt like it had been struck by lightning. He heard that there was a guy in Locke Station that had been struck by lightning twice and it caused his head to look like an egg. He felt his head to see if there was any change, but he couldn't tell. He felt around in the dark for something recognizable, something that might give him an idea just exactly where he was, but he found nothing. He moaned as he rubbed his head because it really hurt, and he was very disoriented. "Please be quiet. He will come down here when he hears noise. He hates noise." At first Decker thought he was dreaming but now there was no mistaking, there was someone else in the room and he had no idea who she was.

"Who are you?" He tried to find the source of the voice in the dark but even if he had more light, he was certain his eyes were blurry and wouldn't be able to see anyway. She gave him the SHUSH and it reminded him of Jeannine when she would do the same thing when they were in the library. "I am Jessica, now please, keep your voice down or he will come down here for sure." Decker sat up, then stood up, but he hit his head on something hard and he fell back to the ground. He rubbed the top of his head and he suddenly felt the need to throw up and he did. He hated throwing up, the taste was awful, and it would stay with him for days. He couldn't remember the last time he threw up and he decided right then and there he would never through up again. His dilemma now was how to get away from the chuck puddle he created. He tried to move away from it slowly while feeling above his head for whatever he just hit his head on. "Whisper or something, I can't find you." This time when he spoke, he was whispering as she had instructed and she responded with her own whisper. "I am over here but please don't come over here." Decker stopped; he was unsure on what to do. He still felt sick, but he thought it was strange that he wasn't scared. He knew he should, but he was too busy trying to figure things out and didn't have time to get scared. He could hear the fear in the girl's voice, but he had to get to know this person. They were obviously kidnapped, and that concept alone just boggled his mind. This was the one position in life he never even considered being in.

"Do you know how long I have been here?" She didn't say anything for a few minutes, and he started to worry that she would not talk to him. "I don't really know. I don't have a watch and he doesn't tell me the time." She stopped for a minute, "If I had to guess I'd say you've been down here about an hour, maybe less." Decker took a few steps closer to the voice and then sat down. She could tell what he was doing because her eyes had adjusted to the dark relatively well. She used to be scared of the dark but now it was only when he would come down and flip on the light that she got scared. For just a few minutes she had to close her eyes to keep the sudden light from hurting them and just about the time she was ready to try and open them, he or the woman he was with, had already found her and taken her upstairs with a sack or bag or something over her head so she never saw either of them. That was when she would get scared because she thought they would surely kill her each time, but each time they brought her back downstairs. Different houses but always downstairs. She felt like she had become a pet to him, and she hated it.

"Who are you?" She said it with reluctance, almost as if she really didn't want to know. Decker scooted a little closer to the voice, he had this strong need to be close to her. The closer he got the more nervous he got. He knew that if he could get nervous, he would get sharper and he would think more clearly. He had always been that way, the more pressure or nerves he felt, the better decisions he made. Everyone would ask him how come he didn't get excited in games when the score was close or there was time pressure and he couldn't explain it, he simply liked being scared and feeling nervous. "I am Decker Davis from Webb, Mississippi." He paused and whispered again, "What's your name? Where are you from? How long have you been here?" He tried to slow down the questions, but he couldn't.

He scooted a little closer to where he thought she was. He knew he was getting close because he could smell her, and she smelled like shampoo. "Please don't get any closer to me. Really! I mean it!" She whispered what she wanted to yell, and Decker decided he was close enough. "Ok, I promise I won't. Just be calm please." He tried to think of what to say, "I promise I won't hurt you." He could hear that she was crying, it wasn't a full-on cry because she was trying to suppress it. "Where are you from Jessica?" He could still hear her crying and through the vibrations in the floor he could feel her body heave. "It's going to be ok, really. Just talk to me please, I like to hear people talk." She whispered as softly as she could, "Drew." She couldn't see Decker, but he was looking around now. His head felt better, and his eyes had almost adjusted to the dark so he could see shapes, corners and the general size of the room. He could see her outline and he could tell she was in the corner closest to him and she had her knees drawn up to her chest and her head buried in her knees.

"Wow, my dad took me hunting over by Drew once. That was a long time ago. I never got a deer though. I just got cold." He could hear her whimpering stop and she chuckled as low as she dared. "My dad took me hunting too and I nodded off to sleep when the night and morning mixed to a fog and I must have let the Shadow Beast get me." Decker could hear her whimper again. "What's the Shadow Beast?" He could faintly see her lift her head and look at him. "Him." Decker reached out as best he could and placed his hand on what he believed was her shoulder. When he touched her, she withdrew quickly but there was no mistaking, he touched her skin, and her skin was like touching a bag of ice from the bait store. He had a sick feeling that she didn't have any clothes on. He wasn't sure what to say so he changed the subject. "I can hear the bullfrogs and I can smell the rice. We must be near the bayou." He could see her relax a little. "You know they would try and treat dysentery during the civil war with Mercury and chalk and then feed them lots of rice to help with the squirts." He didn't mean to say squirts, but it sounded better than the Hershey Squirts or even diarrhea. He stopped and gave her time to respond but she didn't so he continued. "The bayou rice fields supplied an awful lot of rice to the confederates during the war."

Without any warning Jessica scrambled over to Decker and hugged him. She began to cry, and it was then that he found out for certain that she was naked. He didn't know what to do but he could tell from the touch of her skin that she was cold. His heart was beating a hundred miles an hour. He'd never seen a girl naked and was awfully glad it was dark in this place. His first instinct was to scramble away from her, but he didn't. He simply put his arms around her and let her cry on his shoulder where her head ended up. He thought about his sister and how she would comfort him when he started thinking about the good old days when his mother was alive, and it would make him sad and sometimes make him cry. She would hug him tight and rub his back and the back of his head and it always without fail made him feel better. He did the same thing with her. He held her for what seemed like an hour and did the same things to her that Heather would do for him. He finally decided to speak and act. "Hey, hang on!" he let her go and started unbuttoning his shirt. He was wearing one of his Sunday shirts, so it was a nice blue button-down shirt. Luckily, he had a tee shirt on under the button down. He took off the shirt and handed it her. "Here, put this on, it may not smell very well, I was running home and was pretty sweaty but from the touch of your skin, you are freezing cold." She took it and then handed it back to him. "I can't, he won't like it, he doesn't let me wear clothes." She stopped and took a breath, "And he will beat you to death if he thinks you have done anything to me." Decker handed the shirt back to her. "I'd rather be dead than see you naked and freeze to death down here," he leaned a little closer and brushed the shirt against her shoulder so she could feel the warmth, put it on please." This time she took the shirt and put it on. Decker could see her body almost relax when she did. "Thank you, Decker Davis." He was quite a bit bigger than her so his shirt did a good job of covering her, that much he could see in the near darkness. Once he thought she had the shirt buttoned and sounded like she had tucked her knees inside the shirt, he scooted close to her again and put his arm around her. He pulled her close so he could hopefully help her get warm.

"How often does he come down here?" Decker felt in his pocket for his rabbits' foot key chain and couldn't find it. He tried to remember where he left it, but he couldn't, but he did feel his pocketknife that he won shooting baskets at the county fair. He smiled when he thought about that day. The baskets were way smaller than a normal basket, but he was a good shot. He started hitting all the shots and the guy behind the counter kept yelling at him and jumping at him in hopes of trying to distract him, but they couldn't. Decker had already spotted the pocketknife on the prize rack and he was determined to get it. At first the guy behind the counter tried to claim that he hadn't hit enough baskets to claim the main prize so Decker told the guy that his dad was the county Sheriff, and he could settle it with him if he wanted. The barker decided he didn't need any trouble with the law, so he handed the knife to him and told him to "beat it." He pulled it out and opened it so he could feel the blade and remembered that he had just put the wet stone to it a few days before, so it was nice and sharp. He folded it back and stuck it in the arch portion of his shoe. It was uncomfortable but he had seen his dad frisk people before and he knew the Shadow Beast as Jessica called him would surely find it and take it away from him. All he could think about was that he hoped his daddy would find him.

"It's hard to say, some days he comes down here a dozen times and then sometimes he goes for days without coming down here, but he sends her to come down here." She started crying again, he does terrible things to me. I am ashamed of it. I have asked God to forgive me and take me from the earth, but he doesn't." Decker started to ask what terrible things she was talking about so he could prepare himself in case it happened to him, but he thought better of it, there was no point. "You haven't done anything wrong Jessica. God may not show up personally, but I guarantee he will send my dad." The comment made her stop crying and for a second Decker thought that he felt her chuckle. "Why do you say that Decker Davis?" She paused and continued, "How do you know anyone can find us in this dungeon?" Without hesitation, Decker said, "Because my dad is the Sheriff of Tallahatchie County and he is the best lawman in the world." She lifted her head up quickly and even though she couldn't really tell where his face was, she wanted to be looking at him. "Is he a BIG man, real wide and wears a brown uniform and a cowboy hat?"

She couldn't see Decker's eyebrow's rise and the wrinkles on his forehead appear with the confused look he was giving her. "How would you know that?" He pulled away from her a little now so he could try and look at her. "You just described him to a 'T'." She leaned her head back on his shoulder, "We saw him last week," she drew in a deep breath, "me and her." Decker didn't know what to say but he knew he needed more information than that. "She took you into town naked?" She giggled a little and playfully slapped Decker on the chest. "No Decker, I have clothes that she buys me in case we have to pack up and move quickly." She paused for a second, they can't very well parade me around in public with nothing on." She continued, "I have just about outgrown anything she bought me last fall so she took me to town to buy some new clothes. I am not allowed to speak when I am there, only to say please and thank you." Decker shook his head; all this was very difficult to process. He couldn't figure out why in the world someone would treat someone else so badly. "And you saw my dad at the store? Was it I Peals or Turner brothers?" Decker felt stupid for asking which store it was because as soon as he said it, he knew it didn't matter. "I think it was Turner Brothers but I ain't sure. We just passed him on the sidewalk and when she saw him, she got really nervous and tried to avoid him, but she couldn't, he just said hello and tipped his hat." She stopped for a second then started again, "I tried with everything I could to stare a hole through this forehead or something. I tried to let my eyes talk for me, but I got nothing. He just smiled and kept walking." Decker breathed in hard, almost exasperated, "Why didn't you just grab him, yell at him or scream?" He couldn't believe she wouldn't ask his dad for help. He just knew his dad would have helped her. "You don't understand Decker, I couldn't risk it. I just couldn't risk it."

Chapter 22
Gut Punched

DONNIE SR. LAID ON THE GROUND AFTER being sucker punched by the courier. He had to admit that it was a good punch because it dropped him to his knees and when he heard the sirens go off, he simply laid down. He tried to look around and see what was going on, but he had to be careful, if a prisoner moved and a guard felt threatened by that movement during the sirens, it was lights out. They would be justified in their opinion of course to blow his head off so he made very slow deliberate side to side motions so he could survey the yard. The pain in his stomach was still there and still very real. He could see Brett to his right and he wasn't moving at all and he could see Judd to his left and he had his head cradled in his folded arms like he was taking a nap and didn't have a care in the world.

His stomach was really hurting now, he was thinking the courier must have had some brass knuckles or something because from what he was smelling, he was certain he had soiled himself in the process and he was feeling quite embarrassed. He would have to bribe the folks in the infirmary to keep that quiet. This guy had always been a square dealer with him so he couldn't figure out why he would turn on him. This was the only guy he really trusted up until now and had no reason to think he would get double crossed in the yard. He slid his hand under his stomach even though during a situation like this, the inmates were supposed to keep their arms visible. When his hand reached the source of the pain, he realized that it wasn't a punch with brass knuckles that sent him to his knees, it was a stab that did it. He was bleeding from his abdomen and his confusion turned to panic. Then he felt a hand on his back.

"Damn this little prison yard attack of yours backfired huh?" He couldn't tell who it was, but he assumed it had to be a guard. "Now you got everyone in a panic, and they are searching every damn prisoner in the yard one at a time." He laughed under his breath a little when he said it. "This could take at least an hour, maybe two to clear the yard and sound the bell for all clear." He laughed again, "By then, you will have either bled to death with that hole in your stomach leaking like a busted oil pan." He pressed his hand harder into Donnie Sr.'s back, " . . . or you lose so much blood that you end up brain dead," Then he really laughed, "In which case you spend the rest of your brain-dead life as a blow up doll for the queers in the infirmary." He took the pressure off Donnie Sr.'s back and said, "You don't run this prison, we do."

The reality of his wound was starting to set in, and he felt a slight degree of panic, but he wanted this guard to know that he didn't rattle easily. He turned his head to where he thought Brett was and saw that Brett was still lying on his back instead of his stomach. "Brett, roll over before these morons do something stupid." This time the guard bent down quickly and whispered once again in Donnie Sr.'s ear, "I'm afraid your moron son is being judged right now and I don't think he will fare too well." He laughed a little and before he walked away, he said, "Bobby Martin says hello." Donnie Sr. heard his footsteps walk away and he tried to lift his head up and see which direction he was going but he couldn't lift his head up, he was getting weak. "Brett!" he screamed but it only came out as a muffled sound. There was no reply. "Brett! Wake up!" Brett didn't move.

Judd lifted his head when he felt someone patting his butt. He looked back and the guard that had led him down the hall where he was later attacked was standing over him. "Hey sweetheart." Judd put his head back in his folded arms and grit his teeth. He wanted nothing more than to get up and beat the hell out of this guy, but he knew it would end badly for him again. He wasn't a very good fighter, he would never get into a fight without Brett and besides, this man was a guard. Striking a guard was sure to add at least 5 years to a man's sentence and he was up for parole soon. The guard was about to say something when the siren stopped. The siren stopping meant that he could stand up now. He tried to get to his feet, but the guard pushed him back down. "Your daddy got nailed with a pig sticker and if he is lucky, he will probably bleed to death." He laughed as the noise in the yard started to pick up again. Inmates were being ushered back to their cells and that was chatter like Judd had never heard. "Oh, and your big brother, well . . . " he paused, "My condolences." He laughed and removed his foot from Judd's back. Get back to your cell sweetheart." Judd stood up and joined the other inmates that were already being marched back to their cells. He turned to look back and saw that there were two inmates still on the ground. One on his back and one on his stomach, he was certain the one on his back was his brother and he just knew he was dead. He was also pretty sure that the one on his stomach was his dad and his legs were slowly moving so he knew he was still alive. He figured he was in bad shape though because his dad was as tough as anyone he'd ever known and if he could he stand he would.

Donnie Sr. did his best to roll over on his back to help stop the bleeding, but he didn't have the strength, he was fading fast. He couldn't believe that he had been taken so easily. He normally would have sniffed out a double cross as easy as hopscotch, but he sure got beat on this one. There was no way the inmate that got him and Brett did it without the guards help. He was mad but he couldn't focus on his anger now, he could focus on getting even later. If he didn't get help soon, he would bleed out right here in the yard. He had a feeling that the guards wanted him to bleed out for some reason. He thought maybe this new Warden was cleaning out all the internal threats, there were just more questions than answers now.

He turned his head to look for Brett again and he found him. He wasn't moving he whispered his name and his eyes started to blink. He wanted to sleep more than anything, he had never in his life felt this tired. "Ole Sheriff Elmer is gonna have your 'nads' in a vice when he finds out what you ordered done to his baby boy. Damn shame you had to mistreat that boy that way." Donnie was confused by what the guard was saying. He hadn't ordered anything done to the Sheriff's boy. "Just to let you know, you don't run this joint anymore dipshit, I do." The confusion he was dealing with could not keep him awake. He was so tired he closed his eyes. "Now you are good as dead on the inside and on the outside." He didn't feel them lift him on to a stretcher and he certainly never felt them usher him into surgery at Coahoma County Hospital. The stab wound punctured his liver, he opened his eyes briefly in the ambulance, looked around and uttered the only thing he could think of: *Bobby Martin.*

Chapter 23

The Gentleman

JESSICA LIKED THE FACT THAT SHE HAD SOMEONE WITH HER. She had seen many come and go but out of everyone that she shared this dark, dank place with, she liked Decker the most. None of the others ever offered anything, they were all busy crying in a corner or pounding on the walls demanding to be let out. She would beg the pounders as she called them, not to behave that way because the beast didn't like it, he preferred quiet. She tried her best to get a name or something from them so that maybe she could get out and let someone know where they were, but she got nothing until she heard the name Decker Davis. At first, she would always give her name and would practically beg them to repeat it, but they never did.

She didn't hold it against them that they were scared, she was too, but she felt like she had experience now and could help them get free, even if she couldn't. She didn't know why he kept her, out of the 11 that she counted she was the only constant and she prayed every day that she wasn't. She hated him. She had been taught that it is was wrong to hate, but she couldn't help it. The things that he did to her were wrong, they were wrong in her eyes and the eyes of God and because of the things he would do to her she knew she could never get into heaven now. She just prayed that if she ever got away from the beast, her daddy would forgive her for the things she had done. Every time she thought about it, she could start to cry.

"Decker?" She could feel his arms around her, and she could feel his chest rise and fall with every breath and she liked it. Decker was the first boy that had touched her in such a caring way since she was taken from the playground. The beast had tricked her, and she felt stupid looking back on it now. She vowed that if she ever got out of this place she would go to every school and every church and every playground until she got the message to every kid that you don't help grownups look for puppies no matter how cute the puppies are, and it is ok to be rude. She was young at the time but old enough to know better, she thought. She could have just jumped on her bike and hightailed it out of there, but she was trying to be nice.

"Yes ma'am?" She smiled when he responded. She wasn't a ma'am for sure, but it was the gentlemanly way he said it that made her smile. He sounded like her dad when she would listen to him talk to people. Her dad was always kind and respectful. Back then she didn't think much of it but, living with the beast for the last five years and listening to the names he called her, it was a nice departure from reality. "Do you really think that your dad will find you?" She squeezed him as tight as she could, and Decker could feel her grip tighten. He breathed in very heavy to try and steady himself. "Just as sure as the sun comes up in the east, my dad will find me." Decker paused and looked down at her, she couldn't see him do it because it was still dark in the basement and hard to see, " . . . and you." He breathed in again and squeezed her tight and he felt comfortable.

He could feel her body relaxing with every breath and for a second, he thought she was snoring, he wouldn't mind if she did, he could tell by the way she trembled she had been through a lot. In a way he was glad he could make her relax but it also made him nervous and a little scared. "Decker?" He could feel her push close to him as she spoke. "You didn't help him look for a puppy, did you?" Decker smiled and thought about it for a second, she was close in her question. "I guess if you tear it down to its simplest form, yes I sort of did." She didn't say anything and even though he had no reason to tell her what happened, he thought it might feel good if he told her about it. "I thought he ran over Mr. Biggars' dog. Everyone calls him Gabby, but I don't." He paused to reflect, "My dad told me that I was too young to use a grown-up nickname." He stopped and breathed, even smiled at the thought, "Anyway, he trains his dogs to go to the store and get cigarettes for him." She leaned forward and turned her head, so she was looking up at him, "You're joking me!" He shook his head, "No I am not, he really does. It's really fun to watch the dog walk into the store, stand up on his hind legs, with his paws on the counter and hand the clerk the money." She put her head back down on his shoulder, "Now you are really joking me." Decker decided to come clean with the actual story, "Well, ok, he puts a collar on the dog that has a pouch to hold money and cigarettes, everyone in the store knows to take the money and put the cigarettes in his collar and off he goes. People pet him and give him water and snacks all along the way." He paused, "I promise, that is the truth." She chuckled a little, "I still don't believe you."

Even during the conversation with Jessica, he was going over everything in his head and he now remembered what happened on the road as he was running home. He was for certain that the man had run over Bandit and felt a little guilty for being relieved that it was a different dog that was run over. He reached into his pocket to see if it was still there and it was not. He had Jeannine's library card before the incident on the road and now he didn't. The rabbit's foot and the card must have been what he dumped on the road. He hoped that the man with the huge forearm didn't see him drop it.

"Jessica," she didn't answer. He whispered it again, but she didn't answer. He could hear her breathing, it was very heavy, almost a snore. She was definitely asleep. He wished she weren't, he had so much to ask her and so many things to understand. So much confusion remained in his head and he hoped she could help him clear up the confusion, but he guessed by how soundly she was sleeping, she probably hadn't slept comfortably in a very long time. Decker leaned his head back on the wall and stared at the ceiling. He closed his eyes and started going over the trick play the coach installed. He had it down in his head but he wished he were with Heather so he could practice his motions and pretending to be frustrated with the play call or not being able to read the defensive alignment. Heather would always help him with the way he yelled out the calls at the line of scrimmage. She was amazing at recognizing when he was bluffing, or the play was for real. He smiled when he thought of their conversations and he hoped she would be with their dad when they found him. He badly wanted to see her, and Jeannine.

He kept his head against the wall and contemplated his next move. He had no intention of being stuck down here forever and he was certain that the beast's intentions were bad. He hoped his dad would find the rabbits foot and the library card. If he did, he would surely be on his way now and it would only be a matter of time before he and Jessica would be out of this dark, awful place. He felt his shoe for the knife, and it was still there, he looked around the room to see if anything stood out that he could use to help him escape or defend himself, he found neither. He could see that on the other side was what looked to be an open closet so he eased his arm around Jessica so he could go see if there was anything in the closet that he could use. His brain was thinking harder than he could ever remember thinking and he really wished it would stop. She whispered, "Decker?" He stopped moving and whispered, "It's ok, I will be right back." He continued to stand without letting the girl fall over as she had been resting her head on his shoulder. Once he could stand as straight as he could without bumping his head, he made his way over to closet. Even though his eyes had adjusted to the dark basement pretty well, it was still dark and difficult to see. As he stood in front of the closet, he ran his hands along the side wall to see if maybe there was a light switch but there wasn't, but as he tried to walk further into the closet, he realized that it wasn't a closet, it was a small stairwell opening that led to what appeared to be a storm door. He placed his foot on the first step leading up to the door and tried to push the double doors open but they were firmly shut from above. They had a storm door at his house that could be locked from either side, so he was familiar with how they worked. He felt the doors above them looking for a latch or hinge or possibly a lock. He found the double door latch that secured the two doors together and he smiled when he realized that these doors were almost identical to the ones they had at his house.

His dad kept the inside of the door locked with a pad lock but this one didn't have a lock on it. He tried to slide the latch to the open position, but it wouldn't budge, either it was rusted shut or there was something keeping it from opening. He wished he had that pocket key chain flashlight that Heather gave him for Christmas last year. It would sure come in handy right now but unfortunately, he accidently dropped it in the water when he was hunting bull frogs one night during the summer. He moved his hand along the latch trying to figure out how it worked in the dark when he felt a pin. It wasn't easy to feel because if you didn't know what you were feeling for, you would think it was just a part of the latch. This was a cotter pin, he was very proud of himself for knowing what it was, and actually finding it. He tried to pull it loose, but it wouldn't budge. The only cotter key he ever had to mess with was on the tractor and it was on the back hitch. He didn't like messing with that one because it was always difficult to get out. He used both hands to try and wiggle it free and this time he felt it slide a little. He was pulling on the key when he heard the hinges of a door squeak. His heart jumped and the sudden rush of adrenaline caused him to yank the pin free from the latch. He was surprised that he was now holding the pin.

He pushed on the doors, but they wouldn't budge, he figured there must be something on top of the doors or they shoved a 2x4 through the handles from the outside. He pulled the latch and left it in the open position, tried to push it open more time but again it wouldn't budge. He hustled back over to where he thought Jessica would be and slid down the wall until his butt touched the ground. When he was firmly in place, he felt something land in his lap. "He can't know you helped me." Decker felt the object in his lap and realized it was his shirt. His heart was heavy before but now it was getting angry. He remembered the day that Lonnie Buckles and his friends were picking on him and Jeannine at the fort he made. He remembered getting really angry and he was feeling those same feelings right now. He hoped his dad would hurry.

Chapter 24
Crooked Finger

"I HAVE NO IDEA WHY YOU ARE TAKING on another now. You know damn well that we shouldn't be doing this after that brush with the Sheriff from Drew." She paused and took a long drag off the cigarette she held between her middle and ring finger. She dislocated her index finger when she was much younger and because she never had it properly reset, it permanently bent outward away from her other fingers at the middle knuckle, which rendered it useless to hold a cigarette like others. She would take a long puff on the cigarette and it would look like she was pointing at something at the same time.

"Shut up." The voice was low and raspy. He was a heavy smoker too, but all his fingers were straight. He drew in a deep puff of Winston and let it out in smoke rings. He was good at the smoke rings and he enjoyed doing it. He would pop them out of his mouth like little donuts and as one expanded with the air, he would shoot another smaller one right through the center of it. He popped another smoke ring out. "Don't tell me to shut up!" She paced the room like she was nervous, but she was always twitchy and nervous. It was just the way she carried herself. He used to tell her that she looked like a chicken with its head cut off with the way she just darted from room-to-room and corner-to-corner. "I've been helping you do this shit for the last 10 years and you are getting careless!" She moved into the kitchen then came back into the living room with a glass in her hand, but it didn't have anything in it. She tried to take a drink out of it and realize that she hadn't put anything in the glass like she intended. "You've had her for more than two years now and she still bites you every chance she gets." He stopped blowing smoke rings. "I like the rough stuff." She walked back into the kitchen and this time returned with a glass full of vodka. She could handle a lot of vodka throughout the day and hardly anyone could tell she was loaded except him.

"She hasn't been purified yet!" He stubbed out his cigarette and blew a full plume of smoke in the air as he did it. "She is stubborn is all. God will work through me to get through to her and she will bear fruit." She laughed out loud, "You haven't been able to cleanse her since the first day you took her, what makes you think you can do it now?" He got up from the chair, walked toward the kitchen but as he got next to her, he took his open hand and slapped her hard against her ear. She staggered back a few steps because of it. She started to say something but when she looked up and met his stare, she knew better. He had that look in his eye that struck fear in her. When he looked like he looked now, he was capable of anything and she wasn't about to end up face down in a ditch on some rural back road of Mississippi like all the rest of his victims. He kept her for a reason she hadn't completely figured out yet, but God had surely told him that he was to continue his work with her.

"You've been with her every night for the last two years; you've taken her more times than I can count and NOTHING!" She screamed the word NOTHING like she had never screamed before. Most times he would tire of them and be done with them quickly. They would end up in a ravine or a ditch or in a big patch of kudzu only to be found if someone decided to halt the growth and cut back on the invasive plant. Kudzu would grow so fast and so thick that if you weren't vigilant, the plant could consume everything in sight. Richie loved the kudzu; he would search for it far in advance of his actions. He had an uncanny ability to figure out which way it would grow, what it would consume and how fast it would grow based off the sunlight that it received throughout the day. He never told her, but he would plan his purifications around the kudzu and where it was growing. If they ever found them all, they might be able to gather enough clues to find him, but he was certain they would not, except for that Sheriff over in Drew. He had a feeling that the Sheriff of Sunflower County had a good idea that he was up to something.

"And I've taken you too and NOTHING has happened either!" She came over and stood in front of him, "Let's just get rid of them and go away." He was sitting on the couch and she took the opportunity to sit on his lap. She straddled him so that she was looking at him face-to-face. She placed her arms around his neck, and she placed her forehead against his. "Let's just go, baby. Mexico, Canada, Russia, hell I don't care but let's just get away from here." She kissed him on the lips as she said it. "You know I can't, not until I am finished." She leaned forward in frustration and let out sigh. "You'll never be finished."

He pushed her off him causing her to land on the floor. He stood up hovering over her and pointed a finger at her. "We go when I say go, we eat when I say we eat, and we purify when I say we purify!" He stepped over her as she looked up at him. "I pay the bills around here and I am getting top dollar for that boy so shut the hell up. All I need you to do is keep him safe until I get my money and then we will dump him with the rest, until then just keep drinking, you lush." As he was walking toward to the kitchen: "Bring her to me." He continued into the kitchen and did not see her roll her eyes at him. She buried her head in her hands and knew that she needed to do something, or they would be caught. He had certainly become reckless and cavalier, but he had never taken anyone for money, this was a new twist. He came to believe that after so many years of doing whatever he wanted, he was invincible, and she couldn't blame him. His instincts always proved correct, he always outsmarted everyone and seemed to be a step ahead of the law.

Since he commanded her to bring her to him, that meant she wouldn't be needed tonight, and she felt lonely. She also felt nervous, she would have to go down there and retrieve her. Any other night it would not have been an issue but tonight, she was down there with the boy. The boy she didn't expect to be there until he dragged him through the back door, she had no idea Richie was bringing another home. He used to tell her what he was thinking and when he had received a message from God and when he planned on another purification but with this boy, he was a total surprise.

This boy he brought home was a big kid and she had concerns that he would be awake now. There was no way that she could control him. Normally she would just go down and grab number 16 as she called her because she was his 16th. He took delight in the length of time he kept her, but she couldn't understand why he actually wanted to keep her. On normal days, after she retrieved her from the basement; she would take her into the bathroom, wash her thoroughly, fix her hair to his specifications, which was always pulled back tightly in a ponytail, then spray her with his favorite perfume which was Charlie by Revlon, he loved it, except on her, she was forbidden to wear it. Once she had her prepared, she would usher her into his bedroom and close the door behind her as she left.

She went to the door that led to the basement that adjoined the kitchen and stood as she thought about how to retrieve her. She figured that the boy would be scared and disoriented in the dark so she would have the upper hand. Fear was how he controlled everyone, including her. She started to turn the knob of the door handle of the door leading to the basement but took her hand off the door. She walked back into the living room and went straight for it. She opened the small hall desk drawer and retrieved the .22 caliber pistol she kept hidden there. It was the one measure of self-defense that he did not know about. He would not approve, and she kept it hidden from him in a back compartment in the small desk. At first, he was very loving to her, he lavished affection on her like she had never seen; she felt like he was sincerely an angel, as if he was blessed by God and he treated her with such reverence but once he started hearing more messages from God about how it was his job to purify the lost souls of the earth, he became mean, very mean. His affection for her took a turn for the worse in the last few years. Despite his efforts she could not give him a son and she feared this would end their relationship as she knew it.

She opened the door and started down the steps to retrieve the girl as she had been instructed. She tried to make her footsteps coming down the stairs seem heavier than they were. She was very small and knew if the boy wanted to, he could overpower her, so she needed to be careful. As she got near the bottom of the stairs, she cocked the hammer on the pistol she was carrying.

Each footstep that Decker heard coming down the stairs was like a hammer in his head. He could feel the anxiety of not knowing what was about to happen, and worse, how would he react to it. Could he be tough and fight them off or would they simply be too much for him to handle. He heard the gun cock, and his mouth went dry. There was no way he could fight off someone with a gun. "It's time honey, come to the stairs." Decker stood up and started to walk toward the stairs, there was just enough light generated by the lights on above that he could see the base of the stairwell. He didn't know Jessica was beside him until he felt her hand squeeze his elbow and she whispered, "She isn't calling you." She held on to his arm strong enough to stop him from taking any more steps and she passed him. As she passed him, she released her grip on him and whispered in his ear, "Jessica Lynn Muncik, remember that." Decker stood there, not sure what he was frozen by, maybe it was fear or maybe it was simply not knowing what to do, but he froze. He stood there and stared at the light at the base of the stairwell until he saw Jessica appear in the light and step up on the first step. He immediately closed his eyes because he could see her bare butt and knew that he should not look at her that way. He suddenly felt sick to his stomach and staggered back against the wall and slid back down to the ground. He thought about his dad again and he really wished he could ask him what to do, he always knew what to do. He heard the door to the basement shut and the basement went dark again.

Chapter 25
Brother James

AFTER TOM LEFT MAXWELL'S HARDWARE, embarrassed about having blown the antlers off a killer deer, but no worse for the wear; he was confident that he would get a deer this season and he would happily replace the one he destroyed. He made things right with Mr. Maxwell and actually felt like he had made a new friend in town because the two men had more in common than he guessed they would despite the age difference. Mr. Maxwell even suggested that the two of them go hunting when the season opened. He made his way out the back door, through the alley and back to the front sidewalk where he parked the ugly green squad car that Lavera assigned to him when he arrived.

He liked using the Scout but the Sheriff had it today, so he was stuck with the green gorilla as he liked to call it. He sat down in the car and immediately heard the radio come to life. "Deputy 2, come in please." He hated being referred to as number two and even asked if they could switch him to deputy three but Lavera was a stickler for order and the deputy that had been killed in the line of duty was number one and he was number two. He even told Lavera that if they hired another deputy he would quit and get rehired so they could call him number 4.

She would just roll her eyes at him. To him, Lavera had no sense of humor. "This is Tom, go ahead." The radio crackled for just a second, "Deputy 2 you have a call, may I patch it through?" Mary Alice was dispatching tonight but Tom couldn't yet tell the difference between Mary Alice and Peggy, so he took a stab at it. "Yes Peggy, you can patch it through to secure channel." The danger of patching a call through from a land line was that everyone on the radio could hear it and that included anyone you had one of those new police scanners unless you told them to switch to secure channel which changed every day for that very reason. "Copy that and this is Mary Alice, not Peggy". He reached down and switched it to channel 12 which was today's secure channel and grinned at the come back from Mary Alice.

The radio crackled again. "Do you still see her face?" His hand froze on the radio mic. He knew what the reference was about, but he wasn't sure who it was. He began to sweat, and he could see that his knuckles were turning white from gripping the mic too hard. "What do you want?" Tom let his anger come through on the response. "You think you are better than all of us, don't you?" The voice on the other end had a deep and raspy tone. "I bet the good folks of Webb don't even know your family ties, do they?" Tom started to respond but the voice was already talking again, "I bet the drunk Sheriff doesn't know either." He paused, "You can't turn your . . . " the radio went dead. Tom looked down that the mic but didn't move. The radio crackled again, and Tom was about to tear into the voice on the other end, but the voice said, "Deputy 2, I accidently disconnected the line, I apologize for the inconvenience Tom." Tom knew that Mary Alice didn't accidently disconnect the line, she had intentionally disconnected the line. He was sweating through his shirt and he was mad as hell. He was grateful Mary Alice disconnected the line, he hoped that none of the nosy scanners had found the conversation after he switched to channel 12. "Thank you, Mary Alice." Tom threw the mic on the seat and leaned his head on the top of his car.

Tom drove back to the office and all the while thinking of James. There was no mistaking that it was James he just spoke to. James was an angry man and within the last few years he started blaming Tom for their mothers' suicide. He would get letters in the mail no matter where he was, he would always get letters that blamed him for not warning his brothers that day about what they would see. Tom went over all of it in his head every day, he wished he had warned his brothers that day and maybe he could have spared them the site of their mother staring at them with her dead eyes. He would always come to the same conclusion no matter how hard he tried, no matter what he did that day, he would always have the memory of his mom's face burned in his mind and no matter how much it hurt to see her that way, he still did the right thing. He just wished James would leave him alone about it. James wrote these long letters detailing how they had a happy home until Tom came along and everything changed, how the home was happy, they had a good thing, and Tom ruined it for everyone. Tom knew that wasn't true, he knew that the home was always a tough place to be. Their Dad was tough on them and he was tough on their mother.

He walked into the office and it was as quiet as it always was at this hour, there was no one around after 6 PM so he went to the switch board office where he found Mary Alice. She was reading a book with her feet propped up on a small ottoman she brought from home. "Hello, Deputy 2." He shook his head and rolled his eyes. "Can't you just call me Tom?" Mary Alice took her feet off the ottoman and swiveled the chair around, so she was directly facing Tom. "Yes, I could but we all know you hate being called Deputy 2 and it's fun watching your ears turn red when we do it." She laughed when she said it and put her book down on the counter without closing the book. "When you learn how to control that emotion we will stop." She then slapped her hands on her knees and said, "Just consider it a part of your training." Tom laughed, "How in the world is referring to me as Number 2 considered training?" She stood up so she could look straight at him, "Good cops keep a poker face, no tells, no blinks and for sure no red ears." He started to turn around and go back to his desk, "I bet your ears were red a few minutes ago when you got that call." He stopped and turned around, he put his head down and shuffled his feet making him look like a child that had just been caught stealing a cookie. "Yeah, I am, uh, sorry about that." He stuck his hands in his pockets and continued to look down. "Tom, look at me please." Mary Alice stood firm and expected him to comply which he did, "Tom, whatever it is, you need to tell the Sheriff about it." She cocked her head to one side as if she were trying to see all of his face, "The truth is always less painful than the coverup." He shook his head to signal that she was wrong. "You don't understand Mary Alice, it isn't as easy at that." He turned and walked out of the switchboard room but didn't quite make it before Mary Alice said, "And Deputy 2, your other little poker tell is your sweat. You sweat like an August plow Mule when you are nervous." She maintained her seriousness and finished with, "You might want to change your shirt and spray on a little Right Guard." He shook his head and with his back to her he shook his finger over his shoulder but decided to end the conversation. As he walked toward his desk he walked past the Sheriff's office and peered inside. He could use one of those bottles the Sheriff kept hidden, but he decided against it.

He sat down at his desk and started filling out the report on the incident at Maxwell hardware. He pecked away at the typewriter very slowly, one finger and one letter at a time. He hated reports and he hated typing even more and as he pecked away at the typewriter, he thought about her, her eyes were looking at him right now and he didn't like it. He knew she was right though; he would tell the Sheriff first thing tomorrow morning but right now he needed to finish this report, but before he resumed his typing, he caught a whiff of himself and decided to stop and change shirts. Mary Alice was correct; he didn't smell very good.

Chapter 26
Deputy Buckles

ELMER STOOD THERE IN HIS BEDROOM unloading his pockets onto the bureau, he had no idea how he accumulated so much crap throughout the day. It bothered him when he would end up with a pocket full of change when he really didn't remember spending anything throughout the day. He could hear Heather singing in the kitchen which made him stop for just a few minutes and enjoy it. Heather had a beautiful voice, but he realized as he stood there in front of the bureau, he used to share with his wife that he hadn't heard her sing in a very long time and he enjoyed it. She was singing something about being "too late". Elmer had heard it on the radio before, but he didn't know who sang it he just knew that he liked it and even though he might be a little biased he believed that Heather sang it better than the woman on the radio. He remembered all the times that Lois would sing while she was home, she had an amazing voice too and Elmer loved to hear her sing. He was looking forward to Decker coming home, he had a surprise for him that he absolutely knew he would love.

He finished dumping his pockets and put the .38 and holster on the nightstand where he always kept it. After Lois was shot, he wore it all the time. He stared down at the gun and realized that he had never once had to use it although he was pretty sure he would have used it the day he kicked the door of the Jackpot off its hinges. He didn't realize that Heather had stopped singing and was now standing in the doorway of his bedroom watching him. "Supper will be ready in about 30 minutes." He spun around with a startled look on his face. "I didn't mean to scare you Pops." Heather always called him Pops when she was being playful. He started to tell her that she sounded just like Lois when he heard her voice say that dinner would be ready in 30 minutes, but he decided to keep that to himself. "I was lost in thought is all." He smiled at her and put his arm around her neck so he could guide her back towards the living room. "I talked to Commissioner of the State Police down in Jackson today." Heather laughed, I know Pops, I got him on the phone for you," She patted his chest and put her arm closest to him around his waist, "Are you that deep in thought that you forgot?" He laughed, pulled her close and kissed the top of her head. "Yeah, I guess I did." The two walked into the living room where Heather wiggled free of her father's grip and kept walking into the kitchen. "I need to check on the potatoes, I will be right back.

Elmer followed her on into the kitchen, "So anyway, I spoke to the Commissioner about you." She stopped stirring the potatoes and looked at him, "Why would you talk about me?" Elmer went to the refrigerator and pulled out the tea jug. He didn't bother breaking a tray of ice cubes, he liked the sweet tea without ice. "Well, the state police offer a few scholarships every year to kids of law enforcement folks. Same one that helped me get to Duke." She put the stir spoon down on the counter and grabbed the saltshaker and shook out some more salt into the potatoes and then turned towards her dad. "I thought you went on a basketball scholarship?" He took a drink of his tea, "Well that was part of it. I wasn't good enough to get a full ride, so I was lucky enough to get assistance from the State Police

Scholarship fund." She walked over, grabbed a glass from the cupboard where he was standing and poured herself some tea out of the jug that he hadn't put back into the refrigerator yet. "Pops, I can't go off to school, look after you and Decker, and work for the Tallahatchie County Sheriff's office all at the same time. I better just stay at JC for a while." Elmer set his tea glass down on the counter and went over to the potatoes and stirred them, "The Sheriff's office is only for a year. It will give me time to find the replacement for Lavera." He paused for a second, "I know I introduced you as her replacement without any caveat's, but I need you to go off to school and make your way. Me and Decker will be just fine." He turned and grabbed three plates out of the cupboard, "Anyway, the scholarship is yours whenever you decide where you are going." She walked up to him and put her arms around him. "What if I don't want to leave, Pops?" He put his arms around her, "Honey, my heart will ache if you stay and it will ache when you go, my happiness and I am sure Decker's happiness, has a lot to do with you being happy and you can't be happy picking up after us." She started to respond when they heard the knock on the door. Elmer looked at his watch and then looked up at Heather, "Little late for guests, you expecting someone?" Heather shook her head to indicate that she was not. She could see in her dad's eyes, that things out of the ordinary always made her dad nervous. He wasn't always that way but since their mom was killed, he liked order and someone knocking on their door at this hour, way out here was definitely out of the ordinary.

Elmer looked around the kitchen, he had already taken his service revolver off, so he looked on top of the refrigerator and saw the .380 he kept there and grabbed it, "Geez Pops, I don't think a criminal is gonna knock." He smiled at Heather, "I agree but I was caught off guard once, never again." He stuck the .380 in the back of his belt, it was pretty small, so he had to be careful. He knew it was loaded; he always said an unloaded gun is worthless. "Stay in the kitchen please." Elmer walked out of the kitchen and through the living room. He could see the outline of someone at the door, the thin white curtain covered the door so it was difficult to make out who it might be. He reached for the door handle and opened the door. That's when he saw Donnie Buckles, but it was almost as if Donnie didn't see him. Donnie was just staring at the doorway as if he were trying to see through Elmer.

Elmer snapped his fingers in front of Donnie and Donnie blinked and then realized that Elmer was standing in the doorway. "Are you ok?" Donnie shook his head, "Hey Sheriff, I am sorry I am here so late, but Mrs. Hazel asked me to bring this to your daughter." Donnie handed the plastic container to the Sheriff and then Heather showed up. She was still a little apprehensive around anyone with the Buckles name, but she knew she had to forgive sooner than later. "Well come on in, as soon as Decker gets here, we are going to eat and you're more than welcome to join us." Elmer turned to look at his daughter as if he were a little confused then decided he better set a good example too, "Yeah! It's good to have you back in Webb, Donnie. I was hoping to see you in town, but this is even better!" Elmer stuck his hand out for Donnie to shake and he did. Once their hands were locked, Elmer practically drug him into the living room. Heather heard all the stories of war and POW's and she got overcome with emotion, stepped forward, put both her arms around Donnie's neck and hugged him as tight as she could. The tears were rolling down her cheeks when she said, "I am so glad you are home where you belong, safe and sound." Donnie was a little rattled by the embrace, he felt the same way he did when Mrs. Hazel hugged him. He wasn't used to that kind of affection, he liked it though.

"Well Donnie, I ain't gonna hug you but I agree with Heather, its damn good to have you back home." Elmer stepped away from Heather and Donnie as they were still embraced. Elmer wished he had a camera so he could take a picture of the look on Donnie's face. He had never seen anyone look so uncomfortable yet so happy all in the same look, but Donnie managed to be the poster child for that particular look. "Can I get you a beer or some tea? Heather just made a good batch of sweet tea this morning." Donnie shook his head and then as Heather released Donnie, Elmer saw the look he had seen at car crashes, victims on the side of the road, confused and unsure on what to do. Donnie didn't know what to do.

"Donnie Buckles, what's wrong?" Elmer was about to tell him about the phone call he got from Parchman that day, but Elmer could see an expression on Donnie's face that he had seen before but not in this situation. The expression on Donnie's face was one of a person drowning or in deep trouble, but Elmer thought it was completely strange that it changed so fast. It was almost as if Donnie had seen something inside his head that caused sheer panic to set in. Donnie fished in his pocket and handed the contents to Elmer. "I came to give Heather the food and to give Decker his two dollars he dropped in the barbershop, but I am lost on this. I don't like the vibe I just got out there on your porch." Donnie pointed at the card and the rabbit's foot that Elmer was now holding. Elmer looked down at the card, read it then handed it Heather. "Where did you get these?" Donnie turned his head to illustrate sort of the direction he was when he found them beside the road. "I found them beside the road on the way here." Heather reached for the card, "This is Jeannine's!" She put the palm of her hand to her forehead and the tears started to roll down her cheeks again, "Daddy! You don't think something happened to her?" Elmer could feel a heavy weight on his chest and shoulders and he almost took a step backwards, but he steadied himself. The thought that anyone of his kids from Webb might be in trouble like this had never really crossed his mind. "Only one way to find out." Elmer went over to the phone and picked up the receiver. He could hear

Cathy Norman on the other end talking. The new direct phone lines had not made it out to the country yet and they were still on a party line. Elmer didn't mind at all because he never really used the phone once he got home. Heather would get mad if she wanted to call one of her friends and couldn't because Mrs. Norman was always on the phone.

Cathy Norman was a super friendly neighbor with a heart as big as all outdoors, and since Lois passed, she was constantly checking on the Davis's, but she loved to talk on the phone. She didn't care who it was, she just loved to talk. "Uh, Mrs. Norman, this is Elmer, I really need to check on something if you wouldn't mind." Cathy gasped as if she had done something wrong, "Oh my lord Sheriff! I am so sorry I hope everything is ok! I will hang up now." He started to say thank you, but Cathy went on, "Mavis I need to go, the Sheriff needs to use the phone, I will call you tomorrow night and we can talk about your trip to Baton Rouge. Okay?" The line was silent for a second and Mavis replied, "Oh yes please do, and this time don't forget to give me that recipe for divinity." The Sheriff started to speak again but was cut off. "You know the boys are coming for Christmas this year and they just love your divinity." Elmer couldn't wait anymore. "I'm sorry ladies but hang up now or I will cite you both for obstruction." The line went dead on both ends. Elmer dialed the barbershop. The phone rang and there was no answer. He hung up, then looked on the entry desk for a card and he found where he had written the Martin's home number down and dialed it. They picked up on the first ring. "Say Bobby, is Jeannine with you?" Bobby Martin cleared his throat as if he were annoyed but he was really playing with Elmer. "Well hello to you too." The party line encounter with Mrs. Norman made Elmer edgy and wasn't in the mood for it. "Answer Bobby." Bobby didn't hesitate this time, "Yes Sheriff she is sitting at the table right now, why?" Sheriff was relieved and his heart rate immediately went down to normal. "That's great Bobby, is

Decker with you?" Bobby immediately replied, "No Sheriff he isn't, hang on." Elmer could hear Bobby talking to Jeannine, "Sheriff, Baby, says Decker ran home after he walked her to my shop. That was around 8 I reckon. Why?" Elmer's heart rate went back up again. "I have Jeannine's library card," Elmer started to tell Bobby that Donnie Buckles brought it, but he knew that Donnie and Bobby's relationship was very precarious still, so he just said, "neighbor found it on the side of the road and thought she might have dropped it on the way here. Bobby put the phone away from his mouth again and asked Jeannine a question. It was a little muffled, but Elmer thought he asked her about the card. "Hang on Sheriff, I am gonna let Jeannine tell you." There was a pause then Sheriff could tell that the phone was dropped so he took the phone away from his ear for a second then he heard Jeannine's sweet little voice on the other end. She told him about Decker busting into the library and how it shook her up to hear that Donnie was back in town, she knew that she dropped the card, but she saw Decker pick it up out of the corner of her eye and decided she would get it back later. As she was speaking Elmer could feel the lump rise in his throat and he gripped the phone receiver so tightly that his knuckles started to turn white. Heather could tell that there was something wrong and she began to fidget and ask Donnie questions. Donnie explained everything to Heather, the car, the weird guy, the British accent all while Elmer was listening. Elmer was listening to Jeannine and Donnie at the same time and he began to sweat. "Thank you, baby, no I am sure everything is fine." Bobby came back on the line, "Sheriff?" Elmer was still trying to figure things out, but his brain was processing too much at once and he needed to slow down and think clearly. "Sheriff, is everything alright?" Elmer still didn't answer. "Sheriff, if my baby is in some kind of danger I need to know because after that phone call tonight I get the feeling that something is wrong." Elmer snapped back to attention, "What phone call, Bobby?" Bobby looked over at Jeannine who was sitting at the table but pretending to be doing homework. Bobby could always tell when she was pretending because she kept her head very still, when she was really studying, she moved her head with every line she read. She was like watching a typewriter go back and forth as she read. "Baby, I need you to go outside and play for just a minute, don't go too far though." Bobby watched as Jeannine got up from the table, she shot him a look over her shoulder of disproval and exited the front door. "Sheriff, I got a collect call from someone out at Parchman, I almost declined to accept the charges, but I did anyway." Bobby took in a breath and continued, "Said the score was about to be settled and this time the law would be on their side." Elmer interrupted, "What the hell does that mean?" Bobby wasted no time replying, "Hell if I know Sheriff, but he said you'd be coming for me." Elmer looked around for something to write on, but he didn't find anything. "Bobby, do you know who it was?" Bobby hesitated because he had yet to trust the Sheriff, but he went ahead, "I can't be sure, there was a guard out there that was corrupt as hell, Murphy, I think was his name. He had a hand in setting me up with those false charges," he paused and looked out the front window to make sure that Jeannine was still visible, "Crazy man, power went to his head. Someone said he started a prostitution ring with girls that didn't want to be prostitutes if you know what I mean." Elmer opened a drawer to the kitchen cabinet and found a pencil but no paper. He started scribbling on the countertop, "You mean he was trafficking women?" Bobby glanced out the window again. "Hell yes, that is what I mean, the man knew which old ladies had no protections with their men in prison, if the inmate got in debt to him which they all did, he took their women." Elmer was scribbling, "What's his name?" Bobby shot back, "I told you, Murphy." Elmer scribbled Murphy on the countertop, Bobby continued, "He got so good at it, what I hear is he stopped grabbing just the prison widows, he started grabbing girls everywhere, and when I say girls Sheriff, I mean girls." Elmer felt his hand gripping the receiver of the phone tightly. "Bobby, I am not coming after you. Don't believe that for one minute." Elmer put the pencil down and hung up.

Elmer looked around the room for a second and then directly up to the ceiling then back down to Heather, "Heather, take Donnie's truck into the office and pick up Lavera on the way. Donnie is going to take me to that spot where he found this." He held up the rabbit's foot to illustrate what he was talking about. "What's wrong Daddy?" Elmer walked back to the bedroom and as he was heading back there, he yelled, "Turn the stove off!" Elmer grabbed his .38 and holster from the nightstand and put them back on. He gathered the things he normally carried in his pocket minus the change and picked up his badge plus another badge that he kept there. When he came back in the living room he stood there in front of Heather and Donnie then spoke in a very calm voice, "Decker has been taken. He left these for us to help find him." Heather burst into tears and Elmer stopped her. "Now is not the time Heather, we are on the clock, statistics show we have 24 hours to get him back or we don't."

Donnie put his hand on Heather's shoulder and tried to calm her. Elmer didn't miss a beat, "Heather, I need you to get everyone in the office, Mary Alice, Peggy, get Tom on the radio and have him meet us. Alert every county within a hundred-mile radius and give them descriptions of Decker and that description of the car and partial plate that Donnie was just telling you about. Once you get Tom up on the radio, have him meet us out on main road." He checked the cylinder on his .38 and stuck a bullet in the chamber that he always kept empty so that it was now fully loaded, "Heaven help the son-of-a-bitch when I find him." He shoved the .38 back into the holster, "Donnie, raise your right hand." Donnie looked a little confused, "Excuse me?" The Sheriff snapped, "Raise your damn hand!" Donnie raised his hand quickly after that. "Do you swear to uphold the laws of the State of Mississippi to the best of your abilities?" Donnie was dumbfounded but he had also seen that look in the Sheriff's eyes before and he knew better than to argue. "I do." Elmer took a few steps towards the door and said, "Good, you are now a deputy Sheriff of Tallahatchie County. Elmer threw the extra badge at him and said, "Put it on and take me to where you found these and give me every detail on the way."

Chapter 27
The Idea

WHEN HE LEANED AGAINST THE WALL, he could feel
the energy draining out of him. He felt like it was the last wind
sprint of the day in football practice and he almost threw up,
but he fought it off. He was still thinking about his dad and how
long it would take him to find him and then he started having
thoughts that maybe his dad wouldn't find him. Maybe he was
not in Cassidy Bayou, maybe he had been knocked out longer
than he guessed. He didn't like the thoughts he was having, and
he tried to put them away, but they kept coming back. He felt
some tears welling up in his eyes and he tried to fight them off,
but he couldn't. They streamed down his face and he wiped
them away with his T-shirt.

He started thinking that his dad may have trouble finding him
in this cold crappy basement and that he would have to take matter
into his own hands. That thought alone scared him. He really didn't
know what to do. He had no idea what that meant to take matters
into his own hands, but he knew he couldn't just sit here waiting on
something to happen, he needed to make something happen.

Decker stood up and wiped his eyes with the shirt that he
still had balled up in his hands. He would give it back to Jessica

if she came back down. He stood perfectly still for a few minutes and let his eyes stay as open as he could make them. He wanted to take in as much light as he could. He could see shapes but really not much more than that. He decided to follow the wall from corner to corner to get a feel for what the room was like. He let his hand stay on the wall as he slowly walked, he tried not to drag his feet, but he found that it was easier to maintain balance and control of his motion if he slightly drug his feet. He shuffled along the first wall and didn't get very far before he ran into the next wall. He brushed his hand across the surface from one wall to the next. He could tell that the wall was cinder block from the texture, roughness and the fact that it was cold to touch.

He followed what he considered the longest wall which is the same wall that contained the storm door exit. He was careful not to fall into the stair well that led up to the double doors. As he passed the double doors, he tripped on a box that he couldn't see and went sprawling on the floor. Luckily, he caught his fall with his hands and instead of landing on the floor he ended up in the push up position. He drew his legs up toward him and now he looked like a frog getting ready to leap. He still couldn't see very well so he sat down on his butt and felt around for the box that he tripped over. He patted his hands on the ground until he found the box. It was closed at the top and the best he could tell, it wasn't taped, it was just closed flap over flap. He opened it carefully and for a reason he can't explain, he looked around the room as if he was checking to see if anyone was watching. He felt inside the box and found slick papers that he guessed were magazines, he found some cloth, he pulled it toward him, and he could immediately smell perfume on it. He figured it was a girl's shirt or some form of clothing which made him mad because if there was a shirt down here that Jessica could have worn, they should have let her wear it. This one sure wasn't getting any use. He felt a glass bottle and grabbed it. He pulled it up to his chest so he could feel it. It was a pretty good size bottle and it had liquid in it because he could hear it when he shook it. He felt the bottle from the bottom to the top and decided to unscrew the cap. He tried to turn it, but it wouldn't budge. He sat the bottle on the ground beside him and continued to rummage through the box. He touched something that felt like a spool and he immediately knew what this was. He used a spool of twine that felt like this to fly homemade kites when he was younger. His mother helped him with his first one and he became quite skilled at kite making and flying but since his mother died, he didn't enjoy it as much as he once did.

He took the twine roll and stuck it in his pocket, he wasn't sure why, but it seemed like something he should do. He felt around the box that was now empty, but he did find a couple old washers and some screws. One of the screws stuck his finger with the sharp end and he drew his hand out quickly. He slid the box out of the way and continued to walk along the wall, keeping his hand on the cinder block as he came all the way around the room. When he arrived, almost where he started, he began counting his steps. It was exactly 8 steps on the short walls, and it was 16 steps on the long wall minus the side that had the opening for the storm door. He walked from the wall to what he thought was the center of the room and back. His mind was working very hard right now and if you asked him to explain at that moment why he was doing any of it, he couldn't tell you. All he knew is that he felt better if his brain were working and he had a very good suspicion that his dad would tell him to get to know his surroundings better than anyone or anything.

He heard the handle to the basement door turn and make a rough sounding clicking noise. It reminded him of the knob on the door to the pump house at home, it was rusty and old, and in the winter, it was very hard to turn. He softly stepped towards the stairwell where he could catch a glimpse of the little bit of light that would invade the dark basement and possibly help him understand what the stairwell leading to the upstairs looked like. His heart was racing because he only wanted a glimpse of the stairwell and if they were sending Jessica back down, he just didn't want to see her without any clothes on.

The door opened very slowly and he caught a glimpse of the stair well. As expected, they were wood, and the stairwell was steeper than he expected. He quickly counted and there were 10 steps from the first step to the last. Just before he quickly stepped away, he noticed that there was a small nail sticking out of the wall about halfway up the stairwell. The idea came to him at that very moment and the thought of Easy Rider. He would have to put on a good show, but he was sure gonna try. Sitting down here waiting for his dad to find him was not a good idea, although he was one hundred percent certain that his dad would find him. He knew he couldn't sit still.

Chapter 28
Two Tootles

TOM JUST PECKED THE LAST key on the typewriter and was about to pull the paper from the roll but the last time he pulled it too quick the dang ink smudged in certain spots and he had to do the whole report over again, so he just left it in the carriage for a little while longer. He was happy he left an extra shirt in the office because he did sweat more than most guys. If it was summer, he more than likely going to go through several shirts a day because when he sweated, he also smelled. He kept a can of Right Guard and small bottle of Brut in the desk drawer just to help him combat his own body odor during the real hot days.

The door to the office flung open and he heard several footsteps which was very unusual for this time of the evening. It caused him to jump up from his desk and reach for his gun which, at that moment, he realized that he took it off and hung it on the hook as you enter the back part of the office. Before he could get to the hook, the Sheriff's daughter entered the hallway and started yelling for him. Now he was really concerned because this never happened. He wondered if maybe someone had hurt the Sheriff out at his place and his daughter escaped and now it was going to be up to him to go rescue them. He might even have to shoot someone for real. So many thoughts went through his head before he heard her speak. "Mary Alice! Tom! Everyone! Anyone!" He heard Lavera's voice after he heard the Sheriff's daughter. He made it to the front of the office where the two were each now trying to dial numbers on different phones. Heather kept making a mistake with the dial and would slam the phone down and start over, "Oh good Tom, you are here, grab your stuff and go meet Elmer out on the main road east of town just before you get to the Buckles' place." Tom didn't hesitate, he reached for his belt and quickly put it on. He pulled service .38 out of the holster and checked the cylinder. He saw the shell that was spent on the deer antler and removed it. He reached into his belt and pulled another bullet from it and slid it into the empty spot in the cylinder. He quickly closed it shut and re-holstered the .38. "What the hell is going on ladies?"

He could see the tears rolling down the girls' cheek. He could not for the life of him remember her name, he wished he had paid better attention to the introduction that day, but he hadn't. There wasn't much he could do about it now and it didn't seem like the proper time to reintroduce. Lavera spoke up, "We can't be for certain, but we think that Elmer's son Decker has been taken. You need to hurry and meet him please." He didn't say a word, he just nodded and started out the door. Before he could make it out Lavera said, "Take the shotgun, take both shotguns." Tom spun around and went to the rack, fumbled with the key to open it and released the bar that kept the guns safely in the rack. He pulled two Mossberg's off the rack which only left one .30-30 so he decided to grab it too, he thought in a situation like this, firepower was not only prudent, but necessary.

Tom threw the guns in the trunk and jumped into the car. He reached for the keys, but they weren't there. He slammed his hand down on the steering wheel remembering that he left them on the desk in the office, so he ran back in, ran through the front office and quickly found them on the desk. By the time he got back to the car he was out of breath. He cranked the big green car up and put it into gear. After he was firmly on the road and felt like he could breathe and talk at the same time he reached for the radio mic. "Sheriff this Deputy Porter, I am on the road with an ETA of about 10 minutes." He pressed the accelerator to the floor and hit the light switch. He knew he would be there much quicker than 5 minutes but because he was new to the area, he was still a little unsure of precise distances. The radio crackled: "Copy." It was the Sheriff's voice for sure, "Peggy did you get the information on Decker out yet?" The radio went quiet for a minute then it crackled again, "Yes sir, it is out, everyone in the state of Mississippi has it." Elmer could see Donnie looking out the window intent on finding the exact spot where he came up on the car in the middle of the road. Donnie raised his hand, "This is it Sheriff, I am sure of it."

Donnie didn't see Elmer unhook the safety strap over the trigger of his .38. Elmer's mind was going through every scenario in the book and he kept coming back to the fact that the Buckles' were setting him up. That the call from Parchman was to let him know that they were planning something and that this was it. Maybe Donnie Sr. had convinced Donnie Jr. to help him get even with the Sheriff and he was being lured into a trap. Even if it was a trap, he intended to be ready. Both sides of the road were covered in either Kudzu or trees, some willow and some oak but it was enough trees on both sides for someone to lay an ambush. He deputized Donnie on the spot in front of Heather so that even if Donnie were in on it, he would now have to think twice about it. He had a feeling that Donnie could change his mind on a whim, and he was hoping that a badge and a gun would give the Sheriff just enough edge to get the upper hand on any foul play. To anyone else, it may seem like poor logic to give a potential enemy a gun, but the Sheriff knew the Buckles family better than they knew themselves. Donnie was tinkering on either being a mean recluse because of the war or being a good man with a purpose. He was betting that Donnie was a good man, he had seen it before, and he was pretty sure he had made the right decision.

They hadn't made it out to the pecan orchard which put them about 3 quarters of the way back to Webb. The Sheriff looked around and eased the door open to the Scout. When he had both feet on the ground, he put his hand on the revolver and turned toward Donnie who had exited the Scout and was looking at the ground. To Elmer, Donnie didn't look like he was up to no good, but he kept his hand on the gun anyway. "I am sure it was right here Sheriff, that broken fence post was a mental mark for me." Elmer walked around the Scout to stand next to Donnie, "Hell Donnie there are a ton of broken fence posts along this road." Elmer was about to say something else, but Donnie interrupted him, "Not one that is split right down the middle like that." Elmer shook his head; he had a point. They both looked around on the ground but didn't find anything. Elmer decided it was time to talk about the call from Parchman. "I got a call from Parchman today, don't know who it was but they said they were my neighbor and payback was coming my way." Sheriff quickly spun around toward Donnie and used his left hand to grab Donnie around the neck. His oversized hand easily enveloped Donnie's throat as he pushed him hard up against the Scout and said, "You better tell me now if your family has anything to do with this or so help me, I will end you right here."

Donnie let his eyes speak for him as much as he could because the Sheriff was gripping his neck so tight, he could hardly breath much less talk. He managed to say: "Hell no Sheriff!" Elmer released his grip and said, "I had to know for sure. I am sorry." Donnie rubbed his neck and looked at the Sheriff, "Look, my dad ain't the most noble man in the world but he wouldn't get to you through your son," he took in some air that had been stolen from him while Elmer was choking him and then continued, "I can't put it past Brett but since they are both in the same place at the moment, Brett won't do anything without Dad's permission." He looked around on the ground like he was still looking for anything else that Decker may have left for them to find and then said, "Besides, my dad would never hire someone that uses the words "*Tootle Loo*" in a sentence." Elmer stopped, his mouth went dry and he felt the sweat coming up on his forehead. "What?" Donnie repeated the comment, "That's what the guy on the phone said to me too!" Elmer kicked the gravel on the side of the road just as the head lights from Tom's car pulled up behind them. "Son-of-a-bitch!"

Tom exited the green beast as quickly as he could. He got his holster hung on the door handle and it yanked him back inside the car. He was a bit embarrassed, but it was already dark, so he was certain that the Sheriff didn't see his clumsiness. After he got his holster freed from the door handle, he stood outside his car to take in what he was seeing. As he was watching the Sheriff kick gravel on the side of the road the radio crackled, "Tom, have you made it to the Sheriff yet?" He recognized the voice this time because it was Lavera. "He reached back into the car and took the mic in his hand. "Copy that Lavera, I just rolled up." There was a moment of silence then Lavera came on, "Tell Elmer that Heather sent the partial plate information that Donnie gave us and there are 16 potential matches." Tom was looking at the radio when he felt a hand take the mic away from him. He turned around and was staring into Elmer Davis's chest. Tom wasn't sure why, but he hadn't realized how big the Sheriff was until that very moment and it intimidated him a little.

Elmer pushed Tom out of the way causing Tom to bump right into Donnie Buckles, the man he had earlier given such a hard time. Donnie held his hand up to keep Tom from falling although it crossed his mind to just step aside and let the deputy stumble, but this was no time for petty paybacks. Elmer put his elbow on the top of the car and with the other hand he pressed the button on the mic, "Go on Lavera, what else you got?" With his left elbow on top of the car, he was rubbing his index and middle finger on his forehead, something he did when his brain was working things out.

"Heather ran the 16 plates, 12 of the 16 were ruled out because they were registered to cars that were not white in color." She paused and then continued, "The problem with that is that they could have painted the car so it's not totally reliable but then Heather whittled it down to white four door sedans and its down to two." There was a long pause, but Elmer didn't interrupt, he waited for what she might say next, "Again Elmer, the paint thing is the hang up, it's not totally reliable but the two that are left were registered to a Bobby Blanton out of Ruleville and a Lester Murphy out of Tutwiler." Elmer let the names hang in the air a second or two before he asked, "So why are you hesitating?" Lavera responded quickly after Elmer asked the reason for her hesitation, "Lester Murphy reported his car stolen two years ago and Bobby Blanton reported his car stolen two weeks ago." Elmer put his head down on the top of the car, Donnie and Tom looked at each other briefly then Tom took a few steps back away from the car. He turned his back on the two and was facing the city of Webb. He didn't know what to do but he had to do something. Elmer lifted his head up off the car and spoke into the mic, "So what you're saying is that it's a dead end?" Donnie and Tom could hear the pain and desperation in Elmer's voice. "You keep looking Lavera, I don't care if you have to find every white car in the database but there has to be more!"

Elmer threw the mic inside the big green car and slammed the door. He stood in the middle of the road with his head tilted up towards the sky. He was mumbling something but neither Donnie nor Tom could understand what he was saying. "He's got at least a couple hours head start, we can still get him, but we better come up with some ideas." He turned to look at the two men behind him. "No point in heading back to Webb, we know he was on this road, so his options are limited." He started walking back towards the Scout, "Tom you take Cassidy Bayou Road, and we are gonna take 49. Those are the only two directions he would have been going from here." He opened the door to the Scout: "Tear this state up looking for a white car, ANY white car, I want my son found."

Chapter 29
Breaking Point

DECKER STOOD OUT OF SITE of the stairwell as the door opened. As soon as he was certain that someone could hear him, he spoke, "Hey if you let me go now, I promise I won't tell my dad, I won't tell anyone." He waited for a reply, but none came. "Hey come on now." He paused to see if anyone responded but no response came. "I know you can hear me!" He waited and decided it was time to see what he could get away with. He put his foot on the bottom step, so it was sure to be seen and acted like he was going to walk up the stairs. It worked because he immediately heard a woman's voice, "Stop right there!" He stopped for just a second, but he pretended like he was about to keep moving and this time she really let him have it. "If you take another step you will be sorry!" He continued to put pressure on the first step, and she screeched, "I have a gun and I will use it!" Decker stayed still for a few seconds, "I just want a drink of water and to go to the bathroom." He lowered his voice and to sound like he was desperate, he didn't like the way it came out and was for certain that she would know he wasn't telling the truth. He was sweating and was very scared, but he still had time to recognize the fact that he wasn't a very good actor. He knew he would have to get better at acting if he would ever make Easy Rider work correctly, the Charleston defense was pretty dang good from what he had heard, maybe not as good as Clarksdale, but they were still good.

The voice at the top of the stairs slammed the door but before she slammed it, she screamed, "NO!" The room went dark again, and Decker shot up the steps as fast as he could. When he reached the top, he pounded on the door while yelling that he had to go to the bathroom. "Please let me go to the bathroom!" He could hear her say something through the door, but it was badly muffled, so he figured it was a good solid door. He pounded on the door again and this time yelled: "I am so thirsty!" She pounded on the door from her side and yelled something, but Decker couldn't figure it out. He heard the latch at the top of door move and he stood up straight. He thought about closing his eyes just in case she did shoot him, he didn't want die, but he wasn't about to stay put like they wanted. Then it occurred to him that he needed to do this a few more times just to get them in the right frame of mind. He took a quick step back down the stairs, keeping count of each step as he made his way back down to the basement floor: one, two, three, skip, one, two, three, four, five, six, seven and floor.

As the light from the door opening filled the stairwell, Decker was careful to stay out of the light. He heard footsteps, but they were very soft and very muffled. It didn't take him long to figure out that it was bare feet which could only mean one thing, Jessica was coming back downstairs. He had not planned on her coming back down, he was frustrated that he didn't plan on that also but he couldn't do anything about it now. He would simply adjust his plan and wait for the right moment. "I have really got to go to the bathroom and can I please have some water." There was no reply, but the door shut again. The stairwell went dark and he blinked his eyes to help adjust to the dark, but it didn't work, he still couldn't see a thing. He felt a hand touch his shoulder, "They told me to tell you to shut up." He could hear her soft footsteps as she passed him and headed for the side of the wall furthest away from the stairwell. His stomach churned a little because he knew she would not have any clothes on again. And because of the way she spoke she sounded like a robot or something. He couldn't quite figure it out, but it was if she were only a voice and nothing was guiding the voice. He was so thankful it was dark and he could not see her. He slowly made his way to where he knew she would go. He also knew he left his shirt on the ground somewhere in that location and he would find it for her. He hated what was happening and wished he could get them both out of it right now and he had a pretty good idea that if he just stayed calm and kept his mind sharp, he could do just that.

He found the shirt without much effort then tried to listen for her breathing. He wanted to know exactly where she was so he stayed still for as long as it took to get a good fix on her. He was not about to let her sit down in this dank dark place without any clothes on.

He turned his back against the wall and let his legs go a little limp, just enough to allow his back to slide down the wall and end up on his butt. "They told you to tell me to shut up huh?" He didn't hear a response; in fact, he didn't hear anything at all. He started to feel a little panic rise in his chest, and he forced it back down. It was important for a leader to not show panic, he knew that from watching Donnie Ray Richardson. He sat there in the dank basement thinking about all the games he watched Donnie Ray Richardson and how much fun he had trying to mimic his every move. He felt his chest rise and his shoulders started to feel very heavy. No matter how hard he tried, he couldn't stop it. The tears began to well up in his eyes. Just as he was about to let go, he felt her hand touch his shoulder. "It's ok, Decker." He reached up and touched her hand. He had to admit that it was a comforting touch and he appreciated it, but it only made his need to cry worse. He slid the shirt into her hand, "Put it back on and don't take it off no matter what." He paused for a second, "I have to get them to come down here." He could hear her rustling the shirt as she tried to find the sleeves to put her arms in it. He was relieved when she scooted close to him and then he could tell that she had the shirt on.

When she was next to him, she pushed her arm under his arm and locked hers around his. He was still leaking tears and was glad that she couldn't see him cry. He wanted to go home, and he wanted to go home now. He had had enough of this place and he wanted to see his sister and his dad again, he wanted to see Jeannine again. He wondered what Jeannine was doing. Did she know he was missing? Was she out looking for him? He prayed she was, along with everyone he could think of. He wished he could talk to his mother. His dad would tell him what to do, but his mother would make him feel better. He missed her every day of his life. He prayed every day that he wouldn't forget the simple things that she did to make him feel good, like lay down beside him in bed when he had had an especially bad day. She could always tell when he was hurting inside. He endured the bullying for the longest time and tried not to let it bother him, but it did. She would lay down beside him and she would tell him about her day and somehow in the story, no matter how her day was, she managed to tell him that she thought of him every second and she missed him so much that she would pray that the time and the hands on the clock would speed up so he would hurry home.

"Decker?" Her voice was quiet and raspy. He turned his head to look at her even though he couldn't see her. He could smell her, and he could still feel her arm locked around his and he just now noticed that she had her head on his shoulder. "Decker?" He caught himself thinking about how she smelled like shampoo and forgot to answer the first time she said his name. "I'm here." He paused to see if she would continue but she didn't, it was almost as if she were saying his name in her sleep, but she wasn't asleep. He could feel her grip tighten around his arm. "I think we have to get out of here." Decker nodded his head up and down to agree with her even though it was too dark for her to see him make the gesture. "I know Jessica." He patted her arm with is free hand.

"No, I am serious, I heard them talking and something is wrong." Decker looked down at her and again realized that when it is pitch black and you can't see, it wouldn't matter if he looked the other way, she would never know but it just seemed like it would be rude to not look at her when he spoke. His dad would always harp on him about looking people directly in the eye when you talk to them and continue to look at them directly in the eye when they were talking to you. His dad said it was a sign of confidence and a sign of respect. "Of course, something is wrong, they have two kids locked in their basement, that's wrong." She squeezed his arm a little tighter, "That's not what I am talking about Decker." She released her grip and then he felt her lift her head from his shoulder, he couldn't see her face, but something told him that she had adjusted herself so that she was looking at him. "They are fighting really bad." Decker tried to understand what she was saying but he couldn't figure out the relevance of them fighting. "Why is that a big deal?" She drew in a breath of either fear or excitement, he couldn't tell which but she continued, "because I have been with them a long time and they never fight and tonight after she gave me my bath and washed my hair, he didn't do his," she paused and stopped herself from finishing what she was about to say so she could think about her words more carefully, "Well he just made her bring me back down here, nothing more." She put her head back on his shoulder, "and that never happens." She paused long enough for Decker to feel her body shake as she began to cry, "I can't take it any more Decker, I hope I die soon." He didn't have an answer for her, and he felt bad about it.

Chapter 30
Mrs. Bobbi with an "I"

TOM SAT DOWN IN THE BIG green deputy car and let out a huge breath. He didn't think it was possible, but he also knew that there was no mistaking that Bobby Blanton was the same name as the woman his father married many years ago; only they thought Bobbi was a man. He figured he could be wrong, but he doubted it. The chances of two Bobbi Blanton's from Ruleville, Mississippi were pretty slim. He hadn't spoken to her in several years but he knew she was still in Ruleville. He also knew that she was in poor health, her mind was about gone, and she couldn't even remember to take a bath most days. He had a knot in his stomach as he shifted the car into gear and pressed the accelerator. He needed to find out.

He turned into the first filling station that he came to which was just at the entrance of Cassidy Bayou Road off the main road. He couldn't remember if the filling station stayed open late or not and was happy to see that it was closed. The lights to the pumps and the side and back security lights were on but that was it. The side security lamp lit up the pay phone booth just enough to see the numbers on the dial, but it was dark enough so that you really couldn't tell who was using the phone. He was not about to ask dispatch to patch this call through for him. This was a call that no one could hear. He eased the big green car into parking lot and pulled into the back side of the station so that his car wouldn't be visible from the road. He turned off the car and sat there for a few minutes thinking out loud. He liked to think out loud whenever he could, he seemed to work out problems better if he could hear his own voice. "Could it really be him? He was bad for sure, but would he be this bad? Would he actually do something as dumb as this?" He stopped talking to himself and opened the car door. He eased his feet out of the car and put them on the ground. He remembered the embarrassment of getting yanked back in the car earlier by not being more careful with the way his holster slung around.

He made his way to the pay phone and fished around in his pocket for a dime. He didn't find a dime, but he found two nickels and plunked them in pay phone. He heard the nickels make their path through the maze of parts inside the phone until they made it to their destination which he figured was somewhere at the bottom. He heard the perky little bell ding to signal him his nickels were approved and then he heard the dial tone. He started to dial but couldn't remember the number to Bobby's house in Ruleville and had to hang up the receiver. He heard the machine regurgitate the nickels into the coin return and was relieved because he was certain he didn't have any more change. He pulled out his wallet and thumbed through the contents looking for the piece of paper that he had written the number on so many years ago. He hoped it was still in service but as bad as Bobby's memory was, he would not be surprised if she had neglected to pay the bill and it had been shut off.

He pulled the two nickels from the coin return slot and redeposited them in the coin slot. He held the paper as close to the light provided by the phone and began to dial. He missed a number somewhere and had to hang up, let the coins drop, and start the process over again only this time; one coin dropped one and not two. He cursed for a second because he knew he would never get that nickel back no matter who he protested the injustice to. He fished in his pocket and found nothing. He could feel his ears starting to turn red as was common when he was about to get really mad. Knowing what the outcome would be, he first stuck his hand in his right pocket and immediately found the hole in the bottom of the pocket that had been there for quite some time. He wasn't good at sewing and actually stapled the bottom of the pocket once, but the staple would scratch his leg as he walked so he removed it, gave up on that plan and simply carried everything in his left front pocket. Every once in a while, he would forget about the hole in these pants and drop stuff into his pocket only to feel the contents tumble down his leg and into his boot or land on the ground.

He then fished around in his left front pocket and came up with cinnamon piece of candy that had long since fallen out of its wrapper. Rather than put it back in his pocket he tossed it into his mouth in hopes that it would help calm him down. It didn't work because he took the receiver of the pay phone and bashed it against the top of the phone to protest it stealing one of his nickels. Once he was satisfied that he had punished the pay phone enough, he hung the receiver back on the two-pronged hook and walked back to the big green deputy car. He needed to find a damn nickel.

After a lengthy search he managed to find a quarter under the passenger seat. When he stood up from being bent over in the floorboard of the big green beast, he patted the car on the top as if to say thank you for coughing up the much-needed change.

He made it back to the phone booth and immediately deposited the quarter into the machine. As he was dialing, he clinched his teeth together to fight back another anger attack, as was certain he would not use the full amount of time a quarter would allow but he was certain he would not get any change back. Damn phone company and all those rich executives were probably laughing at suckers like him that so easily fell for their schemes.

The voice on the other end was soft and friendly when it delivered a *"Hello."* Tom knew it was Bobbi for sure and thankfully she had not forgotten to pay the phone bill. "Hey Ms. Bobbi, how are you doing?" It took a while for her answer and Tom was worried that her mind was completely gone now, and he may get nothing more than a hello from her out of nothing but pure repetitive instinct. He was about to remind her that it was Tom calling on the other end because she was so far gone now that she may not remember his voice. Hell, she might not even remember who Tom was, but she interrupted before he could speak, "Well it's about time you called me and checked in, I am scared to death!" Tom was shocked at the tone. She didn't sound scared, she sounded more mad than anything. "What are you scared of Ms. Bobbi?" He started to tell her he would help her with whatever problems she was having but she interrupted again. "They called here wanting to know about my car! You told me you would bring it back, so I reported it stolen!" Tom's heart sank. He held the receiver to his ear and leaned his head forward so that his forehead was pressed against the glass case around the phone. He let out a breath and almost hung up on her, but he held the receiver to his ear just a little longer. "You better bring my car back to me or I am calling them back and telling them that YOU stole it!" Without looking, Tom hung the receiver back on the cradle and stood there in the phone booth trying to think about what he needed to do next.

He made his way back to the car, he needed to think out loud again, so he climbed in the car and after he closed the door, instead of thinking out loud he cursed at the top of his lungs. He called up every curse word he could think of and let them fly with the efficiency of an artist painting a canvas. His hands grabbed the steering wheel tightly and he began to bash his head against the steering wheel being careful not to smash his head into the horn. When he felt like he had sufficiently punished himself he began to breathe again. He kept his hands on the steering wheel a little while longer just to have something to grip. "That phone call I got the other day was him!" He could feel the anger rising as he thought through everything he could. "I didn't recognize the voice though!" How could I have been so stupid!" He tried to relax but he couldn't.

If he told the Sheriff, then that was probably the end of his career, but if he didn't tell the Sheriff and something happened to that boy; then he would never forgive himself and that too would be the end of his career. He would no longer be able to serve as an officer of the law with integrity and a clear conscience. On the other hand, if he could get his brain to work properly, he might be able to figure out where he was and he could go find the boy and handle the matter all by himself. First thing was to follow orders. Maybe the Sheriff was correct in his assumption that the white car went towards Cassidy Bayou and maybe, just maybe he could spot the car. He hit reverse and pulled his car out from behind the filling station and worked his way back to the main road. He didn't realize he forgot to turn the headlights back on until he was on the main road and everything was still very dark. He pulled the lever out for the lights and pressed the accelerator to increase his speed until he veered off onto the Cassidy Bayou Road.

It was a very dark area at night, not many lights anywhere. It was a beautiful area in the daytime, but he had only been out this way twice since his arrival in Webb. Once for site seeing, and the second for work. Someone had reported an auger stolen from a barn, so he was sent to take the report; so, he took the report and left because there really wasn't much to it. Even though he was not familiar with the area, he had a pretty good idea when he would start to run into a few houses, and he was getting close to that point. He slowed down so he could examine the cars in each of the driveways and carports.

He pressed the button on the mic: "Dispatch". There was an immediate answer, and it came from Peggy, but he guessed wrong again, "Mary Alice is there a way you can come up with the all the names and addresses of the folks that live on Cassidy Bayou Road?" The radio was silent, he didn't figure that there were that many people that lived out this way, and he didn't know what he was looking for, but he felt better if he was thinking and his thinking led him to find out the names of the folks that lived out this way. "Let me see what I can do, might take a few minutes." Peggy thought about correcting him for guessing wrong, but she decided to just let it go. It wasn't important now.

The radio came alive again but this time it was Elmer. "You got something Tom?" Tom was hoping that the Sheriff wouldn't pay any attention to the radio chatter and he wouldn't have to explain anything. "Uh not really Sheriff, I was just thinking that maybe I would have a better idea if I had names of residents to work with." He paused for a second, "I'm sorry Sheriff, I'm reaching for anything." There was no response from Elmer, it was simply dead air and he felt like he needed to offer more of an explanation than that. "I just don't know the residents as well as you all do is all." The Sheriff still didn't respond so he let it go. What he really needed to find out was if he would recognize a name of someone that would tie a local resident to him. A last name, a first name, anything that would help him connect Bobbi Blanton to anyone in Cassidy Bayou. He knew it was a long shot, but he had to try. He could see how the Sheriff would find it silly for him to want to know names but at this point, but he didn't care. He just needed to find the Sheriff's boy.

Chapter 31
Snapped

"WE CAN'T STAY HERE anymore, and you know it." She tried to make her point as emphatically as she could, but she had never seen him act like this. Nothing was working. He didn't want sex from her or the little whore in the basement. It was like he had something on his mind, and he was hell bent on doing whatever it was that he wanted to do. He had always been strange and ill-tempered at times, but it was never like this. "James!" She screamed at him because he was doing nothing but standing in the kitchen staring at the door leading down to the basement where that little shit kept screaming that he was thirsty and needed to pee. She could tell that it was getting to him and she knew what that meant. It meant that she would have to clean up the mess he made and get them out of town just as fast as she could. Yes, she was used to fixing his mistakes, but this was something different.

Since the day they arrived in Ruleville and spent the night at the crazy lady's house, he was different. She couldn't quite decide what had happened, but she knew something was different. "James, let's just leave them and go." She touched his arm to hopefully snap him out of the trance that he was in. As soon as she touched him, he turned and back handed her across the face. He had hit her before but never this hard. The blow from the back of his hand landed just above her chin right below her nose. It sent her sprawling across the kitchen floor and dazed. She was on her stomach looking down at the linoleum floor with the cute little starburst patterns. She could see a little drop of blood land on the floor just beneath where she was looking. She didn't feel anything which was strange because she expected to be hurt, but she wasn't, she simply wanted to leave now. Her head lifted off the floor, but she wasn't the one making it happen. He was kneeling down beside her as he grabbed the back of her head by her hair. He would usually scream at her a little while and then they would go off to bed and make up, but this felt different. He wasn't himself. He was acting like someone she didn't know.

She started to pull her knees toward her chest to help her gain enough leverage to stand up, but she felt his knee in her back forcing her back down while continuing to pull her hair, lifting her head further backwards to where she now felt the stretching pain. "James! You are . . . " she tried to finish but suddenly she couldn't speak anymore. It was if her voice was an appliance and someone had suddenly unplugged it. Her hands and toes began to tingle as if they were falling asleep. She figured he was putting so much pressure on the small of her back that he was cutting off the circulation to her limbs. He released his grip on her hair and her head flew forward toward the starburst pattern linoleum and as she looked down, she saw a much larger pool of blood. She figured he must have really split her lip open to draw that much blood, but she didn't care anymore. She was tired and very sleepy now. She just needed to rest, and she closed her eyes.

He stood up looked down at his friend and felt sad. He wished she hadn't become such a nag. She was always yelling at him lately and he had had enough. He threw the knife in the sink and turned towards the door to the basement. He was careful not to step in the red pool that had formed so quickly. He had never seen anything like that and the rush he felt from the power was what he had been looking for all his life. He had seen the life go out of the eyes of many of his "children", but she was the one that always did the work. He would simply let her know that it was time to "move on" and she would take care of them during the time she was to bathe them. He always watched as she would do to them what he had just done to her. He got a thrill from watching her do it, but it was nothing like he felt now. His adrenaline was coursing through his veins and he needed a release, needed a release now and he needed it now. Maybe it was time to move on with the Sheriff's boy. He could send that little boy to perdition as God had commanded him to do. He wasn't sure but he felt his release should be seeing the boy's life perish from his eyes. Perhaps the girl he had downstairs was right when he first took her, maybe he was the shadow beast. He liked that name and now he really knew why.

He looked down at where she lay on the kitchen floor, the crimson red pool nearly covered the entire kitchen. He wished he had figured a way to do it in the shower instead of the kitchen, it would have been easier to clean up, but he couldn't help it now. She had nagged at him ever since he brought that girl home. The girl refused to give him a child and that frustrated him, but it frustrated her more. She liked sleeping with him and he spent most of his energy for the last few years on this girl that was obviously not fertile, but he loved her anyway. She was better than all the others and she seemed to have a spirit that the others didn't. The others would beg him to stop and they would cry constantly no matter what he did to try to get them to stop. The one downstairs was quiet, she was like a store mannequin, she never said anything. She just allowed him to do what God had chosen him to do and then she would get up when instructed and would be cleansed and sent back to her chambers where he hoped she would focus on conceiving.

He looked around for answers as to what to do but he found none. He had just made a mess of the house he was given to stay in and hold the boy. He was still unsure as to why he was holding the boy, but there was a vendetta somewhere and he was paid a handsome sum of money to track the boy down and get him to this point. He looked at her again and began to regret his temper tantrum he just threw. She was so good at cleaning everything up and now she was gone. He was trying to think and all he could hear was that dumbass kid downstairs screaming that he needed to go to the bathroom. He hoped the Parchman guard that was paying him was happy. The guard never gave him his name and claimed to be paying for the work through a couple of inmates that happened to have landed in Parchman courtesy of the big Sheriff from Webb that was now his brother's boss. The irony of it all struck him at that moment and he started to laugh. It was a deep laugh that made him bend over and put his hands on his knees. He was told to do whatever he wanted to with the boy but to make sure that the boy never saw his Daddy again. He didn't like boys and never had any use for them, but she always made sure that they took a couple just to keep things confusing for anyone that might be on their trail. They didn't keep the boys long. Sometimes she would toy with them and see if she could ever get them excited but they were usually too young for that kind of stuff so she would give them a shower and when she was done, the two of them would haul them somewhere in the country where the Kudzu would grow like crazy and consume them and any evidence they may have left behind. He took a deep breath and decided to begin cleaning up the mess, he would have to deal with the screaming boy later.

He looked around the kitchen for a mop and bucket, found what he was looking for and began the task of mopping up the mess that his quick-tempered action had caused. He felt sick a few times and thought for a minute he would lose the mushroom burger he had for dinner that night. He powered through the clean-up and thought he had done a pretty good job of turning the kitchen back to what it was before he lost his temper, minus the lifeless woman in the middle of the floor.

He rung out the mop and put it back in the closet. As he was wiping the kitchen sink, he stopped to consider his options. He would have to load her up in Bobbi's car and figure a place to dump her. He figured if he was going to dump her, he might as well dump that boy too. That little shit screamed from the basement the entire time he was cleaning up the mess and he was sick of it. He would take care of the boy, make the girl clean up his mess, toss them both in the trunk and head south toward Cleveland. There were plenty of backroads between Cleveland and Webb with nice tree's, ditches and gullies where he could drop the two off then he and the girl could head to wherever he wanted. She was beginning to warm up to him. He thought it was just a matter of time that she would fall in love with him and then there was no doubt that she would finally conceive. He knew there had to be love between a man and a woman before a child could be brought into the world and he was determined to make her his wife and have children. God had sent her to him, he knew that much, and he wasn't about to squander the opportunity.

He stood over her for a long time, listening to his heartbeat and hearing that boy scream about the damn bathroom while he stood there. He thought about taking her clothes off one last time because his godly urges were very strong at the moment, but he suppressed them as best he could and decided against it. Instead, when the time was right, he would bring the girl to bed with him tonight after he had dumped the bodies and he would perform for her. He would please her, and she would please him. For the moment though, he had heard enough from the boy in the basement. Parchman could kiss his ass for all he cared, he didn't care whether he was paid or not, he was not going to put up with such whiney behavior and worse now, the little rebellious turd was pounding on the door. It was time for him to sleep in the kudzu. He smiled as his manly urges continued to grow, he knew that the only thing that could stop that urge in its tracks was to allow the beast some play time, and it was time that little hellion met the Shadow Beast. Just as he was about to open the basement door, he heard what sounded like a knock at the front door. The knock was soft so he couldn't be sure. His thoughts turned to the front of the house, he tried to remember if the front door was a solid door or did it have any windows to peer through. He looked down at the woman, that his most trusted companion, lying there on the floor. He scanned the kitchen quickly and was pleased with the way he had cleaned up the mess she had made, but there was still the problem of her lying there in the kitchen. She would be tough to explain if the neighbors wanted some tea.

His mind raced, he quickly formulated a plan to hide the woman and silence the ridiculous boy that continued to yell from the basement. If he would have known the boy was going to be this much trouble, he would have charged Parchman a lot more money than he did.

He bent over, placed his hands under her arms, and lifted her as high as he could without straining his back any more than it already was. He drug her toward the pantry and his back was screaming at him to stop, but he didn't dare put her back down for he knew he wouldn't want to lift her back up. She wasn't a big woman at all, but he understood what they meant when they said something was like lifting dead weight. He chuckled at the pun and then wondered how many people besides morticians actually lift dead weight. He laughed again because he knew he had lifted dead weight lots of times, but they were always small kids, he always had her help, but doing this by himself was a challenge. He got really mad at her again for behaving the way she did and thought about just dropping her but then he remembered the pounding at the front door.

He managed to get her into the pantry, but he had to put her in a sitting position because the pantry wasn't big enough to leave her lying flat out. For some reason, he crossed her hands over on her lap so that she looked like she was taking a nap. She looked very peaceful to him and he kissed her on the forehead, whispered that he loved her and would see her soon. He closed the pantry door and slowly and quietly tip toed down the hallway that led to the living room and the front door. He peeped around the corner and peered into the dark living room. He could see the front door and was relieved to see that it was a solid door with no way for a visitor to look inside. He looked over on the coffee table and saw the gun he had earlier. He could hear the boy screaming from the basement, but he was pleased to know that from this spot in the living room you could barely hear him through the solid basement door. Even when the boy pounded on the door it was very muffled from here. The lights in the house, except for the kitchen, were all off so he knew he didn't have to answer the door, but he wondered who would be knocking at this hour. He stayed perfectly still for a while and was convinced that the person knocking had left. He returned to the kitchen so he could deal with the boy now. He forgot about the gun on the coffee table and went back to the living room to retrieve it. Once he had the gun in his pocket, he returned to the kitchen and pulled a knife from the butcher block holder that was on the counter, held it for a minute and smiled as he thought about what he could do to that boy with this long shiny knife. He was certain that he couldn't answer the front door with this kid screaming from behind the basement door. The neighbors would surely question the sound while they were having tea. He would have to quiet this boy before he entertained guests.

Chapter 32
Yes, you could have . . .

ELMER WATCHED TOM DRIVE AWAY in the big green car, the rear CB antenna was as long as a kite tail and flopped back and forth as he drove off toward Cassidy Bayou. He turned to look at Donnie who was not watching the car drive away, he was still looking down at the side of the road as if he had lost a coin and was trying to find it. "What are you looking for Donnie?" He walked over to where Donnie was pacing back and forth. Donnie had not even looked up when Elmer spoke to him. "I don't know Sheriff; I just know that I could have prevented this whole damn thing if I hadn't had my head stuck up my ass." Without hesitation Elmer replied, "Yes, you damn sure could have." Elmer turned and starting walking towards the Scout but stopped and without turning around said, "Get in the truck and help me fix it." Donnie stopped looking at the ground and looked up at Elmer. All he could see of the big man was his back. He knew the Sheriff was brutally honest with people and he had just discovered why. He was expecting some consoling words like, "Not your fault" or "You couldn't have known". He was expecting anything but that and it hurt. The Sheriff was right. Donnie wanted to get mad and say something back, but he quickly put himself in the Sheriff's shoes and decided that if Donnie had a son, he would think and say the exact same thing.

Elmer took his gun out of the holster before he got into the car and set it in the floorboard of the Scout. Even in the trance-like state he was in, he went through the same motions he had always made. He hated all the equipment around his waist and rarely even wore a gun but tonight, he not only wanted the gun, he wanted to use it and, use it now.

Elmer tried his best to keep the bad thoughts out of his head. His mind was exploding like firecrackers, he had taken the time to make amends with Heather, but he hadn't taken the time to make it right with Decker. He wasn't sure if he could live with himself if he could never tell Decker how proud he was of him. Not because he was becoming a legendary local football player but because of the way he handled life. For the way he didn't let the bullies tarnish him, how he stuck by his friends and he never once, as far as Elmer knew, complained about anything. Elmer gripped the steering wheel tightly as his mind continued to explode like a volcano. He thought about all the hours that he and Decker spent fishing and the hours that he would retrieve the footballs that Decker would zip right through the center of the swinging tire he had hung to help Decker learn to hit a moving target. He marveled at how accurate Decker had become and how effortless he made throwing a football look. The death of his wife had really knocked a hole in his stomach and instead of using his children to fill the hole, he pushed them away, drank relentlessly and shrunk away from his obligations as a father, a Sheriff and his obligations as a man. He was on the road to recovery the minute he poured his emotions out to Heather in that store and he hadn't been allowed to finish the job he intended to do. He wanted nothing more than to hold Decker in his arms right now and that feeling alone he realized was eating another hole in his stomach.

"What has changed in the last few days? Weeks? Months?" Donnie looked over at Elmer trying to process the question and couldn't understand for sure what the Sheriff was asking? "About me? What are you asking Sheriff?" Elmer took his right hand off the steering wheel and pointed his index finger from one side of the Scout to the other and then brought it back to him and made a whirlwind motion with his hand, "Around Webb!" He put his hand back on the steering wheel, "You are a cop now damn it! Think like one! That tootle-loo-son-of-a-bitch didn't just dart into town today. He has been here for a while waiting for an opportunity and he took it tonight." He calmed his voice realizing that he was yelling at Donnie and it wasn't necessary. Donnie shook his head to agree. "Well, Milholens' got broken into the other day and someone took a whole bunch of condoms from the stockroom, I heard," he started to continue but the Sheriff cut him off. "Yeah, that turned out to be Darrell Parker. Dumbass got his girlfriend pregnant, somehow got her over to Memphis and had it fixed." Donnie shook his head, he's a little late for stealing condoms then." The Sheriff replied, "Yeah, well, he's got a new girlfriend. Old Darrell won't make that mistake again."

Donnie thought for just a second and laughed when he didn't want to. Breaking into a drug store with so much to choose from and this guy chose condoms. That just seemed funny, but he wished he hadn't laughed. He wanted to redirect very quickly so he added, "And there is some kind of new preacher in town." Elmer slammed on the breaks and pulled the car over to the side of the road. He grabbed the mic from the cradle so quick that the curly chord got hung on the gear shifter and yanked the mic out of his hand. He fumbled around in the dark floorboard for it, but Donnie found it first and handed it to him. Elmer jerked the mic from Donnie's hand a depressed the talk button. "Mary Alice? Anyone?" The response was immediate, "Yes Sheriff?" He couldn't tell who it was because the radio in the Scout was terrible and needed to be replaced. Another part of his job that he failed to do while he was sulking and drinking too much. "Where does that new youth minister live?" The radio was silent for just a minute and Mary Alice replied, "Heather just said that they moved into the old Murphy place. Says they are just renting for now." She paused, "Why Sheriff?" Elmer almost said something into the mic, but he didn't. He looked at Donnie, "The Murphy place is on 49. We need to go pay them a visit.

Elmer punched the accelerator and they topped out at 70 miles per hour in a Scout that wasn't built for speed and a road that wasn't paved for it either. Donnie hung on to side door handle as best he could, but it wasn't helping much. The combination of bad shocks and bad road was beating the hell out of both men in the car, but Donnie could see that the Sheriff wasn't fazed by it one bit. "Come to think of it Donnie, I ran into a stranger lady in front of Heathers store and she had a girl with her," he paused and rubbed his forehead, but the Scout hit a nice pot hole at that moment that caused him to put both hands back on the wheel but he never took his foot off the gas from what Donnie could tell. "The girl looked about Decker's age, maybe older and she gave me a look that I am not used to." The silence hung in the Scout for a few minutes and Donnie said, "What kind of look was that?" Elmer took his hand off the wheel again and this time he rubbed his throat. "I can't put my finger on it, but I am sure as delta mud right now that she was asking for help and I was too damn stupid not to see it." He put both hands back on the wheel and continued, "and that lady she was with had nervous eyes! For Christ sakes! She didn't want to run into the cops and there she was standing right there on the sidewalk of Webb, Mississippi facing one of the dumbest cops ever born!" Elmer slammed his hand down on the steering wheel and mumbled something about not hurting his boy that Donnie couldn't quite make out, but he didn't correct the Sheriff on his self-deprecating comment since earlier the Sheriff had elected not to correct Donnie on his.

"You went to tonight's night prayer meeting, did you?" Donnie was serious in his line of question, but it sounded more like sarcasm. "No, I did not go to Church tonight. What's that got to do with anything?" Donnie knew he needed to be careful and not agitate the Sheriff any more than he already was, after all Donnie knew that the Sheriff's first instinct was that he and his family had something to do with Decker's abduction. "I just don't know how you know that it is the pastor lady if you haven't met her and nobody said anything about the new pastor having a kid." Donnie paused for a brief second because he needed to put the Sheriff at ease, "I am just trying to understand police work and police logic is all. I kinda need to learn what you are thinking." Donnie could feel the Scout slowing down and he looked up to see that they were about to crest the small hill that would put them right in front of the old Murphy place. He saw Elmer kill the lights on the Scout and did as he was told when Elmer told him to roll his window down. "I don't know that she is the pastor lady, but I know now that the girl I saw on the sidewalk was begging for help with her eyes and my gut tells me that when I find her, I find Decker."

As they crested the hill the Sheriff depressed the clutch and let the shifter float between gears, and they began to coast. He turned the ignition switch off and the Scout coasted almost right into the Old Murphy place driveway without making a sound. Donnie was impressed by the silent maneuver the Sheriff just flawlessly executed as if he had coasted into that driveway his entire life. "You aren't in uniform, so you are going to need to be real careful. They could shoot you and claim they thought you were an intruder." Donnie shook his head, "Why are we going in so stealthy and why do you think they will shoot at anyone? Aren't they pastors for cryin' out loud? How the hell do you know Decker is in there?" Elmer quickly shot back, "Men have been murdering one another for thousands of years all in the name of God. Everyone gets it in their head that their God is bigger than your God and the fight is on. Religion is a bunch of hooey my friend and you can write that down." Donnie drew in a breath and let it out. The night was quiet, and the stars were brilliant. "I seem to recall you going to church every Sunday." The Sheriff checked the chamber of his .357. He decided tonight that the .38 was simply not good enough. If he found Decker and his abductor, the abductor would have to die quicker and more explosive than the .38 could offer. "Yep, that was before somebodies God decided to take my wife from me and now my son." Donnie let out another breath, "Sheriff, I am not a murderer and I am not a vigilante, if you hired me to be those things then you can have the badge back now." Donnie didn't blink when he said it and he made sure that he maintained eye contact with the Sheriff. "I ain't asking you to be either Donnie, I just need you to make sure nobody does that to me and if I kill the son-of-a-bitch that took my Decker, take good notes on what you saw so you can testify against me in court because I don't give a shit. I am getting Decker back tonight with or without you." Donnie decided that there was no stopping him this time, so he nodded. "So, what do you want me to do Elmer?" The Sheriff looked at the old house from one side to the other, "There ain't any lights on outside but I can see a light on inside, so I want you to go around back and just give yourself about 10 feet from the doorway. Try to stay out of site if you can but it ain't gonna matter if they try to run, I just need you to stop them, just make sure you don't shoot Decker." He paused. "I am going right through the front door."

Elmer eased out of the Scout and quietly closed the door. Donnie did the same, but he chose to leave his door wide open. The driveway was gravel so there was a little bit of crunching noise between the two of them as they walked toward the house, so Donnie stepped off in the grass to make things quieter, but when he did, he stepped in a gopher hole or something because he turned his ankle nearly sideways and he dropped to the ground in pain. Elmer didn't see it, nor did he hear it because Donnie didn't make a sound although he wanted to. Donnie's training as a marine in combat forbade him from making any noise despite the pain that he was currently in. If anyone could see him up close, they would easily be able to see the tears streaming down his face in silent agony. Donnie wasn't sure if he had just turned it really bad or he had actually broken it; all he knew was that every pain receptor in his body had just gone off like a cannon and he couldn't utter a word of displeasure.

Chapter 33
Clank

MADELYN STOOD THERE IN HER ROOM that was dec-orated like any girl of 13 would decorate a room, but she had nothing to do with it. Janet decorated her room and wouldn't let Madelyn have anything to do with it. Madelyn wasn't allowed to touch anything in the room either, she could only sleep in the bed and retrieve her clothes from the drawers and closet and that was all she was allowed to do. She couldn't play with any of the toys, stuffed animals or dolls that were strategically placed in her room. It occurred to Madelyn that it was all staged for social services. Even though she had been legally adopted by the Johnsons when she was 9, social services performed random checks on them from time to time. Janet wanted to present the best possible image of the all-American family.

She stood there in her room as instructed regretting that she even told Janet about the boy and the girl on the bus. She knew better than to share such information, but she royally screwed up and she was going to pay for it tonight when Reverend Jimmy came home. She never called him that and she never called Janet, Janet. She was only allowed to address them as mother and father, never mommy or daddy, she couldn't even shorten it to mom or dad, or she would get punished for sure. Reverend Jimmy was what he made Janet call him. Madelyn thought the whole thing was weird, but she had learned to live with it. They could be really mean when they were in a very bad mood and she figured it had become her lot in life to try and keep them happy or else they took it out on her. She tried to focus on the positives; they fed her, and they kept her in good clothes. Nothing overly fashionable but she at least didn't stand out as the dorky kid in school.

She heard his car pull into the driveway. The driveway to this creepy home was gravel so it made noise and since they moved there, she quickly learned how to tell when they were home so she would never be surprised. She did this in every home they ever lived in which were several now. She was a quick learner, and she knew how to listen for them. She needed time to prepare so she learned the signals, she could even hear them in her sleep. She stood there and recounted each home and the different noises that they made. In Vicksburg, it was a bump that separated the street from their driveway. When their car would drive over it, it made a double thump, and she knew he was home. In Meridian, it was a willow branch that hung down too far over the right side of the driveway and it would brush against the car side mirror as it rolled towards the house. In this house, it was the gravel that crunched under the wheels of the car tires. She had to admit that this house was the toughest to hear the signals, but she trained her hearing on it. She would be damned if she were ever surprised by them.

She actually thought they were turning a corner in their relationship because up until now they had never let her go to a public school or ride the bus, so she had high hopes. She wondered how she would be introduced in church since she was never allowed to go to church, but something inside her made her believe that they were changing. Standing there in her room, naked as the day she was born, she felt foolish for thinking such happy thoughts. She believed now that God had condemned her for something that she had done, and she would pay for whatever that was the rest of her life.

She heard them talking in what they liked to call the parlor. It was the little entrance way off to the right as you entered the home. For some reason they liked to use that term a lot. Madelyn thought maybe it made them feel rich when they said "Parlor". It wasn't much of a room and to Madelyn and she thought it had a funny smell. It just smelled old. A smell like something had molded and then re-molded. She also knew how to listen to them talk. She always devised ways to eaves drop at every home they had lived in and in this home, it didn't take long to figure out that the sound from the entire house traveled easily though the vents coming from the crawl space and if she used a cup, she could amplify the sound just enough to not miss a word. She was surprised at how much she could hear when she put a paper cup up against the wall or vent and stuck her ear to it. It didn't work very well against her bedroom door because the door was heavy solid wood.

Madelyn could tell that Janet met him at the door and fussed over him as she always did. She treated him like he was some sort of deity or royalty. She would take his coat if he had one and she would put her hand on his forehead to see if he were hot or cold and that would determine her next course of action. If he were cold, she would bring him a nice hot cup of tea laced with a little honey and some kind of Bourbon. The bourbon was always different, and it was always hidden above the china hutch. Neither thought that Madelyn knew but she did. Madelyn knew everything. If he were hot, she would bring him a club soda with lime and some kind of vodka. It too shared space next to the bourbon above the china hutch.

Madelyn quickly removed the vent cover from the floor in her room and stuck her head as close to it as she could. She could hear their words almost as good as if she were standing in the room with them. "Oh, Reverend Jim you are burning up!" Madelyn could picture Janet's hand on his forehead and pulling back her hand like she had just touched a hot stove. She was so full of drama that in order to keep herself from going insane Madelyn would rate Janet's performances every chance she could. A ONE was akin to a child holding its breath to get his way and a TEN was an Academy Award. Tonight's performance was more like a B movie western she had once seen at a theatre when Janet was trying to hide them for an afternoon. Reverend Jimmy didn't care what level of performance she gave, and Madelyn doubted that he even noticed, he just loved to be fawned over. "Yes momma, I feel terrible. That performance I gave tonight was just awful and I think I chipped a tooth." Madelyn had an image of his pulling back his lips, exposing his teeth so that Janet could inspect them like a man buying a horse. "Reverend Jim, I don't see any chips but let me get you something to cool you down." Madelyn heard footsteps so she knew that Janet was headed to china hutch.

Madelyn kept her ear to the vent; she could hear father's footsteps too. He moved to the little love seat that was in the parlor and slid the ottoman in front of the love seat so he could put his feet up. Madelyn could picture him loosening his tie and kicking his shoes off in the middle of the floor. Janet would retrieve them and put them away or she would come get her and have her do it. Tonight, because she had already been told to take her clothes off, she knew she wouldn't be retrieved for that purpose. She would have to endure his temper tonight. Janet would tell him all the wrong things she had done; she would talk about the boy and the girl on the bus and she would get him all worked up and he would come storming into her room and beat her good. Janet loved to get him worked up. It was almost a source of pleasure for her. Janet would always watch with wide eyes as he beat her, he would get this evil smile on her face as it was happening. When he was done beating her and it was time for Reverend Jim to console and "pray" with her, Janet would leave and shut the door behind her.

Madelyn heard Janet's footsteps coming back to the parlor no doubt with a drink in her hand, Reverend Jim was partial to scotch but he mostly drank vodka because he said that if anyone of his congregation happened to stop by unexpectedly, then they wouldn't really be able to smell the vodka on his breath as much as the whiskey. She could hear Janet's words come through the vent, "Little harlot has been flirting with boys and girls today! She more than likely has already obtained carnal knowledge of the boy." It was all that Madelyn could do to keep from screaming into the vent, but she held her tongue. Janet was lying through her teeth and she hated it. She hated that Janet could get him so worked up with crap and then she hated it even more how Janet watched and enjoyed it. "You were excellent in church tonight Reverend Jim." Madelyn heard him laugh and she thought maybe he laughed so hard that he choked for a second, "I nearly knocked out a tooth, I nearly knocked myself out and I scared everyone in the church with my stuttering ramble about nothing." She could tell he stopped long enough to take a drink. "I would not summarize that as excellent." Janet shuffled around the floor and sat down next to Reverend Jim. Madelyn was familiar with this show. Janet would snuggle up to him and rub his legs and wherever else he wanted to be rubbed until he had enough alcohol in him to help him get in the mood and then he would come down the hall and pay her a visit.

Madelyn heard the ice clank in the drink Janet had just fixed for him which meant that he downed it. The next thing she would hear would be footsteps coming down the hall to her room. Madelyn put the vent cover back where it covered the hole in the wall and stood up. She felt the tear roll down her cheek and she quickly wiped it away. She could never show any emotion like tears rolling down her cheeks in front of Reverend Jimmy. Things were always worse if she showed emotion. As she stood there in silence waiting for her punishment, she heard what sounded like tires rolling across the gravel driveway. She was good at hearing things outside but this one was strange. It was like a car pulled into the driveway that was out of gas. It made no sound, just the crunching noise that tires made on their driveway. She couldn't help but pull the curtains to her window back just enough for her to peek out, but it was too dark, and she couldn't see anything. She let the curtain fall back into place and stood perfectly still. She used to pray at this moment right before she was about to be punished but she stopped a while back. She was certain that God, if he really existed, would not let this happen to anyone, including her. Just then her door opened, and the Reverend walked in. She felt the need to throw up just like she did every time he visited her for punishment. Reverend Jim made her feel low and dirty and she knew that because of what she allowed him to do to her, she would never get into heaven so she had stopped praying a long time ago.

Chapter 34
Storm Door

DECKER SAT DOWN NEXT TO JESSICA. His awareness of the room, the dimensions and step count from wall-to-wall and corner to corner were spot on now. He was quite impressed with himself for learning the room to the degree he had. The minute he slid down the wall and his butt softly landed on the dirt floor next to Jessica she grabbed his arm as she had been doing all night. He knew he had only been down here a few hours at best, but to him, it seemed like he had been down there for years. He didn't mind Jessica's behavior, in fact, he had almost come to look forward to it when he sat down. He was comfortable with her and something inside him told him that he was there to protect her. In his head he could hear his mother's voice tell him that everything happens for a reason. His mother's voice was always in his head, but it upset him that her voice was becoming fainter as time passed.

"Listen, Jessica," he paused and let the dank air of the basement hang around them like a heavy coat, "I need you to let me show where the storm door is and that's where I need you to stay." She tightened her grip on his arm to the point that Decker felt her fingernails dig into the inside portion of his upper arm. It was so tight that he almost let out a yep and thought about pulling his arm away, but he didn't. "I don't want to move Decker. I don't want to be away from you." Decker took in a deep breath and then let it out, "You have to trust me Jessica." His voice was at a whisper as he continued, "Look, I know my Dad is coming but I don't know when. That man or that woman or maybe both are going to come down here soon and if we aren't ready, we may not be able to give my Dad enough time to find us." Decker put his hand on her hand, the one that was digging into his arm, he could tell that helped calm her. He started to lift himself up off the ground and he held on to her hand to force her to stand up too which she did. When they were both standing, he pulled her along the left wall and made their way over to the cellar door opening.

Once they were in front of the opening to the storm door, he took her hand and raised it above her head so that she could feel the door above them. "Now don't rub too hard because it is wood, and it probably has splinters and those kinds you can't see hurt the most." She didn't say anything at first but then whispered, "Why am I touching the storm door?" He took her hand a little tighter by the wrist and moved it to the center of the door where the two doors latched together, "This is the latch, when the time is right, you will slide this latch away from you and it should pop right open." He could hear her breathing get heavier and when she spoke, he could tell why she was breathing heavy, she was excited. "Why don't we open it now and just go?!" Decker puller her hand back down, "Because it is latched or bolted from the outside too." Jessica was quiet again and in the short time that Decker had been with her he realized that this meant that she was thinking. He had become so good at understanding her without ever seeing her face or facial expressions that he could almost time how long it would be before she responded, but this time, he was wrong. She took way longer to respond than he was used to now. "Jessica?" The silence was driving him crazy. She finally responded, "Nobody is coming for us Decker." Decker thought about it for a second and couldn't figure out how to change her mind. He would never be convinced that his Daddy wasn't going door to door right now and eventually the knock on the door of this house would be his Daddy and then there would be hell to pay for whoever that was upstairs. "Yes, they will but that isn't important. You have to pull down and push on that latch when I say so. Don't think about anything else but that right now." He paused for a second then added, "Please."

She didn't say anything again but this time since they were both standing at the base of the steps leading up to the double doors, she turned and grabbed in an embrace that Decker was not prepared for. It pushed him slightly against the inside wall of the stairwell where she pressed against him. She had her arms tightly wrapped around him and he could feel her crying against his chest, so much so that her tears were getting his tee shirt wet, but he didn't dare move. He learned enough from his sister that when a woman hugs you like that, you don't move, and you are supposed to try and make her feel better by rubbing her back. It was an awkward motion for him, but he did the best he could. It seemed to be working because she began to loosen her grip and her sobs became more controlled.

Decker held on to her until her sobs were all but gone. He rubbed her back just as Heather had told him to do even though it felt awkward. He stood there holding her realizing that he had never even hugged Jeannine like this. As of tonight, he and Jeannine had kissed right square on the lips for the first time and instead of being able to run home and tell Heather about it, he was stuck in this cold dark basement hugging a girl that he really didn't even know. He felt really homesick and wanted to do a little of his own crying, but he figured it was a bad time with her just now calming down. If he started crying, she might start bawling again and he didn't want that. He was still thinking about the kiss that Jeannine gave him that caught him off guard and sent him falling to the ground and dragging her with him. He was embarrassed by that, but the thought made him smile.

"Jessica, you have to stay here now and promise me that no matter what happens you don't make a sound, I mean that." He repeated that again, "No matter what." Decker had a feeling that the people above would not turn on the lights if they came down and would try and use the dark to their advantage but now that he knew the room as well as he did, he would use the dark to his advantage.

Jessica did as she was told and stayed in the position, he placed her while he made his way to the main stairway leading up to the kitchen. As he was walking towards the stairway, he began screaming that he needed to go to the bathroom. He screamed it at as many times as he could before he made it to the top of the steps and started pounding on the door. He continued to pound on the door, but he would stop every few seconds and listen carefully for any movement because he could not get caught off guard.

Chapter 35
Cassidy Ghost

TOM STRAINED TO LOOK DOWN each driveway as he slowly passed by the homes on Cassidy Bayou. Most of the homes had a garage so he doubted he would be able to see a car in the driveway, however a few had carports so he could see a car if there was any light around the house. It was so dark on the bayou right now he didn't think he could see his hand in front of his face if he tried. He tried to remember if this green car had a flashlight in it but couldn't. He was hoping maybe there was one in the trunk if he needed it, but he would have to do the best he could if he needed to get out and approach a house. If worse came to worse, he had a Zippo lighter. He didn't smoke anymore because when he did smoke, he was certain that it made him slower mentally and physically, but he was also certain that cigarettes gave him gas. Back when he smoked, he would get a gas bubble in his stomach that was unbearable and if it was while he was inside, and there was any one around, he would have to quickly make up an excuse to leave and go somewhere private so he could release all of his "smoke gas," or he might embarrass himself in front of people. He noticed after he quit smoking that he didn't get gas as much, but the non-smoking didn't stop it completely. He could still get a painful gas bubble in his stomach, but it had greatly reduced since he gave up the smokes.

As he was digging around in his pocket to see if he still had the lighter, he noticed the front bumper of a car sticking out from just behind a house that wasn't well lit. For some reason, as he made the slight curve on the Cassidy Bayou Road and the headlights from the green beast, he was driving bounced off the chrome of the bumper for just a second. At first, he didn't think anything of it but then it occurred to him that the house had a carport but there was no car parked under it. It wouldn't be abnormal for someone to park a car behind a house but that would really only be because the occupants had two cars, which was rare in these parts but since there was no car parked in the carport, it just seemed odd and he decided to check it out. He at least needed to see what kind of car it was.

Tom eased the car over to the side of the road and pushed the lever to shut off the lights. He sat in the car for just a few minutes to let his eyes get adjusted to the darkness of the night. He was surprised that after a few minutes of sitting in complete darkness with not even a dashboard light available to help him see, his eyes adjusted and he convinced himself that he could actually see better now so he opened the door to the car. The overhead light that was supposed to come on when the door was opened quit working not long after he got the job for the Tallahatchie County Sheriff's Department. He could bang on it with his fist for a while and get it to work but after a while, not even pounding on it would work. After he slid out of the car, careful not to get his holster caught on the door latch again, he quietly closed the car door and made his way to the trunk. He fiddled with the keys until he found the key to the trunk and unlatched it. He realized he couldn't see as well as he thought he could, so he used his Zippo lighter to illuminate the contents to see if there was a flashlight in the trunk; and there was. It was big bulky thing that he guessed was made during World War I. This thing was a beast in size, it must have weighed 10 pounds but when he twisted the dial to the on switch the light popped right on. It was very bright, almost too bright, he would like to have had a little more stealth before he approached this house, but this light was better than his Zippo. If he held the Zippo too long it got really hot and would burn his hand. He looked in the trunk and saw a shirt that he remembered throwing in there a few weeks back and had completely forgotten about it. It was a half-shirt that he liked to use when he would lift weights. He wrapped the shirt around the old flashlight to help dim the light a little and it worked. It turned the super bright light into a dull light that wasn't nearly as intrusive on the dark. He closed the trunk and turned the flashlight downward so that the light wouldn't accidently scream into a window and alert his presence. He could see a light on inside the house, but it was faint, and he guessed it was on in the back of the house somewhere. He would just take a peek at the car and move on, there was no need to wake anyone.

He made slow and deliberate steps down the driveway. It had a very slight downward slope toward the house and no doubt if the house wasn't there, he would have an unimpeded path right into the waters of the bayou. He could hear the crickets chirping and every now and then a bull frog would call for a mate. As he was walking towards the house, he remembered the story one of the guys at the barbershop about the Cassidy Ghost and how folks have seen it, or maybe it was a lady, but they had heard a lady scream. He couldn't remember which guy at the barbershop talked about it, maybe it was the one that played the guitar all the time, Charlie B, yeah that was it, Charlie B. At the time he laughed at the story but now that he was right here beside the bayou and it was dark, he felt the hairs on the back of his neck stand up and the story wasn't funny anymore. He stopped and unlatched the leather strap of his holster that kept it from falling out. He didn't believe in ghost, but it didn't hurt to be prepared. This ridiculous flashlight was so heavy he was switching the flashlight from one hand to the other to give his arm a rest when he heard a door slam and what he thought was footsteps. He quickly, but clumsily, switched the flashlight to the off position and crouched down. He wasn't sure why he crouched down, maybe it was just out of instinct, but as he was crouched, and he pulled his gun from his holster. He could feel his heart beating in his chest and felt the adrenaline coursing through his veins as he let out a soft breath of air when he realized he was holding his breath. This was one deer head he couldn't accidently shoot. If he went quick trigger again and accidently shot the Sheriff's boy then he would have a life that he didn't want to imagine. A million thoughts went through his head and he was beginning to have doubts about his life's calling. Being a cop was all he ever thought about and now when he was faced with situations that required split second thoughts with ridiculously rapid circumstantial processing, he wasn't sure if he was cut out for it.

He choked down some of the fear that had suddenly overtook his entire thought process and was quite pleased when he raised from the crouching position to an upright position. He told himself that if today was his day then so be it. He believed that one's death was predetermined and no matter how much you tried to prevent it, if it was your time, that was it, game over. Now that he was upright and feeling better about not being scared, he fully intended to walk right up to the front door of that house and alert the occupants that the Sheriff's department had arrived. He also decided that if he were wrong and if there was nothing harmless inside or nothing bad happening, approaching the house with a gun already drawn would be a bad idea and perhaps unnecessarily frighten the occupants and possibly make the Sheriff's department look bad. He slid his weapon back in the holster, but he left the hammer strap just where it was. He wanted quick access. He may have overcome some of his fears just now, but he wasn't stupid. A good peace officer is always prepared. He was about to knock on the front door when he thought he heard the squeaking sound of an un-oiled fence door hinge or maybe a chicken coup door, but whatever it was it made one heck of a racket. He was familiar with the sound of the door hinge, but it was the time of night that bothered him. Most people don't check the chicken coup at this hour and from what he could see, this house didn't have a fence. He put his hand on his gun again and set the flashlight on the doorstep so he could have a free hand to knock and if he heard more footsteps coming from the side of the house, he would be certain they were running away from him. Once again, he was stuck on the "split second" decision mode and he was having trouble processing what his next step should be. His legs told him to crouch again but he overcame that impulse. He thought about running after where he thought he heard the footsteps coming from, but it was so dark that he could easily run right it a tree or step into a hole or a number of really embarrassing things one did while they were in the dark.

After processing all he could, as quickly as he could, he decided to open the screen door at the main entrance and pound on the door so he could announce that the Sheriff's office was on the premises and wanted access. He reached for the screen handle and pulled, but it must have been latched from the inside because it did not open. He then quickly pounded on the screen hard enough to make a dead thumping noise on the door. He was frustrated because the screen was far enough away from the door that he couldn't make the loud announcement that he intended. "Sheriff's deputy, open the door please!" He thought he said it loud, but his mouth was so dry that it came out almost as if he was coughing. He tried to lubricate the inside of his mouth the best he could by moving his tongue around and repeated the request. "Sheriff's deputy! Open the door please!" There was no sound and he could no longer hear the footsteps. He had some decisions to make. He had already crossed running in the dark off the list of options, so he quickly decided that none of what he had heard or seen added up to anything good and he needed to be inside that house. Since the screen was latched from the inside, he couldn't kick the door in, which he had always wanted to do. He loved cop shows where someone had to kick a door in then start shooting the minute they were inside. He wasn't crazy about the shooting part, but he liked the idea of smashing a door open with brute force.

He pulled his buck knife from his police belt where he had made a spot for it since the standard issue police belt didn't have a spot for a knife. He really liked that buck knife. It felt perfect in his hand because it was special made for him by a knife maker in Hattiesburg many years ago. He liked the buck knife, but he liked the switch blade he kept in his boot. He had found the switchblade in an abandoned house when he first became a cop. He cleaned it up and put a new spring in it and it worked like a champ. He kept it in his boot for good luck more than use. He was still amazed that he actually got it in working condition. He cut a slit in the screen big enough to fit his hand through and freed the hook from the latch. He slowly opened the screen door and now that he had direct access to the wooden door, he pounded on it with his fist and made his presence known more clearly. "Sheriff's office, open up!"

Chapter 36

Wrong Door . . .

DECKER HEARD THE LATCH TO THE DOOR that separated he and Jessica from the people upstairs and his heart almost stopped. What he had been trying to do for what seemed like all night was maybe about to happen. He wondered quickly if he could actually do it and second guessed himself. He remembered the man's arm that nearly choked him to death while they were on the road looking at that dead dog and knew there was no way he could fight that guy. He had oversized forearms from what Decker could tell from their brief encounter. Then he wondered if maybe it was just the woman that was opening the door. He knew he could whip her, but she had already said she had a gun and even if she were lying about that, he wondered if he could even hit a girl. He had always been told that hitting a girl was an unpardonable sin from a guy's standpoint, but the people that told him that, his mother, his dad and especially Heather, probably couldn't foresee the jam he was in at the moment so maybe they would forgive him when they found out. Either way, man with big arms or the woman with the gun, he was about to find out if he was as brave as his dad.

Decker quietly, but quickly, counted his steps down to the basement floor, careful to skip over one step. He counted the steps

210

over to where he knew Jessica would be and made quick and deliberate steps toward her. He could not see her so he reached out to where he thought she would be in the stairwell leading up to the storm door and felt the skin of her face. His motion with his hand was a bit less fluid and more herky-jerky than he planned and he nearly poked his finger in her eye. She dodged the intruding finger and whispered "Decker!" He drew in a breath and quickly let his hand fall to her shoulder then bent down to be close to her face and whispered, "It's time now. Be ready."

He hustled to the back side of the stairs leading up to where the latch had been completely released and the door was now opening. There was a slight squeak when the door began to open but not much. From his own experience his mother would have already squirted some *3-in-1* oil on the hinges. She couldn't stand anything that squeaked and would always keep a can of oil handy so that she could silence any unwanted noise in the house. When Decker would play just a little too loud and she was being more playful than usual, she would yell at Decker and tell him that if he didn't settle down, she was going to get her can of *3-in-1*. He smiled at the thought. He missed his mother and he wished she were still alive but at this moment he was glad that she wasn't because she would be worried sick over this whole thing and Decker could see her crying and that vision hurt him. She would either be sitting on the couch with her head in her hands sobbing or she would be in his daddy's big arms, sobbing as she is engulfed by his frame so much that if you were standing behind his dad, you'd never know he had his mother in his arms. He remembered how pretty his mother was and it hurt him right now to think that she would be crying over his current predicament.

He caught himself holding his breath and slowly let out some air so he could steady his heart rate. He was scared beyond anything he had ever been scared of and knew that if he made it out of this basement, the next few minutes would define him for the rest of his life. He wished on everything he could wish that he were alone and didn't have Jessica to worry about, but he did and there was nothing he could do about. If he didn't have her, he could complete his plan and then out run everyone away from the house. He was pretty sure that there wasn't a grown up in Tallahatchie County that was fast enough to catch him in a foot race except for maybe Donnie Ray Richardson and he was not in Webb right now. Donnie Ray was off in college being an all-star quarterback.

He swallowed the lump in his throat and felt the ledge for the string he had placed there earlier. His heart stopped again when he couldn't find it. He fumbled around in the dark looking for it as he could hear the door squeak even more. He saw a little light coming down the stair well that gave him just enough light to see the string. He grabbed it with his hand and squinted because the light that was now filling the stairwell hurt his eyes which made him have second thoughts about his plan. If he made it upstairs and it was well lit, he had been in the dark so long that he wouldn't have enough time to let his eyes adjust to the light and he would probably do nothing more than run directly into walls or trip over a garbage can. He tried to open his eyes as fully as he could to help him get adjusted to what little light was available now. He heard a voice now and he immediately recognized that it was the same voice as the guy that he met on the road home earlier. That was a relief because if the lady came down first, he might not be able to pull this off. "It's time for a potty break little boy." He said it like he was happy and excited but also a little angry. Decker didn't know how he could get all that from the guys voice, but he did, and it made him even more scared than he was now. "Come on up so we can let you pee little boy . . . " he paused for a second, "Or do you need to poopy?" The man laughed but he stopped his laugh very abruptly as if he were faking a laugh. "Don't make me come down there now. You've been whining all night and now it is time to pee, you hear?" Decker heard one footstep and knew that the man had taken one step down the stairs and Decker drew in a breath again. "Fine! I will come down there and drag you up here and make you wish you hadn't inconvenienced me so much!" The man let his voice go up quite a bit to show his anger, but Decker thought that he was play acting. He had seen people get mad and yell and this was nothing like anything he had heard. What Decker heard more than anger was hate. Why in the world did this man hate him? He would have to figure that out later because he needed to focus and not let his mind wonder from the task that lay before him.

He took another step down the stairs and Decker tensed up. He could feel his stomach get tight and his legs got really stiff. He hoped he could move them when the time came and that time was about to happen. Two more steps to go and his life would change forever. "I don't have time for games little boy." Decker heard him take another step and with this step he intentionally took a breath and slowly let out. He opened his eyes just a little more, letting a little more of the stairwell light in. He was happy to see that the little light that was available wasn't bothering him at all. "You won't like me when I get down there little boy." The man laughed a laugh that Decker didn't like at all, in fact it scared him. He could not only hear hate in this man's voice but he could hear crazy. It wasn't the crazy like crazy Calvin who wondered the streets of Webb talking to himself and occasionally peeing in public. His dad told him that Calvin was harmless but to stay clear of him anyway. He said that Calvin couldn't help the way he was and explained that Calvin hadn't been treated very well when he was a child and some of the things that were done to him caused him to be the way he was today. His dad never told him what things were done to him, he just left it at that. Every once in a while, when crazy Calvin would pee in front of one of the towns people that didn't appreciate Calvin's friendly approach to urination, his dad would have to go round up Calvin and take him back to his home. He was with his dad once when he had to go get Calvin and when his dad got Calvin in the back seat of the Scout and was on the way to take him home, Calvin spoke as clearly about a variety of subjects and even knew who Decker was. Decker remembered being surprised that

Calvin knew so much and that Calvin and his dad talked all the way to Calvin's house like they had been life-long friends. Decker knew from the sound of this guy's voice that he was no Calvin and he wanted nothing to do with this man.

He heard his foot take the fourth step and Decker pulled the string that he tied to the nail that was stuck in the side of the wall on the opposite side of the stairs. The man stopped and Decker thought for a moment that the man had spotted the string but when he took the next step his foot got caught on the string and the man came tumbling down stairs just as Decker had hoped. He could hear the man crying out in pain as he slammed against every step on the way down. Decker could see him tumbling almost until he reached the bottom but as he got closer to the bottom it was too dark for Decker to see him, but he could hear him. He was moaning and it sounded to Decker like he was trying to say something, but he couldn't tell. Decker made a dash for the stairs and as he grabbed the railing and made the turn to start his assent, he felt his knee crash into what must have been the guy's head. The pain it caused Decker made him grit his teeth and almost shout, but he blocked it out and continued to bound upstairs despite the protest coming from his knee. If that man's head felt the way Decker's knee felt right now, he had to be in a lot of pain.

Decker reached the top of the stairs to the door that opened into the kitchen. He immediately clinched his eyes shut because the light was more than he had anticipated even though he had anticipated it. He opened them just enough to spot a door that led to the outside. He turned and slammed the door that he had just came from and latched the lock. He spun back around to where he thought he had seen the door but because he was squinting his eyes and spinning around so much, he got disoriented and he couldn't immediately find it. It took him spinning in a complete circle to find the door again and when he found it, he wasted no time getting to it. He reached for the door, opened it and immediately fell backwards. There she was! It was a trap. She was just sitting there waiting for him. He slammed the door and spun back towards the door leading to the basement. He fully expected the man to be chasing him out the door now but he wasn't. It was just Decker and the lady sitting in the closet and the noise of his heavy breathing. Decker was scared but he knew he had to move. Jessica was still downstairs with that man with the big arms and he had to get her out.

Decker could feel his heart beating so fast that he was afraid it was going to explode out of his chest. He wanted to scream, he hated these people and he wished they would just leave him alone! His mind was racing, his heart was racing, and he could barely see and now he couldn't find the door out of this place. Just as he was about to give up he saw it, the door he had missed because it was next to the refrigerator. He was certain that was the exit out of this place and he was at the door in seconds. He turned the knob, yanked it open and took one step out the door. He hadn't noticed there was a screen door there and despite the fact that it had been latched, he went right through and tumbled out the door. He felt silly tumbling out a door like that and he thought maybe he had cut his arm on the screen, but he didn't care. He looked around and was happy to realize he was back in the dark again and he could see better out here than he could see in the kitchen. He got his bearing and ran to the side of the house he thought the storm door was and sure enough he was correct.

He could hear the crickets but he couldn't hear the bullfrogs. He really liked the sound of bull frogs. The pond behind their house always had a huge supply of bullfrogs. He would take his BB gun and shoot a couple every now and then but not often. He wasn't allowed to shoot anything just for the sake of shooting something. He would skin them and make a little fire like they did in the movies and try and cook their legs, but he never really got the hang of it. They tasted terrible to him, but it was kind of fun when he was younger to pretend he was really out in the wilderness roughing it.

He breathed deeply when he thought that maybe there was a chance that there might be a lock on the latch but was relieved to see that it was nothing more than a slide bolt. He slid the bolt free from its housing and pulled up on the door. It flew open. He couldn't see down into the dark but he had an idea of where Jessica would be so he stuck his arm downward and found Jessica or at least he hoped it was Jessica, he couldn't really see her. He tried to grab her arm but he couldn't get a grip and because he had startled her so much she was fighting with him. He regretted at this moment not telling her earlier what his plan was because she could just run up the steps had she had known but he hadn't. He didn't want to speak until they were well away from this house plus he was worried about the lady that was sitting in the closet now coming up behind him while he was trying wrestle Jessica out of the basement.

She kept knocking his hand free of whatever he tried to latch on to, so he grabbed a handful of hair and pulled her up with all the strength he had. He would apologize later for grabbing her hair, but she was fighting him too hard, he hadn't expected that. Jessica let out a small screech but when she finally realized it was Decker she started crying. Decker could hear her crying as he was trying to wrestle her away from the doorway but didn't say anything. Once he had her away from the storm doors he slammed the doors shut on the storm door and latched them. There was no way that guy was going to come after him unless that creepy lady in the closet opened the door and let him out which she might very well do, so he thought they better start running. "Can you run?" Was all that Decker could say and she nodded her head enough for Decker to see that she was saying yes. He grabbed her arm and fully intended to guide her as they ran off, but she grabbed him and embraced him and began to sob. Her head was buried in Decker's chest so the sound was muffled. He didn't know what to do, here he was being hugged by a crying girl in the middle of the night with a man with huge arms locked in a basement and a crazy lady sitting in a pantry to be dealt with and she was hugging him. "We gotta run Jessica!" He whispered it but he was screaming in his head. "We can't just stand here! They are coming!" She didn't move, again, he could still feel her sobbing against his chest. "Jessica!" He pushed her away from his chest enough to see her. His eyes were well adjusted to the dark of the night now and he could see her for the first time. "Jessica, listen to me, I am scared too, but we have to get away from here." She opened her eyes, and he could see the fear in them as clear as he had ever seen anything. "If you run with me now, they won't hurt you anymore, I promise."

Chapter 37

Meet the Parents

DONNIE PULLED HIMSELF UP OFF THE GROUND by rolling over on to his stomach and then working himself into a kneeling position so he could use his arms to help get him back on his feet. His ankle protested every movement, but Donnie ignored the pain and managed to get back to a standing position. He kept his weight on his good leg and tried to slowly shift some weight to his bad leg. The pain was intense, but he had to get moving, he could see that Elmer was almost to the front door and he hadn't even begun to work his way around to the back of the house as he had been told to do. He limped as a fast as he could but had only made it to the side of the house when he heard the explosive sound of wood cracking. He stopped for a split second, but he knew what that sound was. The big Sheriff had just made his presence known. He tried to move faster but with each step came a shooting pain that nearly to his breath away.

Donnie was familiar with pain when he was expecting it like when he was in Vietnam. He was always prepared back then; he knew at any moment on any of his excursions into that god for-saken jungle he might have to deal with pain or might even get killed. He was always mentally prepared for it then but not right

218

now. He remembered when he caught shrapnel in the back of his thigh during one of his missions and he thought his leg was going to catch on fire because it burned from the inside out. That was serious pain then and he dealt with it accordingly but right here, right now, he wanted to scream because it hurt so bad to take a step. He took a few more steps and made it to the backyard just in time to hear a woman scream and what he thought was the Sheriff's voice.

Elmer reached the front door and thought for a second about knocking, but if they really did have his boy in there, he didn't want to give them any warning, they might hurt him and he needed the advantage of surprise. He had been in this house before, lots of times. It always seemed like this house was destined for trouble from the day it was built. With each occupant over the years there had always been some kind of drama, fights, arguments, divorce, squabbles, even one shooting several years back when the owner of the home came home to find his wife in bed with another woman, and another man. It was good gossip for several years because the owner shot the other man right through the cheek. The man turned his head just enough that the bullet went through one side of his mouth and out the other. He was a lucky man because the bullet never even clipped a tooth, it just left a hole on both sides of his face. Elmer hadn't actually seen that one happen because he was away in college, but the news got to him quickly.

After Elmer had been elected Sheriff, he became way more familiar with this house. He hadn't had anything as exciting as a bullet through the face, but he had certainly been to this house to settle disputes and keep the peace. He knew the entrance and where the rooms were so he believed he was not at a disadvantage at all. He didn't bother removing the safety harness over the hammer of his .357, he didn't even think he would need it. He was experienced enough to know now that when you had the advantage of surprise, you had all the advantage you needed.

Elmer took a deep breath as he stood in front of the door. He went over everything in his head. He heard Donnie's voice in his head, questioning his methods and he wondered to himself if he had the integrity left in him to be Sheriff again. He was already guilty of drinking on the job, neglecting the office or as his handbook defined, dereliction of duty. Now he stood there about to smash in the door of a house that he believed his son was being held, but yet, he had no proof that his son was even there. He would do anything to get Decker back and that included breaking the law. He suppressed the thoughts of what might be happening to his son right now and tried to focus on what to do. The urge to just break down the door was overwhelming, but he managed to choke it back down. It was at that moment, without much coaching from his brain, his hand reached up and gently knocked on the door.

He heard shuffling feet coming towards the door and he put his hand on his revolver and took a slight step back and to the side. His natural size at nearly 6 feet 6 inches tall and nearly tipping the scales at 300 pounds now made him an easy target. He vowed he would lose weight by working out with Decker when he got him back. He vowed a lot of things in the last few hours. He even vowed to God that if he would let him have his boy back he would go back to church.

"Who is it?" The voice was whispered or at least it seemed that way from where Elmer was standing. He started to speak but to his surprise his voice cracked and he felt like his throat was made of sandpaper. He managed to work up some saliva to correct the situation and answered, "Elmer Davis, Sheriff's office. Open the door." He heard the latch on the door turn and the door cracked slightly. Just enough to see a woman's face. The woman behind the door was taller than Elmer expected. He was almost looking at her eye-to-eye and that was literal. He could only see one eye through the cracked door. "What can I do for you Sheriff, it's kind of late." Elmer didn't like the way she was not opening the door. Most law-abiding citizens in this part of the country would welcome the Sheriff into their homes, no questions asked. This lady was hiding something and Elmer was not going to stand on the stoop talking to her about the lovely Mississippi weather.

"Ma'am, I would like to come in and visit with you, please open the door." The eye looking through the small opening she had created without unlatching the chain would not offer her any protection if she didn't open the door. "Sheriff, its late and my husband is asleep, please come back tomorrow and we will be happy to answer any questions you have." Elmer put his hand on this holster, "Ma'am, this isn't a social call and I am running out of patience. If you don't open the door I will ask you kindly to step aside." Elmer gave her what he thought was plenty of time to answer and was about to lean into the door with his shoulder when she opened the door.

Once the door was opened Elmer couldn't see anyone but her in the hallway and he stepped through the door into the little foyer. Elmer was struck by how tall this lady was and for a moment figured she must be wearing some high heeled shoes but when he took a quick glance down at her feet he was even more surprised to see that she was in her bare feet. "Sheriff, this is highly inappropriate, and I take offense to your tone and the brutish way you have entered into my home!" Elmer looked around the room to get a better understanding of his surroundings. He had flashbacks of his good friend and former deputy that had been surprised because he didn't pay attention to his surroundings and it cost him his life. Getting himself killed would not help Decker. "Ma'am, I don't really care what you think right now, is there anyone else in the house?" Elmer brushed by her and headed to the hallway. His strides were huge and he was in front of the first hallway door in seconds. He opened the door with his left hand and kept his hand on his holster at the same time. When the door was open he flipped the light switch and realized quickly that three was no one in the room. The lady was behind him now and her voice was getting louder as he reached the second door. This was the room that he knew had the weird access to the side bedroom that had been added on after the house had been built. "Sheriff you must know that this is illegal! You cannot just barge into someone's home and ramble through their property!"

Elmer opened the door to the second bedroom, flipped on the lights with his left hand and quickly scanned that room. He saw the closet with the access to the side room. The lady was still behind him only now she was screaming even louder. "I am going to report this Sheriff and you will be fired from your job and I will see to it that you are prosecuted to the fullest extent of the law!" Elmer had a feeling that the reason her voice was getting louder as he approached the closet with the access to the side room was because she was trying to alert someone that he was about to enter that particular room. Elmer knew from his previous experience with this house that there was no exit from the side room other than to come through the door he was currently standing in front of.

"Sheriff! This is highly inappropriate! I'm afraid I am going to have to ask you to leave!" Elmer didn't pay any attention to the lady screaming at him. He put his hand on his holster and felt the butt of his .357. He tried to walk through as many scenarios in his head as he could as quickly as he could and the one scenario he could not afford to have happen was to accidently shoot his own son but he had to move now. He turned the handle to the door and wasn't surprised that it was locked. Elmer was in no mood for locked doors. He looked behind him to see where the lady was and she was still at a distance and she was still yelling loudly but he didn't hear anything she said. He raised his leg and kicked the door in easily. Splinters flew back at him from the door frame explosion. The door flung open but the force of it opening against its will caused it to nearly close back on him but he caught the closing door with his left hand and pushed it open wide enough to step inside the room.

The room was decorated in pink like a little girl's room, there was metal framed bed across the room with a white matching dresser and chest of drawers. The room seemed innocent enough to Elmer and sure didn't feel like a place he might find his kidnapped son. The only thing that was out of place was the partially naked girl standing over in the corner with eyes as wide as the moon and a look on her face that clearly said she was scared and the shirtless man standing beside the bed hastily trying to zip up his pants. Elmer had an idea what was going on or what was about to go on between the two before his unexpected arrival. This was more information that he wasn't expected to process at the moment and had to blink his eyes a couple times to make sure that he was seeing what he thought he was seeing.

He was extremely distraught that he didn't find Decker but he also knew that he had just stumbled on what looked to be a crime but he couldn't quickly process what type of crime was being committed but he knew he didn't like what he was seeing one bit. "What the hell is going on here?" The man continued to zip up his pants and started to reach for his shirt that was lying on the floor when Elmer stopped him. "Hold it dammit! Do not move another muscle!" The man froze when he saw that Elmer had drawn his revolver and was now pointing it at the half naked man. Elmer looked at the girl in the corner and could see that she was trying to cover herself with her hands and arms. "Find some clothes to put on girl." She didn't move, it seemed as though his booming voice scared her and she was unable to move in any direction. "Find some clothes girl! Now!" Elmer's voice must have snapped her out of her fear mode and she reached into the drawer that was next to where she was standing and pulled a long gown out of the drawer and quickly pulled it over her head. Elmer's blood began to boil when he realized that there was only one possibility of what could be happening before he barged in. The girl in the corner couldn't be much older than Decker and the man standing there with no shirt on and his pants unzipped looked to be roughly the same age as him, maybe even older.

Elmer slid his gun back in the holster. He had learned enough about himself over the years that when he lost his temper he could easily become very aggressive and he would have a hard time controlling his anger. He wasn't the type of man that easily angered but he also knew that what he was feeling inside right now was disgust coupled with anger and if the man that was now having trouble zipping up his pants because his hands were shaking so badly made the wrong move Elmer just might shoot him. Elmer pointed at the girl and told her to come around the bed and stand to his left. He actually pointed to the spot that he wanted her to stand. He was about to take a step towards the man in the room when he heard a soft scuffle behind him.

Elmer turned quickly to see the tall woman behind him swinging a rolling pin wildly in the air as if she were in a sword fight with no one. Because of the way she was standing in the little doorway, Elmer couldn't see why she appeared to be stuck but then he realized that someone was pulling her hair from behind which was causing her to lose her balance. It was quite comical looking to Elmer and if it had happened any other place but right here, he might have laughed but didn't. "Donnie?" At first there was no reply but after he saw a forearm come from behind her and make its way around her neck, he heard Donnie reply, "Yeah, its me." The reply sounded as though Donnie was out of breath or in pain but Elmer was glad Donnie showed up when he did. Elmer had completely forgotten about the woman which he knew was very bad police work, but he had convinced himself that Decker was in this house and nothing was going to stop him from finding his son. If the woman had managed to hit Elmer with that rolling pin she could have easily knocked him out with that thing and he would be in a big mess.

The lady was yelling something about having rights and how she was going to sue and some other stuff that Elmer couldn't quite make out. Elmer turned his attention back to the man just in time to see him fumble with his zipper a few more times and without any sign of trouble or warning the man's eyes rolled back in his head and he crumpled to the floor. "Donnie get that woman out of the doorway!" Elmer was still looking at the man crumpled on the floor but managed a glance at the girl who was looking at the man on the floor too, but Elmer thought for a second that she was smiling. Elmer looked around the room but he didn't see what he was looking for. "Do you have a phone in the house?" The little girl nodded her head to let Elmer know they indeed did have a phone in the house, "Where?" Elmer asked but she didn't reply. "Where is it?!" he said with a bit more force. This time she replied without changing her facial expression of which Elmer thought was a little out of place for current circumstances, she still seemed to be smiling as she stared at the man crumpled on the floor. "It's in the kitchen." Elmer fished around in his front shirt pocket and pulled out a business card, "Great! Now go call this number, ask for Heather and tell her to send an ambulance here and to send Aubrey here." The little girl didn't move so Elmer changed his expression and pretended he was talking to Heather. Heather was tough as nails, but he knew that if he was to gruff with her, she would shut down sometimes and not respond too well. He made sure to remove the intense scowl on his face that came with handling tough situations and he tried his best to smile a little. "Look, honey, I'm not going to hurt you, no one is going to hurt you, I won't let anyone hurt you anymore, I promise." He stretched his arm out without taking a step toward her so that she could easily take the card from him. "I need your help though baby, go call this number." The girl reached up and took the card from Elmer then looked at the doorway to see if it was clear for her to walk out and it was.

Donnie managed to take the rolling pin away from the big woman and to wrestle her to the front area of the house. He was surprised at how strong she was and how hard it was to get her to comply with his movement especially since his ankle was causing him a great deal of pain to put any pressure on it. Each step he took with the woman was like someone was smashing a sledge hammer into the side of his foot. "Lady, I don't want to hurt you, but I will if I have to. Sit down and shut up." Donnie didn't yell or raise his voice in any way. He was calm in his delivery as he had always been that way. Even when he was in one of his many bar room fights of yester-year, he would never lose his cool. He prided himself on his ability to stay calm when everything around him was chaotic. His ability to think clearly and make the right moves, coupled with his incredible calmness had saved his life in Viet Nam countless times. When a fire-fight erupted in the jungle and they seemed to erupt around his unit a lot, he was always sure of what to do and how to respond to it. His words must have had an effect on the tall lady because she stopped fighting him and she slumped down onto the love seat in the front entrance area and she began to sob.

From where Donnie was standing, he could see down the hallway and was fully expecting to see the Sheriff come out of the doorway dragging someone with him or perhaps just nearly beating them to death as Donnie had witnessed before. The Sheriff could be a violent man when provoked and since Donnie had not had time to assess the situation, he wasn't sure what the Sheriff's temperament would be. Donnie hoped he would see Decker walking behind his dad and this horrible night would be over. At least then he wouldn't feel so bad about letting Decker get kidnapped in the first place even though he had no idea that was what was happening earlier when he stopped to help what he thought was a stranded car.

Madelyn stepped through the doorway but stopped as she looked down the hall. Elmer could see that she was still scared of something but when she turned around and took a look at the man lying on the floor, Elmer once again thought he saw her smile. She turned down the hallway out of sight of Elmer. Elmer stood looking around the room trying to think of what to do. He looked down at the man and thought very hard about not doing a thing and simply waiting on the ambulance to arrive. If what he thought was going on in this room was really going on, he would just as soon that the man crumpled on the floor simply. The world would be rid of one more pervert and as far as Elmer was concerned, good riddance. However, he could not be certain about anything at the moment. His son was still missing and he had convinced himself that he would find Decker in this house and he hadn't. He looked around the room one more time as if that would help him decide what to do then he yelled loud enough so Donnie could hear him, "Donnie? Is the perimeter secure?" Without hesitation Donnie replied, "Affirmative, Sheriff."

Elmer stooped down next to the man lying on the floor and checked for a pulse but he couldn't feel one. He was never sure if he was actually doing it right so he checked the man's throat and when he didn't feel a pulse he pressed his fingers against the man's wrist as hard as he could thinking that maybe he was just too excited to slow his own senses down enough to find a pulse, but it didn't help. Elmer let out a deep breath and looked around the room one more time as if maybe if he waited long enough, someone else would show up. He wanted to badly to leave right now and continue the search for his son and having to deal with this right now was almost more than he could take.

Elmer had recently taken a new course offered to law enforcement people by the state that was designed to try and temporarily aid someone that had stopped breathing. In fact, he made the entire Sheriff's department take the course because he believed that it would someday come in handy but this was not what he had in mind. He believed in his heart that had he known about Cardiopulmonary Resuscitation a few years back, he could have possibly saved his deputy and his best friend. He wished he were about to try this stuff on Bubba and not this pervert in front of him now.

Elmer got down on his knees and checked the man's mouth to make sure his tongue was not blocking his airway which it wasn't. He looked around the room one last time to see if anyone else had maybe shown up to take over but they had not. He put the palm of his hand at the base of the man's sternum as he had been instructed and then pressed his other hand on top of that one and began to press on the man's chest. He couldn't remember the sequence of how many times he was supposed to do this before he blew air into the man's mouth and that's when it hit him. He forgot that he would have to put his lips on this guy's lips and the thought nearly made him throw up. Elmer continued to press on the guys chest but he made up his mind right then and there that there was no way that he was going to do any more than that.

Chapter 38

Prison Gossip

PEGGY SAT AT THE FRONT DESK of the Sheriff's office without really knowing what to do. Lavera was sitting with Heather, holding her hand and doing what Lavera always did. Lavera had a knack for seeming calm and keeping everyone else around her calm as well. She was talking in low deliberate tones, telling Heather that they would find Decker and that everything would be alright. From where Peggy was sitting, she didn't think Lavera's words were helping much and she had no problem with that. What was happening right now was hard for anyone to grasp and she sure couldn't put herself in Heather's shoes.

Mary Alice stayed on the switch board and was ready for anything but since she informed the Sheriff earlier that the leads on the white car were a dead end, she felt helpless. She sat there staring at the switchboard hoping and praying for a miracle. She couldn't help but reflect on the fact that she had known Decker his whole life. She brought flowers and a handmade baby blanket to the hospital the day he was born. She and Lois had been friends as long as she could remember. She felt like her family and the Davis family were one in the same. In fact, she felt like the entire Sheriff's office was one big family and she felt more helpless now than she had in her whole life. She had gotten so deep in thought that when the phone rang it scared her a little and she nearly knocked over her coffee cup.

She pressed the answer button on the small antique switch board and adjusted her head set a little. "Sheriff's office" was all she said. She didn't feel like being pleasant and when it got right down to it, she didn't feel like being conversational. The voice on the other end was so soft that she almost couldn't hear it. "May I speak to Heather?" Mary Alice looked over to where Lavera and Heather were sitting and could see that the time that Lavera was spending with Heather was working. Heather was no longer crying but still looked like she was in no mood for conversation. "Heather isn't able to talk right now, how can I help you?" There was silence on the other end and Mary Alice didn't like silence on the phone. She used to work for a radio marketing firm in Greenwood a long time ago and the one thing she learned from that job was that in the radio business you could never have dead air. That concept stuck with her long after she left that company, and she couldn't be sure, but she believed that was why she hated silence on the phone. "Is there anyone there? Hello?" The voice came back on the other end. "I'm supposed to talk to Heather." Mary Alice once again looked over at Lavera and Heather and could see that both ladies had stopped their conversation and were now staring at her. Mary Alice put her hand over the speaker she was using to talk into so that she couldn't be heard, "There is someone that wants to talk to Heather. I can barely hear them." Heather stood up and walked over to the closest desk with a phone and when she got to the desk, she signaled for Mary Alice to send the call to the desk. Mary Alice did as she was instructed and sent the call to the desk. The phone on the desk rang and the light on the phone lit up.

Heather reached for the phone and pulled the receiver up to her ear. She cleared her throat and wiped her eyes one time to gather her composure, "This is Heather." At first there was no voice on the other end but then she heard the same soft voice that

Mary Alice had heard just a minute before. Heather didn't realize that Mary Alice was still listening on her head set but she didn't care either. "I am supposed to tell you that you need to send an ambulance here and to call a man named Aubrey and tell him to come here too." Heather froze, her mind raced as she knew Aubrey was the police chief and if there was an ambulance needed, did that mean they had found Decker? Was he hurt? Or worse, maybe her dad and Decker were hurt?! Flashbacks of that awful day when the town ran out of ambulances because of all the violence and Bubba died at the hands of that creepy mechanic burst in her head like flash bulbs from a camera. Just as she was about to speak she heard a familiar voice on the other end.

Elmer dragged the man through the closet door and then out to hallway. Somehow, he had begun breathing again without Elmer having to give him mouth to mouth. Apparently, mashing on a man's chest enough times will get the heart started again, he thought. The man seemed very groggy, but he was definitely awake. Elmer didn't want to leave him in the room by himself so he dragged him out into the hall so he could keep an eye on him. Once he had the man in the hallway he could see the little girl down the hallway in the kitchen with the phone to her ear so he was certain that she had done as he had instructed.

Heather pressed the receiver to her ear as close as she could, she wanted to be able to hear the soft voice on the other end as best she could. "Where is here? Where does the ambulance need go, honey?" She tried not to rush through the words, but she could feel her heart beating in her chest, she could feel the goose bumps rise on her arms, she didn't want to panic but she was feeling emotions that she remembered feeling when her mother passed away and she wanted nothing to do with those feeling anymore. "Where does Aubrey need to go?" Heather stopped to allow the person to speak but she couldn't wait one more second, she wanted to know what this person knew and she wanted it now. "PLEASE! Tell me where do I send the ambulance and who is hurt?" The sound of

Heather reverberated off the office walls startling everyone including Lavera. Lavera stood up and walked over to where Heather was now sitting in a chair and placed her hand on Heather's shoulder. Just as she was about to say something to help calm Heather the phone in the office rang again which made them all jump.

Madelyn stood there with the phone to her ear and realized that she had not lived in the house long enough to remember the address. She couldn't tell them where "here" was. Madelyn looked around to see if there was anything that could help her answer the questions, but she couldn't find anything. "I don't know what address this is, I haven't been here long." Madelyn looked up in time to see the giant man dragging Reverend Jimmy into the main hallway. She could feel a smile form on her face and there was nothing she could do to stop it. She liked seeing Father being dragged against his will. Father had certainly dragged her against her will many times before and she smiled because the tables were turned.

Mary Alice pressed the button on the switchboard that handled the incoming call, "Tallahatchie County Sheriff's Office." She waited for a reply and then heard the male voice on the other end of the line. "Say have you guys heard about the goings on at Parchman today?" Mary Alice looked around the desk she was sitting at looking for a bulletin or something that could help her answer the question but up until this point she had not heard anything so she responded, "I'm afraid I have not, what can I help you with?" The man on the other end of the line spoke quickly, "There was some sort of ruckus out there and someone said that Bobby Martin finally got back at all them Buckles' boys for what they did to his little girl a while back." There was a pause, Mary Alice wasn't sure what to do or say because this was all news to her and as far as she was concerned, she didn't care at the moment. She was not a fan of the Buckles family and had her own run ins with Buckles, especially Brett. The town had become quite a bit more friendly and safer for that matter since they all had been locked up.

She felt a little guilty about those feelings because she was a good Christian woman and was supposed to be able to forgive and forget but she couldn't. She felt like if maybe someone had got to that littlest one before he was murdered, maybe he could turn out to be fine young man but everyone knew that he was headed down the same path his brothers and father had taken. They were all just mean and deserved whatever they got. "Sir I am sorry there is a lot going on right now and I don't have time for prison gossip, is there something I can help you with." Mary Alice's tone was sharp and testy which got Peggy's attention so she made her way to a phone and picked up the line that Mary Alice was using so she could hear what was being said. The man returned words quickly and almost as sharp, "Well pardon me! I just thought maybe the law would like to know that moron Brett Buckles is dead and Poppa Buckles is said to be close to it!" He paused for a second then continued, "Oh and that simple-minded Buckles boy is probably gonna start liking boys pretty soon or at least he will be forced to." Mary Alice and Peggy both looked at each other with a confused looks on their faces. Mary Alice took a breath, "Sir I don't see what any of that has to do with the Sheriff's office." She paused then said, "We have a lot going on now and we have to keep the lines open, now unless you have a crime to report, we need to let you go now." Mary Alice was about to disconnect the caller when he spoke up, "Conspiracy to commit murder is a crime lady!" The caller yelled into the phone enough for her to pull her headphones away from her ear a little, "and Bobby Martin set it all up!" Mary Alice was about to ask how he knew that but he wouldn't let her speak. "And from what I hear, Ole Bobby ain't a fan of the Sheriff's either and he don't like the Sheriff's boy sniffin' around his little girl, so he took care of that too!"

Mary Alice was relieved that Heather could not hear what she and Peggy were hearing. Mary Alice was searching for words and didn't know how to respond when Peggy spoke up on the other receiver, "Sir if you have information in regard to criminal activity you are obligated to share them with the proper law enforcement agency." It was widely known that Mary Alice and Peggy sounded the same on the phone and that became apparent when the caller continued without missing a beat, "Look lady, I am reporting it to you and you're too stupid to realize it!" Peggy was about to speak when she heard the phone click and make a dial tone sound. Mary Alice spoke, "Hello, are you there?" Both ladies knew he had hung up but Mary Alice felt compelled to verify it with the final comment. The call distracted them both enough that they had almost forgot that Heather was speaking to someone on the other line.

Elmer was a little out of breath from dragging the man through that tiny opening in the closet. When he got him to the hallway, he looked down towards the kitchen to see the little girl on the phone but looking around like she was looking for something. He knew right away that she didn't know her address. Elmer yelled, "Just tell them the old Murphy place!" Elmer looked down towards the front entrance and could see that Donnie was sitting with his back to the wall with his legs extended straight out. "What the hell are you doing?" Elmer then looked down at the man he was standing over who was now staring back up at him. "I better not find out you were fakin' it and made me drag your sorry ass out of that room!" The man didn't blink but he just stared up at Elmer.

Madelyn pressed the receiver close to her ear and mouth so she could hear the lady on the other end and spoke at the same time, "umm the man said it is the old Murphy place." Heather heard that loud and clear, spun around to where Lavera was standing and told her to get Aubrey and an ambulance to the old Murphy place." Lavera started to make the calls immediately. Heather focused her attention back on the soft voice on the other end of the line, "What's your name honey? Who am I talking to?" Heather wanted to scream into the phone, she wanted to know if Decker was there, but she tried to remain calm. Earlier she swore she could hear her father's voice in the background, but she couldn't be sure. The soft voice on the other end replied "Madelyn". Heather looked up at Peggy and Mary Alice who were now both staring directly at Heather. Heather could see that their eyes were wide and fixed on her. She could hear Lavera talking to Aubrey and realized she needed to say something, "It's nice to know you Madelyn. Can you tell me if there is a boy there with you? We are looking for my brother and we were hoping that he is with you?" There was no pause, "No." Heather started to speak but Madelyn interrupted, "There is a very big man here but there isn't a boy." Heather smiled because she knew that there could only be one man described that way in this situation and that was her dad and then the disappointment of her brother not being there set in and she had to choke back more tears.

"Donnie come get your ass over here and help me get this guy outside!" Donnie struggled to get up from the floor, the pain in his ankle was terrible and he had already taken note that he could see that one side of his ankle was swollen to the size of a grapefruit. He used the wall to help steady his assent to being upright all the while keeping an eye on the lady that was sitting on the little love seat with her head in her hands sobbing like she was at a funeral. "Hey lady, get up." The woman looked up at him, the stuff that she put her around her eyes to make her look pretty was not helping at all now. She looked like a horror movie actress he had seen not long ago. Her black make-up around her eyes had made nice giant streaks all down her cheeks. The sight of her scared Donnie enough that when he tried to put some distance between him and this lady, he banged his head on the wall that was holding him up.

The lady slowly stood up and she recognized the look on Donnie's face as fear of her looks because she tried to wipe her makeup off on the sleeve of the dress she was wearing and made it worse. "I've seen worse lady, let's go get your husband out of the floor. Elmer watched as the Donnie and the tall lady made their way down the hall. Donnie was using the wall to help himself and Elmer could easily see that he was trying to keep the pressure off his foot. The site of the lady with black make-up now smeared all over her face was comical to Elmer. He almost burst out laughing but he didn't. He immediately began focusing on where Decker could be since he wasn't at this location. He had been sure he would find Decker here and now that he hadn't he was back to that feeling of frustration and near hopelessness.

"What happened to you?" Elmer looked down at Donnie's leg as if he could discover the source of the problem. "I must have stepped in a gopher hole or something when I got out of the truck. Thought I might have heard it pop, not sure." Elmer shook his head and realized that Donnie was out of commission. "Alright, when the ambulance gets here, you can hop in the back with this guy and go have it looked at." Donnie shook his head no. "No, I am staying with you until we find Decker." Elmer looked down at the man lying in hallway floor then back at Donnie, "Hells bells Donnie, you can barely walk! You are no good to me that way," he paused for a second and then looked up the tall woman in front of him, "Hell, Frankenstein here could knock you on your ass if she wanted too." Just then Elmer saw the light flashing through the open front door. The ambulance had arrived and was just now hearing the sirens.

He turned to see the little girl holding the phone to her ear but not saying anything and figured he needed to get on the phone and fill in some blanks for Heather. He took one more glance down at the man on the floor who still had his eyes open but wasn't moving then proceeded to walk to where the girl was standing in the kitchen. "Let me have the phone baby." She wasted no time handing the receiver to him. Elmer quickly put the receiver to his ear. "Honey is that you?" Heather spoke up quickly, the anxiety of not knowing what was going on was getting the best of her. "Yes Daddy! What's going on? Where is Decker? What's going on!" Elmer felt bad, he wished he could hold his daughter like he had at the store earlier and tell her that everything was going to be alright, but he couldn't. He didn't want to admit it, but he was scared and he was running out of option and ideas.

"Well, we thought maybe Decker was here but he was not but we found something here that we didn't expect. I will tell you about it later." He looked around the kitchen, for what he didn't know, "Anything from Tom, has he called in yet?" Heather started to tell him no, but the radio crackled to life and interrupted her. "County Dispatch, come in County." Heather focused her attention on her dad again because Lavera had already grabbed the big silver microphone stand and was responding. "No, we haven't heard anything from Tom."

Chapter 39
Neighborhood Watch

TOM THOUGHT HE HEARD SOME thumping sounds coming from inside the house but he couldn't be sure. He pounded on the door again and made his presence known so loudly that he could see a porch light from another house pop on just about 100 yards away. He didn't care who he bothered with his noise. He was certain that there was something going on inside this house and he needed to find out exactly what. After he cut the screen and freed the latch, he had unimpeded access to the door. He tried the doorknob but it was locked. He pounded on it one more time and announced himself loudly, loud enough that another neighboring house light flicked on.

He looked around to see if any other houses had lit up, but they had not. He thought about kicking in the door but the illegal search and seizure thing crossed his mind. He didn't want to get shot breaking into someone's house that had done nothing wrong other than park a car in their back yard. Then it hit him, he had not checked the car to see if it was a match to the one that Donnie Buckles described as the car seen on the highway where he found the rabbits foot and library card. He drew in a breath and tried to come up with reasons why his police work was so shoddy and no matter what he came up as an excuse, it all went back to just being incompetent. He would never admit that to anyone but himself, but his last few months in Webb were terrible. He had managed to shoot a beautiful dead deer in a hardware store, he tried to flirt with a girl in town and she blew him off, and to make matters worse, he had been dressed down by a lady at a clothing store when he tried to assert his dominance over what he had been told was the town bully, and as it now turns out, the bully was friends with the Sheriff! All these thoughts went through his mind as he tried to make sense of his life.

Tom knew he wanted to be a cop more than anything in the world and now, the thought that his crazy brother might be behind this whole mess made him sick to his stomach. The fact that he had made some pretty silly decisions could be overcome for sure, but if his family tree was tied to the kidnapping of the Sheriff's only son, then he figured he might as well start selling ice cream out of one of those silly trucks that drove through town and the neighborhoods. He tried to put all those worthless thoughts out of his head because they weren't doing him any good now.

He took one last look around the neighborhood to see if any more lights had popped on. He couldn't remember which ones were on to start with so he just stopped worrying about who he might wake up. The houses out here were so far apart he really couldn't see the next house and even if he could, when he was driving in, he didn't look too closely at the houses as he passed them. He felt for the gun on his hip and it was still there. He made sure that the hammer strap was not impeding his efforts if he had to make a quick draw. He slowly began making his way towards the empty carport area where he would make another survey of the situation and then check the car that was parked behind the back of the house.

After Tom softly walked through the carport and made his way to the back corner of the house, he could clearly see the back bumper of what looked to be a white car. The license plate was definitely Mississippi, but it was too dark to make out the county. Bobbi lived in Ruleville and that meant she lived in Sunflower County but he couldn't make out the small letters at the bottom of the plate. He wanted to turn the big flashlight on but he realized that he left it sitting on the front porch. He didn't want to go back now and get it so he leaned as far down as he could without actually kneeling on the ground. He could see that plate was indeed was from Sunflower County and his heart immediately dropped to his stomach. Could this be the house the boy was being held? He swallowed hard and willed his legs to move because at the moment they were not cooperating. He tried to tell himself that what was happening was not a result of his brother James and that the car being white and the plates being from Sunflower County was purely coincidental.

Tom eased his frame between the house and the car as he made his way to back door. He could see that there was a light inside, but it looked like the door was wide open. The screen door was shut but the inside door was open. Now that wouldn't be out of the ordinary, however, considering the time of the night, it was unlikely, but not completely out of the ordinary. Lots of folks like to keep the breeze blowing through the house out here on the bayou, and not just for the breeze but for the sounds. Tom had to admit that all the sounds of nature out here on the bayou were peaceful and probably calming, but he was too nervous right now to enjoy the benefits of bayou living.

He slowly approached the back door and tried to look inside without being seen, not an easy task at all considering there was a small concrete step that led up to the door. He placed one foot on the step while keeping the other foot firmly on the ground, he wanted to be able to back up quickly if needed. He leaned over as far as he could to see inside. He caught a glimpse of the kitchen cabinets and pulled back quickly. He had overestimated how much he could see inside which meant that it overexposed his head. He was afraid that someone might have seen his head which was a good way to get shot if you were peeping into the wrong house. He waited patiently for any movement or noise, heard none, and figured he needed to stop acting like a thief and act like a sheriff's deputy. He looked around one more time, checked his holster, took a big step and stood right in front of the back door. He reached up and pounded on the screen door with the palm of his hand. As he pounded on the screen he could see that the door would slightly open and close. "Sheriff's office, official business." He didn't yell but he made sure there was no mistaking his presence outside the door. There was no movement or sound coming from inside the house. He nervously looked around for no apparent reason other than to give him time to think this through. He went through the laws in his head as best he could, he had already thought through the illegal search and seizure, but this door was open, there seemed to be a problem and then probable cause popped into his head. He remembered that if he thought something was wrong or someone might be in trouble, he was allowed to enter the premises without worry of being in trouble with the law.

He reached up and pulled the screen door handle; it squeaked ever so slightly which he expected and hoped it would get some-one's attention. He could hear his heart beating in his ears and he was sweating. He put his hand on his holster and kept it there. He stepped into the kitchen and let the door close behind him but he used his butt to keep the door from slamming shut. It was a small kitchen with blue countertops and a linoleum floor that looked like a basketball court he had seen on TV. It smelled clean, like someone had just used a bunch of cleaner, almost too much because the overpowering smell of ammonia was sure to give him a headache if he stayed here too long. He looked down the hall towards the front of the house but there were no lights on. He surveyed the kitchen and saw that there was a pantry door and a door which was latched at the top so he wasn't too worried about that one, it had to be a basement door and he would check that one after he cleared the main house.

He made his way down the hall, "Sheriff's office, anyone home?" He slid his hand along the wall to the right and as he made it to the first bedroom he reached for the light switch and flipped it on. He peered inside, there was no one in this room. He checked each room until he was standing in the living room. It was quiet, he could see there were some magazines that were thrown on the floor and there was an ash tray that had several stubbed-out cigarettes. He slowly spun in a complete circle, "Sheriff's office, I need to talk to someone in the house." He didn't expect a response and that's what he got.

Tom was beginning to think that maybe the owners were down on the bayou frog gigging or some kind of night hunting and he shouldn't be in their house. Maybe this was not the house but then he couldn't explain the big white car parked at the back of the house. His mind raced as he tried to figure out what to do. He thought about heading back to the big green car and radio the Sheriff to come clean about his family and at least let him know that he had found the car in question; but he would much rather radio that he had found the boy. He walked back to the kitchen and he could hear the floor creak under his weight which once again reminded him that he needed to check the basement.

As he walked back into the kitchen, he saw the pantry door and remembered that he hadn't checked it. Most pantry's he had seen were just a tiny closet with shelves, so he was pretty sure there was no need to check it. He stood in the middle of the kitchen and debated whether to go out to radio the Sheriff before he went to check the basement. The car was parked out on the street and it would take quite a while to walk that distance and besides, many times the Sheriff wouldn't even respond to him even when he had one of the ladies in the office try to reach him; his best course of action was to check the basement and leave. After he left he could then come clean with the Sheriff about his family history.

He stood in the middle of the kitchen looking at the two doors he hadn't checked, the pantry door and what he presumed to be the basement door. His head went back and forth a few times as he thought about what to do. His decision didn't center around which door to check but again, his mind went back to the Sheriff and how he could tell him about his family. He told himself over and over that he needed to focus and not get distracted by the Sheriff and especially not worry about his family but to do good police work and find that boy. He knew how to do good police work but he was also self-aware of his short comings. He was also aware that sometimes he let his adrenaline get the best of him and overreacted, but in his mind, that was perfectly natural and expected of him at times, considering the nature of his job.

He started to open the basement door but because he had reminded himself to do good police work he knew that good police work meant that he had to check every door when he was clearing a room so he turned back toward the pantry door, took a few steps toward it and reached for the knob.

The door was partially cracked so he used the knob to merely pull back the door. At first it was dark inside the pantry but as the door opened more widely and the light from the kitchen flooded the vacant little food storage space it became apparent that he had misjudged the size of the pantry. This pantry was larger than most any he had ever seen and it was well stocked with all sorts of canned goods, some bought from the store and some were canned into nice jars and each of the jars were lined up by flavor, he knew that because each jar had a perfectly placed label that described the contents of the jars. The hand writing on the labels was perfect cursive and he was momentarily impressed by the quality of writing but his admiration for the quality penmanship quickly disappeared when he noticed that the pantry was big enough for a woman to be sitting nearly straight up with her hands on her lap. "Holy mother of pearl!" Was all that came out of his mouth. He reached for his gun, but he realized that the woman was not reacting to his presence. He spun around to make sure there was nobody behind him and when he was convinced he was alone in the kitchen, with the exception of this woman, he turned back to the pantry and its lifeless occupant.

He focused on steadying his nerves and tried to breathe normal, but it was impossible. This woman was dead for sure, he could tell by the deep cut from one side of her neck to the other. The slice wasn't easy to see at a glance because her head sagged in front of her with her chin pointed at a downward angle. The curious position she was in made him wondered why she had very little blood on her. It was as if she either didn't bleed when she was cut or someone had cleaned her up and placed her in the closet so that she would be as neat and organized as the labels on the canned peaches.

He stood there looking down at her for what seemed like an hour but it really wasn't. He was still trying to gain control of his adrenaline and was proud of the way he had steadied his nerves quickly enough to not draw his gun and pull the trigger like he had done in the hardware store. He would be damned before he shot another deer head to pieces.

He knelt down in front of her but he had to straddle her extended legs in order to get himself in a position to properly examine her. He felt a little odd squatting over a dead woman the way he was, but he had no choice. For some reason, he snapped his fingers in front of her face as if she might snap out of her death. He felt weird about that too and was glad no one was watching. The last dead body he had seen was his mother and he didn't care for that image in the middle of his good police work and found himself getting mad at his mother again. He was mad that she chose to leave them and was mad that he was the one that found her. Now he was staring at another lifeless woman and she was staring back at him. The only difference he could see between his mother and this lady, this lady didn't appear to have a choice in her departure.

He grabbed her wrist and pressed his fingers against the veins that would pulsate if she had a pulse, but he knew from the look of her that she was dead. He only checked for a pulse because that was considered good police work. He gently put her hand back down in her lap and gave her one last look. She was a pretty lady, she was well dressed, well-manicured and he could still smell the perfume. He thought maybe she owned the house and had been the victim of a break in. He felt a rush of sorrow for her as he knew that she probably didn't deserve to die, especially this way. Flashes went through his head as he tried to imagine how she died, maybe she was in the pantry and reaching for some preserves and the intruder came up from behind her and slashed her throat. That was one of the many scenes he quickly played out in his head but none of the scenes he conjured up in his head could explain how there was no blood anywhere in the pantry and very little actual blood on this lady. He gave up trying to figure out how she died and stood up. He stepped backwards and made his way out of the pantry without disturbing the body any more than he already had.

He turned his attention to the basement door. His heart rate started to go up again and he did what he had done just a few minutes before. He slowed his breathing and focused on doing good police work. Now that he had discovered a dead woman in the pantry then maybe he was about to discover more dead bodies. He felt for his side arm and it was there. He patted it a few times to reassure himself and then lifted the leather hammer guard from the holster leaving the gun easily accessible if he needed to draw quickly. He reached for the door handle and slowly turned the handle. It turned easily making very little noise, but it didn't open. He had to steady his breathing again as he remembered that the door had been latched at the top. He unlatched the door from the top, then turned the handle again. This time the door began to move as soon as he pulled on it. The door creaked and the old hinges on the door resisted the effort by making a creaking noise.

As he was pulling the door open, he decided that he needed to be less stealth and announce his presence, "Tallahatchie County Sheriff's Office! Come on up out of there now!" He could see the first few steps leading down to the basement but that was all. He let go of the door handle and while keeping his hand on his gun he used the other hand to search for a light switch. He couldn't find the switch and realized that it was probably in the kitchen and not on the inside wall leading down the stairs. As he was stepping back to look for the switch, he made another announcement: "Sheriff's office! If anyone is down there you need to come on up! Now!" He looked to the left of the door and saw the switch and quickly flipped it to the on position. The stairwell lit up almost all the way to the bottom and he saw nothing but steps. He liked that he could see the steps easily but he did not like that he couldn't see the bottom floor very well, that made him nervous and his adrenaline began pumping again. He took the first step and the wood step let its presence be known when it creaked louder than the door hinge. Any element of surprise was certainly gone now and if anyone was down at the bottom, they would certainly have the advantage. He really didn't like the idea of taking another step and his body let his mind know that it did not want to participate. His legs froze for a second and he nearly fell down the stair as his legs stayed in place and his upper body began the descent. He stopped his upper body from moving anymore and placed his left hand on the wall to catch himself and steady his balance. He breathed in deeply and let out the breath slowly.

He finally convinced his legs to move with his upper body and he slowly began taking steps down to the unknown. He wished he had that heavy World War II flashlight now, but he had left that somewhere outside the house. He couldn't remember exactly where, but he could sure use it now. He was surprised to find out that with each step down the stairs he took, his motions seemed to become easier. His legs stopped resisting the movement and his breathing slowed to a proper and manageable level. Unlike the hardware store, he knew something bad had happened in this house and there may still be some one bad in this house. He was a cop and he knew how to be one. "Sheriff's office! Is there anyone here?" The room returned nothing but silence. He reached the bottom of the stairs and tried his best to look through the darkness but could not see anything. He could clearly look back up the stairs and see the lights but as far as the basement floor, he couldn't see much at all. He still had his hand on his gun when he was struck from behind.

It was as though he had been tackled from behind. His head snapped backwards and his body heaved forward and slammed into a wall that he could not see until he hit it with the left side of his head and left shoulder. The wall was surely concrete because when his head hit it, he thought for a second that he would black out. Explosions went off behind his eyes like he had never seen and he became very confused but only for a moment. He regained his faculties as quickly as he could and reached down and felt for his gun but it wasn't there. He remembered removing the hammer strap and now wished he hadn't. The gun must have fallen out when he was tackled from behind. He then tried to grab for the person that was on top of him now but just as he did, he felt an arm come up around his throat and he knew he was in trouble. He was pinned in such a way that his left arm was under his body and his right arm couldn't get enough leverage to wiggle out of the choke hold that was becoming tighter by the minute. He managed to pull his right leg up towards his right hand, just enough to get his fingers to extract the switch blade knife from the secret pocket he had sewn inside his boot. He could feel the pressure on his neck getting tighter and he badly wanted to gasp for some air, but the grip around him was so tight that he couldn't even make a sound. His hand was starting to shake before he could flip the latch on the knife making it hard for him to even find the switch. He was about to black out when he felt the knife snap open in his hand and with all his strength he plunged the knife into what he thought was the hip of the person that had him in a death grip. He heard the unmistakable scream of a man but what surprised him was that the man did not loosen his grip despite just having a knife plunged into him. Tom thought he might be dealing with some sort of

ghost or crazed person. How in the world could they continue
to maintain this grip on him after having a knife jabbed in them?
He tried to open his eyes and as much as he could, he was fading
fast and he knew that if he didn't get out of this choke hold he
would soon black out and then he would surely end up like the
woman in the pantry.

He extracted the knife from wherever he had stuck the man
and plunged it in him again only this time he repeated the action as
many times as his arm would allow him too. The man screamed at
the top of his lungs and only after what Tom guessed was the fifth
stab did, he loosen his grip. As soon as Tom felt the grip loosen,
he gasped for as much air as his lungs could handle and then he
exhaled. He couldn't remember a time in his life that felt as good as
it did this very moment. To be deprived of air for what seemed like
an eternity and then gulping it down with gusto was an amazing
feeling, but it was also a feeling he never wanted to experience
again. He rolled out of the man's grip but apparently it wasn't far
enough, the man somehow managed to grab a hand full of Tom's
hair and was yanking him back towards him. Pain shot through
Tom again but this time he could at least breathe. He kicked backwards like an angry mule and the heel of his boot must have struck
the man flush because he groaned and let go of Tom's hair.

Tom thought he managed to roll far enough away to keep this
man from grabbing him again. He pulled his legs up under him
and tried to stand but he quickly found out he was still very dizzy
from either his head smashing into a wall or nearly being choked
to death. Either way he fell back to the ground. He could hear
the man moving behind him but from the sound it more like the
man was trying to get up too. Tom knew that if he didn't find the
strength to get up quicker than this attacker, he would likely be
dead soon. He tried once more to stand and this time he managed
to get his legs under him and used his left hand against the wall to
help steady him. His head was still spinning but he tried to turn
in the direction he thought the attacker would be. He couldn't see

anything, but he could hear some shuffling. "I'm a deputy Sheriff for Tallahatchie County and you are under arrest!" Tom reached down for his gun again but it wasn't there just like the last time he reached for it then he heard the clear and distinct sound of a hammer cocking. The intruder had apparently found his gun before he could. Tom spent the flash of a memory kicking himself for losing his gun and was now quietly praying that he wouldn't get killed, especially being killed by his own gun. So much for good police work. It was then that he realized that he was standing directly in the light of the stairway. He quickly moved to the nearest dark spot he could find but it was too late, he saw the muzzle flash and he felt the thud of the bullet hitting his chest. It was all so quick but it was like he was in slow motion. The flash then the thud, in his mind he should have been able to dodge anything that he could see coming but he hadn't been able. He felt the air quickly leave his body and he collapsed to the floor.

Chapter 40
Wrong way

JESSICA LOOKED UP AT DECKER, she had not been able to see him until now. Her eyes were adjusted to the dark quite well but the tears that welled up in her eyes made her sight too blurry to adequately see this person that had somehow been thrust into the darkness with her but was strong enough to give her hope; hope she thought she had lost forever. She squinted, wiped away some of the tears and tried to see her new friend and hero. She could never see anything in the basement, so this was the first time she was able to look at Decker. Even though it was night, the small lights that were on in the house were putting out enough light for her to see him. She saw the concern in his face, but she also saw the honesty. Even though she wouldn't have wished their situation on anyone, she had at least had some company in the that dark, dank basement since he arrived. Just having Decker put his arm around her was one of the most comforting emotions she had felt since she had been taken. Decker's reassurance of: "I promise you they won't hurt you anymore," reverberated through her head like an echo in a canyon. Even though Decker didn't look very old, she could tell by his mannerism and his current tone of voice, that he meant it.

She started to stand but she didn't have to do much standing on her own because when Decker felt her begin to stand, he practically lifted her off the ground. In a flash, they were both running. First, Decker took them around to the front of the house because the back of the house was all bayou and even though Decker loved Cassidy Bayou, he was certain there were night creatures in and around the bayou that he would rather not encounter during their escape. He saw the white car that had been stopped in the middle of the road earlier and tricked him into looking at a dead puppy in the road. He wondered now if the puppy was even injured and it occurred to him as they were running past the car, maybe that man with the giant arms had trained the puppy to lay in the middle of the road and play dead like that and he wished he could train a dog to do cool stuff like that; not train them to trick kids and kidnap them but to train them to stay very still. After they passed the car they headed straight up the driveway to the road. He thought he heard something that sounded like someone knocking on a door, but he wasn't going to stop and find out what or who it was. He had to get him and Jessica at least up to the main road but his dilemma was, they had to stay off the road so they wouldn't be seen. It wasn't going to be easy, but they had to move and stay hidden at the same time. He could not risk that guy getting up and chasing after them.

As they got further from the house, it became darker and harder for Decker to see. He had ahold of Jessica's hand and she was running as fast as she could but she was no match for Decker. He had to take it somewhat easy. He felt like he was dragging her more than she was running. Once they got to the main road, Decker could see a car parked in the road but he couldn't tell if anyone was in it and he wanted to stay away from being seen for now so he and Jessica went the opposite direction, stepped off the road again and eased down into the ditch that ran in front of all the houses out here. He was glad there hadn't been any rain lately or the ditches would be soggy. It wasn't easy running through the ditches when they were dry, but he didn't even want to think what it would be like if they were wet.

He kept a firm grip on her hand, probably too firm because he would feel her release her grip on his hand but he never released his grip on hers. He was not going to let her go for any reason. If he did, he was certain that the man with the giant forearms would catch up to her and she would be right back where she started. Just as he was adjusting his stride to allow her to stay with him, she fell. He could hear her whisper crying, "I can't Decker, my feet hurt, I stepped on something back there and I think my foot is cut or something, it hurts so bad!" Decker quickly knelt beside her and even laid in the ditch next to her. He had forgotten that when he first met her, she was completely naked, of course he didn't see anything it was just that he figured it out. She had on his shirt right now and nothing else, including the fact that she had no shoes. There were all kinds of weeds and burrs and stuff that could bite you out here and he hadn't considered her being barefooted until now. "Jessica, I know it hurts, we have to move though. We can't stay here, we are still too close to that man," Decker paused and looked around to try and see how far they had traveled and to his surprise he could barely see the house lights they had fled from. They had really traveled quite a long way, but it still wasn't far enough to suit him. The problem that Decker quickly realized was that when they went the opposite direction to stay away from the car parked on the road, they went in the opposite direction of the road that would take them back towards 49 and to the main road back into Webb. He would have to figure a way to navigate around the house they had just left without being seen. After surveying where they were, he laid his head back down in the ditch next to Jessica's but she was face down sobbing and he was looking up at the stars that were visible. "Do you want my shoes? I go barefooted all the time at home." Jessica stopped sobbing and turned her head towards Decker, she sniveled as she semi-chuckled through her tears and whispered, "You have boy feet, I would run right out of your shoes in the first few steps." Decker knew she had a point and he kinda knew what her response was going to be so he was prepared, "then we don't have any choice but to keep going, me with shoes and you without," he paused then continued, "but we can't stay here forever and we have to keep moving."

While he was waiting on a response from her, he raised his head to look across the road, there were very few houses on the other side of the road, it was mainly open fields and pastures. He figured they could shift to the opposite side, give themselves about a 100 yards distance from the bayou and then head straight back for the main road. If they took that approach, they would not be seen when they passed in front of the house they wanted to avoid. That side of the road had lots of trees and it would be slow moving but at least they wouldn't have to run so fast and maybe Jessica could keep up better.

"We have to move Jessica. We have to move to the other side of the road and make our way back to the main highway." Decker heard her take a short breath and then he could see her lift her head and turn it towards him. "Can't you just leave me here and come back for me?" Her voice was raspy and to Decker she sounded like she was just waking up from a nap. She was very groggy. He read about battles on the civil war that were so fierce that some men would get so tired and when they had used up all their adrenaline they would collapse in the middle of the battle and sometimes fall asleep. It seemed odd to Decker that someone could fall asleep right in the middle of all that noise but the way Jessica sounded just now, he was afraid she was about to go to sleep and if she fell asleep, he might not be able to wake her and then they would both be in trouble. "No Jessica!" He was whispering but the urgency in his voice came through. He wanted to scream and shake her but he didn't. "Jessica, we have to get across the road, now get up!" He once again held his voice to a strong whisper. She lifted her head, looked at Decker and then looked at the road as if she was deciding to stay or go and thankfully for Decker, she began to lift herself up from the ditch. Decker sprang up quickly and helped her get to her feet. She almost fell back down a few times as she was trying to stand but Decker managed to catch her and keep her from falling. If he let her fall back down now, he might not ever get her up again.

He pulled her right arm around his neck and over his shoulder and he hooked his left arm around her waist. Once he felt like he had a firm grip on her, the two began to take very slow steps out of the ditch and across the road. She was mumbling to Decker about hunting and how she should have taken the shot, but she couldn't bring herself to shoot that beautiful deer. Her words would fade in and out and her head would dangle almost uncontrollably as they walked. Decker was with his Dad once while when he had been called to the pool hall downtown remove a guy that was passed out on the sidewalk. When his Dad got him up and helped him walk to their car, the guy walked and mumbled just like Jessica was doing now.

As she was mumbling and they were almost to the other side of the road, Decker thought he saw movement far in the distance. He could feel his grip on Jessica tighten considerably. He wondered if the guy in the basement had gotten up from the floor after falling down those stairs and was now after him. The thought made Decker scared and with this tinge of fear, he tightened his grip on Jessica, leaned away from her just enough to lift her feet off the ground and he carried her with her feet now dangling. Her head bounced up and down and side to side as they entered the field on the other side of the road. There were lots of trees and Decker had a hard time seeing some of them, so he had to slow down, plus they were making too much noise to suit him, so he stopped. He looked back at the road to see if he could see any movement, but he didn't. Jessica remained standing beside him with his arm around her waist and her arm draped around his neck and over his shoulder. He didn't let her go while he tried to figure things out a little better because he was certain she would fall. They weren't far enough away from the road and anyone could see them if they were seriously looking so he picked her up the same way he had before by pulling her close to him and leaning sideways so her feet would have to come off the ground. He took a few steps then lowered her feet back to the ground. He quickly spun around, squatted just enough to get some leverage on Jessica and then quickly hoisted her over his shoulder. At least this way he could walk upright and he was more stable. She didn't protest, in fact, Decker wondered if she was asleep because she was being so quiet. He began taking steps deeper into the field but also in the direction of the main road that led back to town. She wasn't heavy to him at all and walking was a whole lot easier now. He gritted his teeth and thought, *I just need my dad to come get us.*

Chapter 41
My Brother's Keeper

THE AIR IN THE BASEMENT QUICKLY FILLED with the smell of gun powder. James could feel the warm blood running down his right leg and he grimaced as he tried to move towards the cop that was likely dead. It was just luck that when he rolled away from the cop to avoid another puncture in his side that he rolled right on top of a gun. He pulled the gun out from under his back and established that it was a revolver style gun so this would be easy. He tried to remain quiet and continue to use the darkness of the basement to his advantage but when he tried to stand, the stab wounds in his hip sent bolt of pain through his entire body. He grunted slightly but he muffled the grunt by keeping his teeth clinched as he was finally able to stand.

He could see in the darkness that the cop was trying to stand and when the cop was almost upright, he cocked the hammer of the revolver so that there was no mistaking who was in charge now. The thought did cross his mind that if the cop had a hidden knife in his boot that he sure might have another gun on him somewhere and he was not about to get shot and stabbed on the same day so he pulled the trigger. He had never shot anyone before and was surprised at how powerful it made him feel. He had seen the life go out of the eyes of all his victims and had enjoyed the power that it gave him, but all his victims had been children and they usually didn't fight back. This was different, he had just been the victor in a battle between grown men and he was still standing. He thought he now had a good understanding of what the ancient gladiators must have felt like when they were the last man standing in the arena. The feeling was more arousing than he had ever expected and despite the pain in his side he could feel the arousal as it sparked his groin to life. He now knew that he had to catch his Jessica and that Sheriff's boy and use them to help him satisfy his needs.

With the gun still in his hand but dangling by his side, he slowly turned to climb the stairs back to the kitchen. Each step was an explosion of pain, especially lifting his leg to advance upward on each step. When he made it to the top and was firmly on the kitchen floor and had good lighting, he looked at his hip and could see that his pants were darkly soaked almost down to his knee and he could see that the blood was already puddling on the floor beneath his shoe. He grabbed a dish towel that was lying on the counter and jammed the towel inside his pants to help stop the bleeding. He looked around the room for a second, limped over to the sink and washed his hands of the blood as best he could. He grabbed the last remaining dish towel he could find and dried his hands. He wished she were here now because she would always fixed things for him. She was good in chaotic times and could help him get organized. He regretted having felt the need to end their arrangement especially since he really hadn't given it much thought at the time. He had always been spontaneous in his actions and urges, that's how he began his journey of purification.

He was certain that the children couldn't get too far if he was patient, he would easily track them down. He had a knack for smelling fear and children emitted loads of fear in strange situations and this was certainly a strange situation. He wasn't sure if the boy knew his way around the bayou since he wasn't from here, but the girl would be lost and totally dependent on the boy. If that boy DID know his way around the bayou, he would either go to the first available house which was quite a distance from this house and it was going in the opposite direction of the main road. The boy would probably try to make it back to the main road.

He shoved the gun in his front pants pocket the best he could. He still loved the feel of it. It was heavy and it was now his friend. It had done as he had commanded, and it had protected him when he was attacked. The gun was now his best friend and he would use it again, not on the girl because he needed her, but on the boy. He imagined shooting the boy in a well-lit room this time so he could actually see the fear in his eyes as he pulled the trigger. He loved that part of his work, the part where he watched the life leave a body and how he knew that he had purified each of his souls and sent them to God prepared for the afterlife. He was proud of what he did for the children as he had spared them a life of deceit, hate, crime, heartbreaks, love and especially sex. With each purification he allowed them to experience the first joyful pain and exhilaration brought about by sex with someone that truly loved them so that they would never have to endure any type of unneeded and unwanted pain with someone that didn't love them as much as he did. He was certain that they were smiling and happy when they met God, after all, God had chosen him to do this work for him.

He grabbed the car keys off the counter where he had left them before, turned off the lights to the kitchen, which immediately made the entire house as dark as the night he was about to enter. He exited the house through the back door, he wouldn't be coming back to this house anymore. Once her and that dead cop started stinking from rot, someone would surely report the smell and they would find them, but he would be long gone by then. He just needed to find that whiney little boy and his Jessica.

He started the big white car he had taken from Bobbi. He felt his hip when he sat down in the car because it caused a rush of pain to shoot through his body like he had never felt before. He thought he might black out and forced himself to focus on healing.

He had always been very good at healing himself. Since God had chosen him for this work, he had been given healing powers that he had never really had to use until now. He focused on seeing the internal stab wounds in his side to heal with each breath he took and then focused on stopping the bleeding. He didn't have much time to waste healing himself though, he would just have to power through it because he needed to find his Jessica.

He eased the car out from behind the house and made his way up the driveway and on to gravel road that winded its way along the bayou. He turned left on the road and slowly drove along looking for signs of his Jessica and the boy. He tried to put himself in their shoes and looked for places that they might hide. His head hurt due to the pain in his side and he was frustrated that he hadn't had the proper time to heal his wounds. If he hadn't had to wrestle that cop, and if the cop hadn't stabbed him, he would have found the kids by now and would have been well on his way back to Ruleville; instead he was floundering around this stupid bayou forced to think like a small child in order to figure out where they were however, he had to admit that if he were a small child he would not have thought to come up with the idea to trip someone on the stairs that way the boy had done to him. He knew the idea didn't come from Jessica because she rarely put up a fight. She did when he first took her but after a while, she became compliant. There was something about that boy that was different than any of the others he had taken and now he wished he hadn't agreed to do this type of contract work; but at the time he was hard pressed for cash and in order to carry on his purification mission for God he needed money. He was a loner by nature, but this seemed like easy work and easy money. He was good at capturing his young souls for purification, but this was not a purification, this was revenge, revenge he knew nothing about. That's why this had all gone wrong now. He was hired to capture this boy and do whatever he wanted to him, but his instructions were to make sure the boy never returns home. He knew he couldn't very well just yank a

Sheriff's kid off the street and leave town. There would be surely be roadblocks so he was using the house on the bayou to let things calm down, then he would simply dispose of the boy later and then just drive right out of town and nobody would be the wiser.

When he found out he was in the same town as his brother and that his brother was now a cop in this tiny little town, he couldn't resist screwing with him a little. When he made that phone call to him, he was having so much fun messing with him, but he had gotten cut off and didn't want to risk calling back again so he let it go. He liked messing with Tom. He felt like Tom always thought he was better than all the other siblings and that he wasn't cut from the same cloth as they were. What he had to consider now was getting caught by his little brother. If those kids told anyone, he would have to head back to Ruleville and forget about Jessica and the boy. He wasn't worried about the boy other than the fact that he had already taken money from the guy at Parchman, and as far as he could tell, the guy at Parchman would probably not take too well to him breaking his contract. He wouldn't sue him, that was for certain, but he knew these types of people had a way of getting even and it never ended well for the person that violated the agreement.

Lucky for him, the boy had not really seen his face because he had kept his hat pulled way down over his brow when he tricked him into helping him with his puppy, but the girl had seen his face for sure. He needed to find her and put an end to her purification process. He really loved her, but she would not conceive no matter how many times he tried so it was probably better if he got rid of her and just waited until God gave him another assignment.

Chapter 42
Gun Shots

AUBREY PULLED UP TO THE OLD Murphy house in his personal vehicle because the police unit he normally drove had a dead battery and he was eager to get to his friend Elmer Davis. The Sheriff's department and the Webb Police department didn't always see eye to eye on how to do police work but there was no mistaking the fact that Aubrey Bigelow as the chief of police regarded Elmer Davis as his friend and would do anything in his power to help him.

Since the minute Aubrey received the call from Heather about Decker having been kidnapped, he had the Webb PD actively involved in door-to-door searches and had placed units at the edge of town in all directions leading into and out of Webb. Aubrey was a "by the book man" when it came to police work and that is where he and Elmer didn't always see eye-to-eye. He didn't think that Elmer was lawless in his approach to the way he handled police work, but Aubrey thought Elmer certainly skirted the edges on occasion, after all, he had nearly beaten Brett Buckles to death a few years back; but Aubrey understood his reasons. Aubrey didn't have any children of his own, but he knew that if someone beat up one of his kids the way that Brett had done to young Decker, he probably would have done the same thing.

Aubrey was surprised to see Donnie Buckles standing outside where he appeared to be guarding a very tall woman, he or someone else had placed in handcuffs. Aubrey turned the car off and shut off the lights. He popped the glove box open and pulled out a 45 caliber Taurus that he kept there for situations like this. From the exterior view of the Murphy home, things looked to be under control, but he was a cop, and he wasn't about to step out of the car unprepared.

He snapped the gun and holster into the belt of his trousers and made his way to the front door where Donnie looked a little ashen under the light of the porch and the tall lady looked a bit frightening because she had obviously been crying causing the makeup around her eyes to streak down her cheeks. "Hey Donnie, what in the world are you doing here and what's going on?" Donnie shook his head in a way that signaled to Aubrey that Donnie was a little confused about the situation, but he tried to offer some explanation. "The Sheriff is inside; he had a hunch that Decker might be here, but it didn't pan out." He paused for a second and motioned his eyes towards the tall lady and then back to Aubrey. "Elmer went in the home to check out that hunch and he found something else." Aubrey looked at the tall lady then back to Donnie and asked, "What did he find?" Donnie shifted his stance and Aubrey noticed the grimace on Donnie's face when he shifted, "What happened to you?" Donnie was about to tell him when the ambulance pulled up. Aubrey rolled his eyes, "Good God! What has Elmer done now?" As Aubrey was looking at the ambulance and made the comment, the Sheriff came out of the house with his arm around a little girl that Aubrey was not familiar with, the girl was wrapped in a blanket and she was barefooted. "Elmer what in the world is going on here?" He paused, looked at the ambulance that had its lights flashing, then back to Elmer and the little girl. "Aubrey this is Madelyn," Elmer looked down at Madelyn and from what Aubrey could see, the look that Elmer gave her was one of pure compassion with a strong hint of protective fatherly anger. Aubrey didn't know why he caught that look so well but it was a look that Dad's gave their kids when they needed to feel protected. Aubrey could tell that Elmer wasn't angry with the girl but something else had happened in that house that had Elmer at what Aubrey liked to call a "flash point". Elmer's blood would boil so hot with anger that he could tear a house down equipped with nothing more than his fists.

Elmer looked back up at Aubrey and said, "She's gonna need to go to the hospital and be examined." Elmer looked at Aubrey and let his eyes do the talking for him. It was remarkable to Aubrey that he could see in the Sheriff's eyes all he needed to know. Elmer was indicating that the little girl needed to be examined for rape. Aubrey shook his head that he agreed and decided it was best not to ask too many questions at the moment, but he sure had a ton of questions to ask for later. Mary Alice is on the way here with Lavera and I'd like them to go with you." Madelyn here can stay with Lavera so she can get a good night's rest and we'll start putting things right for her tomorrow. Just as Elmer was finishing his instructions to Aubrey, Mary Alice and Lavera pulled up.

Lavera was the first to reach the front door area where they were all standing. Without any instructions, Lavera walked straight up to Elmer and Madelyn and immediately took over the situation. She knew that Elmer wanted to get back to looking for Decker, but she knew that he would not leave this little girl until he felt she was safe. He had given her a little bit of information about what he thought was going on in the house while he was on the phone, but he had to speak in a somewhat adult "coded" language because Madelyn had taken to Elmer and was clutching his side the entire time he was on the phone in the house. He didn't want Madelyn to hear out loud that he thought she was being sexually abused in the house, Elmer knew that Madelyn knew it already and he didn't want her to have to relive anything out loud at the moment. In his mind, her healing process had to start with compassion, and it had to start right now, and he was trying to be as delicate with her as he could.

Lavera put her hand on Elmer's free arm in a loving way so that the little girl could see that Elmer trusted her, "Elmer, who is this wonderful little girl you have here?" Elmer smiled and looked down at Madelyn and she at the same time looked up at him but did not return the smile. "Lavera this is my friend Madelyn and I would like you to go to the hospital with Madelyn and make sure that she is ok. She has had a rough time this evening and she needs some much-needed rest." Madelyn looked up at Elmer and then to Lavera but she tightened her grip around the Sheriff's waist signaling that she didn't want to leave the big Sheriff.

Elmer exhaled, he was torn, he knew what this girl had probably been through and he also knew that because he was the one that had just ended her nightmare by crashing into her house and disrupting the course of events for her the way he had, she probably saw him as her protector and now she didn't want to leave him. On any other day he would stay with her as long as she needed, but not today, today he needed to find his son. Elmer kneeled and gently put his left hand under her chin and softly raised her head up so that she was now looking at him directly in the eye. Lavera could feel her heart about to beat out of her chest because the man that was so gently handling this little girl right now was the man, she knew his whole life. The murder of his wife followed by the drinking had taken that man away for a few years but at that moment, watching him show how gentle he could be, despite the fact that she knew he was raging inside, was the Elmer Davis she loved. "Honey, this is Mrs. Lavera, she practically raised me. She is the best woman in all of Webb, I promise you that she will die before she lets anyone hurt you again." Through the depths of her eyes, Elmer seemed to look right into this little girl's soul. "After I find my son tonight, we will come by and check on you," he looked up at Lavera and then back at Madelyn, "She is going to take you to see the doctor tonight so that we can make sure you are ok and then you are going to stay at her house." He started to raise up and let Lavera take her but he knelt back down so he could look her in the eye one more time, "I promise you; no one will ever hurt you again." Madelyn looked deep into Elmer's eyes as the tears began to stream down her cheeks. There was no sobbing, and she didn't even blink, Elmer thought it was if she had hardened herself so much to feeling pain that her body wouldn't give away any emotional signs but no matter how hard she tried, she couldn't shut her tear ducts off. Just as Elmer was about to stand up from his kneeling position, Madelyn through herself into the big Sheriff's arms and began to sob. At first, Elmer wasn't sure what to do, he looked around to see if anyone was going to grab her. He wasn't sure if she wanted him to embrace her, God only knew how she felt about a man touching her now, so he was careful with his actions. He remembered the conversation he had with Heather earlier in the day at the department store and how she hugged him so tightly and sobbed as apologized for not being a good father. He could feel the lump in his throat begin to bully its way up to his own tear ducts and he forced it back down. He slowly put his arms around her and the more be embraced her the tighter her arms clamped around his neck.

He rose from the kneeling position with Madelyn coming along as if she was a natural appendage, she never let go. Her feet came off the ground and just as a small child instinctively does, she wrapped her legs around the big Sheriff. Elmer knew at that moment that although she was a young teenager, young Madelyn wanted nothing more to be a child again. She wanted to get her youth back and Elmer was going to do the best he could to try and return what he could back to her. The road back for Madelyn would be tough but as he stood there with this young girl draped around him, he knew he needed to get going. His son needed him, and he was determined to find him.

Elmer started walking towards Mary Alice's car with Madelyn still draped around him, he looked down at Lavera and motioned his eyes towards the car. Lavera started walking with him. Mary Alice had pulled into the driveway behind Aubrey and the Scout. As they passed the Scout the CB radio cracked to life and both Elmer and Lavera heard Peggy's voice, "Come in Sheriff!" The voice was either excited or scared, it was hard to tell, "Come in Sheriff!" Elmer whispered in Madelyn's ear, I have to answer that, baby, I need you to go with Lavera, I promise she will take good care of you. He shuffled her out of his arms and let her feet gently touch the ground. He reluctantly let go of Elmer but as soon as Lavera touched her arm to help guide her to Mary Alice's car, she embraced Lavera the same way she held on to the big Sheriff only with Lavera, she was nearly as tall as Lavera. The two ladies slowly made their way to Mary Alice's car where Mary Alice was waiting, holding the rear driver side door open. Lavera let Madelyn slide in first and then she followed her into the back seat so that she could help keep her calm on the ride to the hospital. Before Mary Alice could get into the driver's seat, Elmer had already reached for the mic.

"Go ahead Peggy, I hear you." Elmer released the talk button so that he could hear Peggy. "Sheriff, we just had a couple weird calls, one about some stuff that has been going on in Parchman but the other came from Scottie Washburn out at Cassidy Bayou." Peggy paused just enough for the Sheriff to respond, "Don't give a shit about Parchman Peggy, and I don't have time for Scottie right now!" Peggy waited, she knew that when Elmer was angry, he was very difficult to talk to. "Sheriff, Scottie called to say he heard gun shots not too far from his place out there." There was a pause, Elmer took a minute to process Peggy's comments then he felt a little guilty, Peggy knew the gravity of the situation, she wasn't stupid by any stretch of the imagination so she was trying to tell him that she thought both calls might be relevant to Decker. "Sorry Peggy," he paused, and she didn't say anything, "People coon hunt out at the Bayou at night all the time, maybe it was a hunter?" Peggy wasted no time responding, "No sir, said he saw a white car slowly pass by his house at about the time he heard the gun shots." Even though it was dark outside, Elmer's ears turned red and he could feel himself becoming excited and nervous. "Got it! I am on my way!"

Elmer looked back toward the house, the man inside the house was now being loaded into the ambulance and Aubrey was putting the tall lady in the back of his car. "Aubrey! Come with me!" Aubrey looked up at the Sheriff then he looked back at the lady with the horrid makeup streaks on her face, "What do I do with her?" "Let Donnie take her; I need you now!" Aubrey looked back at Donnie who was still leaning against the wall watching them load the man into the ambulance. Donnie heard the Sheriff and was already looking at Aubrey. Aubrey reached into his pocket, fished out his car keys and tossed them to Donnie who caught them in the dark like he had some kind of night vision. Aubrey looked at Donnie and yelled, "Drop her off at the jail and then go have that ankle looked at, I can see the swelling from here." Donnie nodded and pushed himself away from the wall.

Aubrey made his way to the Scout where the Sheriff was already beginning to move the car out of the driveway. Since he had pulled in behind the Scout, Elmer was guiding the scout into yard so that he could go around Aubrey's car. Aubrey reached for the door handle, but the Scout continued to move, he had to jump back away from the Scout or the back wheel would have certainly run over his foot. "Damn it, Elmer! I can't get into the Damn truck if you don't stop!" Elmer stopped for a split second, just long enough for Aubrey to yank the door open and jump in. Elmer wasted no time once Aubrey was in the Scout, he pressed the accelerator to the floor and headed for the main road, never once getting back on the gravel driveway. They hit the ditch at the end of the property causing Aubrey to hit his head on the roof of the Scout. Aubrey felt the top of his head for any immediate knots that may have already risen but he didn't say anything. He knew Elmer Davis well and he knew that Elmer was on a mission. He also knew that his main purpose for being on this little trip was to try and keep Elmer from killing anyone should they find Decker. If someone has hurt Elmer Davis's boy, God help them if Elmer gets his hands on them. Aubrey knew he would not be able to stop him, Elmer was too big, he would have to shoot Elmer and at this moment with his head throbbing from hitting the roof of the Scout, he didn't think even a bullet would stop Elmer Davis.

Chapter 43
Missing: Badge & Gun

 HIS CHEST FELT LIKE SOMEONE had just hit him directly in the sternum with a sledgehammer. He could barely breathe as he blinked his eyes. He couldn't remember where he was or why he felt this way, but Tom knew he didn't care for the pain in his chest or the smell that was currently filling his nostrils. He looked up but the room was poorly lit, he tried to move his head but even that small motion sent flares of pain coursing through his entire body. He tried to take in a deep breath to help orientate to where he was and even that sent enough pain through his body that he couldn't tell whether his eyes were closed or open, but he could see those little squiggles you sometimes see when you close your eyes tight and focus on the darkness behind your eyes. The squiggles were dancing and floating everywhere he looked. He quickly learned to breathe shallow and slowly and that made the pain more tolerable.

He focused on the day and his actions to try and help him remember where he was and why he was lying in this dark smelly room and then it all started coming back to him. He remembered being shot and that was all he needed to remember about the day. He raised his hand to his chest and despite the pain he felt around for where the most pain seemed to be coming from. It was when his hand reached almost to the middle of his chest just above his right nipple that he found the source of the most pain he had felt in a long time. He looked around with quite a bit more focus in his eyes and saw the light coming from above. At first, he thought it was heaven coming for him and he was dead but then he realized it was light coming from the staircase leading to the kitchen.

He would have to get up and get out of this basement if he didn't want to die. He wasn't sure why after being shot, he wasn't already dead, but he was not about to lay here in this dark, dank basement and die. He thought about the man that had shot him and wondered if he was still in the house, then it occurred to him that basement was so dark that the shooter could actually be still in the basement with him. He tensed up for a second but then focused on getting up anyway. If the shooter was in the basement with him, he was wounded, he remembered stabbing him several times, so he was certainly hobbling if not dead. He would just have to take his chances on dealing with the shooter, but he was not going to lay here in the basement anymore. He rolled over on his side so he could get more leverage with his arms to push against the ground and help his get to his feet. The pain in his chest seemed to intensify with every movement but he forced down the pain that so desperately wanted to come screaming out of his mouth and slowly he made it to his feet. He reached around and found the wall with his hand and used it to help steady his balance long enough to get his legs under him.

He stood there with his hand against the wall looking up at the stairway that he would have to climb. He felt the location on his chest that seemed to hurt the most, but he couldn't feel any moisture. He was certain that had to be blood but maybe he had been out long enough for the bleeding to stop. He heard his thoughts and would have laughed out loud if he didn't think it would hurt too much. There was no way a bullet hole would just close on its own.

He used the wall to help him make it to the base of the stairway. He was already tired and didn't know if he could make it all the way to the top of the stairs, but he had to try. He took one step at a time and before long he was taking the last step into the kitchen. He paused at the top of the stairs to look around, maybe someone was in the house with him still, then he remembered the dead woman in the pantry. He took a step into the kitchen and looked around. The house was quiet except for the humming of a fan off in the distance. He opened the pantry door not sure of knowing what he might find that had changed in the last few minutes and nothing had changed, there was still a dead woman in the pantry. e He he

He made his way down the hallway to the find the bathroom, he needed to check out his gunshot wound and make sure he could carry on. He flipped on the light and was startled at what he saw, or more so what he didn't see. He was expecting to see a blood covered shirt, but he did not. His Tallahatchie County Sheriff's deputy badge was missing, it must have come off in the struggle in the basement. He unbuttoned his shirt to investigate further and when he had his shirt open, he slowly lifted his tee shirt and found no blood, only a gigantic bruise on his chest which as big around as a saucer plate. He touched it, and it hurt like hell, he was pretty sure one of his upper ribs were broken but that was it. He tried to re-live the scuffle in the basement, maybe he just imagined that the man had shot him? He wasn't sure if it would help but he took the small hand towel from the hook over the sink, doused part of it with some cold water, folded into a thick square and stuck it between his tee shirt and his chest. It was so tender and hurt so much that he wanted some padding between him and whatever he might bump into. A sudden stir of emotions came over him and he saw his vision getting blurry, his eyes were filling up with tears and he did his best to stop it. He was overjoyed that he was alive.

Even though it shot pain through his chest, he bent over just enough to wash his face in the sink. He needed to get a grip on reality and go find the man that probably murdered that woman who was staying quiet in the pantry and more importantly, the man who had shot a cop. The rule book says that anyone willing to shoot an armed peace officer is an even greater threat to an unarmed civilian. He buttoned his shirt back up and tucked it in his trousers the best he could. He felt really stupid without a badge and wearing an empty holster. He needed to get back to the big green squad car and retrieve the revolver he kept under the seat. He also needed to radio the Sheriff. The thought of letting the Sheriff know that not only did he not find his son, but he had also found a dead body in a pantry, he had been shot in the process and worse, he had been shot with his own gun. The conversation in his head was comical, "*Yeah Sheriff, this is Deputy Tom. Yeah, I found a dead body . . .Oh no sir it isn't your son, I don't know where the hell he is, and oh yeah, I got shot with my own gun, oh no sir, the killer is still out there. Just thought I'd let you know. Oh, how's the search for your kidnapped son going?*" Tom was certain he would be fired from this job as soon as he told the Sheriff his little tale of stupidity.

When Tom reached the squad car, he pulled the handle and realized it was locked, he reached into his pocket for the keys and came up empty. He closed his eyes and took a breath, his keys, his gun and his badge were all missing and now he was standing by the car, in the dark wondering what he was going to do. He looked up at the night sky and said, "*Lord, I am a nice guy, I try hard, I make mistakes like everyone else, but this is just too much, please help me.*" Tom wasn't much on religion and he certainly didn't spend much time praying but at this point he was desperate. He looked down at the ground, picked up the biggest rock he could find, fixed a grimace on his face to help him with the pain of what he was about to do and smashed the back-seat driver side window. The noise exploded in the night and surely reverberated all around Cassidy Bayou. He reached through the back window and pulled up on the lock knob for the front seat. He slowly eased into the driver seat and was relieved to see the keys dangling in the ignition.

Instead of thinking through what he was going to say he decided to just press the button on the mic and tell it all. He wasn't going to try to hide anything any longer. He was in pain and he needed to let the Sheriff know there was a dangerous man, possibly his own brother on the loose with his gun. If he got fired, he would simply move on as he had done with everything in his life. "Dispatch come in." He waited for a split second, started to call again but one of the voices came on, he couldn't tell if it was Peggy or Mary Alice, "Yes Tom," she never called him by his name, she always called him number two, he didn't bother trying to figure out which one he was talking to: "Patch me through to the Sheriff."

Tom was about to request to be patched through to the Sheriff again when he spotted the taillights far off in the distance, close to the main road leading back to Webb. He felt like it was too late for anyone to be out driving now, it had to be the white car, it had to be James. He started the car but before he put it in drive, he reached under the seat and retrieved his extra gun. A nice .38 revolver, not very accurate at long distances but up close it would do the trick. Then he heard the gun shots, instinctively he put the car in drive, flipped on the flashers and slammed on the accelerator, the green beast did not hesitate in the least little bit, it may have been the ugliest car he had ever driven but he never once questioned its power. The beast spun gravel, peppering the trees on the other side of the street and nearly went sideways into the ditch but he managed to correct the slide but let out a slow but very audible grunt. The motion of turning the wheel so hard in the opposite direction sent vibrations of pain from his chest to his brain. Tom grabbed the mic to the police radio and pressed the button, "Dispatch, let the Sheriff know I am immediately responding to gun shots on Cassidy Bayou, suspect is in a white sedan possibly registered to a Mrs. Bobbi Blanton from Ruleville, Mississippi. That's Bobbi with an 'I'."

Chapter 44
One Shoe Down

DECKER STOPPED FOR A MINUTE and put Jessica back down on her feet. She had been awake, but she was rambling on about hunting and fog and being so tired and she talked to her dad a lot. He had no idea what was wrong with her, but he knew she needed more help than he could give her. Up until they made their escape from the house she had been fine as far as he could tell but once they started running it was if she was drunk or something. It reminded him of when Heather went to the dentist and got her wisdom teeth pulled, she came home, and Decker couldn't understand a word she said. She was mumbling and she could barely hold up her head. She slept a lot that day and when she woke up, she was her normal self again. Decker figured that maybe Jessica was so tired now that she just needed to sleep.

He held her up as he slowly eased her to the ground. She would have fallen if he hadn't kept his arm firmly around her waist. He didn't know how far they had gone but he knew they had a long way to go. He also knew that he would probably be all the way to the main highway leading back to Webb if he were alone. He was an incredibly fast runner, and he could keep running for as long as he wanted to without ever really getting tired. He still wasn't faster than Jeannine though. Through all of this he had almost forgotten about her and was now wishing she were here with him but that would mean that she would be in trouble too and he would never want her to be in trouble. He thought about her kissing him and how much it caught him by surprise. He hadn't even thought about kissing her, he held her hand everywhere they went until she would make him stop because his palms would get sweaty and she would tell him to dry them off on his pants and then he could hold her hand again. The kiss seemed like years ago to him, because of what had happened everything seemed so long ago. He had to admit, the kiss was nice though, he wished he hadn't tripped and fell so he could maybe do a better job of kissing her back. He felt like a goober at that moment and desperately wanted a "do over".

Decker caught a glimpse of the headlights far off in the distance. He and Jessica were far enough off the road that there was no way they could be seen, especially if he kept a tree between them and road but he worried that the headlights might be his dad. "Jessica?" She mumbled something but Decker couldn't tell what she said but at least she was awake, "There is someone coming up the road, I need to get a little closer to see who it is." Jessica mumbled again but again Decker didn't understand her. He thought she said something about deer hunting again. It seemed like every time she got confused about anything, she resorted back to deer hunting. "He sat he down as easily as he could, even though she was pretty light, he had either been holding her up or outright carrying her for quite some time now. He put his hands on her shoulders and gently propped her back up against the tree, "Stay here okay, I will be back in just a bit." He wasn't sure if she understood him, so he repeated himself several times. As he let go of her and started to turn, she grabbed him by the neck and started screaming. There was no mistaking what she was saying this time, "DON'T LEAVE ME!" Her sobs were uncontrollable as she continued, "THE SHADOW BEAST!" Decker quickly grabbed her back and pulled her tightly, "Suschhhhhhh!" he tried to whisper but he knew he was coming out too loud. If he couldn't get her to calm down, they would be in trouble if the car coming wasn't his dad. If it were the bad man in the house, he would surely hear her screaming. "Please Jessica!" He looked around to see where the headlights were and he nearly stopped breathing when he realized that the headlights to the car were pointed right at them and just as that realization struck him like a bolt of lightning, he heard the gunshots. This was definitely not his dad.

There was one shot, then there were three more quick shots. Decker pushed Jessica flat on the ground as he heard thuds and what sounded like tree branches falling near them. Decker wasn't a stranger to gun shots; he had been hunting with his dad every year since he was old enough to hold a gun. He had never been shot at though and this sure seemed like the bullets were aimed at him. He kept he and Jessica behind the tree. There was no way he could go left or right because he would have to move so slow that they would be an easy target. His heart was racing, no matter how hard he tried he couldn't make his legs move although he wanted them to move fast. He needed to move further back from the road while keeping the tree between them and whoever was shooting at them. He remembered being scared when he had to face Brett Buckles to defend Jeannine, but this was like nothing he had ever experienced. If he made the wrong move, he could be dead or Jessica could be dead, or they both could be dead, plus when he faced Brett Buckles, he was very fortunate to have had help from Donnie Ray Richardson. He wished Donnie Ray were here now, but then he felt guilty because he was in a bad spot and he would never want to put his hero in a bad spot with him. Donnie had been hurt really bad by helping Decker and Jeannine that day but luckily, he recovered really well and was in his last year of college.

Jessica was clinging to Decker so tightly that he could barely move, he was trying to wiggle free so he could get a better sense of how to move away from the road when he heard the voice. It was a cross between a whisper and a shout, it came out very gruff, but it was very clear. "Come on kids, I won't hurt you, come on out so we can get out of this swamp now." Decker didn't move and the grip that Jessica had on him became even tighter. Decker whispered in her ear to be very quiet. She was pressed so tightly against him that he could tell that she was trying not to sob, and it caused her body to shake a little as she forced down the tears. To his relief, she wasn't making a sound. The voice came again, Decker couldn't tell if it were getting closer, but he could hear the each step the man took. A branch or twig would break under his feet as he approached them. "Look kids, there are snakes and spiders out here in these swamps." He paused and Decker heard some more twigs and leaves crackle under the man's feet, "Maybe even a gator or two out here." The man took another step then stopped, "You know what those gators do to you right?" Decker had never even heard of an alligator in these parts. "They drag you under water, drown you and then stuff you under a log so you can get you nice and tender and then they come back with their babies and chew you up for dinner." He laughed as he was saying it. From the sound of his laughter, Decker figured he was about 30 yards away, but it also sounded like the man didn't know exactly where he and Jessica were. He looked around for a rock and couldn't find one. The bayou didn't have many rocks, it had pebbles but nothing he could throw and fight back with. Decker had no illusions that he could fight a gun with a rock, but he did know that that he needed to do something, or they would be found for sure.

As Decker was looking down, he looked at his feet. He untied his shoe and slowly removed it. He listened carefully for any noise the man was making and felt like he had a good idea of where he was, he looked towards the direction of the house that he and Jessica had fled from and threw his shoe as far as he could throw it. The shoe landed with a few thuds as it banged off a tree and rolled a little further. Decker was happy with the distance he got from the throw, but he was happier that the noise had its intended affect. The man took several quick steps towards the noise which gave Decker time to grab Jessica, hoist her over his shoulder like he was carrying her from a burning building, and he took off. It was dark but he had to move quickly. He gritted his teeth and grimaced as each step he took hurt his foot that was now only protected by a sock. He was making quite a bit of noise as he stumbled through the night with a mumbling girl tossed over his shoulder when he heard another gun shot. He read that in civil war during the volley exchange of battle, soldiers could hear the whistle of the bullets as they whizzed by their heads and he was certain he had just heard the same thing they heard. It scared him and fell to the ground again. He tried not to let Jessica land too hard, but he needed to get them away from those whizzing bullets and the ground seemed to be the safest place for that. He guessed he had put another 30 yards between him and the man with the big forearms which meant that he was over a half a football field away from them. The further the better.

"Come out you little shit! I have had enough of this!" Decker could hear his voice, but it was further away. The man continued to scream, "Jessica baby! Come back to Daddy!" It sounded to Decker like the man was about to cry now. "Baby! You know I love you! God loves you! He needs us to be together!" Every time he yelled; Jessica sank her finger nails into whatever part of Decker Davis she happened to be clinging to. At this moment, she dug her nails into his forearm and his neck. He didn't scream, but he wanted to. He was certain she would draw blood soon if she didn't let go of him. Decker was about to tell her that she was hurting him when he saw the headlights of another car coming up the road at a high rate of speed, then he saw the flashing lights of a police car. Decker forgot that Jessica was ripping his forearm and neck to shreds. He quickly scrambled to his feet and surprisingly as he was scrambling to get up, Jessica let him go without a fuss. It was if she sensed his quick change of mood. If someone had shined a light on his face at the moment, they would see him smiling, his dad had found him. They were going to be alright, he thought. He looked around to see if he could see the man with the big forearms, but he could not. He could hear the gravel crunching under the wheels of the approaching police car. He tried to focus on the flashing lights so he could alert his dad of his location just as soon as it was safe to do so but he didn't want to lose sight of where the man with the gun was.

He looked in all directions hoping to catch a glimpse or a movement, anything to help him decide his next move but he didn't see anything. The man had to have seen the lights flashing in the distance just as Decker had, so Decker thought maybe he ran away but then his car headlights were still visible in the distance so he knew he hadn't left. Decker decided it was time to move again and hopefully put some more distance between them and the man. He reached back to grab Jessica so she could once again pick her up and carry her further away. The thought crossed his mind to just make a dash for the road and the oncoming flashing lights, he was certain that he could get there fast enough to avoid getting shot and that if he could get to the road, he would let his Dad know where Jessica was. As much as he wanted to run without her, he couldn't. Decker wasn't made that way, Decker stuck by his friends even when it wasn't fun to do so; and it seemed to him that Jessica needed a friend more than anyone he'd ever met. He was about to grab her and dash further back into the woods when he heard the siren. He had heard that sound all his life because when he was little, his daddy used to let him turn the siren on. The Scout siren was different than the one on the green beast, it made a higher pitch sound that Decker found fascinating. Now that he was much older, he didn't play with it anymore other than to show Jeannine how loud it was one time. She immediately hated it and covered her ears, so he turned it off. Right there, looking at Jessica in the dark, hiding behind a tree, running from a man that was trying to hurt them, he knew his dad had arrived. The emotion of all of it hit him so hard that he began to cry. He felt the tears roll down his face and was grateful that Jessica couldn't see him in the dark. Hurry up Dad, is all he could think.

He heard the cracking sound of a branch very close to him and he reached over, put his hand over Jessica's mouth and gave her the SHUSH sign by placing his index finger over his lips. Even in the dark he could see her eyes were wide and she was scared, so was he. Luckily, he had picked a good spot to hide, they were right smack in the middle of three trees that it made a natural fort, there was only one way in and one way out. He heard more crackling leaves, he stayed perfectly still. He looked in as many directions as he could without actually moving or making a sound, but he didn't see anything. It was simply too dark.

He was staring directly into Jessica's eyes when he heard the booming voice of his dad. His eyes opened as wide as they ever had been, he could tell that Jessica was very wide eyed now. Hearing his father's voice had given them both a burst of energy that they needed. Decker started to answer but he realized as he was about to yell back that his voice would surely alert the bad man as to their location. Somehow, he had to alert his dad his location without tipping off the man chasing them. He wished he knew where the man was, it would be helpful for him in knowing what to do next. He heard his Dad's voice again and it was so hard not to answer him. He looked at Jessica and slowly pointed at her then pointed to the ground where they were. He made the praying hands symbol and placed his hands against his face and tilted his head sideways indicating that he wanted her to lay down where they were. He then pointed to himself and then pointed off in the distance and turned his hand into a sock puppet without the sock. He was trying to tell her without words that he wanted her to stay put, lay flat and he was going to dash off in a different area so that he could yell back at his dad without risking both of them getting caught or shot. He just needed to put some distance from he and Jessica and if he could do that, he would scream bloody murder for his dad. He was too close to being back with his family to sit here in silence anymore. Jessica looked confused and he couldn't blame her. His attempt at silent hand communication was lousy and he knew it. He grabbed her arm and slowly tugged it towards the ground which thankfully she didn't resist. He softly patted the ground and at that moment she understood to lay down. He was relieved that she was now in a fetal position on the ground. He once again gave her the SHUSH sign and he started to move.

Chapter 45
The North Star

PEGGY HEARD TOM LOUD AND CLEAR over the police radio and she froze. She remembered the reports they received earlier in the night about all the stolen cars in the state and they all had assumed that Bobby Blanton was a man, not a woman. She cringed at the thought of having missed a sign that was in front of them all but didn't recognize it, then it hit her, there was no way for Tom to figure that out from where he was. He had no access to that information so how in the world did he know that Bobbi was spelled with an 'I' and not a 'Y'. "Copy that Tom, I am relaying to the Sheriff." She immediately switched the channel to the Sheriff's radio, "Sheriff, come in Sheriff." He didn't respond but Aubrey did. "Go Peggy, the Sheriff is concentrating on driving, but he can hear you." Peggy immediately replied, "Aubrey, that white sedan that was reported stolen in Ruleville was a woman not a man. Tom is responding to gunshots and he wanted you to know." Aubrey looked at Elmer who had his eyes on the road and if he could have, he would have pressed his foot through the floorboard trying to get the truck to go faster. Aubrey hung on to anything he could find as he tried to respond to Peggy, "Copy that Peggy, ETA, 2 minutes." Aubrey threw the mic on the dashboard where it promptly fell to the floor. "Won't do any good to kill us trying to get there faster Elmer." Elmer didn't say anything, he kept his eyes on the road. They were about to make the turn on to Cassidy Bayou Road and Aubrey could see that Elmer showed no signs of slowing down enough to make the turn safely. Aubrey was certain they were going to turn too hard which might cause the Scout to flip.

Aubrey was silently impressed that Elmer navigated the turn without rolling the Scout, but he was certain that they had made the turn with just two wheels on the ground. "Hit the lights Aubrey," Elmer said as calm as he could possibly have said it. Aubrey was familiar with the Scout, so he knew where the toggle switch for the flashing lights were and he quickly flipped into the on position. After he had done that Elmer said, "Now hit the sound, let my boy know I am coming." Aubrey flipped the toggle switch for the siren and the sound came to life quickly. "Elmer, we don't even know if this has anything to do with Decker, don't get your hopes up." Elmer didn't respond although he wanted to. In fact, he wanted to backhand Aubrey for even saying such a thing, but he didn't. Webb was not a town that saw activity like this, it was a peaceful God-fearing town and for his son to be kidnapped, and his deputy now responding to gunshots was just too coincidental for Elmer. He knew Decker was close and he intended to find him, alive.

When Elmer made the turn on to Cassidy Bayou Road, he immediately saw the flashing lights of the Green beast far off in the distance. From where they were, it looked to Elmer that they were at least a mile and half away from Tom and it appeared that Tom was also moving. He pressed harder on the accelerator, but it was already pressed nearly flat against the floorboard. He could feel his hands throb as he was squeezing the steering wheel. His whole body was as tense as it had ever been. He thought of Decker and the first time he held him in the hospital, the nurse handed him to him, and he choked up more than he ever thought he would. He always wanted a son and now he had one. Decker was quiet, he didn't make a sound, he just stared up at his daddy looking directly into his eyes. Elmer could remember the tears rolling down his cheeks as the moment struck him hard. He pulled that little boy close to his chest and he cried. He couldn't believe that he was holding his son. He also thought about the past few years and how he had neglected Decker and Heather. He felt like he had sort of made it right with Heather earlier in the day, but he hadn't had time to make it right with Decker yet. He intended to have a serious conversation with him that night about his neglect and apologize for his behavior, but it hadn't happened. He was determined to hug his son and tell him how much he loved him and how proud he was of him.

"You got your gun?" Elmer spoke to Aubrey without turning his head, he was completely focused on the road ahead, "Yep, why?" Elmer couldn't believe Aubrey just asked a dumb question like that. They were headed to a location where there have been reports of gunshots and he wants to know why? "How in the hell did you ever become Chief of Police asking stupid damn questions like that?" Aubrey didn't respond right away but he eventually said, "I will take into account your son is missing and your heightened emotional state leads you to irrational and irresponsible thoughts and conclusions." Elmer didn't respond, he didn't have time, by the time Aubrey made his stupid comment, they were right on the green beast.

Both cars reached the white sedan that was parked so that its headlights were pointed out into the woods adjacent to houses on the other side of the street. Tom pulled around to the north side of the car and blocked the road and Elmer blocked off the South side of the road. There was no escape for the car or its driver. Elmer jumped from the Scout, inspected his gun and took a step off in the direction where the headlights were pointed but he turned back to the Scout and grabbed a flashlight from the back-cargo bay. "Aubrey, stay right here with the cars, I don't want anyone circling back behind me and getting away."

Tom walked up to the Sheriff with his hand on his chest and to Elmer, it looked like he was limping a little. "What the hell happened to you?" Tom shook his head as if he really didn't know, although he did, it was just too long of a story to recite right now and the Sheriff didn't look like he was asking for small talk reasons. "I will be fine." Tom looked at the white car and then out to the woods, "He hasn't been here long, that much I know for sure; I haven't seen Decker though. Just heard the gun shots and came as fast as I could." Elmer looked out in the woods, "Decker!" he yelled at the top of his voice, "Decker!" he did it again but there was no reply.

Elmer started walking towards the woods when he heard what sounded like a firecracker going off, he knew what it was. Tom drew his weapon and crouched down. Elmer never moved but gave Tom a harsh look followed by saying: "Do not pull that weapon until we know where Decker is!" He paused for a second and yelled, "There is no way out of here! Give me my son and I will ask the judge to go easy on you!" There was complete silence, "It's the best deal you are gonna get today." He didn't yell that, but it came out stern enough to be heard all the way back in Webb. Just as he was about to tell Tom to circle wide and try and flank what they believed the location to be, he heard Decker. Decker was clearly running but he wasn't running toward his father, it sounded as if he was running away. "Daddy!" There was rustling sounds and then: "He's out here somewhere!" Elmer was so excited he immediately started running toward the sound of Decker's voice. "I'm coming son! Hang on!"

At this point, Elmer didn't care what Tom did, Elmer didn't care if someone pointed and shot a bazooka at him, Elmer only cared about getting to his son. He started running as fast as the darkness and the trees would allow him. He didn't want to turn on his flashlight and make himself an easy target, so he just decided to trust his night vision and the head lights of the white sedan that was pointed in the direction of where he needed to go.

Tom trailed behind him but each step he took felt like he was being hit in the chest with a hammer so he couldn't keep up. He slowed his pace to something that was less stressful on his chest. He still hadn't understood how he heard the gun go off, felt the pain in his chest and was still alive. He was determined to find the answer as soon as he found his brother. Since he hadn't really seen the shooter in basement, he still held out hope that it was not his brother but deep down, he knew it. He knew that somehow James had slid into a world of crime that he had taken an oath to stop and an oath to protect the citizens of Tallahatchie County. If that meant that he would have to arrest his brother, then so be it, but it also hoped that he wouldn't have to kill him. Putting a sibling in jail was one thing, but killing one is another. If he put his brother in jail, he could always hope that he would be rehabilitated and become a better person even if he was locked up, but if he killed him, there was no rehabilitation, he would be gone forever.

Tom watched the big Sheriff plow through the darkness in search of his son. He had really only known the Sheriff as sort of a functioning drunk and since his arrival in Webb he hadn't seen the man that everyone talked about, the man that was kind but fierce, loving and hard. He had heard the stories of the fights the Sheriff had broken up over his time as Sheriff, the money that he would quietly give to someone that was having a hard time. He heard that he once took meals to Charlie B's home every day for an entire year after Charlie B nearly broke his neck falling off the roof of his house when he was trying to fix a leak. He hadn't broken his neck, but he broke both his arms and his back. Charlie B couldn't even lift a fork to his mouth for nearly a year, so the Sheriff did it for him. No, he had never met that man. The man he met appeared to be more concerned about his next drink than anything. Tom knew it was a sad story as to how he lost his wife, and he knew that Elmer was nearly broken by the event, but he couldn't excuse the lack of effort the Sheriff put into his job. The talk around town was that the Sheriff was not going to be re-elected this time and that perhaps the town had had enough of his drinking and lack of engagement. Webb was a peaceful town, but it wouldn't stay that way if the Sheriff didn't do his job.

Tom was watching carefully where he stepped as he tried to keep up with the Sheriff. He had his head down when he heard another gun shot. Both he and the Sheriff instinctively crouched down at the sound. He reached for his gun but only put his hand on it, he was not about to shoot into the darkness and accidently hit the Sheriff's boy. He could see that the Sheriff had done almost the exact same thing, Elmer had his hand on his gun but had not pulled it from its holster. He then heard the Sheriff, "Tom! Take two deputies and swing West!" The Sheriff's voice was as big as he was, but Tom was caught off guard by the two deputies' comment, Tom didn't have two deputies, hell as far he knew he was the only deputy in the county. The Sheriff barked another order, "Bubba! You take two of Aubrey's and swing towards the East!" He continued, I am headed straight ahead, you all have orders to shoot this son-of-a-bitch without question!" Tom realized that the Sheriff was making things up to give the impression that there were more men than they had, and they would surround the kidnapper. He was also letting the kidnapper know that after that last gun shot, the Sheriff was done negotiating.

Decker also heard his father barking orders. He knew that there was only one deputy and he also knew that Bubba had been killed in the line of duty four years ago. Decker looked up into the night sky, he quickly found the big dipper, he knew from what his Dad had taught him when they were out camping was that if he had a good clear night sky, he could find the big dipper and it would tell him where the North Star was. His Dad told him that the big dipper always pointed directly at the north star. If he could find North star, he could find East because something told him that based off what his dad had just yelled, he wouldn't go directly at them, he would come at them from the East. He didn't know why but something told him his dad was sending him a message. He had to go East and maybe if they both went East, they could find each other in the dark.

After Decker located the Big Dipper and subsequently the north star, he figured out which way was East. He was scared to move, what if he got up and ran East and ran right into the man he was trying to get away from? What if his Dad really was coming straight at them and if he went East, he would miss him? What if what he did caused someone to get hurt? So many thoughts went through his head. He took a deep breath, took one last look up in the sky and ran towards East. It was if there was a clear path for him to take, the path opened, and he ran.

Elmer made his left flank move to the East, he wanted to get out of the line of car head lights and possibly use the car lights to spot the man they were looking for. He heard Decker's voice and he could feel his heart beating. This thing felt like he was in an hourglass and the sand was filling the compartment he was stuck in. He had to get Decker back in order to get the sand to stop and to turn the hourglass over. He heard the noise of the bayou, the crickets, and the unidentifiable noises of the night. He felt the sweat running down his forehead and his mouth was dry, the gravity of the moment was extremely heavy for him. He simply could not let Decker be harmed.

He hoped that Decker understood what he needed to do if he could possibly get away from whoever this was. He was certain that Decker was on the run or the guy would not have stopped his car in the middle of the night. Decker had to be the reason he stopped, pointed his headlights in such a way and took then off out into these woods. He also knew that Decker was the reason they were hearing the gun shots. Decker would never quit fighting, that much he knew. His son was as mentally and physically tough as he had ever seen. Decker had the type of grit that kept him going when most others would quit. He was so proud of his son for the way he handled life, the way he overcame challenges, the way he saw people for who they were, not what color they were. He wished his mother could see him now, she would be so proud.

Tom did as he was told and made a flanking move to the west. He looked back at the cars parked in the road with the lights flashing one more time and then towards the dark woods that contained his brother, a brother that had just shot him. He held out the hope that maybe, in that basement, James had no idea it was his brother that he had tried to kill. The emotion of the situation nearly overcame him. Even though the two brothers had grown apart and hadn't spoken in many years, he still loved his brother. He remembered the playful times they enjoyed as boys and how they would spend the whole day during the summers together, exploring everything they could explore.

"James! James Porter!" Tom yelled it with some authority, but he also tried to sound like a brother if that was possible. "Stop this now James!" The woods became quiet after Tom spoke. Tom let the words sink into everyone and he wondered if they had all put two and two together now and realized that they were chasing Deputy Tom Porters brother. "James! There is no way out of here!" He paused and looked around the area in hopes of hearing a voice come from somewhere out there in the woods or footsteps of James coming out in the open, "This shit has to stop now James!" He let the words bounce off the trees but still, there was no reply. He continued to move westward as he had been instructed but he never stopped talking. "You asked me a question that I never answered," he really didn't want to bring out the family history and the dirty laundry it contained in front of the Sheriff, but he had to figure a way to get James out in the open. "The answer is yes!" He stopped for a second, he knew what he needed to do, James was always hot tempered, he couldn't handle being picked on in the least little bit, "Yeah I still see her face, in my sleep, while I'm driving, when I am eating, I see her face every day, every minute and every hour," he stopped to listen, "But not the face you think I see, I see the one that loved me, the one that took care of me, the one that fed me and made sure I had everything I needed," he stopped moving for a second to see if he could hear any movement, "I was her favorite James, she loved me," he made a subtle little chuckle surface that he wasn't sure anyone would actually hear, "You made her do it James, you're the reason she chose death, not me."

Tom stopped walking and just listened, he started to take another step, but a voice broke the night silence. "You are wrong!" Tom froze, he tried to get a directional sense of where the voice was coming from, but he couldn't, he stayed perfectly clear but decided to crouch down just in case James shot at him again. He struggled with the emotion of knowing his own brother was capable of kidnapping a child and capable of shooting his own brother, but he still wasn't convinced that James even knew it was him in the basement that he had shot. "She chose a bullet through the head rather than deal with you one more day!" He paused to let that sink in, hoping that James would reveal himself and he got his wish, "You lie! You always lied! You're a liar today!" The rustle of the leaves and branches cracking was evident to Tom. He put his hand on his pistol and stood straight up, he was not going to crouch anymore, if his brother killed him today it would be while he was standing and not crouching. Tom wanted to put a stop to all of this without killing his brother, despite what he had done, he still loved him, however, Tom had no idea that besides the Sheriff's boy, there was another child out in these woods that had been held captive and abused by his own flesh and blood.

Chapter 46

I got you

DECKER HEARD THE HEAVY FOOTSTEPS approaching as he was moving in an easterly direction; he stopped and crouched, he couldn't be sure who it was, but he sure hoped it was his dad. He knew things were about to happen, he didn't know if they were good or bad, but he knew that things were going to change. He tried to process all of the decisions he had made up to this point, he thought he had done the right things, except being suckered into getting kidnapped, but other than that, he thought he had done what his father would have done.

As he listened intently to every sound around him, he thought of Jeannine and how much he loved her. He had trouble admitting that out loud because it just seemed mushy to him and he had only told her once that he could remember. On the other hand, she would tell him she loved him all the time. He would smile and get red in the face when she would say it in front of other kids in school but that was one of the things that he liked most about Jeannine, she never seemed to care what anyone else thought and she wasn't afraid to say what she thought. But more than anything, he knew deep down in his heart that she made him a better person and he couldn't imagine a life without her. He wasn't completely sure, but he thought she felt the same way about him. It had been four years since she made the teacher move his desk next to hers at the front of the class, four years since he actually punched another kid in the face to protect her and every day since then, they were inseparable, except when she went to her honors classes and he went to his regular classes. He loved that she was so smart because she always helped him study. His struggles with reading continued but because of her, they were tolerable, and he had become a pretty dang good student.

Jeannine was so much like him in the fact that she never saw colors. She had white friends and black friends. In fact, she was friends with everyone, and it seemed they were friends right back to her. Decker was still not very open with people, but he was getting better. He was very guarded. He always thought it was strange how four years ago he had no friends, he was clumsy and reclusive but as he got older, bigger and stronger, he didn't get picked on as much and he had more people wanting to be his friend, at least they pretended to be his friend.

He thought about his sister Heather and how she was his best friend in the world and at that moment he missed her more than he ever thought he would miss his sister. She listened to him when he was hurting, and she held him closely when she detected that he needed to be held. He was bigger than her now, but he had not outgrown the need to be hugged. As he listened to the thud of the feet hitting the ground and the way it crackled, it sounded like they were coming right at him. He paused his thoughts of everyone that was special to him in his life, including his mother and concentrated on being able to see in the dark.

He could see an outline of a person and to his delight he could tell that the footsteps coming at him belonged to a very large person. He told himself that what he was seeing was his dad, but he had to fight off the excitement because what if the man with the giant forearms had a friend that could be helping him. He looked around the ground for something to use as a weapon in case it turned out to be someone bad, but he didn't find anything. He squinted his eyes in the dark to try and make out the figure that was coming at him but couldn't keep a straight line because they were weaving their way through trees.

Decker couldn't contain his voice any longer, he just knew that it was his dad, there could be no other person that would be charging through the Bayou like this man was. "Daddy!" The rustling and footsteps stopped for a second and then came the pop. It was loud, Decker knew exactly what it was, a gunshot. Then he heard the greatest thing he had ever heard in his life, his dad's voice. A voice that was as clear and booming as anything he had ever heard. He tried to stop it, but he couldn't, he had been strong long enough, he needed his dad. He began to cry, he wished he could stop but he couldn't. The tears began flow and he could feel his chest heave with every sob. "Decker stay down! I got you son!" Decker did as he was told although the shots continued to ring out. There were several, so many that he lost count.

He curled up beneath the tree that provided him with shelter from the bullets. He thought that he heard bullets hitting the tree, but he couldn't be sure. He felt an arm cover him and grab him. His first thought was that the man with the giant arms had found him but the voice he heard next made him sob even more. It was only a whisper, but he knew his dad had found him, just like he always believed. "I got you, baby." He felt the arm grip him tightly, but he kept his eyes closed. He was still sobbing, sobbing so much that he couldn't answer his dad. "Are you hurt son? Did he hurt you?" Decker continued to sob but this time he raised up just enough to dive into the chest of the man that he loved, he circled his arms around his father as tight as he could, buried his head in his father's chest and heaved. He felt his dad squeeze him so tightly that he thought he might lose his air but at this point he didn't care. He finally slowed his sobbing down enough to say: "No sir".

Decker had never felt relief like that. It was if all his strength left him the minute his dad embraced him. His muscles went so lymph that he was afraid he may have pee'd and not even knew he was peeing. Then he remembered her, Jessica, the one he had been trying to protect all night. His strength came back momentarily, he scrambled to let go of his dad, he fought the tears and pushed the sobbing back down into his stomach as best he could, but it didn't go all the way down, "Daddy! You gotta hep Jes, she.. she.." He was getting mad at himself because he couldn't complete a sentence without the sobs interrupting what he was trying to say. "See she . . . she . . .out . . .curled . . . up!" He felt his Dad loosen his grip just a little but not much.

Elmer could feel whatever strength his son was using to get through this ordeal leave his body. He hadn't seen Decker cry in a very long time, perhaps since he was a toddler even. He had no idea what this asshole had done to his son, but it was expected that a 14-year-old boy would cry after being abducted. Elmer felt his own tears well up in his eyes, but he fought them back. Now was not the time he thought, there was a man shooting at them somewhere out in these woods and he intended to make him pay for whatever he had done to his son. He felt Decker loosen his grip on him and then struggle to speak. The words were masked by his sobs, but he was definitely trying to tell him something. "It's okay baby, I got you." He tried to squeeze his son tighter, but Decker fought that off and continued to whisper as loudly as he could, "It's Jessica Daddy! She is with me. She is out there!" He felt another wave of sobs coming up so he rushed through the words as fast as he could, "She's out there, don't let him hurt her anymore!" Elmer heard that part loud and clear and he thought, what in good Christ is going on here? He felt the emotions of his breaking heart for his son turn to rage now. There were more people involved and a little girl too. There was no hesitation in his voice when he screamed for everyone in the woods to hear, "Jessica! This is Sheriff Elmer Davis, stay right where you are!" He let the words hand in the air for a second, "don't answer me and don't say another word until you hear me say, THE-SON-OF-A-BITCH-IS-DEAD!" He felt

Decker's grip tighten on him as he continued, "Listen to my voice Jessica, understand me and recognize my voice!"

The Sheriff's booming voice echoed off every tree in the bayou. Tom thought he had just heard thunder turn into words. Tom tensed up at the way it came out. This was definitely the Sheriff he had been warned about. This Sheriff was a very violent man. The voice he just heard had no soul, it didn't even sound human, it was a voice that climbed out from some deep dark crevice, only to be summoned when the situation called for complete destruction. He looked down at the gun in his hand then back out into the darkness of the bayou. "James! Give up, please!" The emotion in his voice was one of a brother, not a law man. "James please make this easy! I promise I will get you some help! This is not the way man!" He looked back down at the gun in his hand and was about to look back up when he heard the hammer cock on a gun that sounded very close to him. He looked up to his right just in time to see his brother James pointing a gun right at him, pointing HIS gun right at him. "You were never as good as you thought you were Thomas." James took a step towards Tom who was still in the crouched position. "You always thought you were better than us, better than the whole stinkin' backwards ass country folks, right Tom?" Tom started to answer but James hit him across the forehead with the barrel of HIS gun. It hurt like hell and Tom saw stars for a second, but he managed to let one already crouched knee drop to the ground to keep him from falling over. "Drop that gun on the ground little brother." Tom had just heard a voice from the Sheriff that he was not familiar with and now he heard a voice from his brother that he was not familiar with. His brother sounded evil, hollow, and somewhat scary. "You know I can't do that James" he lifted his left empty hand to his forehead to see if he could feel any blood and as he suspected, he did. "You already got one of my guns, losing two in one-night ain't gonna happen. You're just gonna have to kill me."

Tom waited on the gun shot but it didn't happen. "Pull the trigger, from my count that clip is about empty. Hell, there may not be any bullets left in it." Tom made himself chuckle, "I have another clip in the car, you can just run on over there and get it but you better hurry your ass up," he grunted as he touched the bump now rising on his forehead, "Because the Sheriff intends to kill you, not arrest you." He didn't quite look up at James, but he could tell that James was thinking things over. "The Sheriff doesn't exactly follow the law in cases like these." Tom grunted again as he continued to rub his forehead but he wanted to keep James talking so the Sheriff could maybe figure out where they were, "From what I understand, Elmer Davis is the kind of man that will inflict as much pain as possible on anyone that riles him like you have and now that he has found out you kidnapped his little boy and now a girl . . . well I would imagine you'll beg him to kill you before he is finished with you." Tom looked at James shoes that had taken a step closer to him, "Never figured you for a pervert James, maybe a crazy killer but sure not a pervert, when did you get the taste for little girls and boys?" He felt the barrel of the gun press against the top of his head now. "Shut up you holier than thou little shit!" James couldn't see him, but Tom was smiling now, Tom knew he was getting to his older brother and just like the days of past, if you could get under his skin he would explode which would cause him to lose his mind. Tom felt like James was the most vulnerable when he lost his mind because he wasn't a very good fighter, he just flailed away never knowing what he was doing, but he also had to be careful that he didn't coach his brother into pulling the trigger.

Tom debated on lifting his knee off the ground and into the crouched position again but thought better of it. "I saw the lady in the pantry James, who is she? Did she catch you sniffin' her daughters bicycle seat or something?" Tom heard the sound of feet moving and then felt the top of James foot smash against his chin which immediately knocked him off his knee and flat on his back. He tried to roll over quickly but before he could get his legs under him, he felt another slam against his already painful chest. Tom cried out in pain but tried once again to get to his feet when another kick landed on his upper left shoulder, it didn't hurt near as much as the last one, but it managed to knock him off balance. Even though Tom felt the pain he knew that he had gotten to his older brother because he hadn't pulled the trigger yet, he was hoping that all this noise was enough to alert the Sheriff to their location. At this point he didn't care if his brother lived or died. "No wonder you chose little kids, you kick like a girl, James." Another kick landed right square in his side and this one knocked the wind out of Tom. He couldn't say a thing, he was now trying to get some air back into his lungs when he heard James say, "Tootle loo, you little shit." Tom closed his eyes even though he couldn't breathe, he knew his brother was about to kill him when he heard the shot. Twice in one night he closed his eyes and waited for death and the second time was no better than the first. He wished he could be in any other place but that one.

Instead of standing at the pearly gates like he thought, he heard a thump and the felt the brush of a leg across his ear and cheek. He thought maybe his brother had tried to kick him again, but he missed. He raised his head; his lungs had replenished the air that had been lost just moments ago and he saw his brother lying beside him. He scrambled to his feet but couldn't see anyone, then he looked down at his brother who was looking straight up at him, smiling. He quickly knelt beside his brother and felt for a pulse, but he didn't have to, his brother removed the smile from his face and said, "Don't put me in the kudzu, they'll get me". He didn't know what to say, it was an incredibly strange thing to say he thought, "What? What does that mean?" The smile returned to his brothers face and Tom felt his brothers hand touch his leg that was knelt beside him. James softly spoke, "I'll see you later." The voice had turned into a whisper and with that last comment James rolled his head away from his brother.

"Is he dead?" Tom looked up, not sure what to do or for that matter what to think. This was his true brother and as far as Tom could tell, without checking, had just died but not before mumbling something about Kudzu. Tom saw Aubrey walking slowly toward them and even though it was dark he could see that Aubrey had his gun drawn and he was pointing it at the two of them. Tom looked back down at his brother and felt for a pulse and was surprised to find one! Aubrey was right on top of them now and was putting his gun back in his holster. "I had to shoot; I really did! He was gonna kill you for sure!" Tom stood and looked at Aubrey, "He still has a pulse! I am going to radio for an ambulance!" He started to move when he heard the Sheriff's voice, "You stay right there Tom!" Aubrey turned to see the Sheriff coming up behind them carrying Decker like he was a toddler. Decker had his arms draped around Elmer's neck with his feet dangling around Elmer's hips. "There's a little girl out there somewhere that probably won't show herself unless she hears the code word." Aubrey threw his hands up in the air and approached the Sheriff, "Damn it Elmer! He still has a pulse! You can't let this man die regardless of what he has done!" Elmer walked up to where the three men were now standing, hovering over the body of Tom's brother. Elmer looked at both of them and then put his hand on the back of Decker's head in a comforting manner and said, "The area isn't secure yet, might be more of them." Aubrey became more animated, "Elmer! I swear on everything sacred about my job I will arrest you for not rendering aide when you had the chance!" Tom looked down and started walking toward the road, Elmer turned to look at him and shouted, "Where the hell are you going deputy?" Without hesitation Tom responded, "to call an ambulance." Tom didn't run, he just walked, he felt like it was the only compromise he had left in him, after all it was his brother and as far as he could see, his brother needed to die but he wouldn't be a good cop if he didn't do his job. By doing what he did, the Sheriff could probably fire him for disobeying a direct order, but the Sheriff would not go to jail for murder either. Tom felt like his family had done enough damage now and even though he had nothing to do with it, he felt responsible.

Elmer set Decker down who desperately tried to hang on to him. Even though Decker Davis was pretty big in his own right, the Sheriff handled him like he weighed nothing. The big Sheriff softly patted him on the back and rubbed the back of his head, "It's gonna be alright now son, I got you." He stepped around Decker who was momentarily blocking him from getting at the man who had kidnapped his son and did God knows what to him. Once he was clear of Decker, he reached into his holster and pulled out his gun. He pointed it down at the man who was laying on his back, there in bayou dirt and pointed it at him, Aubrey saw this and leaped over the man and tackled Elmer to the ground. Aubrey wasn't overly big, but it was impressive that he was able to knock the big Sheriff to the ground. It could be said that Elmer wasn't expecting Aubrey to do anything, as far as the Sheriff was concerned, Aubrey was somewhat of a passivist and could be downright wimpy at times, but Aubrey was clearly strong willed enough to try and stop the Sheriff from committing out right murder. Aubrey had his forearm in Elmer's throat and was pressing down hard. He had landed on top of Elmer which had given him the upper hand for a moment. Aubrey knew that there was no way he was going to subdue this overly large man, but he had to try to talk some sense into him. When Elmer Davis got this way, some say it was a trance like state, that he was blind to everything and oblivious to words and what was worse, he was nearly impossible to stop.

With his throat compressed Elmer yelled at Aubrey, "Get the hell off me Aubrey!" Aubrey felt the big Sheriff beginning to roll the two over at which time Elmer would be on top of him. Aubrey pulled the gun he had just holstered as quickly as he had ever drawn it and in a split second, he had the gun pressed against Elmer's temple and his forearm still pressed in his throat. Aubrey gritted his teeth and mustered up as much anger as he could, "You listen to me Elmer Davis! At this very moment I would have the law on my side if I chose to pull the trigger and leave your brains scattered all over the bayou, THAT will be the last image your son will have of you!" He stopped and pressed his elbow into Elmer's throat just a little harder, "Is that what you want? Hasn't he been through enough now?" Instead of feeling Elmer's body relax as he expected, he felt the Sheriff continue his roll, Aubrey did not want to pull the trigger, it was the last thing he wanted to do but there was no way he would stand by and let Elmer shoot a defenseless man; regardless of how despicable he might be, this man deserved his day in court. The roll continued for a split second and Aubrey cocked the hammer of his gun, now there was a live round waiting to enter the Sheriff's head, waiting to enter into Aubrey's friend. The thought was just about more than he could stand when a quiet soft voice spoke from the woods, "Can someone take me to see my daddy? Please. I'm sure he is looking for me." Both men stopped their struggles and in the blink of an eye, their bodies began to relax.

Decker spun around and yelled her name, "Jessica!" He was so excited that he bolted from where he was standing and where he had just seen two men nearly kill each other and ran to where she was. She stood there in the dark and looking so strangely out of place, wearing a button-down oxford shirt, barefooted and looking as calm as she could ever look. When Decker reached for her, she held her arms out and he embraced her. He hugged her like he had never hugged anyone before, but he would never be able to explain why.

Both Aubrey and Elmer untangled themselves and managed to get to their feet. Elmer wasted no time speaking, he could hardly contain his enthusiasm at the moment, and he asked without even thinking about it first, "Are you Jessica Lynn Muncik?" Even in the dark he could see that the girl's eyes went wide when he asked, he could see that she had a firm grip on his son and didn't seem like she was in a hurry to let him go even though she was excited. He was about to speak again when Decker let her go, but still held on to her arm, "Daddy this is my friend Jessica, she is from Drew and she wants to go home." Jessica didn't want to speak to anyone, but she couldn't help herself now, she couldn't believe that out here in these woods, a man knew her name! "How did you know my name?" Elmer felt his heart about to beat out of his chest, "Holy

Lord" he thought, this little girl has been missing for three years, but he didn't say it, he simply replied, because we've been looking for you."

Elmer looked at Aubrey who was holstering his gun for the second time tonight and then looked back at Decker and Jessica who had now put her arm around Decker and had her head on his shoulder. Even in the dark he could see that she was barefooted, and he guessed that the shirt she was wearing was the only thing she had on. Then he looked at Decker and realized that he was in his tee shirt and the thought of what had happened to that little girl hit him square in the forehead. The pain of what she had been through made Elmer wince and he forgot about the struggle he had just had with Aubrey. He turned to Aubrey, "Can you make sure that an ambulance comes and hauls this piece of shit out of my bayou? Aubrey wasted no time responding, "Gladly." Elmer took a step towards his son and his new friend and calculated everything he could calculate about what she had been through and how he needed to treat her.

His training in situations like this was limited but he knew that her journey back to normalcy if that was possible, began with giving her back control of her life. He would be there to help Decker through this but once he got in contact with her family it would be up to them. "Uh Jessica, I am Elmer Davis, I am Decker's dad. It is very nice to meet you." Jessica didn't respond and Elmer knew not to press. "Son would you like to help Jessica get into the Scout so we can get her to a safe place," Elmer caught the flaw in his comment and continued, "Jessica, would that be alright with you?"

Chapter 47

We got Decker

TOM MADE IT BACK to the ugly green car, he never once looked back to see if the Sheriff would shoot him, at that point he didn't care. He had emotions coursing through his veins that he had never had before. He remembered being scared and not knowing what to do when he found his mother the day she committed suicide, but this was different, he didn't know what to feel. A long time ago he had loved James and he was his blood kin. He had no idea why James was out there in the bayou with Elmer Davis's boy and then to find out he had a little girl with him! Oh, and there was the little matter of a dead woman in the pantry of the house he found Tom in. There was just too much information for Tom to process now.

"Dispatch come in, come in please." He depressed the mic button as he said it. He looked around the area for no other reason than to be doing something. He could feel his body getting numb and his chest hurt even more than it did when he got shot, which was another mystery to him. He could not figure out how in the hell he had taken a bullet at near point-blank range and survived.

Heather jumped to the big silver microphone and pressed the talk button, "Tom! What's goin' on? We are getting calls from all over the bayou about hearing gun shots. I've been trying for the last damn hour to get one of you to answer!!!" Heather never swore and it just blew out of her mouth without hesitation. She was a bundle of nerves, her dad was out there, her brother was out there and there were gun shots! Tom forgot about his pain for a minute and realized that Heather was having her own troubles too. "All is good Heather, we got Decker." Heather heard the news and began to sob. She started to respond but she became overwhelmed with emotions. It was like her entire body was trying to go limp and her brain was doing everything it could to keep that from happening. She pressed the talk button but couldn't get any words to come out. Tom could hear her sobs over the mic and he felt a sense of relief. At least someone had tears of joy flowing at the moment.

Peggy had been dozing on and off for the last few minutes. She tried to stay awake, but it was a battle. She wasn't supposed to work this late and she had been up very late canning the last of her famous pickles the day before. It was a fall harvest that came in better than expected and she made it her mission to get them all put away. Looking back on it today, she wished she had waited and got a good night's sleep because she was tired, but there was no way she was going to leave this office until Decker was found. She loved that little boy like her own as did everyone in the office. She sprung up from her desk when she heard Decker's name and nearly hit her head on the shelf above it. She could see Heather holding the big silver mic by her side as she cried uncontrollably. Peggy grabbed the mic from her hand and pressed the button, "Tom, repeat that please," once again he wasted no time, he needed to hurry, his brother had a hole in his chest and he needed an ambulance, "We got Decker, everyone is ok, but we need an ambulance to Cassidy Bayou Road." Peggy paused long enough to give Heather a hug with her free arm, she could hardly contain her excitement and she thought she might start crying herself, but she had to maintain the office while Heather gathered herself. "Tom what's the address?" He looked around for something to give her an address, but he knew there was nothing. He looked inside the car but that was futile, "Hell just tell them to turn off the main road and look for the police lights." Peggy started dialing the hospital on the phone but while it was ringing, she had a thought that scared her, "Wait! If everyone is ok, then why do I need an ambulance?" Tom thought about how to answer that and he simply replied "nobody you know Mary Alice." He got the person wrong again.

Tom winced as he accidently bumped the sore spot on his chest against the open door of the ugly green squad car. He took in the quiet of the night bayou air, it all seemed so peaceful now. Except for the flashing lights of the Sheriff's Scout and his ugly green car, the bayou would have been normal. He pressed the button on his mic so he could try and explain as best he could what went on without giving away his brother as the man behind all the trouble in Webb lately, "We have the perpetrator in custody, but he has been shot." He released the button to see if she had any questions but then he decided to plow ahead with an update on Decker and the girl, "The victims may have some mental trauma but appear to be physically fine."

Peggy was writing everything down that she heard just as she always did. She had her own version of shorthand that nobody could read but her, but she could always repeat word for word what everyone said in a meeting or conversations on the radio. She raised up from writing and thought about Tom saying there were victims, as in more than one, more than just Decker, she thought? Tom waited on her response but it didn't come so he continued thinking he was talking to Mary Alice instead of Peggy, "Mary Alice, this is a shit storm right now, there is just too much to cover," He continued, "There is one deceased victim, one that might die and two for sure with emotional trauma and to be honest, I don't feel worth a shit either." He released the mic button when his head begun to spin. He leaned up against the car but that didn't help the dizziness and he slid down the side of car to the point he was sitting on the ground. He lowered his head and stopped when he felt his chin hit his chest and closed his eyes.

The ambulance showed up along with the coroner wagon. There was only one ambulance available, the other threw a rod a few weeks back and the motor was being replaced so Peggy took the initiative to send what she could. Aubrey did his best to help the paramedics get the gunshot victim loaded onto a gurney and carry them him out of the woods. Since they were so far back into the bayou it was quite a task to get the gurney and its occupant back to the main road. In fact, the medics actually fell trying to carry the hand gurney. The man they were carrying was not very tall, but he was certainly thick and heavy.

Elmer Davis was helping Decker and the girl get situated in the Scout. Jessica held on to Decker with all the strength she had as they made their way out of the bayou and back to Cassidy Bayou Road. Decker could feel her fingernails digging into his arm, but he never said a word. He had never felt relief like he had just felt, and he was happy for both of them. His Dad had done exactly what he told Jessica he would do when they first met, but for some reason he didn't want to relax any more than he already had because they were not out of the woods yet. He had heard that term before and didn't exactly know what it meant when he heard it but now, as they walked slowly towards the flashing lights of the Scout, he knew exactly what it meant. Not until they were both home and Jessica had her own clothes and most importantly, she was back with her own dad. As they walked, Jessica began to talk more than she had the whole night, it was nervous chatter, but she was opening up now. Elmer walked along with them and listened to everything that she had to say, he didn't want to press too much but what the two kids didn't know was that Elmer wanted to sprint back to the Scout as fast as he could and get in touch with Sheriff R. C. Ross and let him know that he found Jessica Muncik! Elmer was trying hold back his excitement of finding his son and missing child of three years, but it was difficult. He still had a job to do, he had a crime scene to handle, he had a deputy that had a lot of explaining to do and he wanted it all now.

The three of them made it back to the Scout, Jessica talked almost the entire way. She described how she got up one summer morning so excited because her and her cousin who lived just a mile away were going to go to the summer matinee and then they were going to maybe sneak off and go swimming in the creek, but she never made it. She even described how breakfast smelled as she was getting dressed. She talked about how her mother was an excellent cook and that she couldn't wait to sit down and have a meal with her mom and dad again. Elmer wasn't about to tell her that unless they had reconciled their differences, her parents probably wouldn't be together. It really didn't matter that much now but it would be one more thing that this little girl would have to deal with. She chatted so much that Elmer felt like she was trying to put three years of hell behind her in less than 10 minutes. It was like someone opened an emotional spigot that she had been forced to shut off.

As Decker was helping Jessica into the back seat, he felt his Dad's hand on his back and then he saw a set of head lights coming in their direction. The car that pulled up, Decker didn't recognize but the person that stepped out he sure recognized, it was Donnie Buckles and Decker immediately tensed up. Elmer recognized the car and knew that Decker might have a little trouble with the sight of a Buckles which is why he put his hand on Decker's back, "It's okay son, Donnie is one of the main reasons we found you," Decker looked up at his dad with a confused look on his face, "He found the rabbits foot and library card you left for us." For a second Decker was more confused then, he remembered dropping the rabbit's foot on the road when he realized he was in trouble. That seemed like so long ago that he had forgotten about it. He knew he dropped the rabbit's foot, but he had forgotten about Jeannine's library card.

Donnie limped up to the Sheriff and started to speak but Elmer interrupted him, "I thought I told you to get that foot taken care of Donne." Donnie continued to limp toward them, but he had a smile on his face. Decker couldn't remember when he had ever seen a Buckles smile, it just seemed odd to Decker. Donnie replied, "I will eventually but I had to come see if I could help." By now, Donnie was standing right in front of Decker and his Dad. Donnie took one hop closer to Decker, reached into his pocket and pulled out two crumpled up dollar bills. He held them out to Decker who looked confused, "You dropped them in the barbershop, I wanted to give them back to you in person." Decker looked at the dollars crumpled up in Donnie's hand then his eyes traced the length of Donnie's arm all the way to his eyes and when their eyes met Donnie said, "I'm sorry I scared you." Decker looked back down at the crumpled-up bills and extended his hand to take them. He still felt odd about everything, here was Donnie Buckles in the bayou with them, limping and offering his two dollars back to him that he had completely forgotten about and he couldn't understand why Donnie was even there.

Elmer noticed the look on Decker's face, "Donnie is my deputy now son." Decker took the dollars and shoved them in his pocket then looked up at his father. There was silence between them, only the look of a father looking at his son, his only son and the son he thought he had lost and couldn't find the right words to express how he felt at that very moment. He never again wanted to be in this position. Aubrey appeared and broke the silence between Decker and his Father. "Elmer, the man's name is James Porter, he is older brother to one Tom Porter, your deputy." Elmer drew in a breath, he would put the puzzle together soon enough, if his deputy had anything to do with this, he was certain that he would kill him before the night was over, but first he needed to secure the kids.

Elmer looked down at Decker and then knelt to the point where he was now looking up at Decker, "Are you okay?" He paused for second, he didn't want to ask the question that had been gnawing at his gut for the last few minutes, he needed to know if Decker had been molested but he didn't know how to ask. "Did he hurt you? Did anyone hurt you?" He inhaled a large amount of air and he as he was doing so, he had to fight off the urge to cry. He felt the emotion welling up in him and he fought it back down. "No sir, I promise, he hasn't done a thing to me other than keep me in the dark basement for too long." Elmer pressed because he knew that often child victims felt ashamed and embarrassed to have been victimized and would often suppress the event to the point that they believed it never happened to them. "Are you sure son, there is no shame. You can tell me everything." Decker looked at his father then he glanced at the Scout then back to his father, "Daddy, nobody touched me, I promise." Decker glanced back at the Scout and then back to his father, "Daddy, he's hurt her though." Decker searched for the right words and all that came out was, "In ways that a girl shouldn't be hurt." Elmer reached out and grabbed his son and pulled him close to him. "I know son, she is gonna need her family and some real friends right now." Elmer felt his son hug him then pull away for a moment, "She has me now." Elmer knelt again, "Son I know that." Elmer looked around the night air and then back to his son, "I have to know what's happened here son, can you look after her for a little while longer?"

Decker smiled at his dad and then looked around, he pointed at the house light far down the street, "We were in that house Dad, in the basement." Elmer stood up and looked in the direction that Decker was pointing. "That's the Evan's winter place. Are you sure?" Decker nodded; he didn't know whose house that was but he was certain that was the house that he had come from. "We got out through the storm door, or at least I let Jessica out through the storm door, I got through the basement door that leads into the kitchen." Decker watched his dad look back at the house then his dad turned to look back at him. "There is a woman in the pantry, I guess I ran out of the kitchen faster than she could because I never saw her again." Elmer was confused, he knew the Evan's were not at their winter home just yet, but they would soon be. The lived in Minnesota during the summer and on Cassidy Bayou in the winter but it was not quite time for them to return. "You say there was a woman in the pantry huh?" Decker nodded and Elmer looked back at where the man had been shot and where he had found Decker. "How did you get all the way out here?"

Decker told his dad the story as best he could remember, every now and then either his Dad or Aubrey would stop him and ask him a question and he would fill in the blanks for them. His dad stayed very stoic the whole time while Aubrey seemed to be writing down every word that Decker said. Decker counted Aubrey turning the page on his little pad at least ten times. Elmer nodded his head a few times throughout Decker's story but not much more than that. The lights of all the cars were still flashing with the exception of the coroner's wagon. Some of Aubrey's city policemen had arrived and there was someone from the paper, but they were being held back from getting to where the man had been shot by Aubrey's men.

"Okay Decker," Elmer had just listened to his son tell him about the scariest time of his life and he had heard how his son had acted and behaved as he wished he would have behaved in the same situation when he was fourteen. He was proud of his son for staying with this girl he had never met despite the fact that he could have been hurt for doing so. Elmer was ready to scoop Decker and that little girl up in his arms and get then the hell out of this place, but there were still more police work to be done. "Deck, you are the son that every man hopes he will have," he swallowed a big lump in his throat. "I'm just lucky that your MY son." He knelt down and hugged Decker one more time then stood up and looked at Aubrey, "Decker is going to stay here with Jessica, you and I need to talk to Tom." Elmer patted Decker on the shoulder and Decker started to make a move towards the Scout, but his dad stepped in front of him and leaned into the Scout to speak to Jessica, "Are you okay?" She was sitting in the back seat with her hands clasped and trapped between her knees. She nodded that she was okay. "Okay, Decker is going to sit with you, and we will be back shortly okay?" Jessica nodded again and then looked straight down at her lap. Elmer stepped away from the Scout then looked at Aubrey but before he could speak, he was being handed a blanket from one of Aubrey's men. Elmer took it from the man then handed it to Decker where he wasted no time climbing into the back seat of the Scout and handing the blanket to Jessica.

Elmer looked at Aubrey, "Let's go talk to Tom. While we are doing that, send someone down to the Evan's place and ask them to check it out. Approach with caution." Aubrey immediately turned to the man that had just delivered the blanket and instructed him to go check out the house. Elmer and Aubrey walked over to where the ugly green deputy car was still flashing its lights. The driver door was open, and they could see some legs stickling straight out beside it. Elmer was the first one to find Tom on the ground with his back resting against the car. His head was hanging down and he wasn't moving. "Holy shit! Is he hit?" Elmer wanted to say what Aubrey had just said but Aubrey beat him to it. Elmer quickly bent down and put his hand on Tom's neck to feel for a pulse. Once again it wasn't as easy as it seemed but luckily Tom raised his head and took the guess work out of him being dead. "What the hell Tom?" Elmer looked back at the Scout just to check on the kids then looked back down at Tom. "Are you hurt?" Tom didn't reply right away, he glanced at Aubrey then looked at Elmer, "I didn't have anything to do with this."

Elmer looked as closely at Tom as he could. He didn't see any visible injuries that would cause Tom to collapse against the car as he done. "I didn't say you did Tom, but I'd sure like to know more about what is going on." Elmer turned and looked at Aubrey, "Aubrey we need to get in touch with the Sheriff over in Drew and let him know that we have Jessica. Her parents need that information as quickly as we can get it to them." Aubrey nodded and motioned for one of his officers, but Elmer stopped him, "It isn't often in this line of work that we get to deliver good news to a family that has probably been through three years of hell,"

Elmer looked at Tom and then back to Aubrey, "I wouldn't delegate that task if I were you." Aubrey thought about it for a second and realized that the Sheriff was right, actually making a call to the Sheriff and being able to say with glee that a child had been found just doesn't happen. Usually, they have to inform the families that a body has been found and that is the worst possible thing to tell a parent that has lost a child. Aubrey smiled and his officer went away. He turned and walked to the closest police car and grabbed the mic.

Elmer turned back to Tom, "Ok, Aubrey isn't here now, you want to tell me what the hell is goin' on?" Tom tried to stand but the pain in his chest sent him right back to the ground. Elmer reached for Tom to help him up, but Tom shook his head. "My brother was the man in that house down there, there is a woman in the house that I am sure he murdered," he paused and tried to catch his breath because not only did his chest hurt like hell, but he was also having trouble breathing. She might be the owner of the house, I don't know but he shot me in the basement, I don't know why I am not dead." Elmer leaned in even closer now as if he were searching for something on Tom, "Holy mother Tom! You are shot?" Elmer scrambled back to his feet and looked towards the Scout then back down to where Tom was sitting against the car, "I'm gonna go radio to get that ambulance back down here ASAP, hang on Tom!" Tom once again tried to get to his feet but he couldn't so he just sat back down. "That's just it, Sheriff, I ain't bleedin' but I know he shot me with my own damn gun." Elmer stopped long enough to think about what he had just heard but continued towards the Scout.

"You guys doing okay?" Elmer reached into the Scout and grabbed the radio mic, "Hey Peggy, send that ambulance right back here as soon as they drop off the perp, Tom's been shot." Elmer looked back at Decker and Jessica, Jessica had her arm wrapped under Decker's and was covered mostly by the blanket that Aubrey had secured for them. Decker shook his head as if to tell his Dad that they were not ok. "She needs help Daddy." Elmer pressed the button for the mic as Peggy had not responded yet, "Come in Peggy." She answered right away this time, "Yes sir, I was talking to the hospital just now, they are in route back to you!" He shook his head, "Thank you Peggy." He made a quick glance into the back seat. He didn't want to seem like he was staring at them, but he was having trouble getting a grip on his emotions. Having his son back with him was incredible but the fact that his son had rescued a little girl from God knows what horror was almost too much to process. "Hey Peggy- where is Heather?" Peggy came right back with, "She is right here, she needed a few minutes to process everything." The next voice that came over the hand-held mic was Heather, "Daddy, is everyone okay for real? I can hardly stand not knowing what is going on!" Elmer wished he could explain more but he needed help getting Decker and Jessica out of the crime scene and to a hospital, but he needed Heather's help. He needed to process the white car and the house that Tom said he found his brother. "I promise to fill you in later, but I need you to meet Decker and Jessica Muncik at the hospital. Donnie will be bringing them in my Scout, ETA 15 minutes."

Chapter 48
Badge Proof

AFTER DONNIE PULLED AWAY with Decker and Jessica in the back of the Scout, Elmer stood and watched them drive away. He breathed in the crisp night air of the bayou and quickly made his way over to the ugly green squad car. He was surprised to see that Tom was no longer laying against the car but had climbed back into the driver's seat, "Let's go, I have to see that house again." Elmer shook his head, "I'm not letting you drive in the shape you are in." Tom shook his head, "If I have to get out and move to the other side, it will take forever. Get in!" Elmer realized he had a point, Tom was moving so slow it really would take too long and Elmer wanted to see that house badly right now, so he went to the passenger side and got in the car.

Tom eased the car into the driveway this time instead of parking out on Cassidy Road. His chest hurt with each breath he took; he was struggling to breathe. The drive from where they were in the woods was short, but Tom made the best of it as far as filling Elmer in on the details of his brother; how he had just contacted him that night and how he had no idea he was even in town. He told Elmer that he had lost contact with his brother over the years but up until now he didn't think his brother was a killer. Tom had talked himself into believing that maybe James didn't know he was shooting his own brother earlier. He was telling Elmer about how he entered the house earlier when they were met by Aubrey at the entrance to the back kitchen door.

Aubrey looked flushed and despite the cool night air, was wiping his forehead with a handkerchief. "God uhmighty," came from Aubrey's mouth as he looked at Elmer and began his summary of his investigation. "There is a woman in the pantry with her throat slashed clean to the bone, looks to me like if he's applied a little more pressure, he would have cut her head clean off." Elmer pushed past Aubrey and on into the kitchen, but Aubrey continued to talk, "No blood though, just a little around her neck, looks like she was either brought here from someplace else or he took the time to clean up after himself. Damdest thing I ever saw, had to step outside and puke when I saw it," Aubrey said following Elmer toward the pantry. As Elmer knelt down and looked at the victim, "Oh and Tom, here is your badge and conduct book, Aubrey handed them to Tom. "You are one lucky son-of-a-bitch." Elmer was processing what he was seeing, the woman sitting on the floor of the pantry with her throat opened up, then hearing Aubrey say something about being lucky and he turned to see what Aubrey was talking about. "We found them in the basement, looks like the badge and book stopped that bullet from entering your chest." Tom was holding the badge as if it had magical powers and with the thoughts running through his head as he looked at the mangled badge with the huge dent right smack dab in the middle of it; it just might very well have magical powers. Aubrey let his words sink in just a little more then continued, "Flip it over and you can see the tip of the slug trying to peak out the back side." Tom turned the badge over and although the bullet hadn't made it all the way through the badge, it sure looked to Tom as if it had made one hell of an effort. "The book has a dent in it too, I guess the bullet used up all its energy trying to get through that badge and when it hit the book, it just ran out of steam." Tom was holding the book up looking at the dent in it, "Like I said, you are one lucky sumbitch."

Elmer backed out of the pantry and was looking at Tom and the way he was holding the badge that had obviously absorbed the bullet for him, then went over to the small little metal green top kitchen table and slid a chair over to Tom, "Sit down Tom, you probably have some broken ribs." Elmer looked at Aubrey, "Did you get in touch with the Sheriff over in Drew?" Aubrey wasted no time, "Sure did, used that phone right there," he pointed at the yellow phone hanging on the wall, "Man nearly started crying he was so happy, said he was gonna deliver the news to the parents and he was gonna personally escort them over here as fast as they could." Elmer nodded then looked down at Tom who was not saying anything, sitting at the table but still looking at the mangled badge. "Elmer there isn't much in the basement, dirt floors, a small box with some twine in it, the storm door is latched from the outside so there is no way to exit unless you come right back up the stairs here." Aubrey was animated in the way he was describing the basement, "No lights in the basement until we screwed in the fuse and they popped right on, the fuse was disabled on purpose." Aubrey continued, "If Decker and that girl were kept down there, they had to be scared to death. It's dark and dank and when the lights are out, you can't see your hand in front of your face."

Hearing that from Aubrey made Elmer mad, not at Aubrey but the thought that his son and that little girl were stuck down there got to him. He pushed past Aubrey and started to go down to the basement but said, "Tom, get your shirt off and let Aubrey have a look, I will be right back." Instead of going down to the basement, Elmer stopped. Looked for the phone that Aubrey pointed to earlier and saw it hanging in the kitchen at the end of the kitchen counter. He looked at Tom who was resting with his elbow on the table to help steady him. Even though Elmer still thought that Tom had something to do with his son's kidnapping, he had to admit that Tom looked terrible. If this had been the plan for Tom and his brother all along, something had to have gone terribly wrong. Elmer didn't figure there was any way that Tom could have practiced getting shot only to be saved by a badge and book.

Elmer picked up the phone and dialed the office, Peggy picked up on the first ring. "Peggy, I need a number for the Evan's up in Minnesota," he tapped his finger on the kitchen countertop, "Call them now, wake them up and let them know there has been some trouble out at their place on Cassidy." Peggy responded with nothing more than, "Copy that Sheriff." She didn't want to hear what trouble there might have been and wanted to stay away from any details. She wished at that moment she was home in bed where she should have been.

Elmer placed the receiver back in the cradle, turned to look at Aubrey who was scribbling on his pad, "Aubrey, I would appreciate it if you and your men would stay here, secure the crime scene, and collect evidence." Aubrey stopped writing and was nodding in agreement although the Sheriff had never made a request of him, it was usually in the form of a demand. He didn't report to the Sheriff and he didn't have to do a thing the Sheriff said if he didn't want to, but, he did it because Elmer was usually right about his police work and it simply helped to keep the peace between the police department and the county sheriff's department.

Elmer knew that Aubrey had stopped him from murdering a man today and the reality of that was weighing on him at the moment. "I'm gonna go be with Decker at the hospital and I can make sure Tom here gets the medical attention he needs." Elmer stuck out his hand to Aubrey and without hesitation Aubrey took it, "Thank you." Aubrey couldn't remember the last time that Elmer had ever said thank you to him in such a formal way. Elmer turned to look at Tom, "Can you walk?" Tom nodded and slowly rose from the table.

Elmer opened the door for Tom to enter the passenger side of the big green squad car then helped him slowly ease into the seat. Tom winced with every move. Elmer took one last look at the house that had been his son's prison for the night and cursed it under his breath. He knew it wasn't the house he was cursing; it was the things that may have occurred inside the house before he managed to find him. He had so many things running through his head at the moment that he was having trouble keeping them in order of priority. He was certain he would have let that man die in the woods if it had not have been for Aubrey and that always seemed to push out every cogent thought he was having in his head. He was a good cop, and he knew that, after all he had not only found his son, but he had managed to free a young girl from abuse. Hell! TWO young girls! He should be proud, but he was not. He started to blame Decker's capture on his drinking and his inability to be a father and that thought always circled back to the letting the man die in the woods.

He slid behind the steering wheel of the squad car and sat in silence for a minute then he spoke, "And you had nothing to do with this?" Tom squirmed and reached for his chest; his words were strained when he said: "No." Elmer started the car and eased it on to the road. He reached for the mic of the car's radio, but it wasn't in the cradle, he looked down on the seat between he and Tom and saw it sitting there. "Peggy you there?" The radio was silent for just a moment then Peggy came across loud and clear. "I am here Elmer." She rarely called him Elmer but tonight she was trying to be compassionate in her tone, "Peggy has Heather left for the hospital yet?" He waited, "Yes she has." Elmer looked down at his speedometer and pressed the accelerator further to the floor. Tom felt the acceleration as well as heard it. The big green squad car may have been ugly from headlights to tail, but the engine rivaled anything you would see at Daytona. "Did you need something Sheriff?" Elmer looked up at the visor and then placed his eyes squarely on the road, "Yeah, I need to see my kids."

Chapter 49
I know their Names

ELMER HELPED TOM OUT OF THE CAR and into the emergency room. Webb didn't have much of a hospital, but it had one. The hospital in Clarksdale was much more suited to handle the events of the day but for now it would do.

The ride from the bayou was quiet and not much was said between Tom and Elmer. Elmer was still trying to process it all. Tom did manage to reinforce to his boss that he didn't know anything about any of this and that he wished he could change it, but since Elmer didn't respond he thought better of any more conversation and simply closed his eyes and leaned his head back.

The lady at the desk was a polite woman that Elmer had seen around town but hadn't taken the time to meet her yet. He thought that she had just moved to Webb, but he couldn't be sure. He used to know everyone in the town and for the most part, he could tell who would vote for him and who wouldn't but the last three years had been nothing more than a fog of hazy memories and out right lapses in judgement. "Ma'am, where did they take my son and a girl?" The lady smiled warmly from behind the desk, "Well, Decker is in Room 3, Jessica is in Room 2, Donnie is in Room 1." She paused and looked at Tom who was being held up by the big Sheriff. "I'm sorry we don't have a Room 4 so you can sit him down right back here," pointing at a chair behind her. "I will see what I can do to help him until the doctor is finished." Elmer helped Tom get to the chair where she had just pointed, "He might have a couple of . . . " she interrupted, "Broken ribs, we know. It's seems like there are several lucky people here tonight." Elmer nodded in agreement then turned to walk down the hallway to find Decker. The lady behind the desk spoke up, "Sheriff." Elmer stopped and turned back to her, "The doctor is with the little girl in Room 2 with your daughter," the soft smile that the lady had on her face evaporated quickly when she said, "the doctor is doing an examination and collecting evidence for you, give them time."

Elmer nodded and went straight to Room 3 where he found Decker laying back on an exam table with his eyes closed. Decker heard the door close and saw his dad standing next to the table. He tried to sit up because he wanted to hug his dad, but he was so weak that all he could do was lift his arm. He felt like he had just run in some incredibly long marathon and all his energy was gone. His voice was weak, and his throat was dry. The doctor had been in and told the nurse to hook up an IV to help Decker rehydrate. Decker heard the doctor spout off a bunch of stuff that he didn't understand so he just laid back on the table and let them do what they wanted. He knew everyone in the little hospital but more importantly to Decker, he was safe now. When the nurse poked his arm and began to inject the stuff into his arm, he immediately got very relaxed and very tired, so he closed his eyes. It was good to feel safe again.

"I'm sorry Daddy, I was just trying to help that man. I thought he ran over a dog." Decker felt like he was whispering but Elmer heard him just fine. Elmer took Decker's hand in his and used his other hand to run his hand over Decker's forehead. "It's okay son, you did what I would have done, you're supposed to help people." Decker tried to open his eyes as wide as he could, "Heather is here Daddy, she wanted to stay with me, but I asked her to stay with Jessica." Elmer could feel a lump coming up in his throat and his eyes were becoming a little misty. He was looking down at his son, who had just been through more than any human being should be asked to go through and he was still worried about that little girl. He knew that on any other set of circumstances, Decker would have wanted his sister at that moment, but he had turned on some sort of internal protective mode that Elmer didn't realize Decker had, until now. "You did the right thing son. I am here now so just rest. I am not going anywhere." Decker smiled at his dad and closed his eyes. Elmer looked at him sleeping so peacefully and thought of how close he came to losing his only son and let the tears roll down his cheeks.

There was a light tap on the door then the doctor walked in with a graceful stride. The doctor looked at Decker on the examination table sleeping and smiled. He was a tall man as tall as Elmer, but he had a soft demeanor and approach with everyone. He and Elmer had known each other for many years, they met when Elmer was a disaster relief volunteer. Dr. Washburn was assigned to Elmer's team during one of the hurricane's that destroyed parts of the Mississippi gulf back in the early 60's. It was Elmer that talked the doctor into relocating to Webb and setting up a practice of his own. It took a while but a few years later Dr. Scott Washburn set up practice in Webb and handled more tragedy and losses than he ever expected to handle. "Step outside with me Elmer," he whispered. Elmer shook his head no as he continued to stare at his son. Scott touched Elmer on the arm and whispered, "He will be okay, I gave him a slight sedative to help him relax. He needs the rest." Elmer looked at the doc and then back to Decker, he didn't want to ever leave his son again. "Elmer, I have to fill you in on the girl before we get her over to Coahoma County." Dr. Washburn was whispering but Elmer knew he needed to hear what the doctor had to say about the little girl. This time Elmer nodded his head and stepped outside with the doctor.

The hallway was quiet as the doctor spoke; he kept his voice down because he didn't want anyone to overhear things that they shouldn't hear. "Decker has had no injuries other than a chloroform headache; he has not been molested in any way." Elmer let out a sigh and could feel some of his tension leave his shoulders. "The girl, on the other hand . . . " Scott paused, and to Elmer, it looked like he was forcing a lump back down his throat and he was trying not to cry but he continued, "The girl on the other hand has been through a lot Elmer, we aren't equipped to handle her injuries. She needs to get to Coahoma ASAP." Elmer stood there and turned to look at the door which separated the little girl from them, "Do you want me to take her over there now?" Scott shook his head no, but his eyes were tearing up, "I've called them and they are sending an ambulance to pick her up so she should be in good hands very soon." The doc looked at the door then back to Elmer. "Heather has been a remarkable help, that little girl needed a woman's touch and compassion, and Heather is providing it. I gave Jessica a sedative too, but it is taking a while to kick in." The doctor was searching for the right words, and decided on the direct approach, "She's been raped Elmer, I think you already know that. I did a kit on her and gave her penicillin in case she may have some venereal disease but that is about all I can do." Scott put his hand on Elmer again, "She asked to see you, but I am not sure she will be awake now." Elmer looked at Dr. Washburn and scratched his forehead. "What do I say doc? I don't know what to say." Scott looked at the door and said, "Be a dad until hers gets here."

Elmer slowly and quietly stepped into the room and closed the door behind him. The doctor had dimmed the lights but at the request of Jessica, had not turned them off. Elmer felt the tears roll down his cheeks as he saw Heather laying on the small table cuddling a girl she hadn't met until just an hour ago. He could see Heather had her arm over Jessica and Jessica held tightly to Heather's arm. Heather was doing what Lois would have done and that was make that little girl feel protected and loved again. "She's asleep Daddy." He heard Heather whisper. "You okay, baby? Elmer wiped his cheeks with his shirt sleeve and tried his best to show that he was capable of handling the moment. "I'm good. Jessica wanted to tell you thank you. I told her it wasn't necessary, but she insisted." Elmer stepped close to the girls that were sharing the tiny examination table and put his hand on Heather's arm. "Coahoma is gonna come pick her up, she's been through a lot." Heather felt her own tears rolling down her face, "I know, she told me everything and I can't unhear it now. I hope that man dies Daddy," she squeezed Jessica enough to let her know she was still protected, "He called it purification Daddy. Like he was some kind of God." She wanted to scream but instead she started a slow whimper and Elmer squeezed her arm, "I know baby, I feel the same way, but I want him to stay alive long enough to tell us where the others are. There is a good chance he hurt more." Heather hadn't thought of that but before she could say anything Jessica whispered, "He hurt a lot of them. I know their names," she didn't have her eyes open and her voice was very groggy, "Allison, Ruby, Susan, Maggie, Tim, Ja . . . " her voice trailed off and she was asleep again. Elmer looked up at the ceiling and whispered "Jesus, Mary and Joseph."

Chapter 50
I didn't know . . .

ELMER STEPPED OUT OF THE HALL after hearing Jessica's little voice try to recount the list of names that she said the man hurt. He didn't know if they were alive or dead, but he was determined to find out and hopefully provide some kind of peace to the parents. Before he could do that, he would need some answers from Tom. The doctor moved Tom out of the waiting room chair and into the room that Donnie had previously occupied. Elmer saw Donnie sitting in the waiting room chair now with a big white cast on his leg. "What the hell Donnie?" Donnie tried to stand up but Elmer stopped him, "Doc says I broke it clean, should heal up in a few weeks." Donnie's face turned red as if he were embarrassed, "Sorry Elmer, I wasn't much help on my first day in the job." Elmer had to smile at the remark because he thought it was funny that Donnie had been such a recluse since his return from Viet Nam trying to stay out of the public eye and not be seen, and here he was in the middle of the night with a fresh cast on his leg and apologizing for doing a job poorly that he hadn't even applied for.

Elmer slid a free chair next to Donnie, sat down and looked at Donnie with a slight smile. "Bull shit, you did your job well tonight.

You backed me up when I needed it, hell that lady probably would have stoved my head in with that rolling pin." Donnie didn't say anything, "You secured the prisoners, helped free an abused child, then returned with a broken leg to help secure a crime scene and usher my son and ANOTHER abused child to safety." Elmer patted Donnie on the leg, "I'd say you did one helluva job Deputy Buckles." Donnie smiled and breathed a sigh of relief; he really had no idea how the Sheriff would react. He was still upset that he hadn't recognized what was happening when he first saw the car in the road. As if the Sheriff were reading his mind he stood up, looked down at Donnie, "I'm sorry I said what I said tonight, there is no way you could have known or done anything to stop it. I was wrong when I said you could." Elmer sat there in silence for a moment and decided that he needed to tell Donnie about the events of the day out at Parchman. In all of the commotion tonight, Peggy managed to tell the Sheriff about Brett Buckles and Donnie Sr. "Donnie, I have some other news for you that isn't good." Elmer paused long enough to draw in a breath and then he barreled ahead, "There was some trouble out at Parchman today," Donnie slid up in his chair and leaned forward waiting to hear what else the Sheriff was going to say. "Spit it out Sheriff." Elmer looked around the room then back at Donnie, "Brett was murdered today in the prison yard and your Daddy has been air lifted out, he was alive when they medevac'd him out, but I have been too busy to follow up." Elmer was looking directly at Donnie now. He could almost see anguish in Donnie's eyes. He hated that he was tasked with telling him this and especially after all that Donnie had done to help him that day. "Is Judd okay?" Donnie asked. "I don't know Donnie; I didn't hear anything about him, so I take that to mean that he is okay." Elmer looked around for some kind of relief. This was a conversation he didn't want to have but he was having it anyway. "Do you want to take off?" Elmer stood up, "I support whatever you decide Donnie, it's been a tough night for all of us." Donnie stood up but then realized his leg was in a cast and he sat back down. "I don't think there is much I can do Sheriff. I'd just as soon stay here." Donnie's voice cracked as he said it and Elmer felt terrible for him. They may have been bad boys, but they were his family. "I can't tell you what to do Donnie, but I know this, I am sorry about your brother and I hope your father is okay." This time Donnie stood up, he looked at the Sheriff and wiped his eyes, "We don't get to pick our family, do we?" Elmer could see that Donnie was hurting and he didn't know how to fix it. "No, we don't son, but I consider you part of mine now."

Elmer turned away from Donnie and looked at the door where Tom and the Doctor were, "Can you make sure that the kids don't need anything Donnie?" Without hesitation Donnie replied, "Of course, I am not going anywhere until they are out of here." Elmer nodded his reply of thanks and then entered the exam room.

Tom was laying back on the exam table as the doctor held a stethoscope to his chest. "You can't be in here Elmer, wait outside please." Elmer closed the door behind him and pulled up the only chair available in the little exam room. "My deputy Doc, I believe I will just hang out here and get some answers while you do your examination." Dr. Washburn turned to look at Elmer and could see that the Elmer that everyone knew; the hard man that didn't take any guff from anyone and couldn't be swayed easily. "Suit yourself, Elmer."

Dr. Washburn placed the stethoscope in several locations and would ask Tom to take in a breath with each placement of the scope. He listened carefully and when he was finished, he wrapped the scope around his shoulders and looked at Tom, "You have a few broken ribs for sure, I can x-ray but it would be like taking a picture for nothing. I know what I will see and there ain't much that can be done about broken ribs. I will wrap you up tightly and tell you not to cough, bend, lift, squat or run but it is hard getting through the day without doing some of those." He looked at Tom's forehead, you need a few stitches in your forchead which I will do before you walk out of here, but let me tell you Deputy, you could easily puncture a lung with some of those jagged bone breaks in your chest." He fumbled though a drawer, placed some items on a silver tray and slid it over to where Tom was laying. He began to stitch up Tom's head slowly and methodically. Tom winced a few times but realized when he winced, his chest hurt worse than what the doc was doing so he kept very still. As the doctor was stitching, he talked to Tom, "The bullet that hit your badge probably would not have killed you instantly, but if you didn't get treated you would have bled out or passed out due to a collapsed lung. You're lucky Deputy, not many guys get a second chance on life like you have, I'd make the most of it if I were you." Dr. Washburn picked up the small scissors from the table and while holding the remainder of the material used to stitch Tom's head, he snipped the end of it off. Tom felt the tug on his skin but didn't budge.

Dr. Washburn put all the stitching materials on the silver rolling tray and put his hands on his thighs. He spun the rolling stool around so he could look at Elmer, "You two can have the room, I am going to check on the girl. Hopefully, the ambulance will be here soon." As he was standing, all three could hear a phone ring in the background. "Tom, sit up real quick so I can wrap your chest." Tom did as he was told but he moaned as he tried to sit up; so, Elmer and the doctor helped him get to a sitting position and then a standing position because Doctor Washburn told Tom he might as well stand and get the pain of standing over with. Dr. Washburn wrapped Tom's chest as tightly as he could and instructed Tom to change the bandages daily but to get someone to help him and he gave him a prescription for the pain. As soon as he left the room Elmer sat back down in his chair and said, "Keep standing if you want to but tell me all about your brother, the whole damn family, if needed."

Tom told him the whole story, the stepmom, the suicide, the way he found his mother, how his brothers blamed him for not telling them what they would find in the house and perhaps stop them from seeing their mother with her brains splattered all over the bedroom. He told Elmer that Bobbi was a decent woman but was too young for their dad when they first shacked up. She was barely older than Richie who was the oldest of his siblings. He told him that maybe her and James had done some things behind their dad's back but he couldn't be sure.

"I've tried to keep my past out of site, I was afraid that a day would come that everyone would find out that my family was a bunch of hillbillies," he paused, "but in hindsight, that would have been a relief." He rubbed his hand on his chest, "I swear sir, I would run an ad in the paper tomorrow announcing my hillbilly heritage if it would change this. I had no idea that James was doing any of this." He fought back the tears as he tried to come to grips with reality, "My brother is a murderer, rapist, and pedophile. I'd be much happier with my brother as a hillbilly." He wiped the tears away and grimaced. The motion of moving his arm brought pain to his chest. The adrenaline of the night was wearing off and he was starting to feel it. "You'll have my resignation letter in the morning Sheriff." He hung his head, "I'm sorry I caused you all this trouble."

Elmer rose from his chair, he looked around the room then looked at Tom, "Nobody holds your family against you, the past is the past." Elmer turned towards the door leading out into the hallway, "I may never figure out who was really behind this, but I am going to need all the help I can get to try." He opened the door then looked back at Tom one more time. "I'd be proud to have you as my deputy." As Elmer was exiting the room, he nearly ran over the nurse that was working the front desk, "Sheriff, there is a call for you."

Elmer followed the nurse to the desk where she handed him the phone. After he announced himself, he stood there in silence for a few seconds then he let out a sigh, a happy sigh, "Damn right I will, she ain't goin' anywhere until they get here ma'am." Elmer handed the phone back to the nurse and excitedly looked around as if he wanted to pass on the news of the phone call to more people other than Donnie and the Nurse. Dr. Washburn had gone back in the room with Heather and Jessica. "That was Sheriff Ross's wife, she said the Sheriff upon hearing the news of Jessica's recovery immediately got in touch with Jessica's father and they are on their way here with sirens blaring." He looked at Donnie, then to the nurse, "She says they will beat the ambulance here but if for some reason the ambulance gets here before them, do not let them take her." Elmer smiled as he spoke, "We are gonna get to see the results of another miracle tonight!" The nurse used her hand to cover her now gaping mouth, Donnie ran his hands though his hair and smiled even though he was still trying to come to grips with the news of his family. He thought it would be nice to see a family have a happy ending this evening.

Chapter 51
Family Reunion

THE EMERGENCY ENTRANCE DOOR to the hospital swung open so fast that Elmer reached for the gun on his hip as he spun around. When he was facing the door, even though he had never met the man, he could see that it was Jessica's father. There is no way to fake the look on his face, a face that dared anyone to get in the way of seeing his little girl. The man that walked in behind him was Sheriff R.C. Ross, a man that Elmer had only talked to on the phone but to Elmer, the voice matched the person. He was wearing a cowboy hat and was in full uniform even though it was the middle of the night. Elmer stood there and was about to say something when Dr. Washburn spoke up, "I presume you are the girl's father?" The man stopped frantically looking around the room for his daughter and stared at the doctor, "Where is she? Take me too her now!" Dr. Washburn raised his hand as if to request Mr. Muncik to stop, then he spoke in a voice the Elmer recalled as being soothing, almost angelic, "Mr. Muncik, I plan on taking you to your daughter however, I must brief you first." Scott Washburn was speaking to the man as if he had known him his entire life. "Jessica has been through a lot, more than a girl should ever have to go though in a lifetime. She is as mentally tough as I have ever seen,

329

she's had to be." Mr. Muncik could hardly stand still, to Donnie it looked like he was doing a pee pee dance, but Donnie knew that this man had been through hell for the last three years of not knowing. "She has been strong but please know, as soon as she sees you, she will more than likely fall apart because up until now, you were just a memory." Dr. Washburn stopped and looked at Elmer then back to Mr. Muncik, "I don't have loads of experience with this, but I know that as soon as the joy of seeing you subsides, she is going to feel shame, she will feel dirty and unworthy of your love anymore. The doctor continued, "She may even try and pull away, act up, get you to not love her anymore because she is trying to make it easier for you, don't let that happen." Dr. Washburn looked now at Donnie and then back to Mr. Muncik. "She has a long hard journey back and needs nothing more than unconditional love."

Elmer could see that the doctor's words sunk in on Mr. Muncik and managed to calm him enough to cause a few tears to stroll down his face. "One more thing," Dr. Washburn took a step forward and put his hand on Mr. Muncik's shoulder; she has been given a small sedative and she is sleeping right now but you can go in. Dr. Washburn led Mr. Muncik into the room and closed the door behind them. Sheriff Ross stepped forward and stuck out his hand to Elmer, and before R.C. could say anything, Elmer brushed it away and hugged him. Even though Elmer had never officially met R.C. Ross, he felt like they had known each other a very long time. "Thank you for getting him here so fast, Sheriff." Elmer stepped back but kept his hands on R.C.'s shoulders. "It's been one helluva night sir." R.C. smiled a grin that Elmer couldn't help but return.

R.C. was an older man. Elmer guessed he was approaching 70 but was still as active and lively as anyone could be. When he pulled his cowboy hat off, it exposed a magnificent crown of gray, almost white hair that looked as though it never got messy. "Criminals and politicians call me Sheriff, everyone else calls me Clint." He smiled as he looked around the room and started to say something, but they all stopped when they heard the howls and tears coming from room where Jessica was seeing her father for the first time in three years. R.C. lowered his head and fidgeted with the brim of his cowboy hat and then he did something that Elmer didn't expect, "Lord, thank you for bringing these two people together again." Elmer could see that he was actually going to pray, and he immediately lowered his head. Elmer still wasn't much of a praying man but there was a feeling he had that from the minute R.C. Ross walked into the same room with Elmer, he wasn't in command anymore. R.C. Ross was in command now. He envied that ability and hoped that one day he would have the same effect on people. "We ask that you give them the strength to weather the tough times that lay ahead of them and provide them with all the joy and love that they so desperately need, Amen."

During the prayer, Heather had quietly eased out of the room. She had tears in her eyes, she was so excited to see Jessica awake from her medicated slumber and bolt upright off the table and into her Daddy's arms. The two stood there and held each other and cried. Heather felt like it wasn't her place to be in the room and she had done all she could to help Jessica feel safe until her family arrived. When the prayer was finished, she ran to her dad and leaped into his arms. She held him and cried, she cried for what she had just seen, for the relief that her brother was safe and that she was loved unconditionally. The reality of the moment set in on Donnie, Elmer, the Nurse and R.C. Ross. Every single one of them had tears in their eyes.

As Heather was hugging her father, she felt arms embrace her from the side. She lifted her head from her father's chest to see Decker had come out of the room and was now trying to hug them both. She gasped and more tears flowed. When Donnie brought Decker and the girl to the hospital, she was waiting on them as her dad had instructed. She fully intended to lavish Decker with all the hugs and kisses a little brother could stand, but Decker wouldn't hear of it. He wanted her to help Jessica. He wanted the sister that had brushed the tears out of his eyes and made him feel loved for so many years, to work her sisterly magic on his new friend. She was always proud of Decker; proud of the way he conducted himself, how he never quit or gave up despite the bullying or ridicule, but this was different. This was Decker being larger than himself, larger than a 14-year-old boy, this was her little brother being a man. Now with Decker so close and Jessica secure with her father, she jumped from her father's arms and into Decker's. Now she gave him every ounce of energy and love she could pour out in one hug.

The emergency room door flung open again and this time Sheriff Ross reflexively jumped and turned to see who this was. He stepped out of the way as he wasn't sure if this was an emergency or perhaps this girl knew some of the folks in this room. Elmer turned his head and smiled; he was very excited to see her. She was smiling from ear-to-ear, but he could tell that her eyes were puffy from crying. "Decker Davis!" Decker lifted his head from the embrace of his father and sister and immediately bolted towards Jeannine. He grabbed her as tightly as he could and held on, he didn't cry but she did. "I was so worried! I thought I had lost you!" Decker held her tightly, he had never felt this way in this life, he knew he loved Jeannine Martin but up until this moment, he had no idea how much. He thought of her in that dank basement and while he was in woods and wanted so badly to see her again, now here she was, in his arms, crying and kissing him all over his face, including right smack on the lips in front of everyone! That's how he knew there would never be anyone else for him. She kissed him on the lips in public and he didn't even mind!

Bobby walked in behind Jeannine and surveyed the room; he saw Donnie sitting in the chair with a cast on his leg. Flashbacks of all the times he and Donnie had tangled, how many times they went fist to cuffs over the most stupid things and he felt a tinge of embarrassment. He wasn't ready to kiss and make up with the Buckles family, but something told him that it was time to put stupid things aside. His eyes met Elmer's and he tried to convey his internal feelings through his eyes, but he didn't think he accomplished much. He nodded at Sheriff Ross and when he saw Heather, he removed his ball cap. He walked past Decker and Jeannine and headed straight for the Sheriff. "I heard about Parchman today," he looked over at Donnie, nodded and said, "my condolences Donnie." It was quick, but he was sincere. "I didn't have anything to do with any of this Sheriff," he waved his hand holding the ballcap around the room to indicate the carnage of emotions he could see in the room. "Someone is trying to set me up." Elmer took a step towards Bobby, "I know that Bobby." Bobby stopped pointing at arbitrary things around the room and lowered his head then looked at Decker and Jeannine, "I'm glad the boy is okay." Elmer smiled, "I know that too Bobby."

They could see the reflection of the ambulance lights off the entrance glass door, seconds later the paramedics from Coahoma entered with a gurney. Elmer stepped away and knocked on the door that held Jessica, her father and the doctor: "Coahoma is here."

In just a matter of minutes the two paramedics entered the room and were quickly rolling Jessica out on the gurney. She was holding her father's hand as he walked beside her. Everyone in the room stepped aside and stared at her. Jeannine continued to hold Decker's hand as the gurney approached them. Jessica lifted her head up to see Decker standing with Jeannine. She looked up and backwards at the paramedic that was pushing her from behind and softly said: "Stop." The gurney stopped and she sat up, she was wearing a hospital gown now instead of Decker's shirt. "Thank you, Decker, you saved my life." She reached out her arms and without hesitation Decker embraced her. Decker felt her place a kiss on his cheek, two girls kissing his face in the same night was way more than Decker ever imagined. Jessica didn't let go of Decker, but she smiled when she saw Jeannine smiling at them and said softly but still loud enough for everyone to hear, "I finally found the prince I prayed for and he's already taken," she smiled at

Jeannine and kissed Decker one more time on the cheek then laid back on the gurney. Decker held her hand for just a second but let go when the gurney was almost out the door. Jeannine wasted no time wrapping Decker back up in her arms. She didn't mind what just happened, like everyone else in the room, she was proud of Decker Davis. Her boyfriend had seen the devil tonight and had beat him back with nothing more than his courage and brains.

Chapter 52
Chocolate & Biscuits

DECKER WOKE UP IN HIS OWN BED Friday morning to the smell of bacon. He couldn't ever remember smelling something that good. He could actually hear it sizzle on the stove. He flung the covers off and made his way to the bathroom. His knee was still a little sore from smashing it against that man's head. The thought of his knee, the basement and the man's head, stopped him in his tracks and he stood there in the hallway of his own home worried. He could not figure out why he was worried in his own home, but it was as if he were still on the run. He got scared for a second, but he was snapped out of it by his father kissing him on top of his head. "Good morning Deck!" His father continued down the hallway towards the kitchen. "Decker! It's ready!" he could hear Heather loud and clear, but his stomach could hear her louder. He was starving!

Elmer was sitting at the table and by the time Decker arrived, Heather had placed the last bowl of gravy on the table and sat down along with her dad. Decker smiled when he saw one of the bowls was chocolate gravy, Heather didn't make it often but boy when she did, he took advantage of it. He would lather his biscuit with butter and then smother the biscuits in the chocolate gravy. Once he felt like he had just about enough he would start dragging his bacon through the gravy. He could eat at least 10 strips of bacon that way. Elmer poured a cup of coffee, but he didn't read the paper like he always did, this morning he gave Decker and Heather his full attention. How do you feel today son?" Elmer took a sip of coffee and tried to pretend like the question was nonchalant, his dad asked him the same question yesterday over dinner.

Decker didn't go to school on Thursday, his dad insisted that he stay home and rest but today was Friday, he felt much better, and he was kind of tired of being fawned over and babied. Heather reached for the biscuits, "You don't have to do this Decker, you know that right?" Decker looked at Heather as she said, he knew they were trying to be protective of him and he appreciated it, but he badly wanted to move on. Jeannine was calling him so much yesterday that even Mrs. Norman got mad that she couldn't use the party line. He knew they all meant well but he just wanted to get back to normal. He had to admit, he had some bad dreams, but he had bad dreams before this, and he figured he would have bad dreams after this.

He was anxious to get back to school. "I know sister, but I want to. I already missed yesterday, and I missed my game." Heather poured some chocolate gravy on her biscuits while Elmer watched. "You just missed the JV game Decker, coach Bond called yesterday and wanted to make sure you were okay." Elmer spoke to both coaches on Thursday after the news of the evening began to circulate. News crews from all over Mississippi were in town trying to gather information about other kids around the state that have gone missing. Everyone was calling to check on Decker, but Decker had a feeling that many of them just wanted the inside scoop and were hoping that they could get gossip that no one else had. Luckily, his dad was good at handling nosey people. Elmer stayed with Decker all day and did his best to work from home. He went through every missing person reports that he had in the office and spent the day studying the faces of the kids and answered all the phone calls.

"Coach says he'd still like you to dress for the varsity tonight if you are up to it." Decker started to pour some chocolate gravy on his biscuits, but Heather grabbed the gravy bowl and did it for him. She spoke as she poured, "We just want you comfortable Deck, we don't want you rushing back into anything if you don't want to." She set the gravy bowl back on the table then proceeded to use Decker's fork to start cutting up his biscuits, but he stopped her, "I can do that sister, really." Heather realized she was being a little over motherly to her little brother, but she couldn't help it. The events of Wednesday night had scared her beyond belief, and she couldn't imagine her family without Decker. She wanted to hug him and squeeze him all day and had to constantly fight off the urge to do so. "Sorry Decker, I just . . . ", Decker smiled, put his hand on her forearm and lightly patted it. "I'm fine, really. It's Jessica that needs to be pampered." Heather smiled and ran her hand through Decker's hair like she did when he just a boy. "Maybe we can all take a drive to Drew this weekend and check on her? Would you like that?" Decker thought about it and was about to say he'd like to, but his dad spoke up, "She isn't in Drew. They took her to Jackson. Clarksdale recommended it. Seems they have a better facility there to help her," he paused and then quickly said, "But we can damn sure drive to Jackson this weekend and see her if you like Deck?" Decker smiled, took a bit of his chocolate and biscuits, swallowed and said, "Can Jeannine go?" Elmer chuckled, "I wouldn't even think of us going without her."

They all ate and didn't say much as the only noise was the clank of silverware hitting the plates. Decker wasn't in the mood to talk much and was simply enjoying his food. Elmer broke the silence once again, "What do you want me to tell the coach Deck?" Decker took a strip of bacon and drug it through the remainder of chocolate that was left on his plate, stopped and looked up, "I wish it was my game, I hate to dress for a game that I am just gonna stand on the sideline the whole time." He took a bite of the bacon and spoke as he chewed, "I hear we lost the JV game last night, I let them down by not being there." Elmer set his coffee on the table and leaned back a little in the chair, "Son there are 10 other kids on that team that have a hand in winning and losing too. There is no doubt in my mind that they could have used you but you missing the game isn't the reason they lost, they lost because . . . " he paused, "because the Charleston team was better that night, that's all." Elmer wasn't one to let a life lesson go by unlearned, he knew his son had been through a lot in the last 48 hours, but he also knew he couldn't stop being a dad, teaching and helping his son sort out life's puzzles. "If you don't want to dress for the game tonight because you are still sorting out the events of this week, nobody will think less of you, but if you don't dress because you won't get to play, then you aren't really a part of the team."

Heather could see that Decker was trying to process everything in his head and she wished she could help him figure things out more easily, but this was a difficult thing to figure out. Decker didn't respond to his Dad's comment about being on a team because he had some more thinking to do on that subject but there was something that was bothering him that he wanted an answer to, so he asked, "Why me Dad? Why did that man come after me?" Elmer became very still, he knew that Decker would get around to asking this question at some point but even though he thought about it already, he didn't really want to answer it, but he did anyway. "Because you're my son, nothing more than that. They weren't after you." Elmer lowered his head and then looked back up at both Heather and Decker, "I've made enemies in my line of work and some of those enemies want to hurt me by hurting you." He stood up, walked to the coffee pot and then stood with his back to them, "I should have known that. I'm sorry." He didn't want to turn around because he had a tear that rolled down his cheek, so he took the dish towel and pretended to clean the counter by the coffee pot and use the towel to wipe is his eyes. "We just have to be more careful, it's a dangerous world we live in now." When he felt like he was ok to turn around he grabbed his coffee cup and sat down. Heather looked at him then looked down at his still empty coffee cup, got up grabbed the carafe and poured his cup full. She kissed him on the forehead, sat back down and said, "We will all be more careful, won't we Deck?" She smiled and for the first time since they got back home, Decker smiled back at her.

Decker finished what was on his plate and thought about another biscuit, but he decided against it. The conversation at the table made him realize that the quicker he started behaving like he used to, the quicker life would get back to normal which meant he needed to get ready for school and it also meant that he would dress for the varsity tonight. "Will you be at the game tonight Dad?" Elmer smiled then put his elbows on the table, "I wouldn't miss it for all the money in the world, son."

Chapter 53
Pre-Game

A SMALL COLD FRONT BLEW THROUGH Mississippi that afternoon causing the temperature to drop quickly. It wasn't the heavy coat type of cold front, but it reminded everyone in town that it was fall and there was a big football game tonight for the Choctaws. Charleston had beaten them, and everyone said it was because the Choctaws didn't have Donnie Ray Richardson which was probably true, but no one realized that Mike Ford, the quarterback that took over for Donnie Ray when he left, was breaking all of Donnie Ray's records. Decker knew it, he knew that Mike was a very good quarterback but since the team wasn't winning many of their games, he wasn't getting much credit for the things he was doing on the field. Decker sat there in the field house dressing room with guys moving all around, laughing a little but for the most part it was quiet chatter. He hadn't started to change into his uniform yet, he was still thinking about the events of the week. The football games, the JV game he missed yesterday because the doctor said he needed to stay home and rest, and the game today, where he was dressing for the varsity as an 8th grader. It seemed to him to him as he sat there in the locker room that just two days ago that these games were the most important things in the world to Decker Davis, and now, he wasn't sure he even wanted to play. A few of the guys in the locker room had said some encouraging things to him but it seemed to him that most of the guys were avoiding him. He didn't know if it was because of what happened this week and they didn't know what to say or it was simply because he was an eighth grader, and they didn't want him there. Either way, he had grown up being ignored and left by himself, so this didn't bother him much, he knew how to handle it.

Decker looked back at his locker where his jersey was hanging, it wasn't his regular number 12, Mike Ford wore that one, so he saw they had given him number 13. He wasn't crazy about a number as unlucky as 13 but he wasn't going to complain. He figured it would take a while for his dad and Heather to figure out what number he was, but again, he didn't care. He felt a tap on his shoulder and turned to see coach Hayes standing there. Coach Hayes was a thick stocky man with huge forearms, but he was also a very kind man. He sounded rough but he had always been good to Decker and had helped Decker overcome some of his early confidence problems. "You alright?" Decker looked up at him, "Yes sir, coach." Coach Hayes patted him on his shoulder, "Start getting dressed." Coaches Hayes winked at him and immediately turned around and gave another kid some advice on blocking and then disappeared into the coach's office.

Decker sat there for a minute staring at the floor when he felt another hand on his shoulder, this time it was Mike Ford, the starting Quarterback. Mike took a seat next to Decker, he had his game pants on but was still in just a tee-shirt. "Charleston has a strong side linebacker, mean and fast. He likes to get in rhythm with your cadence, he's smart, he figures out your snap count and he shoots past the tackle faster than you can say OH SHIT. By then, it's too late." Decker was listening to him but couldn't figure out why he was telling him all this, Decker was third string on the varsity depth chart and his chances of playing tonight at Quarterback were slim and none but none the less, Decker listened. "You need to know where he is all the time," he patted Decker on the leg. "Number 57, don't ever lose track of him." He got up and as he did, he turned to Decker and said, "I'm glad you are here with us kid," and he returned to his locker.

Decker looked down at the floor again and wondered what Jessica was doing, how she was handling being back with her parents. He thought about breakfast this morning and how he got a little scared in his own house, he would never admit that to anyone, but it was true. If he were scared after one night of being with those terrible people, he couldn't imagine how he would feel if had been with them three years like she had. He had spent the day in school in somewhat of a fog. It was as if he heard people talking to him and he even managed to respond to them, but it was like he wasn't really listening. Even Jeannine tried to snap him out of his fog, but she didn't push too hard. She would say something like, "Are you there?" and when he responded she would either put her arm under his and walk down the hall like she was being escorted somewhere or she would hold his hand. Both maneuvers were forbidden in school by anyone. Boys and girls weren't supposed to display any form of affection in school, but that day, nobody said anything to him. He loved Jeannine and he had to admit, every time she held his hand or touched him, he felt better.

He tried to put all the bad thoughts out of his head and honestly, the thoughts about Number 57 helped him think about something other than the past two days. He still didn't figure he would ever get the chance to be close to that Number 57, but if he did, he was not about to let him crush him. He shook his head at the thought of being hit hard by a fast linebacker and then he turned to his locker, grabbed some of his gear and started to suit up.

The small chatter in the locker room continued as Decker finished his last bit of prep work to get ready. It felt weird sliding the Number 13 jersey over his shoulder pads. His first thought was that it had been in a box for a long time because it smelled funny to him, then he realized he would have to smell that musty smell for the next two hours for sure. He was sitting next to Keith Parker who played left guard and was as big as a house. Decker wasn't for sure if Keith knew him or not and didn't attempt to start up any small talk to find out. Keith reached down for his shoes that were on the floor beneath him and as he was bending down, he let out a very loud fart. It was so loud that the entire locker room went quiet. Keith never said a word, he just continued to fiddle with a knot in the laces of his shoe. Decker tried to hold his breath for as long as he could, but he ran out of air and then had to inhale a huge gasp of lingering Keith Parker fart air. Decker must have made enough gasping noise for several in the locker room to hear which caused everyone to start laughing. Someone yelled "Don't kill that kid Parker! We might need him if Ford and Sherman get killed!" Everyone howled with laughter. Eric Sherman was the second-string quarterback and was the starting punter and kicker. If something happened to Mike Ford, then Eric would step in for him.

Coach Bond walked into the locker room and flipped the switch of the lights on and off to signal it was time to listen. Decker had never been in the room with Coach Bond in a game situation, he wasn't sure what to expect but for the first time in in 48 hours he wasn't thinking about what had happened to him. "Listen up guys," Coach Bond's voice was calm and confident, "Most of what I read today talks about how Charleston has their sights set on a state championship," he held up a newspaper clipping for everyone to see, "Says that they are more talented than we are," there was some shuffling of feet and Decker heard someone spit. "Says that we will be lucky to make it through half time," coach Bond folded the newspaper clipping and put it in his pocket. He didn't say anything for a while and the silence became uncomfortable, then he spoke again, "It's all true," there was a lot of grumbling in the room. "They are more talented. That Number 57 linebacker will be playing for the Bulldogs next year, he's a bad ass." He put his hands together and interlocked his fingers then let his clasped hands rest in front of him, he let a mischievous style smile come across his face and said, "And if I knew where to place the bet, I'd bet every damn dollar I had and my first born on the Choctaws tonight." Every head that was lowered in the room, raised up, and looked at him, "I mean that fellas, you're gonna kick their ass tonight, now go out there and do it." There was no raise of his voice, he said it as matter of fact as he could have said anything. Mike Ford, the leader of the team jumped up with his helmet in his hand and screamed something that Decker didn't quite understand but the rest of team must have understood him because they all stood and bolted out the field house door screaming and hollering like he had never heard. He wondered at that moment if this was anything like the "rebel yell" he had read about in his research of the civil war. A yell that inspired the South and scared the North because it was a sound that was unlike anything anyone had ever heard.

Decker followed everyone out on the field and immediately started looking in the stands for Heather and his dad, he knew about where they would be, but he didn't immediately see them. He tried to remember that he had a job to do so he focused on helping Mike Ford stay loose by throwing the ball back and forth to him. He was surprised by how hard Mike threw. After Mike felt he was warmed up he nodded at Decker and turned toward the field. Decker turned toward the sideline and took another shot trying to find Heather and his Dad. He found them but he was shocked by who he saw with them. They all saw him looking for them and everyone waved except one person and she simply smiled.

Chapter 54

Maybelle?

HEATHER DID HER BEST to carry on the tradition of making hot chocolate like her mother did when she was alive. The temperature had dropped enough that she grabbed a few blankets for her and her dad. He hadn't been to a game this year, so she was unsure of what to bring for him. He promised he would be by the house to pick her up and take her to the game and he kept the promise. He decided he didn't want to go in his normal uniform, that he didn't want to be seen as the Sheriff tonight, he wanted to be seen as Decker Davis's Dad.

Elmer stood there in the kitchen in a pair of jeans and dress shirt. It had been a long time since Heather had seen him in anything but his brown Sheriff's garb; and she liked the way her dad looked other than he had lost quite a bit of weight lately. He looked like a normal man that was ready to go to a Friday night football game. "Daddy did you grab a jacket? It's gonna be chilly tonight." Elmer was looking out the kitchen window and was deep in thought, he didn't answer the question about the jacket, but he asked a question that caught Heather off guard, "You think Lois watches us? Do you believe in God, I mean really believe?" Heather stopped packing her bag, "I do." She started packing again then stopped, "I believe that not only is mom watching, she's helping. I believe that only MOM could have helped you find Decker and TWO other girls that needed help all in the same night." She stopped, walked over to him and put her arms around him from behind, "I know you miss her, Daddy, we all do but we have to move forward as a family." Elmer spun around, put his arms around his daughter, stood silent for a minute then said, "I'm lucky you are my daughter. Ready to go see Decker stand on the sideline?" She laughed and playfully pushed him away. He smiled as he knew there wasn't much hope for Decker to get to play tonight but it was still a big deal that he was even dressed and on the sideline.

Elmer and Heather made their way up the bleacher steps to the spot just under the press box. That's where they always sat, and everyone knew it. They were early for the game so there weren't that many people in the stands yet, but it was sure to be packed as it got closer to game time. Heather spread out the blankets for them to sit on and slid the basket she had with the thermos of hot chocolate under the bleacher seat. Once she was comfortable, she sat down and took in the moment. She breathed the fall air and heard the inconsistent sounds of horns and drums as the band practiced behind the stadium. She had been in this very spot so many times with her family, especially her mother. A tingle came over her skin as if she had seen something scary, the goosebumps were prevalent on her arm as she looked around the entire stadium. She knew at that moment that her mother was telling her she was with her and that things would be alright. She smiled at the thought of her mother sitting beside her and she actually looked at the empty spot next to her as if maybe at any moment, her mother would materialize right in front of her. As she was staring at the empty spot she heard her dad, "Yeah, she is here too." She didn't know her dad was watching her and felt the same way she did. A feeling of relief came over her like nothing she had ever felt before. She leaned her head against her dad's shoulder and slid her arm under his and enjoyed the moment of peace, a moment she, nor her dad, had felt in a long time.

She was enjoying the moment when she saw an older but distinguished uniformed man coming up the bleacher and he had several people with him. He was smiling under the protection of his cowboy hat as he slowly took each step. Heather had only briefly seen the Sheriff R.C. Ross from Sunflower County at the hospital. She remembered him praying and how much better she felt after he had prayed but here he was walking up the steps right at them. As they got closer, she could not believe her eyes when a young girl moved out from behind the Sheriff's frame. Both her and her dad rose quickly as neither could believe what they were seeing. They knew who she was but she looked so much different, they were looking at Jessica Muncik as a little girl that was back where she belonged as opposed to the shell of a girl they had seen just two nights ago. The transformation was amazing and she began to cry.

Jessica saw Heather, the lady that had held her and cuddled her the first night of her freedom, the lady that made her feel loved again with just a touch was standing right in front of her. Jessica made a quick step around Sheriff Ross and skipped every other bleach step on her way to Heather where she practically knocked her over with a hug. The two stood there in an emotional embrace, an embrace that sealed a bond between the two for the rest of their lives.

Elmer stuck out his hand for Sheriff Ross and offered a huge smile, "Sheriff Ross I didn't expect to see you tonight but I ain't complaining!" Sheriff Ross took Elmer's hand but pulled him close and gave him a hug. Elmer wasn't used to being hugged by guys but there was something about R.C Ross that made him relax and feel perfectly normal hugging him. "I told you to call me Clint," as he released Elmer from the hug. Elmer looked down at the older Sheriff, "Well Clint, I am surprised to see you today, especially here. Clint looked around behind as if he was searching for someone but turned back to look at Elmer, "Sheriff this is Mr. Arnie Muncik, you met him already" Arnie reached out to shake Elmer's hand, but he also managed to step around Clint and hug Elmer, "Thank you Sheriff." Elmer could hear a little shake in his voice, but he was also smiling, "Sheriff this is my wife, uhhh" he was searching for words but then came back with "actually she is my ex-wife, Jessica's mother Lois." Elmer started to shake her hand but when he heard her name he froze, "Did he just say your name is Lois?" The small lady smiled, took a step around Clint and hugged Elmer with everything she had in her. "He did, thank you, Sheriff, for bringing our baby back to us." She was clearly crying, there was no mistaking that. She held on to Elmer as they all looked on, Elmer patted her in her back to reassure her, "It was damn lucky Lois, but my son had more to do with her coming back to you than anything I did." She finally let him go and tried to wipe away the tears that had streaked down her face causing some of her make up to run with it. "I'm sorry Sheriff, I told myself I would try and stay together but I, uh, we are so excited to have our baby back." Elmer turned to look at Heather who still had her arm around Jessica, "Me too ma'am, me too."

After they all sat down again, the two Sheriff's sat on the end next to each other but not for long, "Sheriff, I believe I'd like a cup of hot coffee, would you mind walking with me?" Elmer obliged and both men headed for the concession stand. Once they were out of hearing range Sheriff Ross began to fill Elmer in on all the details, "That little girl had been to hell and back my friend. She is remarkably stable considering what she has endured. Doc wanted to keep her in the hospital longer, but she wouldn't have any of it. She told everyone that if they didn't take her to see Decker play tonight that she'd find a way to do it without them." He smiled, "She is as tough as they come." Elmer looked down at the ground, "Wish she had been allowed to be a child, my friend." Clint stopped walking and looked at the Elmer, "Doc says she won't be able to have any kids, the man was Satan for sure." Clint continued to look at Elmer, "How is he? Is he dead yet?" Elmer shook his head. "No sir, our police chief put three slugs in him, and he is hanging on by a thread. I don't think he will make it though." Elmer looked towards the field, "I was hoping we could get some more information from him if you know what I mean." Clint started walking again, "That's another thing I wanted to tell you, Jessica up there, he pointed up in the stands, "She gave us a lot of names, so far we can clear seven missing children off the boards," he shook his head. "Unfortunately, they won't have the same reunion with their families but because Jessica remembered every kid that came through there in the last three years, and get this," he kicked a rock in the path to the concession stand, "She even told us where he dumped five of the seven." Elmer shook his head then rubbed his forehead as he tended to do when he was stressed, "God almighty! She saw all that?" Clint let out a deep breath, "Best we can figure is that he fell in love with Jessica and thought she would be with him forever, that's why she didn't meet the same fate." They both kept walking, "He liked to toss them in the kudzu all over the area, that stuff will cover anything in no time."

Clint ordered he and Elmer some coffee and added a couple to take back to Jessica's parents. When they were walking away from the concession stand Clint continued to speak, "How's your boy?" Elmer stopped and looked at the empty field that would soon be filled with football players. "He's rattled a little. His heart really wasn't in to coming to this game and I hope I haven't pushed into something he shouldn't be pushed into." Clint shook his head, "That's understandable but listen Elmer, that boy of yours is nothing short of a miracle." He paused and looked out at the empty field too, "From everything Jessica told us, Decker outsmarted all of them, set a trap and wouldn't leave Jessica for anything, even though she tried to get him to leave her." He smiled as he looked at Elmer, "I don't know many boys his age, good grief, I don't know many men these days that would have done what he did." Elmer had heard some of the details Jessica told Heather that night in the hospital. Apparently, Jessica was exceptional at recounting details which is why they were able to physically reunite children with their loved ones so quickly. Clint lost his smile, "Do you think the monsters brother knew about all this?" Elmer shook his head in a confused way, "You mean my deputy?" He drew in a breath, "Clint he says he didn't, I have to believe him, hell, you should see the badge that took the bullet his brother tried to put in him." Clint agreed but seemed to still have questions, "What's on your mind Clint?" They were at the edge of the bleachers, there still weren't many people in the stand, Clint set the little carry box of coffee the concession stand gave him on the bottom bleacher, "We've tried not to bother you so you could concentrate on your son," Elmer cocked his head to one side, "Spit it out Clint."

Clint put his hands in his pants pocket as if he were trying to keep them still, "We arrested a guard out at Parchman yesterday, name of Murphy." Elmer shook his head to indicate he didn't know the name. "He thought he was a tough guy, but we slapped cuffs on him and told him our objective was to convict him and send him right back to Parchman with a different uniform, if you know what I mean." He laughed a little as he said it but then he got serious again, "We think he helped set up the murder of your wife or at least he knew about it." Elmer used the chain link fence to help him get steady again, this was not news he expected to hear. "That bullet that killed your wife was meant for you." Elmer could feel a pain in his stomach and the sweat begin to pop out on his forehead, "Clint that was two guys shooting at each other after a fist fight went south . . . " Clint shook his head in agreement but then added, "That's the way it was meant to look." Clint removed his right hand from his pocket and put it on Elmer's shoulder, "I'm sorry I have to be the one to tell you now, but I think you need to know. Paper is gonna run a story on corruption out at Parchman and more than likely your story is going to be in it." Elmer shook his head, "Why?" Clint didn't hesitate, "Vendetta of some kind, just a bunch of creeps in prison trying to get back at you for doing your job." Elmer was struggling with the news, up until now Lois's death had been accidental, "So you are telling me that my wife died because of me?"

"Hi Elmer!" Elmer turned to see who was saying hello and at first, he didn't recognize them but then he recognized her, there were so few people that actually called him Elmer so he should have known, "Maybelle Richardson." He forced a smile, "My good-ness what happened to you? You look like you just got out of high school." Maybelle continued towards Elmer and when she reached Elmer, she hugged him closely and then put her hands on each side of his face, pulled him close to her and gave him a kiss on the lips. It was just a peck but there was no mistaking that she had kissed him. Elmer blushed and was struggling for words, "Uh Sheriff Ross, this is Maybelle Richardson, she and I have been friends since elemen-tary school." Sheriff Ross smiled, tipped his hat and then shook her hand. "I haven't seen you since . . . " he didn't want to relive the day her son rescued his son and it nearly cost him his life, "Haven't seen you in at least three years and now look at you." Maybelle was a beautiful woman in high school and college and still was a beautiful woman, but she had put on a considerable amount of weight after she gave birth to Donnie. Now she was back to her normal size, anyone with a brain had to admit that she looked very good. "Are you ok? Is your health good?" Maybelle knew what he meant, "You want the fat Maybelle back do you?" Elmer blushed again, "That ain't what I meant . . . " she laughed and hugged Elmer again, "I know Elmer, you were always the easiest man in the world to embarrass." They chatted for a few minutes, she heard about what had happened to Decker and she also knew that Decker was dressing for the varsity. "Donnie is gonna meet me here tonight Elmer!" She clasped her hands together, "This is an off week for him, and he wanted to be here for Decker, he wanted to surprise Decker." Elmer smiled, "Well I can tell you that Decker will be surprised for sure, Donnie Ray is his hero." Elmer looked down at Maybelle and remembered them together as teenagers. He and Maybelle had pushed the boundaries for what was considered acceptable behavior back in the day and he smiled, "You want to sit with us?" He pointed up in the stands and she agreed. After Maybelle walked away Sheriff Ross finished what he wanted to say, "Son, it ain't your fault that people are mean and evil. Don't you dare think that way." He let his words hang in the air, he grabbed the tray of coffee, "Let's go get set to watch some football."

Chapter 55

Number '57'

DECKER COULD NOT BELIEVE what he was seeing. He really had not had time to truly understand what she looked like after all, most of the time he spent with her was in a pitch-black basement and after that it was in the back seat of the Scout and after that, a brief moment in the Hospital; but here she was, sitting with his sister, not waving but smiling a smile like he had never seen, somehow she was sending him a message and he was receiving it. Jessica Lynn Muncik was at his game.

He could see everyone: there was Jeannine, she was sitting with Jessica and his sister, he saw his dad, he saw a lady sitting with his dad that he didn't recognize but she was waving furiously, probably more than anyone, so he felt like he was supposed to know who she was, but he didn't. There were other people in the group, but they simply waived and continued to stare. He was a little embarrassed by how many people were sitting there with nothing more to do than watch him stand on the sidelines. They must not have had as much trouble as he thought they would be picking out his Number 13.

He was still staring at his family and all the people in the crowd when he felt an arm around him. He looked to his right to see coach Hayes. "You got a lot of people here to see you tonight. You feel alright?" Decker wasn't sure how to answer that, he was standing there on the sidelines looking up in the stands at a girl he shared a pitch-black basement with just a few hours ago, he thought there would be no way that anyone could understand that emotion and he wasn't really in the mood to try and get anyone to understand it. "I'm fine coach," was the reply he settled on. Coach Hayes smiled at him and patted his shoulder pad with authority. "This ain't no place to pretend boy, when the pads start smashing you better have your mind right." Decker looked at Coach Hayes and decided he was right, he needed to stop thinking about what happened and focus on being a good teammate, at least for now. He became focused on his role of being a backup player, a cheerleader, and in some cases a coach's assistant. Coach Hayes gave him a clip board and it was his job to chart all the plays that were called for the offense. He didn't mind doing that because it helped him remember all the plays. The plays for the JV were the same but the varsity play book had way more pass plays in it. Decker wasn't allowed to pass very much, even in the JV games, Coach Hayes used to say that there were three things that could happen when a team passed the ball and two of them were bad, so Decker spent most of the time handing off to Grant Washburn or running the ball himself. He didn't mind but he would have liked to show the coach that he was a good passer too.

The Choctaws won the coin toss and elected to receive. Once the kick was in the air, Decker could tell that this was a much different game than the ones he played in. The games he played in, well the players were much slower and much smaller. In this game, it seemed that everyone was fast and the collisions between players made a lot more noise.

The Choctaws went nowhere on their first possession and were forced to punt. To Decker, it was a terrible start, they lost yardage due to a couple of quarterback sacks by the Number 57 that Mike Ford had warned him about. He stood there on the sideline and wondered why Mike had not paid attention to his own advice, but he couldn't think about that now. He was trying to remember the last play that caused the sack. He had to ask the coach to confirm what he thought, and they confirmed a *22-play action post.* It was easy to write the next play down because it was a punt. Decker was writing standard cover formation and didn't see the play, but he heard the gasps from the stands. There was a loud smashing double thump sound and when he looked up, he saw a Charleston player sprinting down the side lines in direction of their end zone. The stadium was completely quiet. He was confused for just a minute but when he saw coach Bond trot out onto the field with the trainer, he knew what had happened. Charleston had blocked the punt, and in the process, had knocked the punter and second-string quarterback out. Eric was lying motionless on the field for what seemed like an eternity. The crowd nervously clapped when he finally sat up and Coach Bond, along with the trainer helped him off the field. They walked right by where Decker was standing, he heard Coach Bond tell Coach Hayes that Eric got his bell rung and in the coach's words, "He don't know what day it is."

He felt a hand on his should and he turned to see Coach Hayes again. "Warm up." Decker must have had a confused look on his face because Coach Hayes had a scared look on his face, a look that he knew too well. It was sort of the same look he figured he had on his face when he woke up in that dark basement. "Mike broke his collar bone." Now it was Decker that had the scared look on his face. He knew what it was like to break a collar bone, he had done it a few years back and it hurt. He felt bad for Mike, but it hadn't completely sunk in yet that in two plays, the Choctaws had lost two quarterbacks. They only had one quarterback left now and that was Decker Davis.

Mike Ford came over to Decker before he walked off the field, he smiled but winced when he smiled, "I should have taken my own advice huh?" Decker turned away to look for his helmet, he forgot where he put it and Mike turned to walk away but he spun back around, "Decker." Decker looked up at him. "Everyone knows what happened this week, they know you manned up and took care of that little girl." Mike had a very serious look on his face. "That's some serious shit little brother." He showed his teeth when he smiled this huge smile that Decker had never seen. Then Mike pointed at the field with his good arm and said, "This is just a game." He stared at Decker long enough to see the same huge smile come across Decker's face.

Since Charleston blocked a punt, recovered the ball and ran it all the way back for a touchdown, the offense had to go right back on the field. Charleston missed the extra point, so the game was barely three minutes old and the Choctaws were behind 6-0. Luckily, Decker found his helmet and was adjusting his chin strap when Coach Bond appeared in front of him. He stood in front of Decker for a while without saying a word. They made eye contact and Decker was wondering what he wanted to say, Charleston had kicked off already and Mitch Spivey had a pretty good run back that gave the Choctaws the ball right at the 50-yard line. Decker was anxious to get started, after what Mike Ford said to him, he felt most of the tension in his shoulders and legs go away but he couldn't very well step around the head coach while he was staring at him. The silence was getting to Decker and couldn't take it anymore, "I won't mess up coach, I promise." Coach Bond smiled at him and stepped aside without saying a word.

Decker took one last look up in the stands, he saw his dad and he saw his sister, that's all he really wanted to see. He knew his dad would be nervous and Heather would chew on the fingernail of her left pinky. It was a habit she had that only Decker knew about. He was so busy looking at his family that he failed to notice the tall young man standing on the sidelines next to the trainer, it was none other than Donnie Ray Richardson.

Decker slowly trotted on to the field after getting the play from Coach Hayes. The first play was going to be a simple handoff, in pee wee football they called the play dive right and dive left but in the sophisticated world of high school football this play was called 32 stack. Decker called the play in the huddle, every guy in the huddle was looking everywhere but at Decker and chattering among themselves. Decker knew every guy in that huddle, he had grown up with them, all of them were older than him and worse, some of them had picked on him. Decker didn't hold grudges and even if he did, now wasn't the time to air the grudge, so he called the play one more time, only this time he yelled it so nearly everyone in the stadium could hear it including Charleston. All the guys in the huddle stopped talking and looked at Decker like he had lost his mind. Decker returned their stares, "Well now that Charleston knows we are running a 32 stack we better go show them how it's done." The giant left guard Keith Parker chuckled and said out loud, "Get behind me you bunch of sissies." Keith Parker knew that 32 stack meant that they were going to run right behind him, and he would be responsible for clearing a path.

The play didn't quite work as expected, Decker fumbled the snap from center and had to scramble to find the ball as it was getting kicked around like a pinball. Luckily, he found it and fell on it. He felt the weight of others on top of him and reminded him of the old "pile on" games that the kids used to play so they could all squash him at the bottom of the pile. He couldn't tell who was on top of him but heard them say something about "being next" and then the pile was gone. He stood up and as he walked back to the huddle, he picked the grass clumps out of his face mask. Once he was in the huddle, he called the play he was supposed to, it was the same play as before, but it was on the other side of the center. When all the players left the huddle Decker slowly walked up to the line, he scanned the defense and found who he was looking for, Number 57. Once he had spotted him and he knew where he was, he looked to the other side but something on the sideline caught his attention, that's when he saw him. Decker couldn't believe it; it was Donnie Ray Richardson! His mind raced, his heart rate went up and for a second, he froze, then it hit him. Instead of continuing to the line he veered off from everyone and started slowly walking towards the sideline. Everyone was looking at him, even his own teammates were confused about what he was doing. Coach Bond looked at Coach Hayes, "What the hell is he doing?" Coach Hayes tried to rationalize the behavior, "I don't know coach, maybe he saw something that confused him," Coach Bond disagreed by shaking his head, "He hasn't bothered to call time out!"

Decker shook his head and unsnapped his chin strap and just about the time he got to the sideline he signaled to the referee that he wanted a time out. The referee blew the whistle and Decker stepped out of bounds right in front of Donnie Richardson. Donnie Ray smiled at Decker and shook his head, "I see you are still doing things your own way little brother." Decker took his helmet off, dropped it on the ground, put his arms around Donnie Ray and hugged him. Coach Bond and Coach Hayes had made their way to where Decker and Donnie were standing now. "What are you doing Davis!" Decker let go of Donnie and looked at both coaches, "Saying hello to my friend coach." Coach Hayes threw his hat on the ground in a fury, "We don't have time for that Decker!" Decker didn't flinch, he looked at Donnie, "I'm glad you came. Can you come over to my house after the game?" Donnie laughed. "In the middle of the biggest game of your life you want to invite me over for cake and coffee?" He laughed again, "Damn Decker Davis, you know I will!" Decker smiled, looked at Coach Hayes and Coach Bond, "I got this coach." Decker picked up his helmet, put it on his head and trotted back out to the field like nothing had ever happened. When he stepped into the huddle again, he was in control.

The paper the next day called it a defensive battle and they even used the term *"slobber knocker"* which seemed funny to Decker. The paper was right though, the defenses on both sides played extraordinary football and did not make any mistakes. Decker kept an eye on Number 57 all night as he had been instructed to do and for the most part, he stayed clear of getting pummeled by the big linebacker. Only once did Decker feel his intensity and that was when Decker attempted a roll out pass to his left and lost sight of where Number 57 was. Decker completed the pass but a split second after he released the ball, Number 57 slammed into him but luckily Decker had spun just enough during the throw that he didn't take a straight on hit. Nevertheless, Decker felt the impact well enough that he knew he didn't want to get hit like that again, and he didn't.

Folks were still talking about it being one of the best games they had ever seen, especially how it ended. Charleston managed to kick a 60-yard field goal with just two minutes left in the game. Everyone said it was a miracle because the kid that kicked the field goal wasn't even their normal kicker, he was a back-up wide receiver that had recently moved from England. The kid had never played American football, but the coach saw him kicking the hell out of a soccer ball and talked him into playing. He kicked it funny because he lined up from the side and kicked it at an angle. Nobody had seen that in these parts, but Decker had seen it on TV already. That 60-yard field goal made the score 9-0 in favor of Charleston.

The Choctaws got the ball back with just under 2 minutes on the clock. Coach Bond had his arm around Decker and was talking to him about what to do in the last two minutes. He told Decker that if he saw something he liked or didn't like, he didn't have to call time out to check with him, he just needed to go with his gut, but, and it was a big but, he said he needed to be able to back up his decisions later. Decker was surprised that he had no feelings at the moment, he wasn't tired, scared, confused, nervous or excited. He looked around as the coach was talking to him and took in everything he saw. He enjoyed this moment, he could smell the fall air, he could hear the band playing loud and people screaming all over the stadium. As he was about to turn and trot back out on the field, he saw Mike Ford who had returned to the sideline in his street clothes and his arm was in a sling. Mike looked at Decker and Decker could see him mouth the words, "It's just a game." Decker couldn't hear him, but he knew exactly what he said. Decker smiled and turned toward the field.

Decker could hear the heavy breathing in the huddle, he could see everyone was tired. He hadn't played with these guys very much since they were all older than him, but he was proud of them. Except for Keith Parker, they were all smaller than the Charleston players, but they had held their own. They had gone toe-to-toe with a much bigger opponent and had nothing to be ashamed of. Decker leaned into the huddle, "It's almost over guys, we got nothing to be ashamed of," all the guys were hunched over with their hands on their knees, tired and gasping for air, including Decker, "Hey let's stand up straight, they think we are tired, but we got about three more plays and we win this thing." Decker stood up straight and one-by-one each man followed, now they were all standing up straight with their hands on their hips all staring at Decker. He looked over at the Charleston defense and all the guys on the line were down on one knee including the linebackers. Decker looked back at his guys and smiled, "Anyone ever hear of a play called Easy Rider?" It wasn't the play that Coach Bond had sent in to run but after seeing the Charleston group just as tired, maybe more tired than his guys, he knew it was the perfect time to run it. All his players smiled; he knew they practiced it too. "Ok, make sure you are set, when you see me get right up to Coach Bond, count three and snap it." Suddenly there was new life in the huddle, there were smiles instead of gasps. Jimmy Hanover would get the direct snap. Decker wasn't sure how far Jimmy could throw it or if he could even throw it well at all, but he couldn't show any doubt. "Academy award fellas, make sure Charleston and the crowd see you roll your eyes in frustration." Decker snapped his chin strap, "Ready . . .break!"

Decker slowly walked up to the line, he started calling out things he saw like he had done all game, when he found Number 57, he acted confused and started yelling 57 over and over as loud as he could but then he backed away from the center, unsnapped his chin strap clearly showing frustration and started walking towards the side line. He kept his head down and he could see that the play was working. He couldn't look back and see what his guys were doing but out of the corner of his eye, he could sure see that the Charleston players had all relaxed and dropped back to one knee. The defensive end even unsnapped his chin strap thinking that Decker was going to call another timeout. Decker kept his head down and counted in his head, he knew he only had a few seconds left when the play clock would run out. He made it in front of Coach Bond and was delighted to see the coach was mad as he could be, he was giving Decker a look of anger like Decker had never seen before. When he got his feet set, he winked at the coach which changed the coaches look immediately from anger to confusion. With a confused look on Coach Bond's face, Decker counted to three and took off like he was shot out of a cannon.

At about the 50-yard line, Decker looked back and could see the ball in the air. There was not a single soul near him. The play had worked, now all he had to do was catch it. Jimmy Hanover's throw was not nearly as pretty as Grant's, but it didn't need to be. Decker waited on the ball, caught it in his chest and took off for the end-zone. With a completely confused Charleston team, throwing helmets, their coach chasing a referee all the way down the sideline, the score board changed from Charleston 9 the Choctaws 6. The referees had to huddle in the end zone and go over the facts of the play. Decker was the closest to them and was listening as closely as he could. There was so much noise that it was hard to hear what they were saying but at the end of the conversation, the head referee broke free of the huddle and threw both of his arms straight up in the air to signal that the touchdown stood. The crowd was given a chance to go wild again and they loved it. Mitch Spivey kicked the extra point a few minutes later making the score 9-7 in favor of Charleston.

Decker made his way back to Coach Bond who was smiling when Decker got to the sideline. "Sneakiest damn thing I've ever seen kid." Decker smiled back at him and went to the bench to get some water and sit for a minute. For the first time since the game started, he was feeling tired. He needed just a few minutes of rest and he would be good to go. He turned to look up in the stands and he saw her, Jeannine was sitting next to his sister and Jessica. They both were staring at Decker and when he met their eyes, they both waved and made all kinds of hand gestures that he didn't quite understand but he did understand when Jeannine drew an imaginary heart on her chest. He waved back then turned around quickly, he still had a game to play.

Chapter 56
The Kick

ROSALIND KALINA FROM THE GOVERNMENT office of child protective services who lived in Cascilla came over to see Elmer just after Decker scored a touchdown. She was a huge football fan but was late getting to the game because she was trying to finish all the paperwork on Madelyn Johnson. "That was amazing Elmer! You must be beaming with pride!" She was yelling because the band was playing and the crowd was still going nuts over a trick play they had never seen before, and would probably not see for a long time to come. At first Elmer didn't see her as she was making her way through the crowded bench row to get to him. He turned to see her and smiled because he knew what she had been trying to do. He was hoping that she had good news. "He shook her hand but she waved it off and hugged him. She had always been the touchy type of person that when she was talking to you, she had to have her hand on your forearm or shoulder. He didn't mind because she always meant well. "Thank you, Rosalind, I am nervous as I can be right now!" He had to yell too because it was so loud, and the band continued to play louder by the minute. He had been to many games both as a player and spectator and he couldn't ever remember the stadium sounding like this. "You know Webb is going to have to find a new youth minister, right?" He smiled and nodded, "So I was right about what was going on in the house?" Rosalind frowned, looked down at her feet and then looked back up at Elmer, "I am afraid so." She could see Elmer puff out his cheeks as he let out a huge blast of air in a show of frustration or perhaps disgust. "What's gonna happen to her now?" Her expression changed from a frown to smile, "The state is going to let Lavera take care of her until they can find a home for her." Elmer squinted his eyes like he didn't believe her, "Lavera probably won't go for that you know," Rosalind smiled even bigger, "It was Lavera that suggested it, or should I say, demanded it." Elmer leaned his head back and looked up at the night sky and in the midst of all that noise he let out a huge laugh, "Yep, there is no negotiating with Lavera when she has made up her mind."

Elmer felt a tug on his arm, he looked to the source of the tug, it was Heather. She was pointing at the field, "Here comes the onside kick Daddy!" Elmer patted Rosalind on the shoulder, "Good job!" He turned to the field, no one was sitting, everyone was staring at what was about to happen. He could see hands clasped together in the praying style while the band drummers added a rapid continuous beat to simulate the anticipation of the always suspense packed onside kick. If this were a JV game, Decker would have been on the side that the kick went to because he had knack for knowing where the ball was going to go based off how it bounced, but Elmer figured since the varsity was out of quarterbacks, Coach Bond was not about to risk losing his last one.

He felt Heather grab his arm out of excitement and nervousness, she had already chewed both of her pinky nails considerably. "I can't watch!" She buried her head in her Dad's shoulder, Jeannine buried her head in Heather's shoulder. Elmer felt his heart beating fast, he didn't know what the outcome would be, but he was sure proud of Decker. Decker had handled the game like a pro. He had not set any records or thrown any touchdown passes but he had competed with everything he had in him. It was safe to say that regardless of the outcome, Elmer was proud. He wished that Lois could be there to see this with him, but deep down he had the feeling she was.

He braced for the kick, he glanced at R.C. Ross who was just as tense as he was. He looked at Jessica who was holding on to her mom and her dad and he felt a warmth come over him that he hadn't felt in a long time. Jessica had made it back home against all odds and his son was partly responsible for that. There was no doubt that Jessica had the strength of Samson to get through all she went through but it was clear, without the help of Decker Davis she would still be in captivity. Elmer kept the stoic strong look on his face but deep down he was so proud to be the father of two such remarkable human beings. Heather had held the family together while he tried to crawl into a bottle and Decker had behaved like a man when no one would have shorted him for behaving like a boy.

The kick was a good one, it scooted about 9 yards and popped high up in the air where it seemed to be looking for a place to land. The bodies collided like a train wreck and every man on that field was scrambling as they searched for the ball. The ball ping ponged around for just a second and it disappeared under a pile of boys. The crowd that had been cheering wildly just a second ago were now echoing silence off the stars of the night.

The crowd was silent, the referee desperately tried to untangle the pile of bodies that hid the outcome of the game. Almost no one breathed until the referee untangled the mess and discovered that Charleston had indeed recovered the ball and would take possession with just a minute left on the clock. The Choctaws had fought their way back and come up short. The moans reverberated around the Choctaw side of the stadium. Heather had been looking on as the referee dug through the mass off boys to disclose the mystery. She burst into tears and buried her head once again in her father's chest. Jeannine maneuvered her way in front of Elmer and managed to bury her head in his arms also. Elmer patted the girls but was smiling because he glanced at Jessica who was staring right at him and when their eyes met, she was smiling. She was free, she was desperately trying to be a girl again and she was happy. Her mouth moved and even though Elmer could not hear her though the crowd noise, he understood every word that came from her mouth. "Tell Decker I love him."